THE BUTLER DID IT

SEAN JOSEPH

THE BUTLER DID IT

SEAN JOSEPH

PREFACE

The Butler Did It is a crime novel written by Sean Joseph. Certain events in the novel do mirror and reflect some events which the author has been part of and witness to. Certain facts and names have been changed. The central character Johnny Butler has been created to live the role of a young man born in North London in 1967, who lived through certain events, starting with the gateway crime of shoplifting and leading to a life of crime that funded his various addictions.

Johnny Butler was an unremarkable-looking criminal and made the most of the life he chose to lead. There have been many highs and lows in his life. One of his therapists described his life as similar to the Godfather. One public official described him as Al Capone with the gift of the gab. The story covers prostitution, drug importation and dealing as well as violent crime, contract killing, tobacco smuggling, and way too many financial crimes to list. He managed to evade conviction until he was 42 years old and then his old life began to catch up with him. He faced trial for organised crime in 2010. Then, as a direct result of that event, he manged to turn his life around and found the 12-step program in various fellowships, which helped him look at his life honestly and see how dark it had become. Since then, he has led a different type of life.

Although he has always lived in the fast lane and sailed close to the wind, he has no regrets and believes he has at least lived a life which, although it had to end, if he hadn't lived, he could never have the life he has today – which is so different, has a purpose and is very rewarding. Boring is not a word that would describe this character's life.

The author realised that Johnny's behaviour needed to be worth writing about and the book needed to be written as something worth reading. In both respects, you will probably never have read a book like this in your lifetime. After all, the truth is often stranger than fiction.

The Butler Did It is a work of fiction. Although its form is that of an autobiography, it is not one. Space and time have been rearranged to suit the convenience of the book, and with the exception of public figures, any resemblance to persons living or dead is coincidental. The opinions expressed are those of the characters' and should not be confused with the author's. Some characters, events and facts have been changed by the author for the purposes of entertainment.

CHAPTER 1
THE SON OF A GREENGROCER

Johnny Butler was born in North London on 25th November 1967. He was born with ADHD, but in those days it was not diagnosed, so it was not confirmed until he was 46 years old. He was the youngest son of George Albert Butler and Vera Sophia Butler. George was a kind-hearted, poorly educated man with the gift of the gab. Vera was a beautiful young woman with a difficult background caused by the evacuation process in the war. He had one older brother, Alex. Alex and Johnny were different in both appearance and personality. George and Vera had a greengrocer's shop in Tufnell Park, North London, just round the corner from Highbury, the then-home of Arsenal Football Club. His early memories of childhood are few and far between but one story his mother told him about his early life was when he was in his pram outside his parents' greengrocer's shop. The brake on the pram somehow came off, and it was rolling down the hill towards the busy main road. Luckily for him, his dad was alerted to the fact that the pram was heading for imminent danger. George managed to catch the pram before it went straight into the road, possibly a lifesaving or at least a life-changing moment in Johnny's early childhood. He was grateful for that because if the pram hadn't been caught in time, things could have turned out very different indeed.

His parents were good, hard-working people who came from working class backgrounds and who wanted to get on in life and enjoy their family together. George was a fiddler, or you might say a ducker and a diver. The fires in the shop were always on full blast. They never went cold. The local bookies' runner, Flogger, who came in the shop every day to collect the illegal bets, had shown George how to fiddle the electric meter by sticking a pin in the side of the meter. It stopped the meter spinning and registering the units. That way, they could afford not to worry about electric bills. London in the 60s and 70s was very different from today. Everyone was up the markets trying to save a few bob wherever they could. Buying stuff off the back of lorries was a way of life. Policing was very different in those days too. Coppers had a far more relaxed attitude to crimes such as drink-driving, pilfering, stolen goods and even fights in pubs. CCTV, computers, DNA and modern-day police technology simply did not exist.

There was an Irish pub opposite the greengrocer's, and it was a regular event for two men in the pub with a belly full of beer to have a disagreement, go outside, knock each other senseless in the street, then pick each other up, dust each other down, bury the hatchet, so to speak, then go back in and carry on drinking together again. Nowadays, there would be police involved and charges would follow. Life certainly was very different. George knew a lot of the so-called villains in London at the time, but only to pass the time of day with. He did not mix in their circles, but in the 1960s it certainly was true the police only knew what people told them.

Johnny first went to school in North London – Mount Stuart Primary School. He has a vague recollection of actually going to the school, but he only went for one term. His parents had decided that they were moving from London, and so they did. They thought that the culture was changing quickly, not for the better, and with this in mind, it would be in Alex and Johnny's best interests if they moved out of London and down to Kent. They moved to a village called Lenham, half way between Maidstone and Ashford.

They bought a three-bedroom semi-detached, Number 6 Glebe Gardens, just down from the vicarage and in a very quiet residential area. Johnny started attending Lenham Infant School. His favourite memories were drinking a small bottle of milk in the morning, as well as playing football and running in the playground at break times. He moved from there to Lenham Primary School at the age of about 6. It was just in the next road to the infants school. His behaviour at school was terrible. He could not keep still and he struggled to listen in class. He was a frequent visitor to the headmaster, who used to give him the slipper way too much. In fact, in the end, the fear of the slipper disappeared because it was all over very quickly. It used to sting, but it became part of his school life, and he learnt to accept it rather than fear it. Looking back, there were lots of children who never got sent to the headmaster's office, but he could not see that then. His ADHD was undiagnosed and untreated, and what really may have helped was a visit to the doctors, but no one knew. His form tutor was Miss Walker, whom he did not particularly like. She was a hard-faced, single lady, and he always seemed to be on the wrong side of her. He rarely listened to what she was saying and always wanted to have the last say on anything. So, he became known as a cheeky nuisance child who could not behave or take instructions. His behaviour always got him attention – but the wrong kind. Even at lunchtime he seemed unable to show exemplary behaviour. If he did not like the lunch, he would simply ask one of his friends to eat his or just let it fall under the table before putting his plate and cutlery away for cleaning.

George was a gentle man, and Johnny remembered when his parents came back from parents' evening after seeing Miss Walker one evening when he was about 10 years old. His dad really lost his temper with him. He remembered really being scared as he went up the stairs to bed. His father followed him up the stairs and when he got into bed, George told him in no uncertain terms that his behaviour at school had to improve, and immediately. He had to stop mucking around in lessons and start trying harder in his work. He also had to start listening to Miss Walker and doing what she said. Then George took off one of his slippers and started hitting the bed with it. When Johnny started sobbing, George put his hand over his lips and told him to go to sleep. Of course, he was just trying to get his son on the right track, and the shock did work. The impression being created, he remembered, was that George was slippering him at the same time as raising his voice, but he knew the illusion was for the benefit of his mum downstairs. His end of term report following the parents' evening was terrible, but it did mention a marked improvement in all areas since the parents' open evening. That remark saved his bacon, he guessed. He had done just enough to stop the rot. It was also made clear in the report that when he tried and applied himself, he was a bright and intelligent child.

George had started a small haulage company when they moved from London to Lenham. He had an HGV 1 licence but had never taken his test. He had done national service, and because he drove the large lorries in the army, he just had to apply for the licence. He had arctics and was transporting a lot of fruit from Sheerness Docks for various clearing houses. Vera had found work as a merchandiser for St Ivel. They were a major supplier of dairy products in the 70s. They have long since been bought out by one of the market leaders. During the summer holidays Johnny would regularly go to work with his dad. He loved it. George and Johnny used to go in all the transport cafés, and Johnny used to think it was a wonderful life, sitting in the passenger seat of a Volvo, a Scania or a Ford Transcontinental. When they used to load up in the docks he used to help, best he could, by pulling the curtains on the tautliners. The dockers would be whizzing about on forklift trucks and the cranes would be unloading the ships two pallets at a time on the quayside. The working girls from the cargo ships would be standing on the quayside sometimes. Johnny never knew what they were doing then, but he remembered one day one of the dockers in a forklift truck bibbed at George after the lorry had been fully loaded, shouting, 'Your boy wants to borrow a score, George, then he can go and get himself sorted out,' gesturing towards the working girls on the quayside. Everyone laughed and Johnny kind of realised what he was suggesting. He remembered looking and thinking, *Right, get a few quid together and you can enjoy yourself,* without fully understanding what it meant.

If he didn't go to work with his dad, he would play football with his brother Alex in the back garden. By this time, he had started making friends with the older lads in the village. They all used to go to the local café in Lenham Square. It was called Chequers Café and it was right in the centre of the village square. Lots of local children who were older than him used to go to the café. There were two pool tables, two fruit machines, a space invaders machine, and a pinball machine. Chocolate, drinks, cigarettes and some foods were available. Everyone just left their bikes lying on the cobbles outside the café. Johnny always felt like he had to impress the older lads with his behaviour and antics, so he kind of did all the wrong things to prove himself so that they would accept him as one of the boys. It was in the café he first started smoking cigarettes, playing fruit machines, pool for money, the pinball and space invaders from time to time. The café was owned by Mr & Mrs Bush, a Polish migrant family.

In truth Johnny had a very carefree childhood. The local bobbies never seemed to bother anyone really. It was a small village, and the local officers seemed more interested in drinking in the two local pubs – The Red Lion and The Dog and Bear – or The Lenham Working Men's Club. One early evening, Johnny had just left home and was walking into the village when he saw George coming down the road, obviously on his way home from work. Excited, he turned round and ran towards home again. In too much of a hurry to look where he was going, he ran straight into a telegraph pole, which he head-butted, and crashed to the floor. As he was going to fall flat on his face, he put out his hands and saved his face from smashing on the concrete. George witnessed the event and told him he did well to protect his face with his hands. Johnny liked the praise and very quickly got over the pain.

From Lenham Primrary School, Johnny went to Swadelands School, which was next door and was the local Comprehensive. His brother had gone exactly the same route, and from Swadelands Johnny went to Maidstone Grammar School, after passing the 11 Plus. He had many memories of Swadelands School, including starting going to youth club at the school in the evenings. He was supposed to be growing up and starting to get an education to further his prospects in later life, and in many ways he did. He smoked his first cigarette at the age of 11, had his first girlfriend, Nicola, at the same age, and also then, he started to get the cane from the headmaster rather than the slipper. He started to develop habits he could not afford on his pocket money, namely cigarettes, gambling, girls and lots of chocolate, fizzy pop and crisps, as well as regular trips to the youth club and Chequers Café. Short of options, he turned to criminal activity early. It all started with shoplifting as much as he could. His mother's purse and his dad's trouser pockets became regular targets.

His defence was denial, denial and more denial if ever caught doing inappropriate things. He listened to people but didn't really listen and always did what he wanted if he could. He actually believed if he just kept saying it was not true, then everyone would believe him. Of course, in reality, his teachers and parents knew he was lying but let a lot of behaviour pass.

There was a local ironmonger's shop in Lenham, and Johnny was a regular customer but never bought anything. He would wander in, have a good look round, help himself to batteries and a whole array of other goods. Most had no real value or purpose, but he definitely enjoyed his regular shoplifting trips and always felt really good after getting away with it. Yes, kleptomania was definitely part of his makeup from an early age.

He was at registration one day in his form class when one of the physical education teachers walked in. It was Mr Batchelor. There were two physical education instructors: Mr Richardson and Mr Batchelor. Mr Batchelor was the larger and older of the two teachers. Mr Batchelor spoke to his form tutor and asked Johnny to accompany him to the headmaster, Mr Shepherd. Once they arrived and went in, Mr Shepherd said he knew he stole a torch from the local ironmonger's the day before, after school.

Johnny froze on the spot. He was speechless. He knew the accusation was true but could not work out how anyone could know, since when leaving the ironmonger's no one had approached him or accused him. He had simply taken the torch home, put batteries in it and hid it in one of his board games in the bottom of his wardrobe. Then the headmaster told him that Mr Batchelor had witnessed the theft from outside the shop. He was looking in the window at various gardening products when he saw him through the window and watched him put the torch in his pocket. So now the truth was out, and Mr Batchelor was nothing more than a grass. Johnny thought it was nothing to do with Mr Batchelor and none of his business but quickly realised the man had seen him pick the torch up with his own eyes. He simply looked at the headmaster and Mr Batchelor and said, "I remember going in the ironmonger's and picking up the torch to take to the counter and pay but then realised I could not afford it so I put it back before leaving the ironmonger's and going home.' Not bad for an 11-year-old novice in a tight spot. It was his best hope – to admit being there but create enough doubt and uncertainty that the simple allegation of theft could not stand. Hopefully that would tick the box. Mr Batchelor may have taken his eye off him for long enough to not be certain of the fact that he left the shop with the torch in his pocket. There were no cameras in those days, just large round mirrors strategically placed to help the cashier see different angles in the shop if they were looking and paying attention. He fancied his chances that the torch was well enough hidden at home it would not be found in a casual search – or quite a thorough search for that matter. He saw the possible weakness in the evidence against him, and chanced a defence instead of saying it's a fair cop, guv, and sorry. While he had the chance to speak, he ramped up his denial and went on the attack. He said that he wished Mr Batchelor had stopped and challenged him outside the shop; then there would be no doubt about what he was saying. A point the headmaster seemed to like because he raised his eyebrows. Johnny could smell a way out and instinctively knew that point made sense to the headmaster. Maybe he had just became his own defence barrister by striking at the heart of the prosecution case. He was on a roll now, so he threw this next bit in for good measure. He said, 'I do not own a torch and have not got a torch at home.' Was that enough? He hoped he had just created enough doubt. Unfortunately, not. The headmaster told him Mr Batchelor was certain. Maybe his body language was not as convincing as he had hoped. So, Johnny was told his father would be informed and invited to the school to solve the outcome. He knew the wisdom that the police only knew what you tell them and had simply applied that logic to his teachers. When he went back with Mr Batchelor to see the headmaster a few days later, George was there. He and George had discussed the whole situation at home and George knew he had not been caught with the torch and he had totally denied the theft from start to finish. The headmaster outlined the facts. George very graciously and calmy listened before asking Mr Batchelor why he never challenged him outside the shop and returned the torch to the shop. Then George said that he did not have a torch at home and he believed his son did not steal the torch but had picked it up and put it back. Now the headmaster and Mr Batchelor had just hit an absolute brick wall. Of course, George knew Johnny had stolen the torch but didn't want him facing a possible police caution, so he backed him to the hilt. The headmaster decided the matter was now closed. A kind of not-proven verdict. In any case, Johnny had just learnt the possible art of denying, lying, sticking to your guns and getting a result.

Aged 11, Johnny started to go to the school youth club at

Swadelands. It was on Monday evenings; table tennis, pool, music and the beginning of chasing girls. There was a tuck shop with crisps, chocolate and fizzy pop. Then there were the school discos and girlfriends. Johnny asked what he thought were the two most attractive girls in the school to be his girlfriends. Sian was his first choice. He got his friend to do it, safe in the knowledge he could deny it if she said no. That seemed the best policy to asking girls out, he thought. Sian said she would have been his girlfriend but she was already Simon's girlfriend so she couldn't. He didn't mind that answer so he didn't deny the fact that he had asked his friend to ask her out for him. He just decided he didn't like Simon very much. He thought Simon was a bit smug and was a bit jealous, in truth. Nicola said yes, and she was his first girlfriend. They went to the school disco and kissed in classes. He used to steal chocolates out of the local shops in the village. There was a sweet shop, newsagents, a post office, as well as two convenience stores, a VG stores and Lurcoch's of Lenham. He thought it was very fair that he used to shoplift sweets and chocolates from different shops on different days. At least he was trying not to burden one shop with all the losses. He remembered telling Nicola he did not want her to be his girlfriend. She seemed upset. He had realised that the fun part or the challenging part of getting a girlfriend was getting them to say yes. Once Nicola had said yes, the excitement and challenge had gone. The next day or so, he realised he wanted her again. So, he asked her out again and she said yes. At 11, he thought having a girlfriend somehow gave him status.

His friend Neil had a girlfriend called Karen, and Neil told him he had to get his girlfriend to go up to the playing field with him at lunchtime and he had to get his hand up Nicola's skirt. 'That is where the magic is,' Neil exclaimed. Neil had been doing this with Karen, and Johnny thought Neil was more advanced with girls than he was. He figured Neil was telling him the truth but had no idea what the magic was. And yet he wanted to find out for himself and experience the magic. He asked Nicola if she wanted to go up the school field at lunchtime in the sun. It was a beautiful summer's day and Nicola said no, she wanted to stay in the classroom. So Johnny left it, as he thought this act had to be carried out on the school playing field; he had slightly missed the concept at his youthful age. Then he became bored with Nicola and told her he did not want her to be his girlfriend anymore. Then did it all over again. Once she said yes, he had no interest. The only thing that changed in the end was the next time he asked her she had lost all interest herself and said no and ran off, so that was the end of Nicola and him. Twice she'd said yes, and on the third occasion a firm no. He had no idea he just craved the excitement and thrill of new things, torches and girlfriends being two early examples.

At Swadelands he had his first holiday away from his family. There was a school trip to Jersey for one week. His parents rustled up the money for the trip and he was allowed to go. He remembered some of the sights in Jersey and remembered thinking how sad some of the war stories they'd been told in lessons sounded.

All the school children and school teachers stayed in a local hotel, and Johnny was in trouble for misbehaving from start to finish. The memories of the trip were the zoo in Jersey, the war tunnels and the castle with old canons to fire out to sea. It was Johnny's first real understanding of how dark and difficult it may have been for people in the war. The children explored the underground tunnels with a tour guide who explained about the underground hospitals for people who were ill or injured in the war.

Johnny was still getting in trouble at school on a regular

basis. He just had an inability to listen and behave. He normally gazed out of the windows fantasizing about what he wanted to do and who he wanted to be when he grew up. He had a reputation that he was a right cheeky little monkey to all the teachers. It was obvious that Nicola and Sian were attracted to the naughty little boy that he was fast becoming, with a cheeky little smile to go with it and a look of innocence on his face. He often used to try and say the wrong thing in class and do the wrong thing for attention, even if it was of the wrong kind. He liked to be the class clown and hear the laughter rather than listen and do the work.

His shoplifting became more prolific. The local sweet shop was owned by an elderly couple – Mr and Mrs Tibble. They used to have a penny tray out the back of the shop. The penny tray was full of sweets that were two or three for a penny. Some were a penny, and the expensive ones were two pence or three pence, with the most expensive items being five pence. In reality, this was the beginning of the modern-day pick-and-mix. Being on the elderly side, it took them a short while to get the tray so he could choose what he wanted. Johnny realised that this time was enough for him to fill his pockets and school bag with all sorts of more expensive goodies, including jars of sweets that were lying on the floor in front of the counter.

This went on for a long time. Johnny had a neighbour who was older than him, called Stephen; the tallest kid at school. Stephen had worked out he could lean over the counter and reach the cigarettes while they were getting the tray. It worked a few times. Then, once, Stephen lent over and tried to grab packets of cigarettes but he misjudged his reach in the panic and virtually pulled the shelf down. The shelf collapsed with a terrible noise and all the cigarettes fell to the floor. They scarpered and didn't go back for ages for fear of reprisals.

At Lenham Johnny had joined the Cubs. He seemed to remember enjoying the meetings and friendship. He also loved getting badges for certain achievements, such as learning how to tie knots and various other activities. It was a very good place for young lads to enjoy themselves. That was certainly his overall memory of the Cubs. The meetings were held in the local school halls in the evening. Subs were about 20 pence per meeting. At the age of about 11 he left the Cubs and joined the Scouts. He enjoyed the activities in the Scouts too. The main difference was that the uniform for a boy scout included long trousers whereas in the Cubs it had always been the traditional grey shorts. In the Scouts he went on weekends away living in a tent in a field with other scouts. It seemed all very grown up. He had his own sleeping bag and particularly enjoyed making real fires and playing in the woods with the other scouts. Starting a fire by rubbing two sticks together with paper and kindling seemed like a great magic trick for him, especially as he always had a box of Swan Vestas handy to light his cigarettes. He knew that he just needed a few Swan Vestas matches rather than the whole box, because he could use lots of different surfaces to light the matches. The Scouts were good fun and he enjoyed the regular meetings. He simply struggled to do what he was told and was always in trouble.

With the Scouts he went on a camping trip to Buckmore Park. They had racing Go-Karts. The first time he had ever experienced anything like this. He ended up getting slung off the track. For a dare, he drove round the track the wrong way. His mates all cheered and he thought it was great. The people in charge at the race track were horrified and banned him. He came up with some story and said he was confused; they were not amused. The leader of the group was Akela, which made him smile because he knew his real name was Mr Trevilian, so he never really listened to him either. Mr Trevilian was a very tall, smart teacher who had a passion – to try and help the local lads in a constructive and positive way. It all seemed like some kind of a joke, really, to Johnny. He did know Mr Trevilian was a really nice guy who struggled to deal with the naughty boys who did not follow the rules. During the break at the Scout meetings, Johnny and some of his friends used to climb on the roof of the school and run about up there while smoking cigarettes. There were some large bins close by, which could be placed next to low-level single-story parts of the school building, and from there it was a simple climb to the top of the main school roof. What he and some of the others had not realised was that the main roof was above the main hall and Akela could hear everyone running about on the roof during the break. After the break Akela said he knew some of them had been running about on the roof of the school and, of course, no one admitted to it. Everyone kind of bowed their heads and thought this is a good time to keep their mouths shut. Anyway, he explained it was dangerous and not allowed. In reality he was wasting his breath, but he did point out the danger and pitfalls. He was trying to do the right thing and keep all the lads on the straight and narrow.

The following Friday evening during the break, Johnny, Peter and some of the other lads were straight on the roof again smoking cigarettes. After the break, Akela went through the same speech again. It was obvious there were a few lads doing it, so there were no specific allegations against any individuals. Mr Trevilian made it clear that if it happened again, the group would close, not sure any of the culprits really believed him or took any notice. Perhaps he believed that the threat of closing the group would stop the lads getting on the roof. With the benefit of hindsight, having the break in the hall – thus not allowing anyone outside during the break – would have solved the problem. It was a single door that just needed locking, but he had made the consequences clear, and now was the time for him to show his leadership and authority – so he thought. Of course, the following week he made it clear to everyone again, just before the break. It seemed more like a challenge or a red rag to a bull. As soon as the break started, Johnny and a few lads went racing towards the bins outside to get straight on the roof and light up. After the break, it was announced the group would close. All the scouts had to wait until their parents came to pick them up, and Akela told the parents that there were no more Scout meetings and why.

George listened, but because it was a group of lads doing it, he knew Johnny alone had not been the reason for the closing of the group, just part of it. So, George explained it to Johnny and they drove home happily in George's vehicle, which was called the Red Peril. It was such a great vehicle. It was a small truck with two seats in the front but an open back. George found it really convenient for work with the lorries. If ever he wanted to carry anything about, like tyres or tools, they could just be thrown on the back. At the age of 12 and 13, Johnny thought it was so cool to ride in the back, sitting down or standing up. It was much more fun than being the passenger in a car. If George was only travelling locally in the village or around in the docks, he was allowed to ride in the back, and George drove a lot slower. For longer trips, he had to sit in the front next to his dad for safety reasons. On some occasions he would be dropped off at his friends' houses after being allowed to travel in the back. Life seemed good to Johnny. All his friends loved the Red Peril. The Scouts didn't reopen, and that was the end of that.

Johnny remembered that year close to fireworks night his brother Alex had hidden a lot of fireworks on top of the cupboards in the kitchen. One day, Alex told him to get them off the top of the cupboards, so Johnny stood on the side, clinging on to a unit of three cupboards, which were linked into one unit. He pulled on the unit until he pulled it off the wall. He fell backwards – quite a fall for a young lad – hitting his head on the table and chairs behind him before crashing on to the floor. The really amazing part was that as the cupboard fell on top of him, one of the nails several inches long went straight towards his heart but stopped just before going straight in because the cupboard was partially being held back by a chair. Without the chair in the way, it would have been curtains for Johnny for sure. The nail would have punctured his heart. George and Vera came rushing into the kitchen when they heard the noise of the fall and the cupboard crashing down. George told him and Alex off but quickly realised what could have happened seeing the position of the nail, and the frustration with his two naughty sons turned to relief that no one was hurt. After managing to get up, Johnny explained that he was just trying to get some bangers off the top of the cupboard and was told he was not allowed to climb on the side anymore. Was this another early sign of his guardian angel stepping in just at the right time or just good fortune?

George had left school not being able to read and write. He also could not swim. So, George made sure Johnny and Alex had swimming lessons at a young age at the Great Danes Hotel, which was a lovely hotel in Hollingbourne, with a pool and swimming instructors. Both Johnny and Alex learnt to swim to a reasonable standard.

Johnny remembered when his parents went to Swadelands school for the last parents' evening for him, before grammar school places were being offered to the most suitable students, and he had been chosen as a suitable student to be offered a place at one of the local grammar schools. His parents were thrilled. It was pointed out that his behaviour was a problem but he had the intelligence to be offered a place. Alex was already at Maidstone Grammar School, having gone the same route. The teachers told Johnny's parents that a place at one of two local grammar schools would be offered to him in the post. His mum Vera was absolutely determined that he should go to Maidstone Grammar School – her preferred choice out of the two options. Vera wanted him at Maidstone Grammar School and to follow in Alex's footsteps. Johnny remembered one evening sitting in the living room with his mum and dad and his mum telling George, 'Whatever happens, I want him at Maidstone Grammar School.' She had her heart set on that for sure. She told George he needed to get up the school and sort it out. George was not an educated man, but he did have the gift of the gab so he went for a meeting at the school (or at the local selection committee) and returned home saying it was done. Everyone was so happy. Johnny's parents both knew the value of an education. Shortly after that, a letter arrived confirming that he had been offered a place at Maidstone Grammar School.

CHAPTER 2
MAIDSTONE GRAMMAR SCHOOL

ALEX WAS ALREADY at the Maidstone Grammar School when Johnny started at the school, but he was in trouble in his classes and with his education. He failed dismally in his first attempt at his O Levels. The very year this happened, the school introduced a new year in the syllabus. It was called the recovery course. This was a fantastic break for Alex, and possibly the making of him. He grabbed the opportunity with both hands – as he now sees it – passed his O Levels and went on to get good grades for his choice of A Levels. Alex progressed to the London School of Economics, got his degree and then did his Masters. He met his wife Della at university, and they had three wonderful children – Johnny's nephew and two nieces. Linda is the youngest of the three children, Nicholas second eldest, and Helen the first born, recently married.

It was when Johnny started at the new school that he started getting terrible pains in his stomach. He always seemed to be in pain. He was taken to the local doctor's surgery in Lenham village. Vera was very concerned about his health. The doctor managed to work out he was suffering from a terrible case of his trousers were too tight around his waist. What a relief for everyone. Vera thought it was so funny.

Johnny remembered one day walking into the living room holding a water pistol. There was a big electric fire. He was squirting the water at Alex and, of course, it was going mainly all around him. Johnny wasn't exactly a crack shot. A lot of the water went into the electric fire. It was shortly after that that he was told if there had not been a break in the water, that could have killed him. How lucky was he?

Vera used to type up the invoices for George's haulage business on a Remington typewriter. Johnny still has the typewriter today at home. When his mum passed away in 2019, he remembered the typewriter and all the fond memories from when he wanted to help his dad and be part of the business. After all, the business was called George Butler & Sons (Haulage). Johnny always enjoyed going to work with George. Now, at the age of 12, he wanted to learn about invoices and help his dad run and operate the business. He used to sit at the table watching his mum type the invoices. Johnny quickly learned how to type and add up using a calculator. It didn't take him too long and he had learnt how to type the invoices and send them off to the relevant firms for payment. He prided himself on getting the details right, the columns all lined up, and most importantly getting the figures right. He knew the importance of getting the details right, which would avoid the possibility of the businesses being sent the invoices and returning them because of mistakes or errors, which he knew would delay the payment dates.

Barclay's bank had given George a substantial overdraft limit on his business account to allow for operating on a day-to-day basis and waiting for payment, which seemed to vary between 30 and 90 days from the date of an invoice. Every time George got near his overdraft limit, he would ring and speak to his bank manager in Lombard Street in London, and they just raised the overdraft limit.

George had a double chequebook for his Barclay's business account. The size of the chequebook gave Johnny the impression his father was a serious business man. He never saw anyone else with a chequebook that size. It had about 60 cheques above 60 cheques, a bit like a double decker bus, he guessed. The reality was George was a struggling haulage contractor turning over vast amounts of money but not making much profit. Looks can be deceptive and often are, but what young lad doesn't want to see his dad as a particularly fine business man? George was a wonderful man and dad but his business skills certainly were not as Johnny had imagined.

George's accountant, a guy called Reevsie, used to do the books overnight for tax and VAT purposes. No wonder George was always smiling. He didn't even have to give him the records to get his accounts done. He simply used to phone him up and tell him he needed accounts for the bank or the tax man. What a great system – it was so simple and efficient. It was probably as reliable as the figures that the modern-day tech giants produce, and the results were certainly very similar. Minimal tax payments and everyone was happy. Reevsie was like a magician, Johnny thought. Tax and VAT payments seemed like an option; you could pay or just change the paperwork and not pay. It certainly seemed so, and worth remembering.

The early 1980s were different times, and Johnny remembered George telling him that God had answered all his prayers when a tax office had a bad fire and the Inland Revenue's investigation into his affairs literally went up in smoke. The computer technology was not in then, so if records got destroyed it was all over. A wonderful stroke of good fortune for George, no doubt.

Johnny remembered that George had a massive misunderstanding with Barclays bank once. When George first started trading, he had been a sole trader. Then George decided, on advice from Reevsie, that it would be better to start a limited company, so George did. After trading as a limited company for some time, George believed that the debts of the company – mainly the growing overdraft at the bank – were limited to the company. He had not realised that he had previously signed a personal guarantee, which effectively transferred the liability from the limited company to him personally as a director. The bank manager at Barclays visited the house one evening and made it clear to George and Vera that Barclays did have the right to pursue the house if the overdraft was not repaid by the business. Vera was furious with George. George appeared to take it all in his stride, as usual. What Johnny did not know was that his parents' marriage had effectively finished as a result of matrimonial differences that could not be overcome. It later transpired that communication and differences in interpretation had brought the marriage to an end. Vera blamed George's business and the lorries; George blamed Vera's behaviour. Nevertheless, it was over, and George was only staying at home to keep a roof over Johnny's head and a stable home background while he finished his education. Johnny was not told this at that stage but, somehow, he sensed something was not right.

When he was about 14 years of age, his mother chased him up the stairs with a carving knife and told him that his father would sort him out when he got home. It scared the life out of him. She had never done this before. Then again, he had been very naughty. Vera was probably at the end of her tether, with her marriage difficulties and his behaviour. It was all too much for her. He had been told many times not to play on the wall at the side of the house. It was not particularly strong and he could have been too heavy for it or fallen off the top and hurt himself. Of course, as soon as Vera's back was turned, he was on top of the wall alongside the house. But she came out and caught him. He remembers waiting for George to come home and punish him. He was scared out of his life. He did not know what to expect. After seeing his mum turn on him like that, what would George's reaction be? The episode with the carving knife shook Johnny, to say the least. When George got home, he went in to Johnny's bedroom and told him to try not to upset his mum. He then raised his voice for all to hear and calmy said, 'You need to do what your mum tells you.' That was it – it was all over. This left Johnny relieved and very confused. He was definitely getting mixed signals, but fundamentally both his parents were saying the same thing – with totally different approaches and styles.

He remembered going on a family holiday with his mum and dad. By now Alex was at university and rarely at home. His dad's friend Norman had bought a big hotel in Torquay. It was the hotel where they filmed *Fawlty Towers,* or maybe the show was based on that hotel; he couldn't recall exactly. Next to the hotel was a park, and after arriving Johnny went round there to be nosey one afternoon. He couldn't for the life of him remember the sequence of events, but he definitely said the wrong thing to one of the lads in the park, maybe about his girlfriend, but very quickly, he was being chased by an older lad who was part of a group. He had a knife, and Johnny was scared. As he started running back to the hotel, the knife went whizzing past his right ear and landed on the floor a few feet in front of him. Johnny was so thankful and just kept running for his life, as he saw it in that moment. In any event, it could have been terrible if the knife had hit him in the back of his head or somewhere else on his body.

Another close shave. He was nearly back to the hotel front door when he finally grabbed a quick glance behind him, and there was no one there. He had got back safe and sound. He was in a total state of shock and fear but he never told anyone. He knew he would have to explain what he had done so thought better of it. Johnny decided to spend the rest of the holiday either in the hotel or just going out with his family when they all went out together in the car.

When he was 14, he was in Lenham Square with a couple of mates. At this time in his life all his friends were older than him. He wanted to be accepted by the older lads. They seemed to have more fun, and most of them liked to gamble on pool, fruit machines and cards. Johnny's gambling addiction really began to get a grip of him about now.

He remembered his friend Peter saying that the man in the red telephone box making a call was Tony Killick, who had a reputation as the local nutcase and had just been released from the local mental institution. He suggested it would be fun to annoy him. Johnny agreed, as he always did, with everyone if it sounded like fun or a challenge. He simply went along with everything trying to be accepted as one of the lads. At this time his nickname was "Mutley", after a cartoon character from *Wacky Races*. Mutley was Dastardly's dog and sidekick. They were always up to no good together. Mutley was a dog who had a cheeky laugh. This was probably the reason for the nickname. In any case, it stuck with the local lads in the village. Johnny was very naughty, and when he started laughing, he could not stop.

It is still the same today. If something starts him off, he thinks it is one of the greatest pleasures in life to be in fits of laughter.

Anyway, Johnny and Peter started throwing pebbles at the red phone box Tony Killick was using. A few missed, a few hit, but there was no reaction. Then, all of a sudden, the door of the red phone box flew open and this middle-aged man with a beard turned round. He had tied a scarf round his head and taken out of his holdall the largest machete Johnny had ever seen. He looked like Rambo at first glance. Anyway, needless to say, Johnny was horrified. He turned on his heel and flew. Talk about stirring up a hornet's nest. Johnny ran to the grounds of the local church, oddly enough. He had no idea whether he felt the church represented safety or it was just the fact that it was a short distance away. He ran round the back, and he remembered thinking, 'Please, God, let him chase Peter or one of the other lads.' He hid round the back of the church. He was so fearful that Tony Killick would find him and kill him, chop him up in little bits with his machete. Johnny stayed there for about 25 minutes; it seemed like hours. Then he crept out. He saw Peter and Lyndon and they linked up. No one seemed to know for certain what had happened. Tony never caught or hurt anyone. They were all wary walking up the road, but they never saw him after that. Johnny did not know how hard he'd tried to catch anyone. Maybe the look was just for effect. It'd certainly had an effect on Johnny. Maybe his imagination was, on occasion, totally overactive, but all was well that day.

There was a lad in the village called Gary Holland. He was a couple of years older than Johnny. They never really got on. Johnny was not sure if Gary used to try and bully him or he used to just wind him up and look to start trouble between them. Trouble did seem to follow him about everywhere, and he resented authority as well as obeying the rules, just like Johnny. It was always more fun to break the rules. Let's just say they were as bad as each other. Anyway, one day he and Gary were outside the local VG stores in Lenham and it all started to spiral out of control. No one was sure of the exact reason. Boys will be boys, as Johnny's old headmaster used to say.

Johnny had a new chopper bike at the time. His parents had bought it second hand from the local cycle shop. It was like brand new. They broke the bank to get it for him. He had a vague recollection that Gary said something about his bike, or threatened to take it from him. He dropped it on the floor, said 'Take it,' and ran home. Well, George absolutely exploded, is the only way he can remember it. What followed, Johnny has never forgotten. George rarely lost his temper and was not a violent man. He grabbed Alex, told him to get in the car, told Johnny to get in the car, and they all drove up to the square. George had a purple Ford Escort estate car at the time. He had got it after the Red Peril had passed its best. They screeched to a halt outside the VG stores. Alex knew the Holland brothers; the eldest was the same age as Alex. George did not really know who he was looking for. He was under the impression that Alex had been told if it kicked off, he had to deal with the oldest brother. There were a lot of lads milling about. George grabbed hold of this Gary Holland to get his undivided attention, and in a couple of minutes made it perfectly clear to him that if he ever went near Johnny again, let alone took anything from him, George would put the two brothers and their father through the VG store window. Johnny had never seen his dad like this. Everyone was shocked. Lots of the local lads knew George and were all listening to the conversation. Johnny never had any trouble after that with anyone. He thought George was angry because of the cost of the bike and the idea that someone thought they could just take the bike off his son. Without meaning to, he was sure his dad had sent a message to everyone in the village; his sons were not to be messed about with or bullied.

Johnny caught the bus to school from Lenham to Maidstone every day. He was smoking regularly by the age of about 12 or 13. In those days you could smoke on the bus. He used to sit upstairs at the back on a double decker and puff away. He smoked all varieties of cigarettes in those days. He was famous with his friends for not inhaling. He used to smoke and blow it out very quickly. He used to let the smoke stay in his mouth. He always looked a lot older than his real age and, in some ways, could act more grown up if need be. Soon he was getting in the local pubs and Working Men's Club in Lenham. He could get a crafty drink in the pub but not in the club, because you had to show ID for proof of age in there to get served. He used to get signed in as a guest. His mates would buy drinks and pass them over at the right time, when no one was looking. His friends dared him to dance on the snooker table in the club, and of course, he did. He got caught and was banned – not that he was even a member.

Johnny remembered his first caution at Maidstone police station. He was about 14. A mate of his, Les Kingston, who was a few years older than him, told him that lead was worth a fortune and he knew where they could get it. Les was always in the local café, smoking, gambling and playing pool and cards for money. He came from a large family in the village. They were all tearaways. His sister was older than Les and a really beautiful-looking girl. Johnny used to fantasise about him and her, even at a young age.

So, their master plan was to nick the lead off the roof of the buildings at Swadelands School. Les said he knew where they could sell it. It was simple. Sounded like easy money to Johnny. He thought it was a matter of climbing up, grabbing it and climbing down. The thought of getting caught or that it was against the law didn't seem to enter into it. As usual, he just said yes. They did it… or they tried. They were both on the roof of a school building when Les spotted the local caretaker running towards the building, shouting at them to get off the roof. He was not sure if he knew what they were doing. Johnny remembered the man from his time at the school. He was an elderly man who walked and ran with a limp. Les and Johnny were off like a shot. They seemed to have no problem getting away. The real problem came later that day. Les got arrested by the local bobby. The caretaker recognised Les from his time at the school. He never recognised Johnny, but Les gave him up to the police.

Johnny was mortified. Even at that young age, Johnny knew you didn't give names to the police. It just wasn't done. They applied a little pressure and Les cracked straight away. Johnny would not have given him up if the boot had been on the other foot. He would have said a lad he'd met, didn't know him before that, or that he was trying to get him off the roof because he took something from him.

He lives a law-abiding life today, but over many years he has seen people grass and do deals. He never approved of it at all. It never fails to amaze Johnny how you get these so-called villains who are hard as nails, and yet they are the first to cave in under a little pressure from the police. Of course, people should obey the law, but if you choose to break the law and get caught and convicted, take the consequences on the chin; that was how Johnny saw it.

Johnny stood trial in 2010 for organised crime with other co-defendants. He never said one word against any of them to the police or in court, and neither did they him. He got a certain satisfaction from that; they all stuck together as best as they could. No deals done and no one gave anyone up. He and his co-defendants made the police and the Crown prove their case without any help or cooperation from any of the accused. Johnny always remembered watching *The Godfather* with George, who loved the film – and so did he. George always admired the acting talents of Marlon Brando. Johnny learnt a lot from the film, including keeping your mouth shut, minding your own business, and never telling anyone what you were really thinking.

This time, he tried to deny any involvement in attempting to steal the lead but he was in such a tight spot; everyone seemed to know he was there. The caretaker recognised him, and the police believed the old man and Les. George knew straight away. He always did, Johnny realised. At the time, Johnny thought George believed his lies. Looking back, George always knew. He let him off, was probably nearer the truth. It was agreed Johnny would accept a caution. A date was set, and his mum and dad took him to Maidstone police station. It was a sergeant who sat down with all of them and read Johnny the riot act, but his memory is that it was all quite civilised, really, and not that bad at all. The sergeant was a very smart middle-aged man who was clearly well versed in the practice of giving cautions to minors. Johnny remembers being told he was on the wrong path; he was lucky with his school and parents. He had to change his ways. As usual, Johnny listened but did what he wanted instead.

At about this time his gambling was out of control, he was smoking, drinking a little, and he had terrible behavioural problems at school. He was constantly in detention, fighting, stealing, writing his own letters for bunking off, stealing dentist cards from the local dentist and filling them in for made-up appointments, and making up the most ridiculous excuses and reasons why he could not produce his homework. He was such a problem, looking back, and he never knew. He remembers one day in prison, in about 2011, a bloke called Joe said to him 'I bet you was a nightmare as a child.' He was in HMP The Verne, and the night before he had been running around shouting abuse at prisoners late at night. He thought it was just a bit of harmless banter, knocking on their doors and running off. At the time, his comment surprised Johnny, but looking back he understands what the man meant.

Johnny started working at the local newsagents in Lenham. It was called Thompson's and it was owned by Tony Thompson. Johnny didn't know this at the time, but he had previously been convicted of manslaughter or murder. He was a man who had little hair in the middle of his head; in his fifties, he guessed. He owned two newspaper shops – one in Lenham and one in Harrietsham, the neighbouring village on the way to Maidstone. Johnny's mate Shaun Scales, who was one of his paper boys, put Johnny forward to cover his paper round while he went on holiday. Tony paid Johnny to learn the round with Shaun before he went on holiday, so he knew what he was taking on.

It worked quite well. Johnny and Shaun shared the paper round for a couple of weeks. He remembered it didn't seem to take too long. At this time, Johnny had a racing bike. He covered the round for Shaun while he was away. Very quickly, he was filling up his paper bag with more than the newspapers; chocolates, crisps, fizzy pop, cigarettes, and very occasionally he managed to get cash from the till too. When Shaun got back there was no regular job for Johnny, but Tony said he would pay him to cover for people who didn't turn up or went away on holiday. It was great. He was reserve, and for months all he did was get paid for doing the odd day here and there. Then he was given an *Adscene* round in the village. It was extra money and could be done after school. *Adscene* was the local free paper and it had to be delivered on Thursday or Friday. Johnny had a better plan: why deliver it at all? For weeks he used to put the papers in the garden shed. It was more money for old rope, or so he thought.

What happened next was kind of strange. He went fishing with Peter Pitcher one Saturday night at the local lakes. They never caught much. It was just a chance to have a camp fire and sit up smoking all night. He totally forgot that he had to cover a paper round on the Sunday morning. The outcome was that he was cycling home with Peter, and Tony Thompson was driving along in his car covering the round that Johnny was meant to cover. He spotted Johnny and Peter. He undid his window, told him he was finished, and he mentioned the fact that there had been a lot of complaints about people not receiving the *Adscene*. Johnny tried to look shocked and amazed at the thought that he had not delivered them exactly as he should have. Anyway, George had found the *Adscene* free papers in the shed and was not pleased with him. He never forgot Tony Thompson had told him to pop in and pick up his wages for the week; he remembered to do that part. It would have seemed rude not to, really.

Johnny and Alex were never allowed to open the front door at home. Their parents told them that it was best to check who it was first. Johnny thought it was because there maybe someone nasty there or someone who might kidnap him at the front door. The reality was that there was a pin in the electric meter. It was a trick George had learnt in London. At the time it was fashionable to drill a small hole in the side of the electric meter. Then, by placing a small pin through the hole, the spindle which was measuring electric use could just be stopped. The pin was in about six weeks every quarter. It made the electric bill permanently half price. The fear was that Johnny or Alex would open the door to the electric man, who wanted to read the meter, let him in, and the pin might be in. Of course, it is funny looking back, but at the time it did create unnecessary anxiety and fear in Johnny's mind. He recently met a meter man who came and read the gas meter in his new home. Nowadays there are no pins in the electric or gas meters at his place. The man read the gas meter, then went on to tell Johnny all the tricks people are up to nowadays. He explained they just disconnect a certain pipe and that is the new swizz. It struck Johnny that with the cost of gas and electric going through the roof, you would never stop this type of behaviour in certain homes where people are struggling with their bills.

Johnny started gambling at a very early age. It appeared to fix all his emotional inadequacies and make him happy. It lit him up inside. There was a café in Lenham square, with fruit machines, pool tables, space invaders, a juke box and pinball machines. Johnny had found his first love. The fruit machines, pool played for money, smoking and playing cards for money. He had expensive tastes as an early teenager. His pocket money would not run to it. So, his crime spree slowly got worse and worse. Shoplifting, stealing from his parents, and theft from other places slowly started to become a way of life. A lot of the lads in the café had jobs, but they were all older than him and had left school. He was still at school.

There was a family called the Dawsons. There was Paul, Stephen, Barry and their sister. Their dad Reg was the gamekeeper for the governor of the Bank of England at the time. His estate was called Tory Hill. It ran for miles and miles all around a village called Doddington, which was just a couple of miles up the hill from Lenham. They regularly went dog racing at Maidstone, Haringey and Walthamstow dog tracks. Johnny started going with them, and it really got out of hand. The bets simply got larger and larger, and he had to get his hands on more and more cash. From the dog tracks he was introduced to betting shops. He always looked older than his real age, so placing bets in bookmakers, at dog tracks or getting into pubs and 18-year-old-rated films at the cinema became reality for him at about 14 or 15. He had no idea he was totally addicted to gambling at such a young age. All he ever wanted to do was gamble, and he had to gamble for larger amounts than all his friends. He wanted everyone to know he was a player; he so badly craved the rush of gambling combined with the approval of all his older friends. He certainly had the bug – that was for sure.

Johnny remembered on the 1st April one year his brother Alex coming into his bedroom one morning and telling him that they had all overslept and Mum had said it was not worth going to school because it was too late. It was music to his ears. He just simply turned over and went back to bed. Only one small problem – it was not true. A bit later on, his mum came into his bedroom. She had not realised he was not up and ready. His brother's story became reality. It was now too late, and Mum said he could have the day off, which was unusual for her. She always encouraged her boys to attend school.

There was a night club in Maidstone called The Warehouse, and Paul, Barry and Johnny used to go there to drink, dance and meet girls. It was expensive for drinks. They were all at school. But they had a secret weapon: Paul was a really good-looking bloke. This was the plan. Paul used to be able to get great-looking girls' attention very quickly. Then he would tell them they had to go and ask certain blokes if they wanted to dance. The blokes in question would have just bought drinks at the bar. The blokes always looked shocked but always agreed. While they were dancing, Paul, Barry and Johnny polished off their drinks. Lots seemed to twig but let it go. Some would not let it go. Amazing rows followed, and there were a few fights, but Paul was a bit handy so they never ended up in too much bother. After the club finished at 2 am, they could not afford taxis home. The Warehouse was located just on the river, in Maidstone. So, they used to break into the boats moored on the river and try and sleep until the morning.

As a child, Johnny used to look forward to visiting his grandparents on Sundays. They used to go to his mum's mum and dad's first for lunch. They lived in Abbey Wood. His grandma used to do a wonderful Sunday lunch. She was a great cook. It was his Grandma Scott who taught him to say please and thank you. He remembered he kept saying, 'Can I have an orange squash?' She would ignore him. After a few times, she would say, 'Did you say please?' Then when he learnt to say please, when he got an orange squash, she would say, 'Did you say thank you?' For all his faults in life and problems along the way, he has for the most part tried to have good manners and say please and thank you more than most. There is a saying, 'Manners maketh the man'. Johnny thinks it is true.

Then they would go and visit George's mum and dad, Grandad and Grandma Butler. They were very generous with money, which Johnny always remembered thinking was handy. Then they would go back to the Scotts and Bingo in the church hall, which Johnny took way too seriously. He never used to win, but his nan was very lucky at bingo and often made a profit out of the evening. Grandma Scott loved her bingo. All Johnny's memories of visiting his grandparents were good ones.

Johnny got a job in the summer holidays working as a cleaner helper at Lee Davey caravan sales in Harrietsham. It was a fair job, he thought. He was bored silly but wanted the money. He used to fall asleep in the caravans while he was meant to be cleaning them. He was always tired, having been out late the night before with Paul and Barry. The manager, Les, caught him a few times and let him off. They used to make a joke of it. Perhaps Les was very kind, or perhaps Johnny just had a way about wriggling out of awkward situations. He had been in enough by now and his imagination was very creative, to say the least.

George had left school without being able to read and write but he taught himself to read and write afterwards. He told Johnny that, when he took his mum on their first date to a dance club in Woolwich, they were asked to put their names and addresses in the book upon entry. George just wrote the information in an illegible manner, a little bit like doctors' writing – you can't read it but you know it looks genuine and don't question it. At a young age, Johnny used to love typing invoices for his father George's haulage firm and adding them up, applying the VAT and invoicing firms for the work done. He could type at an early age and liked the power he thought it gave him. It was for substantial amounts of money at the time, in the region of £20,000.00. Then he used to chase the firms for payment. He was learning business skills at a very young age. He found it far more exciting than school.

He used to love going to work with George when he was in his teens. George used to mainly transport steel from Sheerness Steel, as it was then, or all kinds of fruit from Sheerness Docks to local storage facilities or to the London markets and occasionally a bit further. The further the journey the worse the rate for the job, so George preferred London market jobs wherever possible. Johnny definitely had found his best friend in life at an early age but he did not fathom this out until much later, when he realised not everyone was as fortunate as he was to have a loving dad and best friend in one man. Whether everything George told him about life would be as true for him as it had been for George, the basis for the advice was life experience and the burning desire for him to be able to understand life and make the most of it.

Most of the haulage contractors, or at least the ones George knew, were stealing pallets of fruit, bananas, and lorry loads of both if they could get away with it out of Sheerness Docks. The boats were bringing in thousands of tons of fruit at a time, and there were loads going straight on the back of legitimate loads. Two tricks Johnny noticed early on were that a tautliner would hold 22 pallets of fruit. Lots of the loads were 20-pallet loads, so the drivers were bunging the checkers when loading, getting 22 pallets and paperwork that would say 20. The checker got his whack and the driver got two pallets to sell at the market. This was going on daily for years. It was just common practice in those days.

There was one bloke, Barrio, whose nickname was "Split Pin", who had his own book, stolen or paid for, so he would load up a full lorry load, bung the security bloke on the gate, and regularly drive off with a full lorry load of fruit for himself. It all came on top when he mixed the paperwork up one day and wrote the wrong information on it. The checker in the docks knew what was going on and told him. He let it go because Split Pin had acquired his nickname because of his personality and he had a reputation as not the sort of guy you would want to inform on. The checker did not want any trouble. It just stopped that particular fiddle on that occasion.

With the bananas, it used to be done on weight, so the scam was to have tanks on the trailer filled up with water when weighing on at the beginning, emptying the water out when weighing on after loading, and the difference in weight was about 40 or 50 boxes of bananas. Offering to put the seal on the back of the container for the seal man meant there was an opportunity not to fully seal the load until the 40 or 50 boxes of bananas had been removed first, before arriving at the delivery address. Johnny used to enjoy the transport cafés and the hustle and bustle of all the lorry drivers, life in the docks and the markets. It had a certain hustle and feel to it. It seemed to him half of people were working there were on the take or the make.

George rarely went in the motorway services. Everything in there was more expensive than in local places. The fuel, the food and the drinks were totally overpriced and often not that great. It seemed to be left in hot trays and was almost cold if you bought it. Similar to nowadays, really. Those motorway service stations seem to think that because they are on the motorway and have no competition, they can charge whatever they want. It just seems to be the most expensive place in the world to fill your car or lorry up. One day, George, Barry and Johnny were in the services to use the toilets and decided to grab a bite to eat and a drink. They were queuing for the food and drink. Barry, Johnny and George all picked up large sausage rolls. They seemed very expensive but Barry said they all had to eat them before they got to the till. The cold drinks were self-service. So, everyone ate their sausage rolls before getting to the till. Johnny kept topping up his coke from the machine. Then he wandered off to the toilet with his fizzy pop. That way, by the time George and Barry got to the till lady, three large sausage rolls, two teas and a fizzy pop had become two teas. That made the services quite good value for money, and not too expensive. Johnny loved learning tricks like this. George would always be able to cover or explain they were hungry and Johnny just needed the loo if challenged, but they weren't. Johnny often used this formula for eating in the services later in life. As Tesco's say, 'Every Little Helps'.

George explained to Johnny that you could tax the lorries in different categories. The full rate for an artic to transport full loads of goods about was about £3,000.00 for the year. You could also tax the same lorry just as a tractor unit, not to carry full lorry loads of goods, for about £100 per year. George chose the second option on the basis he could say he was using the vehicle just to load trailers in the docks, not actually carrying them on the roads. Then he could always say if caught that it was a one-off, that a vehicle broke down and this vehicle was just being used as a one-off instead. Johnny remembered that was a great money-saving scheme. Of course, the reality was George was struggling to make the job pay doing everything straight and was cutting corners and taking risks just to stay in business.

The CB radios were being used by lorry drivers at this time, in a craze sweeping the country. There was a film called *Convoy* out, and it was highly fashionable for lorry drivers to communicate all day long on CB radios. They could let each other know about road delays, traffic works and keep in touch. The most important thing seemed to be letting each other know where the police (smokeys) were. Log books were still being used at this time, before the tachograph system took over to record use of the vehicle, and these were hand-written by the drivers on a daily basis. Plenty of scope for adjustment there, as you can imagine, with working hours and breaks just being recorded by the drivers and not the vehicles. Users of the CB radio had a handle, which was their user's name, and talked in a language Johnny loved. It seemed like a code, and he loved using the CB and talking in that language. Barry suggested his handle should be "Monty", and so it was.

There was a friend of George's called Ronnie. Ronnie got caught stealing lorry loads of bananas out of Sheerness Docks. He got caught red handed. What they could not work out was how he had been managing to get out of the docks without the correct paperwork. The reality was he had one of the security officers on the gate in with him. Ronnie had him in his pocket, so to speak. It was simple if you knew that the security guy would just let

Ronnie in and out of the docks without any or the correct paperwork. The outcome was that Ronnie would never say how he did it, and the police never found out. Ronnie served a longer prison sentence for failing to cooperate with the police and was banned from the docks for two years. George said that was the correct thing to do; no need to help the police. They only knew what they were told. In those days it was true. Nowadays, technology, computers, mobile phones, new laws and new court procedures have all balanced the proceedings on the side of the law. Years ago, it was favouring defendants. Even down to the caution change that was introduced so the accused could have their silence used against them in court. Before, silence had been a right, and juries were not supposed to hold it against them. Of course, the reality was, it gave people time to sort their story out and walk into court with fully prepared alibis and prepared defences after seeing the case against them. Johnny knew it was the right thing to do deep down. You don't give people up – or grass, as it was known. The irony was after Ronnie got released from prison and was allowed back in the docks. The guy on security had kept his nose clean and been promoted. Needless to say, Ronnie made a fortune, and the security guy earnt a right few quid as well.

George also shared with Johnny that he had tried international haulage as well. Johnny remembered George going abroad for a period of about six to eight weeks. It had meant to have been a simple trip to Greece, reload and return. He did it with a guy called Paul, whom he knew from Sheerness Docks and who was in the haulage business himself. Paul had a nickname: "The Animal". He had a reputation that he could be nasty if necessary. The trip had been a total disaster for many reasons. Nothing had gone to plan. The timetable did not work out. They had many problems, including punctures, breakdowns, and they actually fell out over some of the differences. Both of them lost money over the venture. When they returned home, Paul turned funny with George. He actually threatened to harm George's family. It was a very heated telephone conversation. George had told Paul that he would be happy to meet him in a phone box and discuss the differences with him there. He needed a few hours before he could meet him because he wanted to pick up a hand grenade on the way to the meeting. When they were both in the phone box, George was going to pull the pin and let it go off if that suited Paul. That was the end of the threats and business association.

Johnny went to Terry White car sales in Newington with George when he was about 14. George had seen a V12 Daimler there and wanted it. They went to buy it and the deal went on forever. George and the salesman were haggling for ages about the part-exchange value of George's car. George loved to haggle and have a deal. Nowadays people just seem to pay the asking price of cars and accept the offers on their part-exchanges. Johnny learnt to negotiate young in life to get the best deal he could. He thought there was a certain satisfaction and skill in buying, selling and trading. Over the years he spent several hours negotiating in business, on cars and properties. Always trying to save a few quid, so to speak…

Another memory he had from childhood was when he was watching a film one day with George. The John Maynard Keynes quote, 'If you owe your bank a hundred pounds, you have a problem. But if you owe a million, it has,' was in the film, and George laughed and said 'That's right.' That always stuck with Johnny. He liked the idea of playing big.

Another couple of jobs Johnny tried as a kid were fruit picking and painting with the local travellers. He enjoyed the fruit picking and working on the farm. He got to drive a tractor, and he really liked the idea of being paid for what you pick. He thought incentive-based pay was great. It gave him a chance to work hard and reap the rewards. The job painting with the travellers was a good day rate, he remembers, and as much as you could eat in the café. The travellers were up to more tricks than Paul Daniels. Lying and cheating was just a way of life for Tom, the bloke Johnny worked for with Peter Pitcher. Still, they always got paid, and when you are hooked on gambling, that was the only part that seemed to matter. He loved the card games with the local lads and no one minded where they played. Sometimes it would be in friends' houses or the local café. On other occasions the local toilets or at the church entrance. People wanting to use the toilets or enter the church seemed ok with it. Some offered comments and some just walked round them, but they were so into the action they were not really too bothered about the odd interruption.

He had his first real fight with Sean Leks at Maidstone Grammar School. Realistically, he had only two options: take a good hiding or refuse to fight. So, he chose to fight and give it his best shot, so to speak. The fight was not going well for him in the pavilion in the school fields when it got stopped by the teachers. They both got marched before Dr Murdoch, who was the deputy head. Dr Murdoch was a massive man about 6 feet 3 inches, very large build, an almost larger-than-life character. Nothing like the headmaster, Dr Thaw, who everyone called Mad Phil because he was a Master of Arts and a Dr of Philosophy, which read Dr P Thaw M.A.D. Phil. Dr Murdoch never wore a tie. He was a history teacher and a very good one at that. He had taught Johnny and his brother previously, and Johnny always remembered him because the lessons were on Tuesday afternoons. Dr Murdoch always said that Tuesday afternoon was his favourite time of the week because all day Monday and

Tuesday mornings he worked for the government, paying his tax and national insurance. Tuesday afternoons he started to earn his own money for spending.

Dr Murdoch told the lads they could get over the problem or go down the gym, put boxing gloves on and knock each other senseless in the gym with Queensbury Rules. Of course, he had already embarrassed Johnny and Sean into agreeing to forget their differences. As soon as they left his office, they agreed to fight again after school at the field just down from the school. In for a penny, in for a pound was Johnny's thinking. He had a massive fear of not fighting. He was too worried about what all the lads would think if he bailed. He knew his reputation was on the line. As Dr Thaw said to him on more than one occasion, 'Boys will be Boys.' So, after school, everyone seemed to know it was on at the field. When he got to the field, he was shocked. It was absolutely packed. It looked like half the school was waiting. Sean was already there. The bags were flung on the floor, the blazers came off, and they were at it again. The rules were simple: the two lads would be fighting with their fists and feet until one had had enough. So off they went.

Johnny struggled from the off. He was getting hurt and it was a bit one-sided. Sean had a reputation for being a local hard nut and fancied his chances against him. A nose bleed, some bruises, and pain as well would all follow very quickly for Johnny. All Johnny kept thinking about was his image with everyone at the school. Anyway, he was really getting hurt and taking a lot of pain, which made him wild. He stood up and hit Sean with all his anger and force in the punch. The punch landed fair and square on Sean's nose. Sean's face changed totally. He had blood pouring out of his nose and was now suffering pain and fighting someone who wouldn't give up. All the lads watching the match were really enjoying it. This was a real fight, not a couple of punches. Sean asked if Johnny wanted to end it now, and he said yes. Why he said yes, he will never know. He did not realise how much he had hurt Sean and the fact that the tide had turned. He thought he was losing but was not sure that was how everyone else saw it. His reputation was good after that. He never had any trouble with anyone. What he had displayed without realising it was that he was not prepared to stay down. He may have got knocked down a few times, but he kept getting up and trying. Without knowing it, he was showing his willingness to keep going and a great attitude to have, no matter how it is applied in life. The single biggest secret to life is to keep going and not give up.

One day in the village, he and a few of the lads spotted a group of foreign lads camping in a grass field area. They thought it would be a good idea to jump all over their tent while they were in it. They did so, it all got out of hand, and they ran off. They had ruined their tent. Johnny was not sure what happened but, somehow, they all got caught. He thought one person may have been recognised and he gave everyone up. The police got involved. They were all going to be done for criminal damage and the tent got sent off to be repaired. The manufacturers lost the tent, as the tent was now evidence. A new tent was provided free of charge by the manufacturers, and they were off the hook by the skin of their teeth.

Johnny went to judo classes with George on Friday evenings, now the Scouts were closed. A bit of self-defence and exercise seemed like a good idea. He never really could get it or take to it. He got the uniform, a white belt, and off he went. He tried it a bit but had not mastered how to fall and was regularly getting slung all over the place. Still, in time he got a few yellow tags on his white belt. He entered in a competition and fought a few people who played with him. He was totally outclassed, even as a beginner. He lost all his bouts and decided he was not cut out for martial arts. It seemed like a lot of work and training, something that never appealed to young Johnny. He would rather play cards or the horses and chase the excitement and thrill of winning money and gambling.

Johnny lost his virginity at the age of about 14 or 15. It was to a girl a few years older than him called Claire. Claire had a reputation, so to speak, for being a very experienced young lady in these matters for a girl so young. Anyway, one Friday evening Johnny's parents were out and Alex was at university. His friend Gary Mannering was dating Claire's best friend Michelle. Gary had a car and a job. It was agreed the four of them could have a party at his place on this particular Friday evening. It was not much of a party. When everyone was there, they very quickly split into two couples and went into separate bedrooms. In his bedroom, Claire and Johnny put music on. It was his Blondie LP. Gary and Michelle used Alex's bedroom but had to promise to tidy up afterwards. Claire was not his girlfriend, but Gary got Michelle to get Claire to have sex with him so they could use one of the bedrooms themselves. It did not go particularly well, he thought. He was totally inexperienced and struggled. They did the deed. He remembered thinking, was that it? Still, he had now lost his virginity and he felt proud about that. Claire was not particularly pleased or amused either. It was all very quick and they never saw each other after that, except in passing.

Sean Leks and Johnny were mates again now, after their "Rocky" experience. They were down at the Stoneborough Centre in Maidstone one lunchtime when they met this girl. Sean was doing most of the talking. Very quickly, she agreed – or offered – to take Sean and Johnny up Moat Park and have sex with both of them. They had never met a girl like this before. The three of them went up to Moat Park. He and Sean actually spun a coin to see who would go first. He lost. Sean and this girl had sex behind a tree. He thought, 'This is not for me.' The idea of having sex with a girl who had just had sex with his friend did not sit well with him. After Sean finished, he made an excuse and Sean and him went back to school.

Alex had a 50cc Suzuki moped when he was sixteen, and got a Suzuki 250cc motorbike when he was seventeen. One day, Alex was driving through Bearsted when a car pulled straight across him, giving him no chance of stopping. Alex's legs were broken badly. He was lucky to keep his legs and be alive. After that, Alex got a car and left the motorbikes alone. George bribed Johnny, really, when he was sixteen. The deal was he did not get a moped when he was sixteen but they would buy him a car when he was seventeen. This is what happened… although he was always out on his brother's motorbike when he thought he could get away with it.

One night when Johnny was out on his brother's motorbike, he came home and his parents were in the garage. He turned the engine off, rolled down the drive at Glebe Gardens into the garage, and got caught red-handed. He got told off and told never to do it again. Long after that, Vera told Johnny that when he went indoors, George said, 'That takes balls, to do that, taking the bike without permission and riding it underage.' He was driving a 250cc motorbike on the road underage with no licence. He never listened at school – or very rarely – and only occasionally listened to his parents. He knew he shouldn't take it out but was constantly seeking new thrills and excitement, and breaking the rules was just a way of life by now.

Johnny managed to get 8 O Levels at the first time of asking, which astonished everyone at school and home. He cheated a little in some exams and did well in others without any unfair advantage. He was a very gifted individual, looking back, especially as he had not attended all the lessons or done the work. He just did not apply himself in the correct manner. The busy head and his ADHD made paying attention and living in the moment very difficult for him. He started doing his A Levels. He had chosen History, Politics and Economics.

Johnny was in the lower sixth form doing his A Levels. He had won at the dogs. He decided to have a monkey, slang for £500.00 on a horse. He liked favourites. He also liked Lester Piggott and Willie Carson. He walked into Coral's Maidstone, and placed £500.00 on a horse Lester was riding later that day. Coral's were a modern, large chain of bookmakers, and all their prices were displayed on TV screens. Some of the other bookmakers, small independent ones, were still putting the prices on boards and had a board man with a marker pen continuously changing the odds of each horse on the wipe boards. The race was about 3.40pm. Johnny could watch it after school. He thought about nothing else all afternoon. After school, he got down to Coral's with five minutes to spare. He watched the betting. He had taken 7/4 at lunchtime. The horse drifted on course. Then got smashed off the boards, and backed in to 6/4 favourite. The race was off. It was no steering job. The horse was struggling about three furlongs from home. Lester threw the kitchen sink at the horse, got the rails and held off all challengers in the last furlong. He had won. Johnny tried to give the look of never any danger and he knew he would win, but that had not been the case at all. Johnny got back £1,375.00 including his stake. His life had just changed in one horse race. This was the way to live, he thought. He was wasting his time with A Levels. He was going to be a professional gambler. It was his destiny.

CHAPTER 3
LEAVING SCHOOL

AFTER THE WIN in Coral's in Upper Stone Street in Maidstone, Johnny could see the future – or so he thought. The last thing on his mind were A Levels, working hard, exams, university. He could be a professional gambler, work a few hours per week, and live the dream. His behaviour at school got worse and worse. He simply did not want to be there. He was reading the *Sporting Life* one day in a politics lesson. In those days the *Sporting Life* was the daily Bible for horse and dog racing. It was printed every day. Johnny was not hiding the paper. He was trying to select a winner or two for that day. His politics teacher and form tutor, who also happened to be the local Labour political candidate, Gordon Best, was furious. He recommended to the headmaster Johnny be suspended.

Johnny had spent most of his time at Maidstone Grammar being punished for his inappropriate attitude and behaviour. It started with getting caught smoking, not doing his homework, skipping lessons, taking days off school and writing his own notes, always giving back chat and disrupting lessons, fighting, and getting caught filling out his own dentist appointments. It all seemed to just be part of the normal education process. Well, it was for him. He was a regular at detention, visiting the headmaster, lines, the cane, he was put on school report, various letters used to get sent home about his behaviour and conduct, and now suspension.

What a cheek, he thought. He would have to see the Head, Dr Pettit, later that day to find out his fate. Gordon Best had actually been very helpful to his brother Alex a few years earlier. Johnny always thought he had it in for him, but looking back, he thought Mr Best was probably trying to help or at least instil some discipline in him. When Johnny sat down with the Head, he had already accepted the recommendation to suspend him. He told Johnny as much and gave him a letter addressed to his parents. Clearly reading racing papers in the lessons and ignoring the teachers was not something anyone was prepared to tolerate. Johnny opened the letter in front of the Head and said if he suspended him, he would not go back. Bloody cheek of the man, he thought. Johnny may have not wanted to be there but he wanted to leave on his terms. Dr Thaw said his decision was final and tried to have a go at him for opening the letter addressed to his parents. Johnny had been opening George's mail for years at home for his business. Hard for him to see what the problem was. Anyway, it all seemed to pan out how he thought. He was suspended for two weeks. He refused to go back. Johnny's parents, the local council and school governors tried to encourage him to go back. He was absolutely bloody-minded. He had said he would not go back and he would not change his mind. His stubbornness had seen him go from one of the best schools in the country at that time to the dole office. He simply thought he knew better; he did not want to back down from what he'd said to the Head about not going back, and in truth gambling and leaving school was his preferred choice.

He was living at Lenham on the dole. His recent winnings had all gone back to the bookies, and more. He was not exactly living the high life; his dole money was about £25.00 per week. After about six weeks of lying in bed, George told him it was all over. He had to find a job, go to work and sign off the dole. Johnny started looking for a job and came across a vacancy for a window cleaner for a firm in Lenham Heath. He went for an interview and was offered a start. He was sent out with a nice old boy, Les, a decent bloke, and they got on for a while. The wages were not great – about £50.00 per week. The firm had lots of school and hotel contracts. Johnny was cleaning a hotel in Blackheath and somehow the rate for cleaning the hotel came up. He wanted to get the contracts himself and get his own firm up and running. Johnny approached a few hotels and could not get any work. George told Johnny it takes years to build up contracts, business contacts and a business. Johnny was not convinced, but George was right, and as usual, Johnny wanted to run before he could walk. He left the window-cleaning job shortly afterwards. His first job had lasted about 6 or 7 weeks; not exactly a career plan, but he gave it a go.

After his window-cleaning effort, Johnny was still a learner driver. He had a red Ford Capri. It was K registration and he loved the car. Johnny's parents had bought it for him as they agreed they would because he did not have a moped at age sixteen. The asking price had been £250.00 and George paid £200.00 for it. Johnny used to whizz about everywhere in it whether he had a passenger who had a full driving licence or not. One evening, he was out in his car with Peter Pitcher at his side in the passenger seat. Peter had passed his test a few months earlier, so everything was legal and above board, with the red L plates displayed on the front and back of the car. They had been to Maidstone looking to try and chat up girls. Their regular trick was to pull up by girls and pretend they were lost and ask for directions. They knew where they were but it broke the ice a little and, sometimes, they met some nice girls and just had a laugh and a joke with them. Peter, in the passenger seat, could talk for England. They had some harmless fun and used to get a takeaway.

On this particular evening, they were driving home through Bearsted when the police pulled them over. It was quite late, about midnight. The police officer who came to Johnny's window really had a terrible attitude, and so did he. Johnny very quickly started giving him some lip. He asked for Johnny's documents. In those days the police used to look at the tax in the window after stopping a car, then ask for a copy of the driving licence, insurance and MOT certificate, depending on the age of the vehicle. The police computers that nowadays tell the officers all about the car, driver or registered keeper, tax, insurance and valid MOT simply didn't exist. Lots of people were driving about without driving licences but had their friend's name, address and date of birth to tell a police officer if they got stopped driving. Those details would be recorded on the document issued by the officer, and their friend would attend the nominated police station and show their documents. It was a long time before photographs appeared on driving licences.

Johnny was young, cocky, and he could be rather full of himself. He certainly had no time for the police. He at that age thought that they were simply a necessary evil. George had told Johnny that when he was younger, and it made sense to Johnny. The officer asked Johnny to get out of the car, and he did. Johnny started giving the police officer some lip, showing off in front of Peter, who was in the passenger seat. He knew he and the car were fully legal so thought he had nothing to worry about, so he started threatening the officer with cheek and arrogance. The copper threw Johnny on the bonnet of the car, put his hands behind his back and put handcuffs on him. By this time the other copper had got out of the car and was keen to know what was happening. Johnny screamed police brutality and said, ‘Who do you think you are? Starsky and Hutch?’ The whole thing got so out of hand over nothing at all, really. It was in reality just a routine traffic stop. The second copper suggested it might be an idea if he were released from the cuffs and went on his way. Johnny was a little so-and-so, that was sure, but the police officer’s reaction was totally disproportionate. So, he was released and sent on his way, probably a just outcome for all. Peter told everyone about the comment he had made, and Johnny was over the moon about that part. He thought his inappropriate behaviour was giving him a great reputation and the respect of all his friends.

A few of Johnny’s older friends had a full driving licence, so he guessed his parents thought or hoped he was always out with one of those friends by his side. The car was a great hit with the girls, and he used to try and take as many girls out in it as possible, hoping for lots of activity that young teenage boys and girls like to get up to. One night he went dog racing with the Dawsons and stayed at their house that evening. He woke up early in the morning and decided to get home. He jumped in his car and set off for home. It was about 7 am. The windows were still not clear. He had not waited for the windows to clear or sprayed them with ice remover. It was a cold, frosty morning. The heater was not the quickest, and he had no patience, just wanted to get home, so off he went with the choke fully out.

As he left Doddington and came down the hill to the A20 to cross in to Lenham square, the passenger front window had not cleared yet. He leant over to wind the passenger front window down, but the seat belt would not stretch and he could not reach. Instead of taking the seat belt off so he could reach, he tried to see through the window. He was still half asleep himself. He thought he could see and there was nothing coming. He looked to his right and that was all clear. He drove straight across the A20, or he attempted to. Cars were traveling along the A20 from his left to right, or from Ashford to Maidstone. He pulled straight out in front of a man in a Ford Orion, causing a bad traffic accident. Both cars were write-offs. The only saving grace was that no one was hurt. Instantly, Johnny realised he was not insured without a passenger with a full driving licence. As he got out of his car, a woman leaned out of a window of one of the houses nearby and shouted, 'Don't worry. I have called the police.' Johnny totally panicked, ran to the other car and told the driver the truth. He said, 'Please remember I had a co-driver. I know it was my fault. I accept that, but you may not get paid if I did not have a co-driver.'

Johnny thought the other driver didn't appear too interested but he agreed to the fact he had in fact had a co-driver with him when the accident occurred. Johnny knew someone who would say if necessary that they were with him in the car that morning. The police arrived, took details, and it was clear what had happened. They were all good. Johnny said his friend had left because he went to work. No one seemed that interested. Next thing George pulls up. He was on his way to work in the morning. He was delighted no one was hurt. Johnny told him what happened, and George knew straight away his son had been on his own. His look said it all. Anyway, he pressed him on the issue, and Johnny kept insisting Peter was with him. The cars got towed away. The insurance forms got filled out and everyone got paid. Johnny bought a new-shape Ford Cortina with his insurance cheque. It was about another £200.00 more than he got paid, but it was a great buy. He bought it from his next-door neighbour, who let it go cheap because he had just been promoted and given a brand-new company car as part of his package.

When Johnny applied for his provisional licence, he filled out the forms honestly. He used to write 7s as French sevens, with a line through the stem of the seven. He used to think it was highly sophisticated. Anyway, this time he didn't, and the upshot was that his date of birth come back as 1961, not 1967. He never noticed it to start with. The date of birth used to form part of the driver licence number. One day Johnny got stopped by the police in his car. Asked for his date of birth, he told him. The officer said Johnny was wrong. They got into a heated discussion. Then the error came to light. Johnny told him the facts, which were true. The man understood and told him to get it changed. Johnny never did, and later on in business it helped him to pretend to be 6 years older, particularly when driving taxis underage. Johnny always looked older, and he guessed this helped. He never changed his license until 2012, when he was released from prison. He had to apply again after a three-year drink-driving ban. He had the medical and was passed to hold a licence. When it came through, he thought no more, sent it back with his birth certificate and got it corrected, 28 years after the policeman had told him to get it changed. Still, better late than never.

Johnny failed his driving test the first time but passed on the second attempt. He was still only 17 years and a few months old. He had regularly taken Alex's Ford Capri out when no one was watching. Alex was in London at university and had left his Ford Capri at home. Johnny knew where the keys were and regularly used to take it out for a spin, even driving to and from school in Maidstone in it before he was suspended and left.

Alex had caught on. A few things had given Johnny away. Alex knew the exact position he had left the car in, the mileage and the fuel in the tank. What student wouldn't? Alex was living on a grant and struggling to make ends meet. So, when the car was parked differently, there were more miles on the clock and less fuel in the tank, you didn't need to be Sherlock Holmes to work out someone had been using the car. Since George or Vera could have just used the car and told him why, yet hadn't, it wasn't them, so that just left Johnny. Alex accused him of driving the car without his permission. Johnny pulled his best face of 'Who, me? Why would I do that?' and denied it. It was clear the car had been used but there was no proof that Johnny was the culprit, apart from the process of deduction in Alex's mind. Alex had been at university for a long time without returning home and Vera couldn't remember if she may have used the car in that period. Johnny was off the hook once again and just smiled at Alex. Vera's admission that she could not remember was the end of the matter.

Johnny had first driven a car in Sheerness Docks at the age of about 12. George would let him sit on his lap in the driver's seat and Johnny would do the steering and the pedals. Not exactly like when Johnny took lessons with BSM, but he really enjoyed the experience and responsibility. There were lots of open spaces in the docks, which meant if there were mistakes or erratic driving, there were no people or expensive property about to crash into. After that, Johnny was allowed to move the HGV arctics George owned; not drive them about, but move them forwards or backwards a little. One day while waiting to unload the lorry full of grapes at a fruit storage facility in Faversham, George was chatting to Barry (one of George's drivers) and

Johnny was just playing around them as he often did if George was talking to someone. George's lorry needed to be moved forward, so George asked Johnny to move the lorry forward. What a great honour and responsibility for him! He would be doing it on his own and trusted. It was about 40 feet or so, so it was just put in first and crawl forward at a very slow speed, stop and put the air brake on. What could go wrong? Johnny, by mistake, put it in reverse gear rather than first gear and started reversing the fully loaded artic into the vehicle behind. Barry had parked his lorry just behind George's. There was not a great gap between the two lorries. Johnny had turned up the eight track playing Frank Sinatra tunes and his window was wound up, so he could not hear George and Barry shouting for him to stop. They were literally witnessing one of George's vehicles being used to crush another. Not many vehicles would recover from having a 40-ton artic being hit face-on by a tautliner, even at a slow speed. But Johnny realised he was going backwards. He hit the brake, took it out of gear and put the brake on. The gap was down to about three or four inches between the Ford Transcontinental and the tautliner with the other Ford Transcontinental at the front of it. George opened the cab door, and Johnny smiled as he always did when he saw his dad, and jumped out. George jumped in. George put the vehicle in 1st gear and drove it forward. The near-disaster had been averted. Afterwards everyone was laughing and joking about it. Even George saw the funny side, with a huge amount of relief as well.

The next job Johnny took was as a milkman. He got the job working for a firm in Tenterden. It was about a 40-minute drive each way for him. The manager told him whatever happened, if he could not make it to work, he had to let them know in advance. Johnny did the training for two weeks with a really nice milkman who was covering the round that he was going to take on. It worked well. He was showing him all the ropes. He was a really nice guy who had worked for the firm for about 25 years. He showed Johnny everything he needed to know about the round, collecting money, the cold box products on the back of the milk float, and introduced him to the customers as the new milkman. It reminded Johnny of learning the paper rounds. After two weeks' training, he was given his own milk float and round. The first two days were great. Johnny used to like being up in the early morning and finishing about 1 pm. On the third morning Johnny set his alarm to snooze. Johnny thought his dad may have turned it off later but it was probably him. Next thing he knew, he woke up about 12 o'clock. George told him the manager rang from the milk depot, and that he was finished. He had to take his bits back, which was mainly the uniforms, and he would be paid what he was owed. George did not seem that bothered. George probably realised 3 am starts and Johnny were not a long-term deal.

Johnny's next job was as a delivery driver for Wiseway Stationery in Maidstone. He used to drive the transit like a man possessed, get the deliveries done in record time, and then skive off for hours in the van. If he went back early, he was expected to help in the warehouse. This was not the job he wanted so he never went back early. He always went back just in time to fill up for the next day. The owner sacked him after a few weeks. He didn't like his attitude and had learned that at the weekend and some evenings his van was allegedly being used for some very strange activity. He had reports from the police that the van was used in a theft of tiles from a builders' merchant and even an armed robbery. Both events allegedly occurred in Harrietsham, the second one in a petrol garage.

Johnny remembered the local police officer coming round to investigate the complaint made about the builders' merchant. He was the local bobby, PC Hollis. He knew George and Johnny from previous dealings with both. George went to the door; Johnny was sitting on the stairs out of sight. He listened intently. George said it must be a mistake as he was with him all last night, when the tiles were stolen. What had happened was Johnny, Paul and Steve realised how much Kent Peg tiles were worth and knew a builders' merchant who had thousands of them lying on pallets in their yard. There was a metal fence surrounding the yard, but not that high. It was next to Harrietsham train station. So late at night they had formed a human chain to pass the tiles from the yard to the back of the van and managed to get about 2000 tiles. All went well. No one interrupted them and they already knew where they could sell them the next day for cash. The only thing they had overlooked was that during the theft a train had pulled into the platform and a passenger reported to the police when he got to his stop that at Harrietsham he witnessed three men taking the tiles from the builders' merchant over the fence and putting them into the back of a white van which had Wiseway Stationery written on its side. The witness could not identify or see the men in the dark, just their silhouettes, and could not see the registration because he saw the side of the van, not the back or front. After a brief conversation, PC Hollis accepted George's word, said it must be a mistake, and left. Johnny never faced any charges over either allegation. George knew, of course. He told him he needed to sort himself out. Johnny never knew it but things at home were going to change very dramatically.

The van also got used as a getaway vehicle from a robbery in a garage not too far from Harrietsham train station. Johnny, Paul and Barry realised that there was cash in the tills at the petrol garage on the A20 in Harrietsham. The petrol was put in your vehicle by the petrol attendant in those days. Most people paid by cash. The plan was, Johnny would hide in the van about half a mile away from the garage. Paul and Barry were going to get close to the garage, wait there until there were no cars waiting for service, then nip into the shop area where the attendant would sit waiting for customers by the till, sweets, car products and cigarettes. They were going to cover their faces and demand the cash from the young lad who was serving. They all figured that he was young, would be scared, and give the cash up by opening the till. So, when the garage forecourt was empty, Paul and Barry went in with their faces covered and demanded the contents of the till. Only one problem – the cashier said no. Johnny was unaware of everything, just sitting in the van waiting for them to return. Paul was infuriated and a proper handful. He simply grabbed hold of the guy and put his face straight through the window. Then he opened the till, took the cash and ran to the van. When Paul told Johnny what had happened, he was shocked. He would have run, he thought, not put the guy's face through the window. Deep down, he did not really approve of that. It was ok to steal from the garage but not to do that. Still, it had happened, and the stolen money amounted to about £300. Just like the money from the sale of the tiles, it vanished very quickly in the night clubs in Maidstone.

It was at this time that Johnny's parents split up. This broke his heart. It devastated him. George said Johnny needed to go into the lounge because he and his mother wanted to talk to him. How Johnny knew what was coming he would never know; it was probably the way George spoke to him. It just felt bad. This was a new experience, but he knew and wrote on a piece of paper *Mum and Dad are splitting up* before walking into the lounge. When he got there he was told to sit down on the sofa. George and Vera were sitting in the two armchairs. They both explained that Mum and Dad were going to split up and George was leaving. In temper and anger, Johnny threw away his scribbled bit of paper and started crying. He was right, unfortunately. Dad moved out. Johnny was not emotionally equipped to deal with this. Somehow, he felt guilty or responsible. It was not his fault at all but deep down he wondered if he had caused the split. It was between them, they'd told him that, but he just did not listen. He felt so guilty and carried guilt around about that for a long time. Johnny was not sure how his brother found out. He was at the London School of Economics at the time. George was heartbroken that the marriage failed, and Johnny remembered a bit later on George saying to him that if he had his time again, he would probably get some houses in London and have a few girls working (on the game – as it was known) for him rather than get married. George also told him to keep away from drugs, and that best to keep out of prison or he might end up having a load of trouble in there he could do without. Johnny had seen the film *Scum* and put two and two together.

Johnny realised that a lot of the lads in the local café were builders or tilers. He had no knowledge of either but they all kept on about employing labourers and tilers. If you have the pair, you have a firm, he thought. Johnny was 17. He advertised at the job centre for both, started ringing firms for work, and got work. Now he was a tiling company. How hard could it be? Only one slight problem with employing people to do a job you cannot do yourself: how would you really know if they were any good? He soon learnt.

Johnny had no problems with getting work. Everyone was subbing off everyone. The building industry was booming. He got a job doing a new roof on a beautiful old barn conversion for a farmer in Upper Harbledown, near Canterbury. It only lasted a few days. He remembered the farmer screaming at them after a while, 'Just because it is a barn, I don't want fucking cowboys on top of it.' Johnny thought it was quite funny, and he was right. Clearly, he could see the lack of ability in the team he had assembled. He never even knew some of the terms and names of different tiles they were supposed to be using. It was all over very quickly and with no money earned whatsoever.

The next job was worse. They were doing a strip and retile on a roof in Ashford. A semidetached house. The bank holiday weekend was coming up. They started and the lads did not want to work over the three-day holiday. So Johnny came up with a plan. It all looked easy to him. He was going to work hard for the three days, get a lot done, so come Tuesday they would be cracking on. He went there on Saturday and continued stripping the roof and covering it up using sheets to weatherproof it before they put the felt and batten on and then laid the tiles. He worked hard. He went home looking forward to Sunday and Monday. Johnny went back Sunday and did the same. Sunday night it poured down with rain. Two rooms upstairs flooded and needed to be totally redecorated. Johnny and his team got slung off the job and sacked. The bloke he had subbed this job off knew he did not have a clue. He said he knew deep down he was just blagging, but he liked him and thought perhaps his lads did know what they were doing. They parted on really nice terms, but of course, there was no more work.

Johnny still thought he knew he could do it. He managed to get another job in Sturry. It was a beautiful farmhouse, a great job, and he thought he was beginning to understand roofing. He was picking things up very quickly, learning from his mistakes. His friend Paul Dawson wanted to help. He was home on leave from the army. He had signed up in the army for seven years. His brothers all came to help as well. It all seemed to be going well. After a couple of days, they looked like a firm at last. Johnny genuinely never knew one of the lads on the job went in through the roof and took a load of lady's jewellery. They all went out clubbing that night, blew all the money, but Johnny did not know how they got the money. It was the cash from the sale of the jewellery. They all went back the next morning and the police were waiting for them. For once in Johnny's life, he did not have a clue what they were talking about. He soon realised what had happened. They were charged with theft; everyone denied any involvement and the matter got dropped at a later date by the Crown Prosecution Service. If convicted, Paul would have faced discharge from the army. Johnny was furious. He felt let down by the person responsible. He lost the job. He actually went back and tried to save it but their bridges had been burnt. His roofing company collapsed that day. He has never done any roofing work since. The lads in the café all seemed to earn good money out of it. He had earnt nothing, but it had been more experience under his belt.

He bought his first house when he was seventeen. He wanted to buy it, rent it out and build up a portfolio. He applied for a mortgage with the Anglia Building Society. He applied for a 95 percent mortgage and was approved. The house was £33,000.00. He had the £1,650.00 deposit. Everything was looking good. The building society wrote to him and told him that he could not take out a mortgage until he was eighteen. He never realised, and neither had they when he made the application. He went to the seller and told them the facts. It meant a two-month delay. They were ok with that. Everyone understood why there was a delay and they all agreed to proceed on Johnny's eighteenth birthday. In the two-month gap, he blew the deposit in the bookies on the horses. He was in bits. He didn't know what to do. He went back to the Anglia Building Society, told the manager some halfway plausible fantasy. She said fine, have a 100 % mortgage, and he did. She had saved the day. But Johnny never learnt his lesson.

He had managed to put the deal together and he bought the house. It was a three-bedroom end-of-terrace house – 56 Jefferson Road, Sheerness. He was a property owner at 18. The theory was good. The rent nearly equalled the mortgage and he would make up the shortfall. But he had no idea about tenants. He just thought, get a tenant and they pay, and they look after your property for you. What a great deal!

A young woman applied to rent the house. He had put an advert in the local paper. She seemed ok and he took her on trust. She said she had a job. She paid the rent for a while. There were no problems. Then she lost her job and her boyfriend moved in. He was about 6 foot 2 and fancied himself. She signed on benefits and was claiming housing benefits. This all seemed in order. Johnny had never understood the money was hers and would go to her. He thought housing benefit would and should be paid to the landlord. He never received any rent for weeks. He rang the council, and they explained they would not talk to him. It was her claim, not his. They did tell him she was getting the rent paid to her directly. That was her choice. He went over to see her a couple of times but could never catch her in. Mobile phones were not out yet and she did not have a land line. Johnny soon began to think she was avoiding him, and he was right. It had gone on for months and house prices were falling. This was not exactly how he had planned everything. He went over one day with the keys and let himself in. There were several bodies sleeping on the floor, either drunk, high, or both. It was like some kind of squat or doss house. Johnny was furious. He started ranting and raving. The big boyfriend got up and Johnny told him he was not being paid his rent. Johnny told them they had to leave. He told Johnny in no uncertain terms to f*** right off. Johnny was on his own and decided to take his advice – well, at least until he could think straight. He left and went home. He spoke to George about the situation. George sorted it for him, as he always had. George knew a bloke who understood his plight. He was not a ruthless property owner being hard on tenants. He was just trying to get on. Johnny did a deal with the bloke. Whatever happened, he said, they would leave. In reality, he did nothing except turn up. He was a local character with a reputation that preceded him. They went round there, let themselves in. The guy copped hold of the boyfriend and told him, 'You can either leave through the front door or the window, but you are leaving.' They were all out in less than ten minutes. The property had been neglected and vandalised badly but Johnny had got possession. The reality was it was worth about £27,000.00 now and was a tip with lots of damage. He pondered the situation, then went and gave the keys back to the building society. The lady behind the counter listened and asked him for a forwarding address in case there was a shortfall in the sale price and the outstanding mortgage. He gave her a fictitious address in Ireland and was glad the whole experience was over.

Shortly after that, he received a summons to appear in court accused of unlawful eviction and depriving a person of a roof over their heads. The tenant was on legal aid as well as drugs. Johnny went to court. It was adjourned a couple of times, then the boyfriend of the woman became ill and there was a long delay. The case finally came to court and failed on a technicality, something to do with the fact that he was not on the rent agreement and never had been. It was he, not she, who was the complainant. So, the case was dismissed. He was furious. Johnny was smug as a bug. As Johnny left Sheerness Magistrates Court on his own and walked across the road towards his car, the boyfriend jumped on him from behind, got him on the ground and gave him a rather quick good hiding in the middle of the road, then quickly ran off. What Johnny particularly remembered was all the cars driving round them while this was happening in the middle of the road. No one stopped at all. When the guy ran off, Johnny got up, jumped in his motor, confirmed no broken bones, and went home. He was going to go back with someone and find him and carry it on, but he never knew where the guy lived, and so never did. The matter was now finished.

George used to have a fuel account in a garage for his haulage business. It was on the Isle of Sheppey. Nowhere near where Johnny lived, but Johnny was allowed to use it from time to time. One night he was over at Sheerness and ran out of petrol. He was on his own, had just a few shillings in his pocket and it was early in the morning. He had been to a local night club and not thought it all through properly. He had spent too much in the club trying to chat up girls. All the garages were closed. Johnny had a garden hose in the boot and a petrol can. He had learnt the art of syphoning petrol and was quite good at it. He used to have a knack of getting the pipe out of his mouth before the petrol started flowing through. All he needed was the right car. In those days most cars did not have locking caps, just a cap that turned. He found one near Sheerness town centre. He gave it a go but could not get any petrol out. Strange, he thought. The car probably didn't have much petrol in it. Johnny left the car and started walking, on the lookout for another one. Next thing, a police van pulled up with about four of five officers in it. The copper driving got out and asked what he was up to walking along with a petrol can and a piece of garden hose. Johnny said he had run out of petrol and needed to get some petrol to get home, so he was walking until he could get some assistance. He said Johnny was equipped to syphon petrol. Johnny put on his shocked look and tried to look amazed at such a suggestion. He was taken to Sheerness police station, and George was called. Johnny was held, interviewed and charged. The case went to

Sheerness Magistrates Court. Johnny denied the charge. Due process took over and a date was set for trial at the Magistrates Court. It got out of hand, with the Crown calling all the officers. They never found the car he had been trying to syphon from. That weakened their case. All they had was Johnny was walking down the street equipped and had intent, which was the officer's opinion. Johnny denied under oath. George gave evidence about his fuel account, proving Johnny's right to use, his previous usage and the amount he spent on fuel monthly. The Magistrates could see it was such a weak circumstantial case. Johnny was found not guilty. He always remembered the petrol can and hosepipe were exhibits in the case. As Johnny and George left the court, the police officers were talking in the waiting area. The driver of the police van looked at them with disbelief. George and Johnny were both laughing – why not? George said to the officer, 'Do you always carry the can?' He was not amused. Johnny had escaped the wrath of the law once again.

CHAPTER 4
EARNING A LIVING

JOHNNY WAS unemployed again after the roofing experience, and needed a regular income. He started seriously looking in the job centre at all types of vacancies. He found a job for a warehouseman in Maidstone, working evenings. He enquired further, and an interview was arranged for him. It was working for Bucks Distribution on the Parkwood Industrial Estate. The job entailed working in a warehouse loading and unloading delivery vehicles. He arrived on time for the interview and was seen by Tom Dewey, who was the general manager. It was very much a standard job interview, and he was offered a start. The wages were good for the kind of work it was, he thought.

He started about a week later. He was given a uniform, a quick look round the warehouse, introduced to a few staff members and the evening staff foreman, a man called Terry. He seemed quite a decent bloke, and most of the crew seemed to be friendly enough in their own way. It turned out that this firm specialised in handling certain goods for Marks and Spencer's and all the fixtures and fittings for certain banks. NatWest was one of them. A lot of the stuff in the warehouse was very expensive but purpose built just for certain customers. It had no real value apart from to its clients.

The work was simple. It was quite hard at times, very physical. The evening crew had a certain workload to do every evening, unloading a certain number of lorries, then loading the fleet that operated from the warehouse for the next day's deliveries. Once that was done, they could all go home except one person, who would have to stay until the next crew came in for their shift. So it was job and knock, and they used to crack on with the job to get home early.

After a few days of working in the warehouse Johnny met one of his school friends, James Taylor. James lived in Bearsted and his father was one of the founding partners in Ward and Partners, one of Kent's most successful estate agents. He had been off when Johnny started but he was the stock controller for the evening shift. He worked in the office, which was built in the warehouse. James used to check all the stock in the warehouse and checked that the correct information had been entered on the computer, and that it all matched exactly. Any discrepancies, he used to backtrack and find out if it was a computer error or stock error. Then he could alter the records to suit, giving a written explanation of why there was an alteration for future reference. It all worked quite well. James had memorised all the store codes so that when he was entering stock on the computer, he really could do it quickly. During his breaks, James used to show Johnny how to do it, and he would enter some data on the computer. Johnny quite enjoyed working on the visual display units. He thought it was a better job than working in the warehouse loading and unloading vehicles. Within a few weeks, James was offered the daytime stock controller position. He was over the moon, because he liked the job but did not like the evening shift. He accepted, and recommended to Mick, the Transport Manager, that Johnny could easily do the job in the evenings. Mick asked Johnny and he was chuffed to bits. He saw it as a promotion. The pay and bonuses were the same but working in the office in the evenings meant he did not have to answer to anyone. Terry did not really know how much work he had to do, so he could always wangle being busy if Terry needed help.

Vera moved from Lenham to Canterbury and Johnny went with her, so now his commute was about 30 miles each way rather than 10 miles each way.

It was about September and all was going well. Johnny used to work five evenings per week. Marks and Spencer's had so much stock on order for their stores for Christmas, they were struggling for space on a short-term basis. They asked Bucks Distribution if they could just use their warehouses to look after the stock, mainly lorry loads of jumpers and clothes, for a short while until they could reduce their stock in their warehouses and make space to store it themselves. Of course, it was all agreed, but not with much real organisation. Lorries were just delivering lorry loads of clothes. It was just being neatly stacked, not really counted or checked. This was happening on a daily basis, several times. Very quickly, a few of the staff realised this stuff was worth a small fortune. Johnny's gambling was in full flow all the time he could fund it. It was far too tempting. Johnny and a few of the staff just started helping themselves to the stock. It was so easy to sell. Johnny started doing several regular trips of an evening and night-time with his car full up. There were no cameras in the warehouse. The security man on the gate was an elderly gentleman. Johnny thought his purpose was mainly to keep unauthorised people out, not worry about staff leaving. He used to offer to get him drinks or food from the garage. The man never wanted anything. He had a flask and his sandwiches. The everyday stock in the warehouse had no real value to ordinary people. The clothes were high quality and everyone seemed to like Marks and Spencer's clothes, especially on the cheap. It was all Marks and Spencer's winter range, mainly jumpers and cardigans. Greed took over completely and most of the night shift were all diving in. The foreman, Terry, was the only person not helping himself. It went on for weeks. No one really knew what was supposed to be there, certainly in terms of the volume of items. They just kept taking it out, and they just kept delivering it. In the end Terry helped himself, but only to a few bits, just a couple of items for himself.

Johnny was trying to run his own commercial operation, and so were some of the other lads. It was very good for a while. The only problem Johnny had was that he was losing all the money he was making in the bookmaker's every day, so it was all for nothing, really. He could just not see that at the time. About the beginning of December, vehicles took all the stock to Marks and Spencer's warehouses or shops. It just got loaded up and shipped out. That seemed to be the end of it. No real drama. Everyone just went back to their usual duties. A few weeks later Johnny arrived for work about 4 pm, as usual. He was informed the whole crew for the evening shift had to go and see the General Manager Tom Dewey in his office. The fraud squad had been called in to investigate the losses. Johnny thought the other shifts had all been at it as well, but that was only his gut feeling. They were all sitting in the office. Mr Dewey explained there were losses of stock which totalled several hundred thousand pounds. The logic was the evening shift unloaded the vehicles, so they were somehow responsible. Johnny thought sure, what brain surgeon worked that one out? Then Mr Dewey told the police officer that Johnny could not be responsible in any way because he worked in the office, not the warehouse. Johnny liked that logic very much. The police officer asked him if that was true, and he agreed. He was told to leave the office and he did. Everyone seemed to have that shocked expression and little-boy-lost look on their face. Obviously, no one knew anything and could not assist the officer with his enquiries. The whole crew lost their bonuses indefinitely while investigations continued. Johnny handed his notice in and left two weeks later. No one was charged with any offences.

He was now living in Old Dover Road in Canterbury with his mother. He had no job and no real income to speak of, but his addiction with gambling was alive and well. By this time, he was smoking 50 or 60 cigarettes per day.

Johnny was thinking he needed some sort of income quick. He went into McDonald's one day and saw they were hiring so he thought he would give it a go for a while until he could get into something. He had just blown a fortune on the horses, so now a job in McDonald's looked appealing. He went for the interview. He did not think it was an interview. He thought McDonald's took on everyone who went for a job. A lady interviewed him. He was too honest and arrogant, looking back. He said something like he would do it for a while until he could get something decent. Needless to say, he got turned down for the job. He was well shocked. He thought she was going to tell him his starting date. He doesn't blame her, looking back; he had made no effort or attempt to be interested in working there.

Johnny used to go to a William Hill's in Dover Street just round the corner from his mum's house, and he hit a purple patch on the horses. In no time at all he had lots of cash lying about at home and the madness was telling him again it was all going to be fine. He was going to be a professional gambler after all. This was after a couple of weeks winning regularly. He used to play his winnings up and the bets got bigger.

He remembered going to Bridge Country Club one Saturday, where he met a girl called Nicola. They did not speak much. They swapped phone numbers. She rang him the next day. He vaguely remembered her. They spoke a little. He told her he was going to the football with his brother to watch the Arsenal play. They arranged to meet up at some point a little later and they did. Very quickly, Johnny moved in with her at her place in Faversham.

Nicola loved markets. Johnny had some cash. She told him he would do well if he sold baby clothes at the market. Looking back, he should have been modelling and wearing the clothes rather than trying to sell them. As a man, he was just not growing mentally or emotionally. He was still just a kid inside. He used to buy his stock in Commercial Road in East London. They must have laughed when he walked in the store. He had a pocket full of cash burning a hole in his pocket and no idea about buying clothes, especially to sell at a profit. He bought some great-looking stuff. He spent thousands on stock. He was over the moon. Mothercare had better watch out, now he was in town.

The market business soon became another headache. He had to get up at really early hours to travel to markets to see if he could have a pitch. Then if he got a pitch, it was usually a duff one, one right out the back. The regular market traders had it all sewn up for the best pitches. Some of them had been going years, something he had totally overlooked. To make the whole thing worse, the trade prices he paid for his stock were about the same as the other baby clothes stall holders were selling theirs for. He had done very little research and was snookered. He put on a brave face, marked some of his stock at the same price he had paid for it. Then people would say ‘that is dear’. Then came the rainy and windy days where everything gets blown all over the place, as well as days where his total takings did not match his stall rent. He got that down with it all, he could not care less. He used to set his stall up, ask a stall holder to look out for him if they could. Then he was off round the bookmaker's all afternoon if he had the money. For a while, his winnings were subsidising his losses on the market so he looked to be a successful market trader. Nothing could be further from the truth. He never made a penny from day one. When his good fortune ran out on the horses, he could not get rid of his stock quick enough. He virtually gave it away. He got back about 30 percent of what he paid and was glad to be out of it.

The relationship with Nicola ended abruptly. It had never been a healthy relationship for either of them. He thought he was helping her with money every week and they kind of lived like a couple for a while. They were both better off away from each other, looking back. Nicola's father had been in the retail business and he did rather well at it. He worked hard every day and just kept growing. Johnny always remembered Brian saying to him, 'The only place to be in your shop is on the till.' He knew from experience.

Then Johnny saw an advert for a radio controller at a taxi firm in Canterbury. It was for night work. He rang and got an interview for a day or two later. The firm was City Cars. He was interviewed by the owner, Peter Andrews. They chatted. It was a pen, paper and radio system, not computer despatch like a lot of firms operate nowadays. Johnny had no real knowledge of Canterbury and said so at the interview. His saving grace would be he could pick things up very quickly. He was given a trial for the job.

Lynn was the manager. She was married to Des, one of the evening drivers. Peter thought he would get it. Lynn said to Peter she thought he would not be able to do it, Peter later told him. Peter gave him the benefit of the doubt and he got the job. He took to it like a duck to water. In a few weeks he was bang on with his local knowledge and ability to do the job. He knew no one at the firm so he was fair to everyone, which is a big thing in that job. What he did realise very quickly was that if Des did alright, he would be sure to let Lynn know. This was his insurance policy as he saw it. He never discussed it with anyone but he used to make sure Des did well. He never told Des or anyone else. Peter had said Lynn thought he would not get the job so he wanted her on his side, not against him. It was probably a smart move, looking back.

So, Johnny was now about 19 years old, a radio controller at a local taxi firm which were owner-drivers. Peter used to have only one or two vehicles of his own. The office was in Military Road. Johnny used to work from 4 pm to midnight. He could smoke in the office as much as he liked, and he did. The wages were about the norm, he thought. This was way before the minimum wage and so on came out. He was playing the horses most afternoons if he could afford it. Then it became apparent some of the drivers used to go to the casinos in Margate and Ramsgate after work. Johnny had never been to a casino. About a half-hour drive each way. They said they got a free breakfast. You did in the sense there was no charge for the breakfast itself. In reality, the breakfasts turned out to be the most expensive he would ever have. He was hooked instantly. Blackjack and roulette were so addictive for him. It was all so quick, and because you gambled with chips, they seemed to lose all value whatsoever. It was just so hard to stop once he started. He never really had that lucky start some people have. He just kept losing but wanted to go anytime he had the money. The casino took over from the bookmaker's for a while. It used to feel great going to the casino after work. Johnny thought he was living like a lord. Even when he lost, he enjoyed the new experience.

At that time City Cars was a busy firm and the drivers were earning well. Johnny calculated that if he were to buy cars and plate them as private hire vehicles or taxis, he could rent them out at a profit. This would make his earning power far greater at the firm. He bought a brand-new Peugeot 405 and rented it out to two drivers, one for the day shift and one for the night shift. This was when he took full advantage of the 6-year error on his driving licence. He needed to be over 21 to drive or insure a taxi. That all went very well so he bought another brand-new Peugeot 405 and did the same. Then he bought a second-hand Orion from a driver called Titch. It was cheap, had done a lot of miles, and was a bit unreliable. Still, with the three cars rented out and him working nights, he started to do very nicely. It mostly went in the casino or bookmaker's but he was earning well every week.

One of the blokes he rented a Peugeot to on the night shift was called Barry Thomson. He was looking for somewhere to live. Johnny suggested they buy a house in Canterbury and rent the rooms out. He could have a room there himself and it would be a good investment. So they did. They got a 100% mortgage and bought 49 Whitstable Road in Canterbury. It was a terraced property with 3 bedrooms upstairs. There was a lounge and a dining room downstairs that had been made in to two more bedsits. It had a garden shed that was also used by someone to live in. Johnny used to call it a one-bedroom chalet. The man from the council laughed and said it was a garden shed. You get the picture. This house also had a small extension out the back that was like a utility room. It already had three or four tenants, mainly young females. They filled the vacant bedsits. Barry took the shed and they were showing a profit every month after paying the mortgage. Life was looking up. Johnny used to take Nicola out again, but only on dates, one night at a time, so to speak. There was never going to be any real future in it. He always liked dining out and she used to like going out for the evening with him, and stop in the lay-by on the way home. Then not seeing each other for a while.

City Cars seemed to be doing really well. Lots of contracts on the go, phones were busy, and everyone seemed to be jogging along nicely. Peter found new premises, a modern industrial unit in Roper Close, Canterbury, which he made into several offices and they moved in.

After a few months, one Saturday night, Peter and Johnny fell out. Johnny could not remember exactly over what. He thought maybe he was beginning to upset people at the firm. Maybe he was becoming too big for his boots. Maybe some drivers were jealous. Probably the truth, as with most things, was somewhere in the middle. Anyway, Johnny said he didn't need the job anymore. Peter said something and he took it the wrong way. So, he left, and so did his cars. He clearly had not thought it through at all. The two Peugeots were taxis and both on finance. The Orion was a private hire vehicle and could only work from a radio system. Very quickly, Johnny realised he had no regular radio work for the taxis, no job, no income. He had two vehicles on finance. He was in trouble. But Johnny's pride was never going to allow him to go and try and apologise to Peter and ask to work there again. He would rather go skint trying on his own.

He managed to keep a couple of drivers for the Peugeot Taxis – one was Barry and one was Trevor. He charged less rent and said he would sort something out with regard to extra work. They were just working the taxi ranks in Canterbury. The Orion, Johnny was using not for work but to drive about in. A friend of Johnny's he had met on the taxis, Nigel Craddock, who was still working on City Cars, suggested he meet a friend of his, Mikey.

Mikey had previously been a driver for Waldron Taxis, fell out with Bobby Waldron and started on his own. He had two taxis; one he drove himself and one he had a bloke called Barry driving on a 60/40 split. Mikey was a local lad, knew a few people in Canterbury, a lot of local lads in the pubs. He had a mobile phone and was building his business up on that basis. He wasn't a big man, but what he lacked in size, he certainly made up for in attitude.

The purpose of the introduction was to form a new taxi company in Canterbury. Johnny had never met Mikey before the meeting or spoken to him. He may have seen him on the taxi rank or in Canterbury but that was about it. Nigel was a great go-between. He arranged a meeting at Mikey's home in Blean one morning and he was there with them for the introductions and meeting.

Well before arriving Johnny had a plan, and so did Mikey. It all happened so quickly. They sat down in his front room, started talking, the purpose was agreed, a plan was formulated, the vehicles were valued, and they agreed premises at the rear entrance in a room of 49 Whitstable Road. They agreed equal partnership. They agreed starting dates in principle. This all took less than an hour or two. Mikey insisted on the name Lynx Taxis. He had been using this name for his taxi work for a while. He liked the name because one day when he was driving around Canterbury, one of the Lynx Distribution Group lorries cut him up. Mikey pulled in front of the lorry to stop him. Then went to drag the driver out of the cab and give him a good hiding. Before Mikey managed to do this, the lorry driver jumped out of his cab and gave Mikey a good hiding instead, left him lying in the road and drove off. That was how come Mikey named his cars Lynx Taxis. He had a landline number at home, which he was using, with the calls diverted to his mobile. They carried the number over to the office.

They were meant to have planning permission to run a cab office from a house, but they just seemed to overlook that point at the beginning. Within about four weeks they had a business trading from 49 Whitstable Road, 5 vehicles, a decent bunch of drivers, the phone started ringing, and an atmosphere that was hard to imagine. It was just a bunch of guys trying to enjoy life and succeed. The one thing Mikey and Johnny did share in common was a desire to be successful. Nigel also worked with them to start with. He had his own cab and, looking back, he wanted them both to succeed. He was a great asset to the company, and made the fleet up to six. They had icon radios, good reception as Whitstable Road was on a hill, and they wanted it bad, whatever it was. There was passion, creativity, desire and two young lads who wanted success and money.

They were so different, chalk and cheese, but with a few differences of opinion, it worked. When push came to shove, there was not a lot they were not prepared to do, really, to achieve success. Johnny had a certain something which was hard to put your finger on; not conventionally good-looking, but he had a certain presence which ensured that those he met, even briefly, always remembered him, a quality that might prove useful one day. Mikey was wayward and could be violent if need be. Johnny found this out the very first day they opened.

A driver called Ray was arguing about something on the radio with Johnny. Mikey and him were both in the office. Mikey said, 'Get him round here and we will sort it out now.' That sounded like a good plan to Johnny. Get Ray round the office and discuss the differences and work it out from there. Ray was a giant of a man, about 6 foot 2, and had been in the armed forces previously. Mikey just hit Ray and clearly shocked and hurt him, not what Johnny or Ray were expecting. Mikey told Ray to stop moaning and do the job they wanted. Ray changed his attitude and agreed. He told Mikey to calm down. Johnny sat there wondering what was going on and remembered thinking, *not sure this is what I signed up for*.

Johnny's mind was constantly ticking over for more and more shortcuts and success. He used to create the strategy and Mikey was very much a front man. He mainly dealt with the drivers. Johnny and Mikey probably had such a fear of failure, they could only succeed. They formalised their agreement at the solicitors and traded as a 50/50 partnership.

Strange what people find acceptable when they are a bit hard up, just started a business and have addictions to feed. Johnny's gambling and smoking knew no bounds. He was on 60 fags per day and the gambling would swallow up anything he could earn. He also started to visit call girls and hookers on a regular basis.

Within a few weeks of opening, they had managed to upset all the local firms and people were talking about them.

Mikey knew a lad called Darren Gray, who worked in Barclays Bank in Canterbury. He was a young, bright lad. He used to work on the radio on Sundays for them. He had been a customer of Mikey's previously. Darren used to use Mikey to go to and from his girlfriend's Teresa, who lived on the other side of Canterbury to him.

CHAPTER 5
BUSINESS WAS VERY GOOD VERY QUICKLY

WITHIN A VERY SHORT space of time things were looking up. Johnny was not sure how he would describe Mikey and him but it was a winning combination. Trade started to pick up very quickly and slowly they began to increase their market share. It would take them another couple of years of hard work and ducking and diving but they were going to be the busiest firm in Canterbury by far on turnover and job count, which in terms of a taxi business is a good measure.

They started to add vehicles to their fleet on a regular basis. They only bought new vehicles, mainly Ford Mondeos at that time, and the council started to add restrictions for taxis. Some of the restrictions included size of vehicle, colour of vehicle, black and white chequered stripes on the sides of vehicles and age of vehicle. They soon had a great-looking fleet of vehicles. They started financing them all through Lombard North Central. They never missed one payment in the 10 years that Johnny was there. After about two or three years, the manager at Lombard North Central told Johnny they could have whatever they wanted. She suggested a half a million pounds credit facility and then just said, 'Have whatever you want. It will not be a problem,' and it never was.

They used a mobile mechanic called Mick to do most of their repairs and servicing. He used to do most of it in the street in the early days. Unfortunately, as the fleet grew so did the number of accidents the taxis were involved in. On reflection, lots of the drivers had drug issues going on, one way or another. They had a fleet policy with the Prudential at the time, and Johnny knew the lady at the claims department staff way too well. At one stage, Johnny used to have to ring them every Monday to fill out the claims on the phone. They found a local firm called Stocks Garage to do all their bodywork repairs. They built up a great working relationship with them. They were a family-run firm and did a good job. Their premises were at Unit 6 Nackington Works in Canterbury, a large industrial unit owned by Paul Mathis, a local, self-made property owner. His son Andrew used to run the business for him from Castle Row in Canterbury.

They started to gain contracts with the local council, Kent County Council, and a whole host of local and national companies. They were running a genuine 24-hour service with the office manned and vehicles always available. They started putting free phones in the local supermarkets and the local hospital. They paid for the privilege but it all seemed to be on a sound financial footing. In Canterbury at that time there was only one university. It was the UKC or University of Kent at Canterbury. They had thousands of students studying up there during regular term times, and in the summer, it was packed out with visitors or language school students.

The students spent fortunes on taxis. The bus service to and from the UKC was poor and there were no clubs or bars on the campus. All the bars and clubs were in the city. Competition among the firms was very fierce. Johnny came up with the idea that if they had free phones at the UKC near the campus phones, they would clean up. This was before everyone had a mobile. In those days pay phones were the norm. The individual colleges at the UKC had banks of phones, about 20 in a cluster, and of course, it was 10 pence to make the call.

Johnny approached the University of Kent with the suggestion that they could install free phones at the university in various locations. This would save the students money and provide a better service for students – that was the approach he took. There were also concerns around security if students did not have change late at night. This way they would not have to worry about phone charges.

He remembered the first meeting he had with the governor at the university. The morning before the meeting, Johnny went into Marks and Spencer's in Canterbury and bought a really nice suit especially for the meeting. The meeting was at 3pm. It went really well. They made good ground. Johnny felt he had conveyed all his points really well, and the governor at the university was very receptive to the idea but told him it had to be referred to a board for discussion and voted upon, although he made it clear to Johnny that he supported the idea wholeheartedly. Johnny was very pleased with how the meeting had gone. He knew Mikey was going to be impressed and pleased with his endeavours.

On the way back to the office, he dived into Marks and Spencer's to take the suit back and get a refund. He threw on his jeans, put the suit back in the original bag, and walked in. He thought it would be a simple transaction and he would get an instant refund. He had the receipt, after all, and he had only purchased it a few hours earlier. Well, the lady who served him was not impressed at all. She said he had been wearing the suit and could not take it back. Of course, she was right. He looked at her in absolute astonishment and said he had tried the suit on for his wife to see and she did not like it. So, he wanted to take it back. The assistant would not have it. She stood her ground very firmly, and he did the same. He told her one or two things and they agreed he could have vouchers, not a refund. When he left the store, Johnny thought it was only because it was Marks and Spencer's that he got a result. They had a great customer service department, and it was only the little doubt that she had that saved the day. He knew they would bend over backwards not to upset their customers, and go the extra mile, even for the men who are showing their wives the suit… who are not actually married.

Johnny knew a few people at that time who used to make a living out of going in Marks & Spencer's, picking up clothes, pretending they had previously bought them, and getting refunds. He knew one bloke from Canterbury called Robert who made a career out of it. He used to think it was a job. He used to drive everywhere. He had the gift of the gab and was a decent-looking bloke, so he played the charm card with the ladies serving as well. He did it for years, made fortunes and blew it all in the bookies. He was a degenerate gambler, womaniser, drinker, with a penchant for drugs as well. It was how he funded all his shenanigans. The last time Johnny saw him many years ago, he was putting himself through university doing the same thing in different shops in different areas.

Johnny had a few meetings with the governor at the university to discuss and iron out the wrinkles, and then it went for the vote. They knew the day the decision was going to be voted on and waited for the call that afternoon to find out the result of the vote. The governor had said he would let them know the result after the meeting. He rang and told Johnny that the idea had received full support and was approved. Then he dropped the bombshell. The committee had decided that the local cab firms should all be given the opportunity to tender for the right to install free phones and operate the service. Johnny was gobsmacked – over the moon about the result, but he had not envisaged having to tender against all the other local firms to get the deal.

The governor was a little embarrassed. They arranged to meet in his office a few days later. Johnny protested the best he could, making allowances for the fact that the man was the last person he wanted to fall out with. Johnny and Mikey were both disappointed and Johnny was on a mission to save the day. The governor had a great deal of sympathy with his plight. It was a short meeting; he was a well-educated gentleman with a sense of fair play. He knew full well that if it was not for Johnny approaching him, there would not have been any such service to be put out to tender. So he and Johnny did a deal. The very last day before which the tenders had to be returned, he agreed to let Johnny know the amount of the highest bid. He was good to his word. The tenders went out and firms were given about 28 days to return their bids. Johnny and Mikey held on, with their forms fully completed, except the yearly figure they were prepared to pay the university to operate the service. Johnny rang the office the afternoon of the day before the bids had to be in at 12 noon. It was like a spy conversation. He got through. Johnny introduced himself on the phone. The governor said hello, told him a figure and put the phone down. It was over in a few seconds. They added £200.00 per year to that figure and Johnny delivered the bid by hand about 10 am the following day. They never spoke to each other again after that. Johnny and Mikey received a phone call a few days later from someone else to confirm that their bid had been successful. A letter and contract soon followed in the post. They had got a three-year deal. This turned their firm from a pretty successful cab firm in Canterbury to ultimately *the* cab firm in Canterbury. It felt like they were the Tesco's of the cab business in the area.

It was shortly after winning the tender at the university that the garage they used for their bodywork and crash repairs told them they were moving to larger premises on the other side of Canterbury and were looking to find tenants to take over the lease of their original building. It was a substantial unit with lots of parking on a small industrial estate that could be used as a garage and taxi office rolled into one. Mikey and Johnny didn't think twice about it. They agreed to take it. The rent and rates were not cheap, but there was no premium for the lease. They just lodged a deposit with the landlord. It took a few months to complete on the deal, with Stocks Garage waiting for their new lease to be drawn up and their references and application to be completed. The mobile mechanic they were using literally worked out of the back of his van, trading as Mobitech. They invited him to take a large area of the floor space in the new unit and trade as his own garage, with a gentleman's agreement that their vehicles' servicing and repairs would be prioritised. He accepted and took on an equal partner called Ian. So, when they moved in to the new unit, Mick and Ian traded as Mobitech Garage Repairs. It worked well for everyone. Johnny and Mikey had concessionary rates and priority for their vehicles. Mick and Ian had a garage with guaranteed work each week from the taxis.

Darren, the Sunday lad, agreed to be their new full-time manager. He had built up a good relationship with most of the drivers and they offered him more money than he could earn at Barclays Bank. A guy nicknamed Bobby Box bought the first London taxi to be operated in Canterbury. It was an amazing thing at the time. No one else in Canterbury had gone down this road before. The London taxi was purpose built, looked the part, could carry five passengers instead of four, and was also designed for wheelchairs. They were about £12,000.00 more than a saloon car at the time. Lynx had a large fleet of Ford Mondeos. Johnny and Mikey thought the London taxi was the future at the time, so they bought a fleet of them over the next couple of years. They reached seventeen taxis in all – six London taxis and eleven saloon cars. They had daytime drivers using the vehicles from 7 am to 5 pm and night-time drivers using them from 5 pm to the early hours of the morning, depending on when the clubs kicked out and the last trains of the day had been and gone. The London taxis proved a hit with the students, five travelling for the price of four, and the local councils liked them for the wheelchair accessibility. On their best weeks they could top five thousand jobs, but they averaged four thousand-odd jobs per week. They were turning over a million pounds per year, and in truth, neither of them was particularly content with their lot at the taxis but it did generate a great income mainly in cash. In fact, the last thing Johnny or Mikey possessed was the gift of contentment in life. Johnny lived in the bookmaker's, for card games or at dog tracks. Mikey was in the pub every day, as well as dabbling and taking cocaine. Mikey had a beautiful wife and baby and started a thing with one of the girls who was a tenant at 49 Whitstable Road. She was the sister of one of the drivers, Colin. Her name was Maria. Johnny's gambling just got bigger, the bets he placed were larger, and he found himself playing in regular card games where a lot of the players were large car dealers, drug dealers or successful businessmen looking for some action. There was probably 50-100 k in cash at a lot of the games, and a lot of unusual characters playing as well.

A guy called Stuart Fallon came to work at the cab firm doing radio shifts in the evening for cash. He was living on disability and was a total hypochondriac, as far as Johnny could work out. If anyone ever talked about health conditions or disabilities, he either had the condition, had the disability or had something worse. As far as Johnny was concerned, he was just totally self-absorbed and a benefit cheat, who just played the system for what he could. He did have genuine heart conditions but he did an awfully good job of impersonating a totally normal, physically active person when he was bombing about in his disability car, gambling in the bookmaker's or puffing on his cigarettes. Stuart had a love affair with gambling in general and the bookmakers as well. He was a character, and he did have a good understanding of the taxi business, so he was a welcome addition to the team.

Johnny and Stuart would often meet up in a bookmaker's shop in Canterbury quite by chance. Stuart had a council flat on a cheap rent in Hillbrowe Avenue, Sturry, just outside Canterbury. Johnny and Stuart did a deal when Stuart got a mortgage to buy the flat on maximum discount from the council. Johnny was guarantor for the mortgage, since Stuart was on benefits. Then Johnny gave Stuart £9,200 for himself. The flat cost £20,800. So, Johnny ended up with a £30k mortgage, for which he was responsible. Solicitors drew the agreement up whereby Stuart could live there for the rest of his life or until he chose to leave, whatever came first, at which point the flat was Johnny's. Stuart convinced Johnny that at best he only had a couple of years to live, and it seemed a good deal to Johnny at the time. Stuart was going to go on a world cruise with his money. In reality, Stuart blew his money in the bookies and would live well over another twenty years.

Mikey and Johnny had space at the unit for their own diesel tank. They ordered a one-thousand-gallon tank, brand new, and started to buy their own fuel directly from local fuel distribution companies. In those days they could save about four and a half pence per litre by doing this. It meant a saving of about £10 - £15k per year on fuel. They had a great relationship with Barclays Bank by this time, and their references were enough to get them a £25k monthly credit facility with various suppliers. So they were saving on the fuel and only paying for it the following month. They had previously been buying from local garages, paying more and paying as they went.

They also signed up to take credit card payments. They were one of the first firms to do it in Canterbury. It was a bit of a performance, really. The slide machine was in the office. They had a low floor limit, and it generally got done over the radio, with mistakes being made and payments refused because details had been recorded wrong at the point of sale. Johnny also thought a lot of the local toe rags knew the floor limit and were using stolen cards for taxis all the time. They went through a phase of having so many small payments under their floor limit returned and not credited to them, they began to wonder if it was worth it. Half the time Johnny would rip them up when they came back. If Mikey saw too many, he would blow up and it was simply not worth the aggravation with him as much as anything else. By this time, Mikey's drinking and cocaine use was flat out on a daily basis.

They installed fruit machines in the office too. At the time they were £100 jackpot, and then they upgraded to £250-jackpot machines. They were a great racket. Money for old rope every week. Lots of cab drivers have addictive personalities and like to have a flutter. Some drivers used to do their entire wages on them. Very quickly, they were generating between £500 and £800 per week just from the fruit machines. There were plenty of drivers who never played them at all. A local fruit machine provider used to sell them second hand. Of course, they were not licenced, but a handwritten sign stuck on them lower down said 'for Johnny and Mikey's use only'. No one seemed to worry about the signs and they were in their private office.

One Sunday night Mikey told Johnny there was a fortune to be made out of the cocaine business. Mikey asked if Johnny wanted to go in business with him buying and selling it. Johnny had never taken cocaine at this time in his life, and had a fear of it, so he declined. He never really understood how much money there was in the white powder but George had told him many times to keep away from the drugs and the drugs business, and he did. They never discussed it again after that night.

One Monday, out of the blue, Mikey told Johnny he was going to buy a new Mercedes for himself from the local dealer called Viking's. Mikey asked Johnny to go with him. Most times Johnny used to do the deals on the vehicles, so Johnny guessed he would go with him for the ride and try and cut a good deal for him on the model he chose. After they banked one Monday morning, they drove down to Viking's. Mikey had been researching different models and seemed to know exactly what he wanted. He and a salesman got totally engrossed in a conversation about models, extras, colours, prices and so on. Johnny was a bit bored, really, and not particularly interested.

They had a coffee, cake and doughnut area in the middle of the showroom so he was positioned quite near there and was tucking in. He was eating too much cake, too many doughnuts and drinking lots of coffee. A salesman came over and started talking to him. He could see one of his colleagues was busy with Mikey. They knew who Mikey and Johnny were because the salesman who approached Johnny had previously worked in the Ford dealership down the road, and although they'd never bought a car from him, he used to see them regularly buying new cars from his colleague at Ford's. They always used to use the same salesman, Chris, who had the desk next to him at Ford's. He asked Johnny if he wanted to buy a new Mercedes; Johnny said no, thanks, he was just keeping Mikey company. Johnny did not know it at the time but this guy was good at his job. He accepted Johnny did not want to buy one but invited him to test-drive a couple of different models. Johnny certainly had no objection and thought it would pass some time. He got the keys for the first one, a new 180 model, and off they went.

Johnny thought it was nice, it was ok. After that test drive, the salesman said he should take out a 230. So, he got the keys and off they went. Johnny was hooked instantly; at the time he was driving a new Ford and there was no comparison. The car glided along. They ended up back at the show room at his desk. About 45 minutes later Johnny had ordered a brand-new one fully loaded with all the extras. This was his first experience of buying a car where the price quoted was for the basic model, and as you kept adding extras, the bill just kept creeping up. The extras were about £9k. He also included a private plate with his own initials on it. The car was going to cost him £32k, and Johnny had to wait about 10 weeks for it to be built in the factory in Germany. He part-exchanged his Ford, did the best deal he could – they were very hard work, he thought – and signed on the dotted line. He financed the car through Lombards over 24 months. The payments were over a thousand pounds per month. Johnny was as happy as Larry. The salesman certainly knew his job. He knew if he got in one, he would buy one. By this time Mikey had decided he was not going to buy one and they left. A few days later, Mikey went in to Ford's and bought a brand-new Ford Escort Cosworth.

So now they both had nice cars at the office, business was good, both were earning a fortune and both blowing it on their addictions. In all honesty, Johnny was so wrapped up with gambling, he could not see how bad his problem had become. He was not really paying that much attention to Mikey's behaviour, and had totally forgotten about the conversation about cocaine. One afternoon when Johnny was in the office, three new Porsches turned up outside. A scouse lad called John came walking in and asked where Mikey was. He was very well dressed and polite. What shocked Johnny was the fact that the guys with him were wearing smart jackets and had guns in holsters under their arms. Johnny rang and spoke to Mikey on the phone, and he said he was on the way to the office to meet him. When Mikey turned up, they all disappeared into Canterbury. Mikey later told Johnny that John always had his own armed heavies with him; they were like his own private army. He was a guy Mikey referred to as 'we do business together.' Johnny wasn't really interested but didn't want them round the office. Still, he never said anything. What could he say?

He and Mikey ran the firm together but kept out of each other's private lives. The signs were there for Johnny and everyone to see, but he ignored them. After all, what concern was it of Johnny's how Mikey carried on? Johnny had not really thought through the consequences of Mikey's behaviour, and neither had Mikey. Lots of people knew he had a gun under the passenger seat of his Cosworth. When Mikey used to leave his car at the office, one of the lads, Gary, who used to clean his car for him, would often pop into the office and say, 'What should I do about the gun?' Johnny might be watching the horses on the television and say to him, 'Don't touch it, whatever you do.' Instead of confronting Mikey about the gun, Johnny stopped going to the bank with him on Mondays. He did not want to travel with him in his car. They used to bank quite a bit of cash on a Monday, but they did not need armed protection. The whole thing was ridiculous. So rather than going to the bank together on

Mondays, they started banking separately. They would take it in turns – Johnny one week and Mikey the next.

At this time, they had a great lad driving for them. His name was Shaun Gill, and little did Johnny know at the time how much of an influence Shaun would become in his life later. He was to become a major influence in Johnny's life, and a great friend and asset. Shaun left the firm around this time to start his own landscaping business. This was about 1993/1994. Johnny saw him once or twice in passing, but apart from that would not speak to him until 2012.

There was a lot of cash going through the business and they had VAT and tax inspections, which were probably pretty standard. Johnny was thinking if they got down to the truth of the matter, they would probably hang them both. They used to have their own formula for paying tax and VAT So, when the man from the VAT office informed them of an inspection of their records, before he turned up, all the fruit machines had gone, Mikey was on the missing list, no one was allowed anywhere near the office, and Johnny sat in the office working on his own on the radio, with all their financial records. They had accountants which did all their records very thoroughly indeed, but they worked on the figures that were given to them. Obviously, the system works on the basis of full disclosure of all the facts.

Johnny was so nervous. It was a routine check-up but he was totally paranoid. About half of the drivers were signing on the dole at that point. Johnny was smoking like a chimney, which was par for the course. The VAT inspector was there for several hours. He was a very patient and methodical man. He seemed to mind his own business but just kept checking records and documents. At the beginning Johnny offered him a coffee, but he declined. Johnny thought inspectors were not allowed to accept anything from anyone at all. It was all very professional. After a few hours he said he had discovered some problems. Johnny's heart sank. He then pointed out a couple of errors in addition, and Johnny could not even follow what he was saying so he just tried to look interested and surprised and thanked him for pointing the mistakes out. They were for a few hundred pounds. Then he said he had an area of concern. He explained that VAT was chargeable on the coffee machine sales and he could not see them disclosing it in the records. Johnny sort of shook his head and put on the little-boy-lost look; inside, Johnny was so relieved. The inspector clarified the position. Then he informed Johnny he would be writing to them pointing out the mistakes and the duty that was due. He would not fine them, but interest would be added. It was such a relief. The inspector had done his job and was on his way. Johnny knew deep down VAT evasion was a serious problem and if they worked out the formula Johnny and Mikey were using, it would have been curtains and possible prison sentences for both of them.

The next inquiry they had was from the national insurance people. All their drivers were working on a self-employed basis, and they were not paying anybody's stamp or national insurance except for a few working in the office. By this time their accountant had merged with a lot larger company in Rochester. It was a much more switched-on outfit who had taken over their accountant's practice, but they called it a merger to try and keep the clients. Their new accountants were Singh and Co, and their offices were in Rochester in Medway. The owner was Ravinder Singh, an Indian gentleman. Johnny liked him, he was straight to the point, he was professional and a chartered accountant who understood the needs of all-size businesses, including Johnny and Mikey's. It was now a limited company. They had started out trading as a partnership and on advice formed the limited company, so they had equal share holdings and were both directors.

The enquiry was held at the accountants' office upstairs, in a private room. A small team of people turned up from the national insurance agency. It was led by a lady who was rather large and full of her own self-importance. When they sat down, issues about people signing on and working were raised. Johnny had brought all the contracts they had with drivers working for them on a self-employed basis. They had been drawn up by solicitors originally. They kept blanks, and just inserted name and address. It was all very simple, really. The idea was to keep the drivers and the limited company separate for tax and national insurance liabilities. The problem was half the drivers were signing on, and most of the others were disclosing such little income on a part-time basis they could claim benefits and housing support in addition to their wages. The treasury was certainly not getting rich from the firm or the drivers' contributions.

A short while before the enquiry Johnny asked the drivers if it was all right to disclose their employment and contract to the national insurance. He was astonished how many just came clean and said no, that they were signing on the dole. In the 1990s, the council used to issue private hire and taxi licences but not inform the social security people. Later on, that practice changed, so if anyone is signing on today, the DWP are aware that the person has a private hire or hackney carriage licence, and if you have the licence, there is only one reason for having it – the fact that you are using it. So that loophole was closed later on.

So, at the accountants', the number of contracts Johnny turned up with and the number of self-employed drivers they had shrunk, amazingly so. The reality was the NI team had names of drivers who had come to their attention for working and signing on. Johnny did not have any contracts for these lads, so the team leader asked Johnny point blank and named them. Three names were correct, but Johnny had no contracts or records of them. Johnny said that if they had worked for them previously, they would keep a record of when they started and finished. They used to write a starting date, then when someone left, just write a leaving date and place them in a separate folder. This fact was the truth. Johnny had only brought the current contracts with him.

She knew Johnny was lying, or, perhaps, he thought she knew, because he knew he was. He felt particularly uncomfortable. She was not happy. Ravi sat in on the proceedings and seemed to be able to charm her and deal with her an awful lot better than Johnny did. Then she questioned the validity of any of the contracts. Her argument was that if the drivers were only working for them, they were dependant on them and therefore employed by them. At this time, they had about 45 full- and part-time drivers. If her point was valid, they were finished. The tax and national insurance contributions for years for all the drivers would have been enormous. This argument about what constitutes self-employment has since been to and fro through the courts several times. Now they would not be allowed to work on a self-employed basis. Another loophole that has been closed.

Johnny started explaining how lots of the drivers had other sources of income from other work and therefore earnings from the taxis formed only part of their total income. Then he messed up so bad, he said something that virtually confirmed her argument. Amazingly, she missed the point. Johnny was not sure if Ravi did or did not, but he casually took the conversation into another area. Johnny's heart was beating at a million miles an hour, or it seemed that way. Then he came up with this chestnut. He said that they'd recently had a VAT inspection and the VAT inspector raised the issue, which they investigated thoroughly and concluded that the contracts were legitimate. When he had been in the office with the inspector, the man had asked to see them and studied them for a few minutes. Johnny thought he was looking at figures, not the legality of the document. Then the man handed them back to Johnny and said thank you. So Johnny, as usual, interpreted that situation rather well, and made it sound halfway plausible. She accepted his argument and the enquiry ended. There was a bit of small talk before everyone left. Johnny had left his new Mercedes at home that day. Mikey and Johnny used to earn on the payroll what the tax allowances were at the time. It was their own interpretation of the tax system and meant they never paid any tax, just a few pounds here and there.

When Johnny went back to the cab office and told the lads their names had been brought up and that they were onto them, they all left. Johnny thought they would sign off immediately and declare their employment. They all did the opposite and left the job, preferring to stay on the benefits.

A lot of the local scallywags used to bring some very nice things to the cab office for quick cash sales. Johnny and Mikey could always rustle up cash from somewhere, and things were always flying about on the cheap, so to speak. Then one evening Johnny walked into the office to find Mikey had rails of very expensive suits and jackets everywhere. It looked like Top Man. Anyway, the upshot was they had bought all these clothes. All the drivers were walking about in swanky expensive suits. They all went in time. They made a few more bob. It was not a lot of money for the aggravation involved, Johnny remembered thinking. It was all out of control, really, and there was a lot of fun being had at the same time. Between them, they just didn't seem to know when or where to stop.

It was about this time the night controller, Ken, left the firm.

Bless him, he was an alcoholic and was always on the booze in the office. He hid it from everyone the best he could but it was out of control, and it all came to a head in rather a brief time. His replacement was a chap called Dougie. He was an elderly gentleman, looked like you might want your granddad to look. It turned out Dougie had been involved in running brothels for someone and it had all come on top. He was quite a character, and Johnny thought in the ten or eleven years that he owned the cab firm no one was ever asked to provide references or questioned about their past. They did not judge anyone. Everyone was paid cash as much as possible, and it was all about whether you could do the job, not where you'd been or where you'd come from. It was almost expected that there would be something amiss with most of the staff. They employed people on their ability to turn up and do the job. Many people who worked there had behavioural problems. Mikey and Johnny seemed to attract them like a magnet. There were some who were regular guys and girls but they seemed to be the minority, Johnny thought.

So, after a short time Dougie convinced Mikey and Johnny that the brothel business was a good move. What were they thinking, looking back? Mikey and Johnny did not want to run a brothel. They bankrolled a brothel in Gravesend. They were just the investors. Dougie was their man, and it was all going to be wonderful – riches for all. It was a fiasco from start to finish.

They gave Dougie the money. He took over. He did everything. In truth, you couldn't trust Dougie to go to the chippy for cod and chips and get it right. He was not a dishonest man; he was simply incompetent, Johnny later believed. After a while, they kept investing with no return. There were lots of stories and reasons for delays. There always were. Then it was up and running… and still no return. Johnny and Mikey began to wonder. They agreed Johnny would go over and check out what was going on, so he did. He had the address; it was just down the road a bit from Gravesend police station.

He knocked the door. A large bloke came to the door in his dressing gown. They started a conversation, which was short and sweet. Johnny couldn't remember the full conversation but it ended with him slamming the door in Johnny's face and telling him to sling his hook, so Johnny did. He went back to the office.

Mikey and Johnny weighed up the situation. They could not get hold of Dougie, so they both went back to Gravesend. When the bloke opened the door again, Mikey put something to his head, fully loaded, and told him the facts of life. He changed his attitude totally. It turned out he was the manager, there was not much trade, and Johnny thought he was sleeping with one of the staff and this brothel had a lot of different owners. It was almost laughable. It was the only brothel in Gravesend with several owners and investors, and no trade. It was like a small Ponzi scheme. The sort of racket Bernie Madoff got put away for, only he was on a grander scale.

Dougie paid Mikey and Johnny the money back. They used to stop it out of his wages at the cab firm every week. Johnny didn't think Dougie conned them; it was more the act of a fool. That was certainly the view Johnny took when he became aware of all the facts.

CHAPTER 6
BOTH OUT OF CONTROL

JOHNNY WAS VISITING female escorts on a regular basis and also inviting them to come to the office, when he could shut the unit up and guarantee some privacy for an hour. One night he went to see Lydia. She lived in the Rochester area, about forty minutes' drive from where he lived in Canterbury. He had spoken to her on the phone. It was late, as he was working until midnight on the radio. She sounded great on paper and had a good telephone manner, with a sense of humour as well. When he arrived, she was very pleasant company, absolutely stunning and dressed to kill. He lay on the bed for hours talking to her about life, chain-smoking cigarettes, absolutely smitten. She declared after a while her real name was Sophia. Lydia was just a name she used while working for the escort agency. He left later that morning bowled over by her. So, he chose to go back and see her again the following week. She told Johnny she was going through an acrimonious divorce with her estranged husband Arthur, had been dating a guy called Joe, who she thought might be married – she knew him from telephone conversations at work. She started working for Annabelle's escorts to improve her financial situation. She was really very intelligent, good company and had a great sense of humour. She had been approached by Annabelle, who had suggested she would do well at escorting, in a restaurant. Annabelle gave her a card with her number on and said 'Give me a ring,' and she had.

By now Johnny had become a member of the Barracuda Casino in Baker Street, London. He first started visiting the club and gambling in there with Steve Andino, who also owned a taxi firm in Canterbury, called Bells Taxis. It was a very exclusive casino in London. Steve had proposed Johnny for membership, and also Steve had introduced Johnny to dice – or craps, as it is known. Johnny loved it. He was instantly hooked to the dice and the atmosphere that could surround a dice table when a player was on a roll. It was in the Barracuda with Steve one night, high from playing dice and winning, that he started playing roulette for large stakes and won twenty-five grand in a few minutes. Steve dragged him to the cash desk and out of the casino. Johnny couldn't sleep for a couple of days with the high of having packets of five thousand pounds in fifty-pound notes in his pockets.

So, he knew he liked Sophia and decided he didn't want to see her as an escort but to take her out. He didn't know if he was in love or obsessed by her. The only thing he knew for certain was that he enjoyed himself when he was in her company. He used to send her flowers from a florist close to her. On one occasion when he went in the shop, there was a card for him from Sophia – thanking him for the flowers and asking 'What next?' along with her phone number. For their first date Johnny took Sophia to see Joseph at the Palladium. Jason Donovan took the lead and it was a great show. Then afterwards, out for dinner.

He really enjoyed the show, the dinner and her amazing company. It was a great night and the beginning of their dating.

There were a few postmen working at Canterbury sorting office who were looking to make a few quid on the side, so to speak. They had been forgetting to deliver the credit cards to certain addressees and having spending sprees of their own. It was the early 1990s and Johnny knew in those days a card would arrive in the post ready to go. It would not need to be activated. It was all on a signature, pre chip and pin. The cards were all blank, so it was just a matter of signing the strip and off you could go. Usually, the agreed credit limit was on the paperwork with the credit cards, and for debit cards the address generally acted as a good guide to whether the addressee had a healthy balance or was living on the bread line. Johnny and Mikey were approached by one of the local postmen called Jake and offered the cards.

It was like having a licence to print money. The postmen all seemed to know which envelopes contained which cards, and they were all getting greedier and greedier, as one does. The going rate for a card was £100.00 and there were always lots available. That all seemed fair enough, but on the odd occasion when cards did not last long, Jake used to give them a part-refund. Mikey was not that interested in the cards but Johnny liked the racket. There were always goodwill gestures and everyone made hay while the sun was shining. Johnny was not sure how many people were involved in the whole thing but it went on for months. They were spending under £50.00 in about 20 stores per day for 3 days, then cutting the cards up. They started on Thursdays, so the card would generally be good for Thursday, Friday and Saturday before the slips starting being banked and presented for payment, which would give the game away. It was all cigarette and booze purchases, which meant the resale value was generally very high, which maximised the returns. To top up on returns, the cab firm accepted card payments at the firm and Johnny used to process enough business through the firm to pay for the cards. It was a very lucrative racket but the proceeds all went on gambling and living it up.

Johnny went into work one Wednesday morning to find out that the night before at the office, there had been problems between an independent driver called Steve and Mikey. Johnny was not sure what really happened but Mikey had been arrested and charged with assault. It was either over stealing jobs at the West Station or Steve said something about Mikey. The long and short of the allegation was that Mikey had left the office, went to the station, gave him a good hiding, then left in a hurry. That was not Mikey's recollection of events. Mikey was interviewed and released on bail. When he returned to answer the bail, the police had statements from Steve, doctors at the hospital and some witnesses at the station, and charged Mikey.

Mikey had instructed Irwin Mitchell & Co Solicitors in Canterbury to act for him. This was a firm of solicitors that they both would have a number of dealings with over the years. At that time, they certainly had the reputation of being the best criminal solicitors in Canterbury. So, Irwin Mitchell & Co prepared Mikey's defence according to his instructions. The defence centred on Mikey, Johnny and about ten drivers all giving statements, which would build a defence for Mikey in Crown Court. The drivers all said that, to their knowledge, Mikey had not left the office. If that were true, then it could not have been him at the West Station. Mikey was on bail. There were a few minor conditions but nothing out of the ordinary. The main condition was not approaching or contacting witnesses. The court process is notoriously slow if a defendant enters a not-guilty plea and the matter is sent to the Crown Court.

In the meantime, one night Mikey lost the plot with one of the firm's ex-drivers, a bloke called Paul. He lived on the London Road estate. Mikey either had a row with him and did something to his car or assaulted him as well. Paul reported the incident to the police, and Mikey was duly charged with criminal damage. At this time, Mikey's cocaine habit was in full swing and he was losing the plot, with mood swings and aggression becoming the norm. One night he threatened to kill Paul for reporting the earlier incident to the police. Paul was genuinely scared. He went to Canterbury Police Station and asked to withdraw the complaint against Mikey. A senior officer at the station sat down with Paul in a room and asked him what was going on. Paul told him that Mikey had threatened his life and he was in fear for his life and so did not want to press charges. The officer told Paul he could not withdraw the earlier allegation; he took a new statement from Paul and Paul and his family were offered police protection. Mikey was arrested again, charged with threats to kill and refused bail. The magistrates at Canterbury were not prepared to give Mikey bail under any conditions, so Mikey was remanded in custody. Irwin Mitchell & Co managed to get a judge in chambers to hear an application for bail about two days later. The judge gave Mikey conditional bail. He was not allowed to approach witnesses and was not allowed to enter Canterbury. He had to reside at his mother's place about 8 miles away in Whitstable. He could not go to work at the cab firm. He spent the whole time waiting for the trial, drinking every day from about lunchtime. By now Mikey was drinking to excess every day, and his own cocaine habit was about £2,000 per week, he later told Johnny.

The case came to trial several months later at Canterbury Crown Court. The cases were not heard together. The first case was about the allegations of violence against Steve at the West

Station. The jury did not hear about the other allegations involving Paul. The case went on for several days. Johnny spent days waiting outside the court to give evidence. Lots of drivers from the firm sat and waited to give their evidence. The defence had all their witnesses at court from the beginning. Johnny's evidence was about procedure in the firm and office. He was not there on the night in question so he had nothing direct to say about the evening in question, only that Mikey was the only person working so had to stay in the office for the firm to operate. Johnny also explained how certain procedures worked. The sheets for the night in question had been rewritten. The Crown Prosecution had proved that in court. They had expert witnesses to testify, and they could say with a large degree of certainty that two sheets, the relevant ones, had not been written by the same person at the same time. Johnny had no idea how the case was going. After the summing up, the jury being very quickly returned with guilty verdicts. Clearly, they had not believed anyone from the cab firm and saw through the tissue of lies. It was after this that the other charges were read out. Paul was in the courthouse with police protection, ready to give evidence. Mikey, who was going to contest the allegations, entered a guilty plea to threats to kill, and the criminal damage was left on the file. Mikey did very well to escape without a prison sentence, although it has to be said the injury Steve suffered was a minor one and Paul had never been hurt; it was just words said in anger. Mikey received a suspended sentence, fine and costs.

Johnny did a lot of his dating with Sophia on the cards. He used to book theatre tickets in the West End on the cards and eat in the best restaurants in Park Lane and West London all the time. At first, he never used to let Sophia know, but as they got to know each other, she used to leave the restaurant first with the car keys, just in case there was a problem with the card, which meant at least Johnny only had to worry or think about himself rather than Sophia as well in her high heels, just in case a runner was going to be required. He often took her to the Barracuda casino, as well, to eat in the restaurant and gamble.

Johnny actually got arrested at Safeway's in Maidstone one day with Tony, Sophia's son, while they were both using stolen credit cards. Tony was a decent lad who got hooked on drugs. Sophia and her ex-husband had two sons. The eldest was unfortunately killed in a motorcycle accident on the M2, and Tony probably never really got over it or dealt with it on an emotional level. It happened when he was young and was the end of his world at the time.

This fateful day, they were driving about in Johnny's new Mercedes all around the supermarkets in Kent, purchasing booze and fags. They were both using stolen credit cards. A cashier at one branch of Safeway's in Maidstone suspected something was wrong, alerted the other Safeway's in the town, who contacted the police, and they were waiting for them at the Safeway's in Maidstone town centre. After they left the store, the police came from everywhere. Johnny thought it was a slight overreaction for what was being alleged. You'd have thought the two were terrorists, by the number of officers involved and the way in which they handled the arrest.

They were charged with attempted deception; Johnny's Mercedes was confiscated on the spot. Johnny had Irwin Mitchell & Co act for him in the matter. They got his car back fairly quickly and the charges were later dropped due to a lack of evidence. He remembered thanking God for both outcomes.

It turned out that there were hundreds of cards going missing and the post office had undercover police officers working at the sorting office to nail the culprits. It all came on top for a few of the postmen but Johnny was relieved that Jake the postman never actually got arrested or charged. Johnny never really followed the case but several postmen were convicted and went to prison. The police had been aware of the situation for some time, and had installed cameras in the sorting office at Canterbury and had undercover officers working at the sorting office while they gathered their evidence and built their case.

By now business was good, earnings were up at the firm, and with the money from credit cards and other various hare-brained schemes money was plentiful. Johnny was gambling as much as ever. He had developed a penchant for greyhound racing. There was a dog track at Canterbury and he was regularly down there trying to hit the jackpot or at least win a few quid. He used to turn up in the motor and was known as a high roller in terms of the size of the bets he placed. The number-two bookmaker's pitch at Canterbury Dogs was owned by an Iranian bloke called Keki Irani. He was a lovely bloke. He could talk for England and was a colourful character. He had pitches at Canterbury and Ramsgate (Dumpton Park) dog tracks, and a betting shop in Margate High Street. He was strapped for cash and not doing so well with his bookmaking ventures. He came up with a scheme whereby he would sell half his Canterbury pitch to Mikey and Johnny. Of course, you could not do this legally at the time, so they would act as his agents, effectively, when they were there on their own. The deal was that they gave him £5,000 cash and they would have the pitch every other week. They were responsible for the expenses, rent, etc, when they operated the pitch. They also agreed to keep his clerk when they worked. He was a nice bloke called Steve Bolton. He knew the job and it all worked out reasonably well.

They called the venture Lynx Racing. Johnny had always loved gambling and simply saw bookmaking as a natural extension of that. He thought it would be money for old rope, which it wasn't. Mikey's father had previously been a bookmaker and Mikey had some limited experience of bookmaking from his father. Strangely enough, one of the guys who used to go to Canterbury Dogs used to work for Mikey's father in one of his shops. Years prior to that, a bet was placed in one of Mikey's father's shops, and this guy, Bob Dale, was aware that the selections were winning and the bet was rolling up, but the last selection was a 33/1 shot and made the winnings enormous. He took the view that the horse would not win, but it did. It had put Mikey's father out of business at the time, because he had no limits for horses in his terms of business.

Lynx Racing was Mikey, Monty and Johnny. Johnny loved gambling, bookmaking and smoking 60 cigarettes per day, Mikey was bang on the booze and coke, Monty loved gambling, smoking, cigarettes and cocaine. What a threesome they were. Johnny was virtually left to his own devices with Steve as the clerk, Mikey would be the bag man counting the money, and Monty relayed the prices. They rarely agreed about anything. As the night went on it got louder and louder, and they were constantly having steward's enquiries after every race about why they lost so much or why they had not won more. Johnny actually used to love those times but they could not make it pay. They kept losing more and more money as the months went on.

Johnny remembered thinking bookmaking was like money for nothing, but the way they carried on that was the last thing it was. They were novices, which did not help. They actually lost a lot of money in their time at Canterbury dog track. One night Johnny was walking out of the track with Mikey when the photographer for the local paper, Neil, grabbed Johnny by the throat as they were leaving. He grabbed Johnny from behind. Johnny was in the restaurant and bar area located upstairs at the dog track and apparently had said things Neil thought offensive to the barmaid, Kate. Johnny and Mikey had both been drinking. She was a stunning girl and everyone was always trying their luck with her, and Neil liked her a lot. Everyone knew her and knew she had a fella. Neil thought Johnny's behaviour or language was inappropriate. Before Johnny had a chance to do anything, Mikey grabbed Neil, knocked him over with a right hander and jumped on top of him to give him a good hiding. There were a lot of people there, who stopped it going too far. Apparently, the owner of the dog track, Wally Maudsley, wanted to bar Johnny and Mikey because of that incident. Later on he changed his mind and never said one word to either of them. Maybe he thought banning them might come back to haunt him. No threats were ever made to him, but he was obviously aware about some of the background and reputations as well as stories.

Johnny was at Canterbury Dogs one night when Keki had the pitch, so he had just been down there gambling on the dogs himself. A new trainer had started recently. Her name was Amy Spiers. She had come down from Catford Dog Track. All her dogs had trialled in over a period of a few weeks, and she had a few runners on the card. When it came to about the tenth race that night, it was an A3 contest. There were some substantial wagers placed by some new faces on her runner in Trap 3. The faces placing the wagers, it turned out, were all Irish lads down from London. They were the owners and heavy gamblers. Johnny found out afterwards that they had been told the dog would win. When the traps opened, the three dog hit the lid and went two or three lengths clear in a matter of strides. By the time the dog got to the first bend, it was four or five lengths clear. Going down the back straight, the dog went clear. It was a procession. Johnny thought the winning margin turned out to be about eight lengths. The dog had found about

60 spots on its best trial time. The dog was locked up immediately for drug testing, and a steward's enquiry was announced. Of course, this had no bearing on the bets placed. At dog tracks, all bets are placed on the first past the post system, so the Irish lads all drew their money and went off with smiles on their faces. Johnny was mightily impressed by this turnout and performance. It had been a proper coup, and Johnny witnessed the manner in which the dog had won. He got very busy asking questions about the trainer and the owners.

It turned out that a bloke he knew a little, called Lance, knew the full background to the story. Amy Spiers had previously raced her dogs at Catford. Her partner was an Irish lad called Tony and he was in effect training the dogs. His official title was 'kennel hand'. He was the main man and he had a reputation for being very warm with the dogs, but he was banned from having his own licence. Johnny went over to Tony and Amy, who were in the restaurant that evening, sat and talked to them. He told them he wanted to buy a dog and for Amy to train it for him. He wanted to wager large bets on dogs that could win by margins as big as he had witnessed that evening.

After that he started buying greyhounds and placed them with Tony and Amy for training purposes to race at Canterbury Dogs and all tracks for the open-race class dogs.

The cab firm also bought shares in a horse that was owned by a group of businessmen from Canterbury. It was not an expensive horse, and about 8 or 9 local businessmen all bought a share in the horse. A guy name Julian, a local roofer, had put the syndicate together and had found a local trainer to train it. The horse only ever ran for the syndicate twice, if you could call it running. It was a hurdler, and not a very fast one at that. After two races it was obvious the horse was not capable of winning a race, and so they had retired it. On both occasions it had simply been beaten by a massive distance in very low-grade races.

One evening Sophia was explaining to Johnny how her house had been burgled a couple of years earlier and she'd had all her expensive jewellery stolen. Then a guy from the Prudential came round to discuss her claim on her household insurance, and after an interview at her home they had paid out. It had been for several thousand pounds. Johnny liked the idea of this and made a mental note about the event. He also knew people who had made fraudulent claims for watches and jewellery by either stating they had been lost or stolen and got paid out as well. It was shortly after this that Johnny and Sophia started living together in Kinch Grove in Canterbury. They rented a two-bedroom bungalow with a view to looking round and buying a place to live. Sophia and her estranged husband had put their former matrimonial home on the market as part of the divorce proceedings and settlement process. Arthur was working abroad at the time.

Now that the credit card scam was over, Johnny found a small loophole with stolen chequebooks and cheque guarantee cards. He realised that if you placed bets in bookmakers on a Thursday, in reality the cheques would not come to anyone's attention at the bank before Monday. So, by placing bets for £50 at a time in various bookmakers, mainly William Hills, you could place them on Thursday, Friday and Saturday safe in the knowledge that there would be no problems until Monday, Tuesday or Wednesday. If you picked a big football match, you could bet on all outcomes, i.e. home win, the draw and away win, and on Monday morning, after the event and result, just go back to the shops with the correct slip. He simply wrote on the back of the slips where the bets had been placed. After allowing for an about 8 or 9 percent loss on the overall stakes, he just drew cash winnings. This scam didn't last for too long. It was lucrative for a while but very quickly the betting shops stopped taking cheque and card payments.

Johnny was gambling a lot with his own money with small bookmakers on the phone, because they did the bets tax free; they did not declare the bets to Revenue and Customs. In those days betting tax was 10 percent, which got reduced to 9 percent later on, before being slowly abolished altogether. The tax was crippling for all gamblers. By doing away with the tax element, the gambler had a far better chance of winning. The bookmakers were not declaring or paying the tax, so it suited everyone really. A lot of small bookmakers would trade like this, which gave them a good chance of getting and keeping some of the larger gamblers in the local area. Why would anyone want to pay tax if they didn't have to? Of course, bets placed at the dog tracks and horse races were exempt from betting tax, but all bets placed in shops should have been subject to the tax. It just simply meant that bets were written out but not placed through the till, which meant there was no record of them for betting tax – or betting duty, as the Customs used to refer to it.

Johnny and Mikey thought it would be nice if Sophia and Kelly met each other, so one Tuesday evening they booked a table for four at The Limes in Lenham, where Johnny had lived as a young man. The Limes had become a very upmarket hotel and restaurant in Lenham Square and seemed like a good choice. Both couples drove there separately and met in the restaurant. When they all sat down for dinner, Kelly was beside herself with rage. She just came out with 'Of course you know Mikey is carrying on with the girl from the pub.' She was referring to Nikki, the barmaid in the Maiden's Head, who was a lot younger than Mikey.

Johnny was speechless. He instantly decided it was a good

time to go to the gents. Of course, Johnny was aware Mikey might be having another affair with the girl from the pub but it was not his business if it was even true, and just like Mikey's cocaine dealing, Johnny preferred to look the other way and not get involved.

Kelly knew about a girl called Maria Evans, who lived at the house in Whitstable Road a few years earlier, but they had managed to work through that one. Now Mikey and Kelly had a baby boy at home called Shane, as well as their daughter Catherine. Johnny didn't blame her really. While standing in the gents in The Limes having a cigarette, Mikey quickly came rushing in behind him lighting up a cigarette too. Mikey said, 'What are you doing leaving me on my own?' then started sniffing cocaine. Johnny was lost for words; he had not realised what he was signing up for by going out as a foursome. After a while they both went back to their seats and just sat down and ordered. The conversation had changed by now and Johnny just drank a lot, as did everyone, just to get through the evening.

CHAPTER 7
INSURANCE FRAUD

Now that Sophia and Johnny were living together in Canterbury, he decided it would be a good idea to obtain valuation certificates on all of Sophia's jewellery, which was very expensive, and get home contents insurance with the Prudential for the bungalow in which they were living. Mikey told Johnny he knew a jeweller called Carl Jones who worked at Pearce's in Canterbury, who would be a good guy to go and see to obtain valuation certificates for the jewellery and who would provide a reasonably priced service. Johnny decided to take his advice and took all the jewellery that Sophia owned into Anthony Pearce jewellers in Canterbury to obtain the certificates. The jewellery was left there some time, and valuation certificates were obtained after a couple of discussions about some of the pieces. There was an Inca god brooch encrusted in various jewels, which had a valuation of £9k. The jeweller was fascinated by the piece and asked Johnny about it. Johnny knew Sophia had purchased it in the Channel Islands after receiving her insurance payout from the burglary at her place years before. So Johnny casually remarked to Carl that he had got it in Guernsey while over there. Also, Sophia had previously worked in the Middle East and had bought jewellery there, and this jewellery was not hallmarked. Both points seemed incidental to him at the time, as he did not understand the jewellery business. By now he had purchased Sophia a beautiful diamond ring and they were engaged. Johnny had kept the receipt for the ring, which he had purchased from a jeweller in Maidstone, and that obviously was on the valuation as well.

Then Johnny staged the burglary one evening, but as he had never done this before, it didn't go quite according to his plan. He broke a window at the bungalow one Saturday evening, then got in to make it look authentic. He then removed a whole host of items in a car and thought the best place to store the items until a later date would be at Sophia's former matrimonial home. A lot of the items were Sophia's property. So, this is what he did. The property was just about to go on the market and was secure. What Johnny hadn't figured was that Sophia's estranged husband Arthur was home at that time from his job abroad and intended to go to the property to retrieve a few things of his from the garage and property. So, on the Sunday morning, he saw the items all in a room neatly stacked, and either helped himself or disposed of them. Johnny was unaware of this at the time.

Johnny subsequently reported the burglary to Canterbury police to obtain a crime number for the insurance company. Later that Sunday afternoon, a Detective Constable Cousins based at Canterbury Police Station attended the crime scene. He asked him what had been stolen. Johnny told him lots of jewellery, pictures and various goods. He asked for a whole list of the items stolen. Johnny wrote a complete list of all the goods that had been stashed at Sophia's place in Rochester and added most of the items of jewellery from the valuation certificates which were hidden at the bungalow. Scene of crime officers later turned up and dusted for finger prints and forensics at the point of entry. There was a bungalow next door to their bungalow, and an elderly lady lived there on her own. She was asked if she saw anyone breaking in but she had not witnessed the event and could not give the police any help with their enquiries. A couple of days later Johnny dropped a copy of his list of stolen items into the police station for DC Cousins. He then obtained a claim form from the Prudential and filled it in. The total claim was for forty-nine thousand pounds. Johnny had increased the cover with the Prudential and listed all the items that were over a certain valuation to comply with the requirements of the policy. He did know that the policy had not been in force very long but kind of figured you couldn't legislate for when you may be burgled and was totally unaware that the Prudential had a separate department to deal with claims made in the first 12 months of cover. He later found this out from a casual conversation he had with an insurance assessor, many years later and purely by chance.

By now Kelly had given up on her marriage with Mikey. Nikki at the Maiden's Head had been the straw that broke the camel's back for her. She kicked Mikey out and started divorce proceedings. Mikey started living with Nikki in hotels for a while before deciding to rent a place to live with her at Shatterling, near Canterbury. Business at the cab firm was good and Mikey wanted to hide his ownership for any up-and-coming divorce proceedings. Mikey could backdate the sale of his shares by several months, which meant that on paper Mikey had sold his shares in the company while he was still living with Kelly. So, as a mere paper transaction, really, Mikey sold his shares to Johnny. Then, once his divorce was over, he could just buy the shares back from Johnny. Johnny didn't mind. It may have been very complicated and embarrassing to have Mikey's ex-wife as a shareholder in the business, and even more embarrassing if the business was looked at in any great detail by a court or solicitors. Johnny did know it was better the devil you know, and at least with Mikey they were both on the same page about how the business would be run. This action would later prove to be a small blessing in a total mess that was going to ensue.

Johnny was enjoying owning dogs that were being trained by Tony and Amy. He liked Tony's attitude for training greyhounds and it all became about gambling on the dogs when Tony said they would win. In reality, some did and some did not. He was learning quickly and at his own great expense that dog racing and predicting winners was almost totally unpredictable. There were some great moments of triumph and some financial disasters which he had not allowed for.

A Kent-based firm of insurance assessors had been instructed to deal with the insurance claim at Kinch Grove. Johnny was contacted by a guy called Barry Langford, a loss adjuster for the firm, who made an appointment to visit him and discuss the claim. So, he was pleased with this and thought after the visit he would probably be paid out in about a month or two, depending on the figures offered being acceptable and realistic. Not exactly how it worked out. It was just the beginning of two expensive and protracted trials.

Barry Langford and Johnny met at Kinch Grove one afternoon, discussed the claim for about two hours, and Johnny thought it went very well. This Barry Langford guy, rather than worrying about the value of the claim, started investigating every aspect of it. Johnny was totally unaware that Barry Langford had been a serving member of the metropolitan police before becoming an insurance loss adjuster. Apparently, that is a common type of back ground for a loss adjuster. He went and spoke to DC Cousins and introduced himself as ex-job. Then he went to Carl Jones and spoke to him in great detail. Then, as a result of Sophia's connection to Johnny, he ended up interviewing members of Sophia's family and her ex-husband. At this point he found out about the goods stashed at the former matrimonial home in Rochester. He obtained statements from several family members. Then, as a direct result of the conversation with Carl Jones at Pearce Jewellers, he ended up in the Channel Islands looking for the jewellers that sold the very distinctive and individual Inca god brooch that formed part of the claim. The jewellers had in fact closed down and he could not find out when it was purchased or by whom. He also realised that Sophia and Arthur had both worked in the Middle East and that the jewellery without hallmarks was probably Sophia's, not Johnny's. He then found out about Sophia's previous insurance claim with the Prudential and looked at the valuation certificates she had produced when making that claim. He wanted to prove that some of the items on both valuations were the same items and were therefore Sophia's property, not Johnny's. He also took a further statement from Arthur as to the provenance of some of the items on the claim, to try and prove they were not his. Sophia and Arthur's divorce became very acrimonious over a long period of time, and Arthur was more than willing to stick the boot in wherever and whenever he could. Maybe he saw the Prudential assessor Barry Langford as a vehicle he could use to bash Sophia and Johnny with. The investigation went on for ages. Johnny contacted the Prudential several times to discuss the claim but continuously hit a brick wall: it was being dealt with by the loss adjusters. Frustrated, he decided to pursue the claim by other means.

He and Sophia had been looking at some really nice properties to buy. He wanted to use the cheque from the Prudential for a deposit on a home. He realised that wasn't going to happen. Out of all the properties they had looked at, they found one which was a bank repossession. The builder of the property was overextended and they had foreclosed on him. It was on the market with Amos and Co Estate Agents. It was a beautiful five-bedroom detached property with substantial gardens at the top of a bank that surrounded the property. Johnny made an offer for the property and told the estate agent he had a mortgage agreed in principle and was in a position to proceed immediately as he was currently living in rented accommodation. The offer was accepted. Of course, he had totally overlooked how hard it would be, even in those days, to get such a large mortgage with such a small deposit and being self-employed.

He very quickly realised that his employment situation was the main barrier. He visited a few buildings societies and banks and was turned down. The agent was keen to know when a valuer was going to value the property. Both parties had instructed solicitors, which bought him a little time, but he needed a mortgage offer to satisfy the agent and a mortgage to purchase the property with. He went to see a mortgage broker, Stephen Law, and realised he could just change his employment situation on paper and create his own records to satisfy the lender. So this was what he did.

He made the application via the broker to the Halifax Building Society. He created the company he worked for, his pay slips and P60. The stationery for the firm had the land line phone number at Kinch Grove, just in case they rang for verbal confirmation, as did all the documents he had provided. He told Sophia what was going on and asked her to start answering the phone at home with the company name and pretending to be a telephone operator for the company. The Halifax did ring a day or two later, and it all went well. They just asked if Johnny was there. She simply replied that he was out of the office. If they wanted to leave a message, she would make sure he returned the call. They explained it was just the Halifax ringing for verification and confirmation of his employment. They seemed quite happy to accept her very sincere and genuine-sounding verbal assurance. Shortly after that, they sent a valuer to the property to Johnny and the estate agents' delight, as time had been dragging on. Shortly afterwards a mortgage offer was issued. Once he had the mortgage offer, Johnny went back to the agents and managed to get a further reduction in price. He realised it was a bank he was buying it from and took a chance with a lower offer than had been originally agreed. The bank did accept the lower offer and the purchase went through. When he went to collect the keys, Johnny got a very frosty welcome from the agents. He felt that maybe they had to take a reduced fee as a result of his revised offer, but it was only a feeling he had. So, he and Sophia moved to High Hopes at Chilham, just outside Canterbury.

Johnny sought legal advice about the claim with the Prudential, and after explaining the basic details to a solicitor at Brabners Solicitors in Dover, he was advised that there were three possible options: wait and do nothing, make a complaint to the insurance ombudsman or take the insurer to court. He instructed Brabners to pursue the claim on his behalf. They wrote to the Prudential and started the ball rolling; Johnny pursuing the claim one way or another. Letters and correspondence about the claim did start, very slowly, going backwards and forwards between Brabners Solicitors and the Prudential.

An unusual situation was created on Derby Day that year at Canterbury Dog Track. Canterbury Dogs had decided to put on a meeting in the afternoon. Tony and the racing manager decided it would be a great situation to create some money-making opportunities. It had been discussed weeks in advance and was quite simple, really. On Derby Day, no one was really interested in the racing at Canterbury greyhound stadium. The Derby held at Epsom race track was such a huge spectacle in the racing calendar, all the bookmakers from Canterbury would be working there. Even the lead bookmaker at Canterbury, Michael Duncan, who used to work for Satellite Information Services (SIS), would be at Epsom working for SIS. The betting shops in general would not be looking at bets on greyhounds at Canterbury as thoroughly as they might have. If the racing manager could give three of Tony's dogs great opportunities to win races, Tony was going to prime the dogs and get them ready. Everyone would be able to see that they had stand-out opportunities of winning the races, which were graded races. Their prices would be very short, reflecting their chances. It was also thought that attendance would probably be very poor on a Wednesday afternoon, with the Derby on. So, if the prices offered for a dog's chances were artificially increased by the bookmakers, that would create a false betting market and artificially high starting prices.

Johnny was approached by Tony and let in on the scheme. It was put to him that if he were the lead bookmaker for the afternoon, he would be able to influence the starting prices greatly. Johnny approached Wally Maudsley and asked if he could have a pitch for the afternoon, as lots of the other bookmakers would not be able to attend. Wally said yes; after all, the track needed bookmakers to provide a service for the customers at the track on that afternoon. Wally could not have foreseen what was going on. Then the starting price man at the track was let in on the coup; after all, he would be the one to return the starting price of the winners. His name was Sammy. He loved a bet and he knew he could earn as well.

So, the scene was set. The racing manager was going to give three of Tony's dogs amazingly easy races to win, Tony was going to make sure they were trained specifically for the races on the day, Johnny was going to create a false market for the races, and Sammy was going to return the starting prices according to his opinion of a rigged market, focusing mainly on Johnny's prices available at the off. The three selections were going to be placed in multiple bets in many bookmakers – patents, singles, doubles and a treble, as well as doubles and trebles. They could also be placed in Yankees with one a non-runner, as well as Lucky 15's with a non-runner, which may disguise the real bets a little at a quick glance.

Just before the meeting, one of the dogs got injured and one became sick, so could not race, which changed the whole plan. It meant that all everyone was left with was one selection. The plan that was left on the table worked a treat on that afternoon. The race in question came up and the dog looked to have a great chance of winning the race in question. The realistic price for the dog was about even money. There was a very small crowd at the track. Johnny opened up the betting at six to four. The punters liked that price and started backing the dog at that price. Johnny and some friends had spent the entire morning going round various bookmakers, placing wagers on the selection, just trying to get as much money on the dog as they could at SP. Everyone else concerned had made their own arrangements.

The racing manager and Tony placed their bets where they could for as much as they chose, Johnny guessed. Sammy had placed a large bet for him with a bookmaker called Paul Humphrey's. Paul Humphrey was a local bookmaker. Everyone knew him. He had a couple of bookmaker's shops locally and attended meetings at the dog track, where he did a lot of business. A lot of his account customers used to meet him at the dogs to receive their accounts for the week, as well as their winnings or settle their accounts. Paul always seemed to have a pocket full of envelopes with different names on them, and just walk round bumping into people and giving them their envelopes. He had a reputation for laying a good-sized bet. He had been in business for a long time, had a solid reputation financially and, of course, most of the account business was tax free. Johnny had met him at the dogs previously and started gambling with him on a regular basis, mainly on the horses in the afternoon if he was at work. Johnny had never considered placing a bet with him for this caper.

Paul was not at the track that afternoon; obviously, he was at work in his shops. The betting market for an average dog race only lasts about two to three minutes. Johnny was taking bets on the selection which was in trap one, and the more money he took, he just kept increasing the price. He quickly managed to get the price of the dog out to three to one. At this point the other bookmakers did not want to increase the price anymore. One of the factors which threw some bookmakers and punters was everyone knew Johnny and Tony were very close, so some of them may have thought that the dog was a non-trier. Tony had two dogs in the race, and Johnny was continuously reducing the price of his other dog, which had very little chance in reality, but it gave the impression Johnny did not want to lay the other dog. Maybe, people thought, he knew something they didn't. Anyway, with a small crowd and very little time left before the off, Johnny made the dog four to one, then five to one, and just as the hare was approaching the traps, he changed the price from five to one to eight to one. No one else did. They were still three to one and nervous of that price. The traps went up, the dog came out well and got a small lead, which he further increased. The dog won the race in grand style, winning by a very healthy and comfortable distance. As soon as the race was over, Sammy returned the dog as eight to one, and Johnny's bag man and price man who knew nothing about it were busy pulling faces and smiling. A lot of people then approached Johnny, making various snide comments and remarks. One of the bookmakers flew upstairs to the racing office to complain and said virtually they were doing whatever they wanted now. It was a joke. The reference was to Tony and Johnny. Johnny didn't mind that sort of criticism; after all, everyone was entitled to their own views on any subject.

A regular gambler at the track – Tony McManus, who was not there on the afternoon in question – joked with Johnny about what had happened that afternoon at a later meeting one evening. Tony's nickname was 'Concorde' because of the size of his nose. He was a tall, thin man who always wore a long overcoat and resembled Fagin from Oliver Twist. He always had an angle or scheme on the go to make a few pounds. He had been gambling since early childhood and was a well-known character at the track. Johnny slowly got to know Tony well over the years, after they first met at Canterbury greyhounds in the restaurant.

There was also another guy Johnny knew from card games in Chatham. He owned a snooker hall in Chatham and loved to gamble. He had great potential as a snooker player and had trained with people like Steve Davis when he was in his prime as a player, but he'd never managed to fulfil his potential or make it on the professional scene. He was aware of the coup on Derby Day and got talking to Johnny about it because he knew Lance and was keen to know everyone's business. His name was Russell Nowak.

After about five or ten minutes everything calmed down and the next race just took place. People started to hear about what had happened very quickly. Johnny got round all the bookmakers the next day and got paid all his winnings at the princely odds of eight to one. He later found out that Sammy, with whom he'd never discussed it, had written on his account envelope not Sammy but CHEAT. Johnny laughed at that. Paul never discussed it with Johnny; after all, he didn't place any bets with Paul and it just never came up. Paul knew what he was like in any case. Then, a couple of days later, the front page of the Sporting Life newspaper covered the story. The headline was Canterbury Coup at the greyhounds on Derby Day. One of Kent's largest independent bookmakers was Alan Bown. He had a large chain of shops based all over Kent, which he later sold to Coral's when he got out of the business. Johnny had money placed in all of Alan Bown's shops and Alan Bown was furious. He worked out quickly that the problem was the price of the dog and said as much. He complained and said he wouldn't mind if the dog had been evens, but he resented paying eight to one about an even money winner. As with most front-page newspaper stories in those days, very quickly they just became fish and chip wrapping. Wally Maudsley was furious with Johnny yet again but never said anything to him. He didn't even ban him from the track.

By now Barry Langford, the insurance loss adjuster, had finished his investigation into the burglary. He took the findings of his investigation and report to DC Cousins at Canterbury Police Station. Now DC Cousins started to look at his findings.

Monty and Johnny were trying to do a deal with Keki Irani over his betting shop in Margate High Street. The pitch at Canterbury greyhounds was not a successful business venture in terms of finances but there was an awful lot of fun to be had with the racing, cheating, ducking and diving, as well as meeting various characters at the track. Being a bookmaker or involved in that world was a drug of its own, certainly for Johnny. The idea of buying a betting shop seemed very appealing to Monty and Johnny. Maybe it could be the first of a successful chain, or maybe not. Johnny could not work there very much, maybe on a Saturday or the odd day here and there, because he was committed to the cabs. Monty had no money – or readies, as Keki used to refer to money. Monty was driving about in a hire car five or six days a week all over the south of England, picking up goods in shops, then returning them for refunds at the counter. He was good at it. He had been doing it for years and only had a couple of minor convictions for it. He had rented cars from Avis Car Hire for years and had never actually bought a car on finance, mainly due to his poor credit history. That was how the betting shop was going to be paid for. Monty wanted Johnny involved because of his so-called good character, and he wanted a new car of his own. They agreed Johnny would buy the car and Monty would make the payments. Johnny went into Invicta Motors in Canterbury, the main Ford agent in Canterbury, and bought a new XR3i. Johnny owned the car on paper. Monty was a named driver on the insurance and would pay the finance payments each month. Once paid for, Monty could have it. It suited Johnny. Monty told Johnny that once the betting shop was paid for, he would pay the car off quickly so he could then own it.

A deal was agreed whereby Keki would be paid weekly instalments until the agreed price had been paid, then, at that point, it would be transferred legally to Monty and Johnny. At that point, Monty would not get a betting permit or licence because of his previous criminal convictions, whereas Johnny had no previous convictions and was seen as a person of good character for licencing purposes. Monty was funding the deal. He was desperate to have a legitimate business and income and stop breaking the law on a daily basis.

Monty had two daughters with his estranged wife Dianne. He was going to try and make a go of his marriage again. His two daughters were Carly and Natasha – or Tash, as he called her. So that was the name. It was Cartash Racing. He took great pride in changing the name on the facia, door and windows on the betting shop. He loved telling everyone about the name of the shop and his two daughters. The betting duty people were aware that the shop had all but been sold, but until all the payments had been made, the shop and licence were still Keki Irani's.

The shop was nearly opposite a snooker hall in Margate High Street. A lot of gamblers, small-time villains and colourful characters used to frequent the snooker hall and the betting shop. The nearest betting shop to Cartash Racing was a Ladbrokes, just up the road. In reality, a lot of the customers went in both, depending on their mood, but you could get a back show on a price at Cartash Racing, and that was their unique selling point. It was probably the only real tool most small independents had to compete with the large chains such as Ladbrokes, William Hill or Coral's. In their shops a punter could only take the current odds of a selection, whereas by offering one back show, Cartash was offering the punter better value on single-win bets, particularly if the price of a selection had shortened. It also affected the profit margins. Of course, by offering that service, it made it harder to win enough money each week to pay all the bills and show a profit.

Keki had employed two local people – a couple, Yvonne and Noddy – to work in his shop with him. Monty and Johnny took them on full time to run the shop. So, with all the expenses of running the shop, rent, Satellite Information Services (who were responsible for providing all the prices and live races from horse and dog tracks daily), utility bills, betting duty and wages, the shop needed to win a lot each week to break even. This was something neither Johnny nor Monty had particularly considered. With the added stress on finances of offering one back show on selections, it quite quickly became clear that most weeks the shop did win money but not enough to pay all the bills and make a profit. This was probably the main reason Keki was letting it go. If it had been a gold mine or money for old rope, he probably would never have tried to sell it. He was selling for the money, not for any other reason. So, the shop was run by Noddy and Yvonne and it won and lost, won and lost, then it would break even a lot, but overall, it could not pay its way. Some days trade was very thin. A lot of this type of shops simply didn't have customers with unlimited funds. They would lose a little and disappear for a while.

Johnny and Monty used to meet in the evenings to discuss it nonstop. In those days there was a casino in Margate and one in Ramsgate. They would inevitably have dinner in one of the casinos and lose what they had in the casino, then promise each other they would stop doing that. It was good fun, like the dog track, but not a sound business venture. After a while, only a few months later, Monty lost heart in the idea of going out stealing every day to buy a betting shop that lost money every week. The novelty had worn off and reality had sunk in. They discussed the whole thing several times and, in the end, just gave Keki the keys back. He kept what he had been paid to date but also incurred the betting duty bills that had not been paid. The HM Customs and Excise tried to pursue Johnny for the money but he explained that he had not signed a licence and was not responsible for the debt. They pursued Keki for the debt and he took the shop back on but now the Customs and Excise noted how Johnny had acted in this deal, and in their view he was no longer a fit and proper person to be operating or trading in the bookmaking world.

The XR3i was still on finance. Monty had been doing a lot of miles in it, not looking after it much, and Johnny wasn't amused but it was agreed that if Monty paid it off quickly, he could then keep the car. Monty missed a payment on the car and Johnny was furious. Johnny always prided himself on making payments on time. It was why and how he had built up a great credit rating at work and in his business life. The betting shop had amounted to nothing and Monty now, Johnny thought, was taking the proverbial. The car had come with two sets of keys. Johnny had given Monty a set for the car and had a set at home, somewhere in a drawer. The car was fully insured and Monty seemed to have totally forgotten about his agreement to pay the car off quicker or even just keeping making the payments. So Johnny took the keys one night about midnight, went up to Monty's place, took the car, drove it to Faversham, and found a wooded area. He had a gallon of petrol. He poured the petrol inside the car and lit it. As he was walking away quickly, the car blew up like a bomb. That was the end of the XR3i.

In the morning Monty phoned Johnny and asked if he had the car. Johnny said no. So, Monty reported it stolen to the police. About a day later the police found the car in the woods at Faversham. They thought it may have been young joy riders who stole it because it was an XR3i. Monty knew instantly. He told Johnny about it. Johnny just said, 'Well, at least the finance will get paid now.' So, no harm done. Pity you couldn't pay the car payments on time. That was the end of their business dealings and friendship, really. Johnny did meet Monty by chance many years later, but only briefly, in passing. They just passed the time of day. The insurers did pay out but told the finance company they were not happy about the circumstances of the claim. Johnny never knew this until a later date, when he tried to buy a car on Ford Finance and was declined for this reason.

CHAPTER 8
ARRESTS AND CHARGES

JOHNNY HAD BEEN PLAYING cards a lot in Medway and had agreed with Russell Nowak to buy two greyhound puppies that would be trained at Wimbledon by Terry Dartnall. Terry had an excellent reputation at getting dogs ready for a coup. He had appeared on the greyhound pages of the racing press many times for appearing to land successful coups. In reality, after Johnny's brief experience with him, he didn't particularly rate the guy. He realised lots of people probably had a lot of successful and unsuccessful stories they could share but tended to overlook the unsuccessful and the coups that went wrong.

On Tuesday, 20th December 1994, which was Sophia's birthday, the first of the two puppies, which had trialled in at Wimbledon Dog Track over the few weeks previously, was in its first race. It was in about an A5 grade. Terry told Russell the dog would win – he'd had a lot of time in hand with the dog – and Russell told Johnny. Johnny was working at the cab firm that day and was excited all day about the prospect of going to Wimbledon Dogs that night after work and gambling on the dog.

He was so wrapped up about the dog he simply overlooked Sophia's birthday. She was furious.

His car was having some work done on it. When he finished the day shift, Johnny asked a driver called David Ruler to drive him from Canterbury to Wimbledon Dog Track, wait for him, and bring him back later on that evening. David had worked for the firm for ages. He was always on speed, or so it appeared. He was a likeable lad who was always reliable, and a very quiet, non-confrontational character. So, Mikey took over the office for the evening shift from Johnny and he set off for Wimbledon Dogs. He got to the dogs and decided that he would place several thousand pounds on the puppy and clean up.

Well, he had totally overestimated the betting market. He had never been to Wimbledon Dogs before and assumed the bookmakers would take large wagers on dogs. It wasn't like that at all. It was bloody hard work. Whether that was because of the size of the bets or because the selection was a new puppy trained by Terry Dartnall, he never really knew. Anyway, he could only get £2k on the puppy and was disappointed about that. Well, the hare came round, the traps opened and the puppy was very green. He was in trap 2 and never really got going on the way to the first bend, he took a slight knock at the first bend, never really recovered and never ran a great race at all. He never looked like threatening the leaders or winning that evening.

Johnny was so disappointed. He had been led to believe it was a foregone conclusion that he would win. Then, after the race, Terry Dartnall started moaning about people knowing the dog was meant to be winning, and a row ensued. Clearly Russell was not as close to him or friendly with him as he had made out. All Johnny could think of was that the puppy didn't win. The rest just seemed like a proper old load of eye wash. He was now relieved he could only get £2k on the puppy. He was so wound up by all the hype and promise which had just failed to materialise.

In the next race there was a dog in trap 3 which looked like it had an excellent chance of winning. It opened up evens. Johnny wanted his £2k back. He had an even £2k on the dog out of desperation, not knowing anything about it. The race was off, the dog came out well, led at the first bend and won in good style. Johnny was relieved and glad he had got his stake back. He didn't rate the whole experience with Terry Dartnall and Russell very highly. It just seemed very unprofessional to him. He lost total interest and confidence in the idea and walked away. Neither of the puppies turned out to be that great. They never really fulfilled their potential after he walked away. So, he found David outside, waiting in the taxi, and was now on his way home. It had not been a good night at all but he had limited his losses. The drive back took about one and a half hours and he had calmed down a bit but had totally forgotten about Sophia's birthday.

When he got home Sophia let him have it. She said she had had enough of him and his behaviour, and was leaving. A big row was going on about his behaviour and she would not let it drop. It was about 11.30 pm. Then a London taxi was suddenly on the drive at High Hopes and it rather surprised Johnny and Sophia. What was he doing? He and Sophia stopped arguing for a minute. Johnny went outside and realised it was Ted Davenport, one of the drivers at the firm. He spoke to him. Ted said there was a problem at the office and the police had shut the office down. No one could work and no one knew what was going on. The police had cordoned the office off and no one was allowed in or out. So, Johnny told Sophia he was going to work because there was a problem. He didn't know how long he would be.

He jumped in the back of the cab, and Ted drove him to the office, about a 10-minute steady drive. When they got to the office Ted dropped him off and drove away. Johnny walked up to the tape and saw a lot of police officers everywhere, some in plain clothes and some in uniform. They asked him who he was. He replied, 'I own the place and the business.' They let him through. When he got to the office, he was shocked. Mikey was standing with his hands behind his back in handcuffs by the heater. There was a number of police officers in the office searching and talking. On one of the desks there was a large amount of what looked like cocaine in clear plastic, a gun with bullets lying next to it, and an open shoe box full of cash. Then the police opened the safe and took the firm's money as well.

Johnny tried to explain that money was the firm's cash but it was to no avail. He never found out that night what had really gone on but was there when Mikey was arrested for fire arms charges, and drug and money laundering charges. So, the shit had really hit the fan now. Shortly after Mikey was taken away by the police, the firm could resume business again. The whole thing was complete madness. The firm had major contracts with the Kent County Council and Canterbury City Council for transporting disabled children around. The only piece of good news was that Mikey had sold his shares to Johnny on paper. Of course, they were still partners in reality, but only they knew that for certain. The police were not interested in Mikey's employment status at that stage.

Anyway, Mikey was charged and taken to court. The papers were full of it. It was a big scandal at the time in Canterbury. Then the phones started ringing with questions about what had been going on. Johnny just stuck to the line that Mikey was employed there as a manager and as a result of what had happened, his employment had now been terminated. This separated Mikey from the business totally and people kind of seemed to accept he was just an employee and not a partner in the firm. So, Mikey's case was sent to Crown Court, on advice from his legal team, and in light of the circumstances, he was going to plead guilty to some of the charges. The Crown Prosecution Service agreed to leave a couple of charges on the file. That was his best deal. He took it.

Johnny went to the Crown Court when Mikey pleaded guilty, and at that time one of the police officers in the case went to speak to the judge in his chambers before sentencing Mikey. The judge actually said in open court he had been made aware of Mikey's cooperation with the police and was going to sentence him accordingly. Johnny was horrified. He understood that Mikey had grassed on certain people in the drug world for a reduced sentence. Johnny didn't approve of that behaviour at all. Mikey received a six-year-nine-month prison sentence for pleading guilty and cooperating with the police.

Mikey had just been given six years nine months in prison, was going through a heated split and divorce from Kelly, and had his young girlfriend Nikki in tow – who was a total liability in Johnny's opinion. One day she went to see Johnny and offered to help at the firm. Johnny looked at her and just politely said he would let her know. He should have walked away from Mikey, paid him a fair share for his half, and just moved on, but Mikey didn't want to sell. It was a difficult situation. They had a great business, which they'd built up from scratch, they were really earning well, and now Mikey had nearly ruined it all. Johnny and Mikey did a deal about reduced earnings for Mikey while he was in prison. Mikey had lost the plot and didn't want his earnings to go to Kelly and his two children. For some reason, he wanted Nikki to have his money. He was determined to make a go of it with her.

Johnny found the whole thing very embarrassing. Kelly would phone him and tell him that she didn't have the money for nappies for Mikey's son. He felt for Kelly. He knew she had not been a loyal wife or always honest with Mikey, but he was worse than she was. There were lots of stories about her behaviour and morals flying around Canterbury while they had been together – and some were true, Johnny had found out. Still, he said he would speak to Mikey about it. What everyone seemed to be overlooking was that Mikey was now coming off drugs and on prescription drugs as a substitute and his mood swings were all over the place to say the least. Mikey saw Kelly needed something to help with the children and asked Johnny to kind of split the money, but still Nikki got more.

To make matters worse, Johnny and Sophia had now been invited to go to Canterbury Police Station and discuss the insurance claim. The police, namely DC Cousins, had spoken to Brabners Solicitors and advised them that they wanted to interview him and Sophia with regards to an attempted deception on the Prudential Assurance Company, under caution. Both he and Sophia attended Canterbury Police Station, were represented by Brabners Solicitors, on advice gave no-comment interviews and were both bailed to return to the police station at a later date. DC Cousins had now taken the same statements from the same witnesses as the loss adjuster and taken statements from the loss adjuster as well. The papers were passed to the Crown Prosecution Service for a decision to be made about the case. The dates to return to the police station kept getting extended and changed, then a date was fixed and agreed. Johnny and Sophia both returned to the police station, were interviewed under caution, were both represented by Brabners Solicitors, and both charged with attempting to deceive the Prudential Assurance Company of £49k by knowingly making a false claim on a home contents policy issued by the Prudential Insurance Company. Peter Macready was the representative who attended on this occasion. He was an elderly gentleman who had spent a lifetime practising law and had seen and heard all the stories from defendants pleading not guilty to divorce cases where, he explained, 'You really do wonder if both parties were in the same marriage.' This was his way of explaining that the husband and wife's recollections of events and the marriage differed amazingly.

Johnny and Sophia both decided to instruct Brabners Solicitors for the criminal proceedings. At a later appointment, after reviewing the evidence and disclosure from the Crown Prosecution Service, Johnny was trying to convince Mr Macready of his innocence and enquired about his and Brabners' ability to defend the scurrilous accusation. He always remembered the reply from Peter (it made him smile deep down). He said in all his years defending criminal cases, he did not believe any of the people they defended had ever been convicted of a crime they did not commit, not once. He then smiled and said he did believe he had defended a number of defendants over the years who were guilty of the crime but had not been convicted. That was about the best Johnny could hope for, and he knew that deep down.

As a result of the criminal charges, the civil proceedings that had been started between Brabners and the Prudential were suspended pending the outcome of the criminal case.

The case against them had many different types of attack and challenge to it. Firstly, they were saying that Johnny did not actually own some of the goods he was claiming for; they were in fact Sophia's. Then they were saying that there was no burglary, but the goods allegedly stolen had been placed at Abbots Close in Rochester by Johnny or the defendants. As a result of witness statements about goods having been left at the Rochester address, it was clear that either he and Sophia were lying, or Arthur and Hayley – his daughter and Andrew, his son in law were. Both sets of people could not be telling the truth. Then, after reading statements from other witnesses, including Mr Barry Langford, the loss adjuster had built the whole case for DC Cousins and gave it to him as a *fait accompli.* After all, when he'd introduced himself to DC Cousins, he had told him he was ex-job, so that would have given the detective constable a reassurance that he knew what he was doing, was impartial, fair, and investigated the facts without bias. The small point Mr Langford had forgotten to mention was that he was forced to resign from the metropolitan police force while a serving officer after being convicted of being involved in fraudulent insurance claims, where lorry drivers were pretending to be hijacked and claiming on the insurance. He was one of the team of officers investigating the alleged hijacks and thefts and recommending to the insurance companies that they were genuine crimes and the insurance companies should pay out. It had been a big scandal at the time and it was beggars belief that he only received a suspended prison sentence at the time, as well as losing his job, rather than a custodial sentence.

So, their defence had now been given an amazing boost. The Prudential did not know about Mr Langford's background, and the officer in charge of the case did not know about it either. Johnny had instructed Michael Mann to act for him in this matter. He was a very experienced QC, a larger-than-life character, a little bit like Rumpole of the Bailey, only with a louder voice. He had worked in law all his life. He told Johnny he would do his best for him. He came highly recommended and certainly knew how to charge. The retainer and daily rate were very expensive, so Johnny thought. In fact, he did wonder if he may have done better to work hard at school, go into the legal profession and become a QC. It may well have been more lucrative, he thought. Maybe his mum and dad were right, after all, when they'd told him to work hard at school and get an education. Sophia had instructed Adelle Fulton. She was married to a judge and had the reputation of being a rottweiler. She would later become a judge herself at Canterbury Crown Court. So, on paper at least, a formidable defence team was on the case.

The defence was a simple one now. Clearly Arthur, Hayley and Andrew were lying or confused. Arthur clearly had something to do with the burglary; revenge maybe, or possibly just trying to take property he may have thought he had a right to. Then, with the assistance of the thoroughly dishonest Mr Langford, who just wanted to deny the claim, a story and statements had been produced. There were a lot of twists and turns in the prosecution case, and claims that clearly certain events had been looked over and evidence obtained with only one outcome in mind. This had all been done in a very unprofessional and dishonest manner, with a total and blatant disregard for the truth. Who would the jury believe?

While all this had been going on, in June 1994, one of the most high-profile murders in American history had been committed. The murder trial of the century, as it was referred to on TV and in the press at the time, started later in 1994 and concluded in October 1995. OJ Simpson was accused of murdering Nicole Simpson, his ex-wife, and Ronald Goldberg at her home in an upmarket part of Los Angeles. The trial was on Sky TV news channel every day, starting at 2 pm in the afternoon. Johnny had never really heard of the famous football star in America, but had seen him in the small parts he played in the Naked Gun films. He just didn't really understand how famous or successful he was in America. Once the reports came out and Sky News just kept reporting the story over and over, Johnny became fascinated by the whole thing. Then Sky said they were going to cover the trial live every day, and Johnny watched the whole thing unfold. He had never been able to watch a live trial before, but because of the media speculation and hype, he spent months just glued to it all.

In 1994 it was brought to Johnny's attention by Stuart Fallon, who still worked at Lynx Taxis, that there was a betting shop in Sturry Road in Canterbury which may well be for sale. The owner was an elderly guy, Martin, who had been very successful in the poultry business in London, as well as the bookmaking business. He had a chain of shops which he had sold slowly. The chain was called Tower Bookmakers.

Johnny set up a meeting with this guy at his home in Chestfield. The shop had been closed due to his age and not so good health, really. It was the last one of his betting shops. When Johnny turned up to meet him, he was greeted by a very well-dressed, elegant lady, his wife Dot. She took him through to the lounge. Johnny was taken aback by the home. It was the most tastefully decorated and furnished property he had ever been in or seen. Everything was perfect. It reminded him of when he had stayed at the Savoy with Sophia after going to the theatre in West End on several occasions. Dot's taste was impeccable, he realised. Martin was a real rough-and-ready gentleman. You could tell, Johnny thought, that in his day he had been a ducker and a diver, but he had become very successful and was also a real gentleman.

They sat down at a beautiful table and agreed a deal. The licence needed to be transferred, SIS reinstalled, and a good clean-up was needed, but the basics were all there and it definitely had potential.

Johnny asked Mullis and Peake in Romford, a firm of

solicitors specialising in betting permits and betting licences, to arrange an application for a permit and then to transfer the licence for the shop (which was still in force) to him. He decided to keep the name Tower Bookmakers since it was already called that, and his permit could then be in the name of Tower Bookmakers Ltd as well, since the betting shop was going to be owned and operated by Tower Bookmakers Ltd. It just meant the directors of the company would have to be vetted rather than people applying for a betting permit.

Johnny had first come across Mr Alan Martin at Mullis and Peake as a result of the failed purchase of Keki Irani's betting shop in Margate High Street. Keki had always used Mullis and Peake and recommended the firm for all matters relating to the gaming and bookmaking industry. They were very highly thought-of in this area, and it turned out an awful lot of people in the industry used their services.

So, after making the initial application and advertising the application in the sporting newspapers, Customs and Excise made it clear to Mullis and Peake that they would object to Johnny Butler, as in their opinion he was not a fit and proper person to operate a bookmaker's shop or hold a permit. The failure of paying the betting duty while trading in the shop was coming back to rear its head. So Johnny stood down as a director of Tower Bookmakers Ltd and Sophia was appointed as the director. She had no criminal convictions, no previous dealings with Customs and Excise, and no track record. They could not object to her with any success. The application was changed, Mullis and Peake represented Sophia at the application process in Canterbury Magistrates Court Licencing Section, and it was approved. Johnny decided not to go to the hearing, thinking it just better to keep out of the way. Once the betting permit had been granted, the shop, which was already licenced, could be operated legally by Tower Bookmakers Ltd. The company had been purchased through Singh and Co Chartered Accountants in Rochester. They were the same firm he had been using for the taxi firm for a few years and had proved to be very professional and knowledgeable in all tax and company registration matters in which they had acted. SIS then did the installation and setting up of the TVs and information provided to bookmakers, including live displays of the daily horse and dog racing in the UK.

On 14th February 1995 Tower Bookmakers Ltd in Canterbury opened up for business. Johnny had installed some fruit machines in the premises, and had opened a totalizator account for Tote bets. He knew his way around a betting shop like the back of his hand and everything was set up and good to go. Sophia later joked it was a Valentine's Day gift from Johnny to her. Not sure that was how he meant it or saw it, but it was up and running so what difference did it make?

Later that year, when Stuart Fallon was at a car dealer in Sturry Road, Canterbury, called Team Traction, he noticed there were several Bentleys and Rolls Royces in really good condition for sale. He rang Johnny at home and told him there was a beautiful Bentley for sale at Team Traction, opposite Asda's in Canterbury, which would really suit him.

Johnny was off. He had never considered a Bentley before but was on his way down there within an hour. He saw a beautiful Bentley 8 in beige, with cream leather, for sale. He couldn't afford it in cash but absolutely loved the car. He didn't want to test-drive it. He just wanted to own it. He told the sales guy he kind of liked it but it was too dear. He didn't know where to start with his opening offer. He could finance it, he thought. That wouldn't be a problem. Buy it today and worry about paying for it tomorrow. The salesman was the owner of the garage, and Johnny thought it hard work negotiating with him, but about one hour and 30 minutes later a price had been agreed. He knew the finance wouldn't be a problem, and about an hour later the garage rang Johnny and confirmed everything had been approved. So now he had a beautiful Bentley 8 to park on the drive. In reality, it was not an everyday car and he hardly ever used it. He changed the number plate to hide the year of the car. He bought a cheap Irish plate, UJI 1667, which he liked because he was born in 1967.

The betting shop in Canterbury had not been open very long when a local gaming machines licencing officer visited the premises. He introduced himself and wanted to meet Sophia. He was aware that Johnny Butler had a reputation with Customs and Excise and had previously bought a lot of fruit machines from Richard, a provider in the Thanet area; these were £100 and £250 jackpot machines, the ones Johnny had at the cab firm. Somehow, he thought or had received information that these would be used in the betting shop. At the time, the largest jackpot size in betting shops was £10.

But his assumption was wrong. The fruit machines in the shop were only £10 jackpot and fully licensed. The licencing officer nevertheless criticised Johnny to Sophia and suggested he was not a man of good character. Johnny and Sophia were living together and had been for years but had not married, had different surnames, and it appeared the man hadn't quite put two and two together. He actually tried to chat her up and asked her out. When Sophia told Johnny, he thought bloody cheek, but he knew the guy didn't know they were a couple. She was distancing herself from Johnny in the conversation and acting dumb, so to speak, when in reality the last thing she would be described as was dumb. She was just way too cute for this guy. In reality, half the time it is better to let people think they are clever when they don't even know the real facts of the matter. Johnny, deep down, thought, well, at least the guy had good taste in women.

In 1995 a dog track opened at Sittingbourne. Its name was Central Park. Johnny heard they wanted bookmakers to apply, so he did. He made the application in the name of Tower Bookmakers. He decided when he traded there, if he was successful in obtaining a pitch, that he could just be the company representative on that occasion, so to speak. There was a lot of demand for the pitches, and bookmakers had to pay a premium to the track to get a pitch. He wanted in and paid the going rate. It was quite a few thousand but Central Park was a new track with lots of new possibilities. Johnny was allocated pitch number two. Of course, he would have liked pitch one but was happy with two. The first night of racing and the opening of Central Park had been delayed a few times but a date was finally set. It would open on Tuesday 3rd October 1995. On Tuesday 3rd October 1995 OJ Simpson was acquitted of murdering Nicole Simpson and Ronald Goldberg, after the jury finished deliberating and hearing rereads of evidence and testimony.

Johnny had bought himself a camel hair overcoat to match his Bentley, and drove to Central Park, ready to go. He had pockets full of thousands of pounds in cash, and a new stand to place on his pitch, with a new bag. He had his best suit on and felt like a million dollars. Bookmakers had reserved parking in a separate area of the car park, which was fenced in and could be locked. That was perfect for his Bentley. By the time the first race started, the track was packed and business was good. Johnny was in his element. He loved every moment of it. He was well known by a lot of people there. The first night money and bets were changing hands nonstop. The punters had their successes and so did the bookmakers. Johnny came out well on top and was very happy with the proceedings. Then a few guys suggested going for an Indian in Sittingbourne. Johnny was in a good mood and thought that would be a good way to celebrate. So, he drove to the Indian, parked outside and went in, then all through the meal he worried about his car being scratched or vandalised outside the restaurant. It was the first time he had just left it in the street of a town with a not-so-great reputation and he realised that, in that respect, the car could be a burden as well as a blessing. It was food for thought.

CHAPTER 9
ATTEMPTED DECEPTION CRIMINAL TRIAL CANTERBURY CROWN COURT

GEORGE HAD a new female companion in his life and her name was Patricia. They started to live together at Aylesford and had moved to a place in Leybourne. George and Vera had not yet reached a financial settlement as a result of their marriage ending. Their only real asset was a property in Canterbury, which Vera was living in and renting out rooms to students. George owned half of it. George asked Johnny if he would buy his half off him at the fair market rate, which would release the money George had in the property but allow Vera to stay there, rather than asking her to sell it and move out. Johnny agreed to take out a mortgage for half the value of the property, which half the rooms let would cover, as they would the expenses of running the property. It meant Vera and Johnny now owned the property but it was clear that he had a far larger burden of the mortgage as Vera was leaving her equity in the property.

Vera had been letting to students as a stream of income. Pat, as everyone referred to Patricia, used to work for a woman called Sue who was married to a guy called Richard. Richard was the managing director of a successful battery company with an office in Maidstone. The company used to spend a lot of money on their senior staff and directors travelling to and from the airports as well as various places in the UK. Richard told George he would use his services if he wanted to start a chauffeur business. George spent the proceeds from the sale in Canterbury on Mercedes cars for the chauffeur business and the rest on modernising and extending the property in Leybourne. New garages and a new drive were laid to finish it off.

George asked Johnny if he could invoice the battery company via his company on his behalf, which meant he wouldn't have to start a company officially, register for VAT or declare the income. Johnny naturally agreed – anything for his father. He would bank the cheques, declare the income, pay George the value of the invoices in cash, and everyone would be happy. Rather than get involved in the invoicing, Johnny just gave George the blank headed notepaper with the VAT number on and the company details. It meant George could just do whatever he wanted. When cheques arrived for payment with invoice numbers and dates on, Johnny would let George know how much the cheques were for and what invoices and months they were for. He then banked the cheques, declared the income and paid George in cash.

In 1996 business was good. Johnny was doing well with the cab firm, with the bookmaking ventures, and had hit a purple patch playing in high-stakes cash card games and winning regularly while gambling on the horses. In general, he was enjoying life. He and Sophia were on bail and a trial date was set for 1997. It was during the period between being charged and coming to trial that Sophia had fallen pregnant. Unfortunately, she miscarried one day after going into hospital with pains. She lost the child and stayed in hospital overnight. It was a terribly sad experience for both of them. Johnny had agreed to go out with the two mechanics from work, Mick and Ian, that evening, and he did. They went out for a meal and drank too much. Sophia asked Johnny to pick her up from hospital the following morning about 09.30 am. He overslept and Sophia ended up making her own way home. He was still in bed. Sophia went mad at him, and rightly so. Johnny had set the alarm but had turned it off when it went off. He knew he got it wrong and regretted his actions; he'd just not thought it through properly.

The criminal trial had been delayed mainly so the witnesses could all attend. Some witnesses were flying into the UK for the trial and had to get time off from work at the same time as other witnesses would all be available. The trial was at Canterbury Crown Court in front of Judge Barclay. It started at 10 am one Monday morning. Johnny knew nothing about the judge except that he lived locally in Bridge, near Canterbury. He was often in the local papers after hearing cases and sentencing people, after convictions or offering his words of wisdom after acquittals. He knew all the barristers very well. The case was expected to last two to three weeks. The jury was sworn in after one or two members were excused, as well as one juror who recognised Sophia from years ago. Opening arguments were straightforward enough, really. They were not facts; just what the Crown Prosecution intends to prove beyond a reasonable doubt to the jury by the end of the presentation of the evidence and after having heard all the evidence in the case. Of course, in criminal cases the burden of proof is high, and it falls on the Crown to prove their case, not the defendant or defendants to prove their innocence.

The first witness to take the stand was DC Cousins. The prosecutor asked him to introduce himself, and explain who he was and his role in the investigation and the case against the defendants. At this point Michael Mann QC and Adelle Fulton asked the judge about issues with the whole investigation and case built against the defendants. The judge decided in light of the suggestions being made by the defence counsels that the jury should be excused until the issues had been resolved, as clearly, he was unaware of the facts that would follow and did not want the jury hearing matters which may cause bias for or against the defendants.

Once the jury left the court, the defence counsels stated to the judge that although this officer was the officer at Canterbury Police Station who gave the papers to the Crown Prosecution to consider further action or charges, he was not in fact the person who gathered the evidence and dealt with witnesses. All he had done was copy witness statements onto police paper exactly as they were taken by Barry Langford, the loss adjuster. Then the judge was made aware of Barry Langford's role in the case and his background. Then his criminal convictions were put before the judge. The argument became simple – the investigation had been tainted from the very start by a dishonest man who only wanted one outcome. He did not investigate without favour either way. He was just on a mission to produce one outcome regardless of the facts. Clearly, the honesty of DC Cousins was not at stake, but the procedure that had been followed was, as well as the integrity and honesty of Barry Langford.

The nail in coffin seemed to have sunk in when Michael Mann asked DC Cousins what happened when he first met Barry Langford. DC Cousins said he introduced himself as the loss adjuster and made it clear to him that he was ex-job. It was then established that by Barry Langford stating he was ex-job, he had put the serving officer's mind at rest that he knew what he was doing around investigations and could be trusted to do a thorough job. His previous position as a police officer had instantly given DC Cousins peace of mind about the investigation. DC Cousins accepted the principle that as he was ex-job he could be relied upon or trusted. Then it was put to DC Cousins about Barry Langford's previous convictions, which he'd obtained while a serving officer in the police force. DC Cousins was asked if, had he introduced himself as the loss adjuster, ex-job and explained the reasons and circumstances of his dismissal from the force, would he have trusted the man and relied upon him with regards to witness dealings, statements and the gathering of evidence with the same peace of mind and trust that he had as a result of the simple statement 'I am ex-job.' His answer was 'Yes, I would have.' The judge did a double take. He shook his head as if to say he didn't believe what he'd just heard. DC Cousins was effectively saying that he would trust a thoroughly dishonest ex-police officer with multiple convictions for fraud and dishonesty the same as he would an honest police officer.

The judge knew cases could not be built by dishonest people who break all the rules to get the result they want. All police investigations are meant to be conducted with honesty, integrity and credibility. At this point the judge stated he was beginning to have a feeling about this case. It was pointed out by the defence counsel that this went to the very heart of the defence in these proceedings. The prosecutor was offered the opportunity to take instructions from the Crown about the case. There was an adjournment to allow for the phone call to take place and the prosecutor to explain the circumstances and take instructions. So far so good, Johnny thought.

The judge was almost inviting the prosecutor to end the matter there and then. After the adjournment, the prosecutor explained he had explained the situation, the circumstances, and the Crown said that they wanted him to continue with the prosecution. He had found out about the convictions of the loss adjuster and it got more complicated. As a result of the convictions, trial witnesses were given new identities, and their identities were protected because of the witness protection program. The case papers had a seal on them, and all papers relating to the case were protected and could not be looked at without the express written permission of the Director of the Department of Public Prosecution and a High Court judge. Mr Mann said the defence would naturally like to see the papers and put them before the court if appropriate. It was explained to the judge that all the case papers were in a storage facility in Hounslow with a seal on them.

It meant certain permissions had to be sought first of all, and that if approved, then someone would have to examine all the papers individually and look at what evidence could be shared and what evidence could not due to the sensitive nature of the trial which involved several police officers, paid informants, and protected certain witnesses' identification. Judge Barclay agreed with the defence that they should be allowed to examine the papers and see exactly what had gone on and how the loss adjuster had acted and behaved. The prosecutor said that a great deal of time would be required to allow this process to happen. The prosecutor seemed to be arguing that after the long, drawn-out process to date, it would be acceptable to stop the trial, have an adjournment which may be for several months, then debate possible disclosure, and then start the trial again. The judge disagreed. He said the Crown had until 10 am Tuesday morning to bring the documents – which were sealed, in storage – to the court and disclose them to the defence. That was it. The judge had made his order. Everyone knew the Crown could not and would not do that, but the judge invited them to try or stop the prosecution. Without producing and disclosing the documents, an imbalance in the proceedings would be created that would not allow the defendants to get a fair trial according to the rules of disclosure. Court was adjourned until 10 am Tuesday morning and the jury were sent home.

The following morning it was clear that the documents were not forthcoming and the Crown were not in a position to proceed further. The judge stated that due to the non-disclosure, the pleas entered by both defendants, a jury sworn in and the trial started, he would find the defendants both not guilty. This was the correct procedure in the circumstances. Johnny and Sophia had both been found not guilty. The judge ordered that the defendants receive their costs from the public purse.

It was all over. Johnny shook hands with his barrister and just said thank you. Sophia stated that her barrister said to her, 'I am pleased for you.' Just as Johnny was walking out of the court, his barrister shouted at him across the court, 'Mr Butler, if you have any problems getting your money from the Prudential, come and see me,' and smiled.

Johnny had phoned George on the Monday evening and explained what had happened at court that day and what was expected to happen on Tuesday. George was naturally pleased for his son. George had given a statement to Brabners Solicitors with regard to the ownership of certain property on the claim form. His evidence totally contradicted other witness statements in the case, and if true, meant the witnesses were either mistaken or lying. In any event, if George would have been believed, it would have ruined the credibility of some of the Crown's case. Johnny had always turned to George for advice and guidance in life. He was Johnny's go-to whatever was going on in his life. As far as Johnny was concerned, George knew everything and had always protected him. He was his father, mentor and best friend. When he had got serious with Sophia, Johnny later found out that

George had told Sophia, 'If he lets you down, it will be with his gambling.' When he had losses at the track, the casino or in the bookmakers, he would often borrow large amounts of money from George to put the damage straight. Then he'd work tirelessly, nonstop, until he had paid George back. Johnny always paid his father back in full, and very quickly.

Soon after that, George had rung Johnny and asked him if he would get an American Express platinum card and then get him one as well as an additional card holder. Johnny didn't think he would get one. David Beckham was doing the adverts for the card, and Johnny was doing well, but not that well. He thought that only celebrities and really high-profile and successful people could have an American Express platinum, as the card had no pre-set spending limit. He applied and got it. He was pleased, because he could now get George one and he always wanted to help George out where he could.

Shortly after the criminal trial collapsed, while Brabners Solicitors were busy retrieving costs from the public purse, Johnny instructed Brabners to pursue the Prudential for the amount claimed at the time of the alleged burglary. The Prudential did not want to settle the claim as a result of the criminal trial collapsing. After several months of correspondence, they stated they would not pay the claim. At this point Johnny could have walked away, made a complaint to the insurance ombudsman or issued proceedings. George had told Johnny to leave it but Johnny wanted the £49k. He asked the solicitors how much it would be to issue civil proceedings in the High Court against the Prudential and fight the claim if they chose to defend it. The solicitor pulled a face and said how long is a piece of string? Johnny thought about it for a few moments, remembered Michael Mann's words, and the gambler in him wanted to win at all costs. He instructed Brabners to issue proceedings against the Prudential. It was agreed to leave the money from the criminal defence costs as part payment and he would fund it as it went on right up to and including the civil trial, if the matter was not settled before.

One evening Johnny was working at the cab firm and one of the drivers said that other firms were listening in over the airwaves to jobs being given out on the radio, and if they could get there quickly enough were stealing the jobs. This had been a common problem recently, with the number of no pickups or dead runs, as they were referred to in the business, increasing all the time. Taxi firms and drivers picking up other firms' customers and bookings had always been common place in the business, especially by drivers whose taxis were not carrying any markings or displaying the names of their firms, or who were just independent drivers. Lots of students and some customers just wanted a taxi quickly and were happy to see one turn up. They would approach the driver and tell them their name and the driver would confirm that he was there to pick them up.

One of the drivers said to Johnny that Mark Eastman had just picked his fare up at the university and it was now a dead run. Johnny saw the fare was going to the Westgate kebab house in Canterbury. Johnny knew Mark Eastman, who had previously worked for the firm, and exploded. He didn't know if Mark had been listening in and stealing the jobs or had just turned up at the university at that moment and took the fare. Johnny took it very personally, jumped in his car, drove like a man possessed to the Westgate kebab, and saw the customers getting out of Mark Eastman's taxi. Johnny screeched up, jumped out of his car, ran over to Mark's taxi and exploded at him. He told him in no uncertain terms what he was going to do to him if he ever did it again, grabbed Mark after opening his car door, and ripped his taxi radio out of his car, dropping it on the floor. Just at that minute, the police were passing. They stopped. The confrontation between Johnny and Mark finished. Johnny was arrested for assault and criminal damage. He couldn't believe it. The police took a statement from Mark Eastman and charged Johnny with assault and criminal damage. He appeared in the local magistrates and pleaded not guilty. Johnny instructed Irwin Mitchell & Co to defend him. It was decided the matter could be heard and dealt with in the Canterbury Magistrates Court. A trial date was set and the magistrates would hear the case. Johnny knew it would come down to his word against Mark's and thought he would take his chance. His defence was effectively Mark was lying and exaggerating the whole thing. There had been a disagreement but Johnny had not assaulted him and not damaged the radio. It was just simply a heated exchange of words, nothing more, nothing less.

Purely by chance, nothing else whatsoever, the day before the trial Johnny walked into the Coach and Horses in Harbledown, just on the outskirts of Canterbury, to use the toilets. To avoid the embarrassment of just walking into a nice country pub just to use the toilets, as he ran towards the toilets, he ordered a coca cola and packet of salted nuts. So, after he used the loo, he could have the coke, eat the nuts and be on his way, so to speak. After using the toilet, he went back to the bar, took a stool at the bar, started drinking his coke and opened his packet of nuts. Then he looked round and noticed Kenny Eastman sitting at the bar having a drink. It was Mark's father. How ironic, he thought. He had not seen Kenny for years. Kenny had worked on the buses and taxis for years. He knew Mikey and Johnny well but had never worked for their firm. He had known Mikey many years previously.

They exchanged pleasantries and Kenny asked Johnny how Mikey was doing in prison. They chatted for about another five or ten minutes. Johnny finished his drink and left, wishing Kenny well. The next day Johnny was at the local Magistrates Court at 09.30 am, the agreed time to meet the barrister Irwin Mitchell & Co had instructed to act for Johnny in the matter. It was a simple defence. Johnny had no witnesses. The Crown had Mark Eastman and the arresting officers. They had no other witnesses – just the police who'd turned up after the event, so to speak, so they could only speak about what they'd found when passing, not what had happened up until that point. Then the Crown said that their witness had not turned up at court. He did not want the matter to go to court and did not want to be involved. The Crown decided to proceed in any case and rely on the arresting officer's evidence. They gave their evidence, which was brief and to the point. They stated they were passing, stopped, got out and spoke to Mark Eastman, then arrested Johnny. They then took a statement from Mark, interviewed Johnny and charged him with assault and criminal damage.

Johnny then took the stand and said it was nothing like what they had explained at all. He made it very clear that the police officers were not there when the disagreement had happened and were relying on Mark's statement. Mark had no injuries. They had merely grabbed each other. Johnny explained the radio was lying in the road as a result of Mark's actions, not his. He really thought he came across well when giving evidence and, when cross-examined, he believed he had the answers. After he finished being cross-examined, the case was concluded. The magistrates said they would retire to consider their verdict. During that time, he was outside the court room and asked his barrister, 'What do you think they will do?' The barrister looked at Johnny and said, 'I think they will fine you.' Johnny was speechless.

Johnny was asking whether he thought they would convict or acquit – that was the question he thought he had posed. The barrister had very quickly stated he thought they would convict him and fine him in one quick breath. Johnny was surprised and disappointed.

When the magistrates told the court clerk they had reached their verdict, everyone filed back into the court. The magistrates came back in and sat down. Johnny had to stand. The female magistrate who was the middle of the three magistrates on the bench stated that they found on the evidence that the case had not been proven. It was not a guilty, nor a not guilty. It was a not proven. Johnny had never heard this before. He would take it and be happy with the outcome. He had a sneaky feeling that when he'd walked into the pub purely by chance and found out from Kenny that it was his local, Kenny may have taken the view he was making a statement without saying a word about the case. He never did find out if Kenny had advised Mark it wouldn't be a good idea to give evidence, Mark decided it would not be a good idea to give evidence, or Mark knew that he had stolen the fare that evening and had an attack of his own conscience. That was, in any event, the end of the matter.

CHAPTER 10
1998 DERBY DAY

JOHNNY BELIEVED that the civil claim with the Prudential would soon be settled or would be heard in court. This matter was going to become protracted and expensive for both sides.

In 1997 Vera decided she had run her course with letting rooms to students. She wanted to sell the larger property and downsize to a smaller property in Canterbury. She no longer wanted the hard work or the aggravation that went with being a landlady. She was older now and decided she wanted a peaceful way of life. The property in Old Dover Road, Canterbury, was put on the market and sold relatively quickly. All she had to do was find a smaller property that she liked and agree a price with the vendor. Johnny later would find out that she miscalculated what she would end up with in terms of net proceeds from the sale and, in all honesty, could not afford to buy a new home without a mortgage or getting a cheaper place elsewhere.

He never paid too much attention to the sale of the property, expecting his mum to have her new place sorted out in time for the sale and completion of one and completion on her new place.

Halfway through the sale process, Vera told Johnny she had nowhere to go. She had not found, made an offer or started purchasing a new place. He was a little shocked. It was agreed she could move in with him and Sophia, store her furniture in the double garages at High Hopes, and live there until she had time to find a new place and buy it.

This was what happened. The property in Old Dover Road was sold. She moved in with them, with her cats as well. She said she would stay in her room upstairs most of the time. That was not what Johnny wanted. He made it clear to her she should treat the place as her own. The thought of his mother keeping out of the way made him uncomfortable. Of course, she was just trying to let him and Sophia have their own lives and privacy. A very tricky situation but on the whole, it worked well enough.

Then, one day Vera was sitting in the living room looking at two sets of property details. She did not seem in a rush to find somewhere, he had thought. They started chatting and she showed him the details of two cottages. He casually remarked, 'Go and view them, pick the one you prefer, and make an offer and buy it.' Then she explained to him that she could not afford to buy either of them without getting a mortgage. She didn't want a mortgage, and maybe at her time of life wouldn't get one, especially as she only had a little part-time job. She suggested she was going to get a mobile home to live in. Johnny was shocked and felt terrible. After all the money he had earnt and lost gambling, as well as the lifestyle he was leading and had led since the age of about twenty? He didn't want that. It was not his fault or responsibility but he felt like it was, somehow.

He asked Vera how much she had in the bank. He could see the asking prices of both of the properties, which were almost the same. She told him her cash balance at Lloyds Bank. So rather than get involved or make a song or a dance about it, he grabbed her chequebook out of her handbag, went down to Lloyds Bank, wrote a cheque to her for £20,000.00 from his Standard Chartered offshore bank account, and paid it in her account. Then, later on, when he got home, he told her she now had the money to buy either of the cottages, whichever one she preferred. She objected to what he had done. He said it was a gift. She said she did not want it. They later agreed that it was a loan that would be paid back to Johnny when she passed away. It would be noted in her will and he would receive the money back before her estate was split between him and Alex. There was no record made of the payment or agreement. He was not bothered. Life had been good to him and he realised he would get half of her estate later, as and when she passed away. She chose her new home, and it was a property in Ivy Lane. She would live there for many happy years, right up until nearly the end of her life, when she would have to go into a care home because of poor health.

In late 1997 and early 1998 Johnny kept bumping in to Tony McManus, who was now living with his new lady, Carol, in Canterbury. They would bump into each other at Sittingbourne Dog Track or Bown's, the bookmakers in Canterbury. At the time Tony was working at the horse races for Chris Lane. Chris, like Johnny, had a cab firm. He was based in Chislehurst. He was a middle-aged man who was always well dressed and well groomed. He had pitches at various horse racing tracks in the South of England, which he'd inherited from his family. That was how horse racing pitches changed hands. They were very valuable commodities that could only be handed down to family members. You could not legally buy a pitch from a bookmaker. If family members did not want them, they could be handed back to the race tracks. There was a very long list to get pitches at all race tracks. In reality, no one handed them back.

Tony said to Johnny that he could go to the horses and lay

horses privately with Chris. By that he meant that he could go to the race tracks and tell Chris what favourites or short-priced horses he wanted to lay at the meeting that day. Chris would then back them with him but expected better odds than the price he had laid to the punters or other bookmakers. So, in theory or on paper, Chris would lay a horse at even money, then want 11 to 10 from Johnny. This would give Chris a margin and meant he had laid the horse at odds on rather than even money. Unfortunately, Chris was not good to do business with. He turned out to be greedy, very selective about the truth, and he always had a glass in his hand. Johnny never knew what he was drinking but thought they looked like large vodka and tonics. But he wanted the action, so he agreed to do it.

Chris was either trying to have a party every day or had a drink problem. After a few races he was almost embarrassingly legless, or at least tipsy. He'd then stand up to do business on the pitch, laughing and joking with everyone, embarrassingly so. In theory it was a good plan and business opportunity. The team, as it was then, was Chris standing up on the pitch, laying the bets; Teo, an ex-accountant from Scotland now living in Maidstone, was the clerk recording all the bets and keeping Chris up with his liabilities; Tony McManus was the price man and responsible for back bets – or hedging, as it is known in the trade. This was where a bookmaker would have other bets with other bookmakers at the track, to adjust his liabilities on certain horses. In those days the internet and betting exchanges didn't exist. Even the bookmaker's boards were marker pens on wipe boards, so the bookmaker would just rub the prices out with his finger or a cloth and change it one way or another. The introduction of electronic boards was on the horizon. It was not long after this that bookmakers started displaying their prices electronically on digital boards, which is the system currently in use today.

Bill, an elderly gentleman was the bag man. He would stand to one side of the bag hanging down at the front of the pitch and count the money, check the notes, give change and generally try to look like he knew what he was doing. He had been around the races most of his life. He was retired. Chris knew him well and trusted him. He would also set the joint or pitch up at the beginning of the meeting. He knew all the sayings and Johnny loved listening to them. A lot of them never made sense when Johnny started, but he would come to learn through his own experience what they actually meant and how relevant they would become. The first one was 'Race tracks tame lions,' then he would say 'You can't beat results,' and the one that made Johnny smile was, 'How do you become a millionaire as a bookmaker? – Start with two million.' Johnny was always hanging around the joint between races waiting for Chris to return from the bar, which sometimes he never did. He would simply get chatting, forget the time and not come out and trade on that race.

Tony and Johnny used to travel to Teo's house in Maidstone in the mornings before racing. They would drive to the track where the racing was that day and meet Chris and Bill there. If the track was one of the tracks a longer way away, they would sometimes meet near Chris's home, where Chris and Bill would be waiting in a lay-by or agreed meeting point, and all go together. Chris had a seven-seater vehicle, which he used for racing, which could cope with all the staff and the joint as well. Sometimes Chris would take his wife along for the larger, more glamorous meetings, like Royal Ascot. That was a complete disaster. They both loved a drink and half the time just sat in the restaurant or bar eating and drinking. Chris used to pay Teo petrol money if he drove his own car. When they all met up together, Chris used to get Teo to drive and he would sit in the passenger seat. They all used to read the Racing Post and Sporting Life on the journey. There was always a good atmosphere and banter between them. All of them except Bill were gamblers and working out what the winners would be, or at least what they thought they would be.

Of course, what Chris and Johnny were doing was technically illegal. Johnny never had a permit. He could not claim to be representing Tower Bookmakers, since Tower Bookmakers did not have any race course pitches. It was just what it was; two guys chasing some money. Johnny didn't have the expenses of operating a pitch at the races or any travelling expenses apart from the journey to Maidstone to meet Teo, but he was laying greater prices than the horses actually were. He paid his own entrance. Chris, on the other hand, paid the travelling, paid a daily rent for the pitch, paid all his staff entrance fees, paid their daily wages, and there were a couple of incidentals as well, such as paying for the daily sheets with the runners printed on and a small fee for the joint. In those days it was costing Chris between £250 and £350 per day in expenses before he would see a penny. If he went four or five times in a week, his expenses could be anything between £1k and £1,500 before he would see a profit.

Johnny very quickly realised a few people were doing the same thing as he was with other bookmakers, and there were other bookmakers who would do exactly the same thing with him as he and Chris were doing. He was introduced to a bookmaker called Bill Papps. Bill was a lot easier to deal with. Bill was not a drinker. He just liked coffee or a soft drink. Bill was struggling to make it pay at the track, with his expenses often getting paid but him not actually seeing any money himself. Johnny had cash. Bill was struggling. Johnny very quickly realised Bill would do anything he wanted once they got to know each other and Bill saw he had the money to back it up.

Bill had a clerk called Eamon, who was a young Irish guy with a great sense of humour. After every race Eamon and Bill used to argue like cat and dog about everything. Both of them seemed hell-bent on having the last word. Johnny found it amusing. In a strange way, they were like an old married couple, constantly bickering, but it was clear to everyone they had a great friendship and a lot of love between them deep down. Bill was an old-fashioned bookmaker. He had been around a long time and seen all the changes. Every day he wore a jacket, trousers and tie that somehow never seemed to match. He wanted to look professional and smart but managed to look like he was trying hard and still not achieving it. He was a loveable rogue and had a unique character all of his own. Johnny had never met anyone like him. Over the time he and Bill got to know each other, Bill told him that the bookmaking at the track used to be a gold mine. The percentage that bookmakers used to bet to in the years that had gone by was a lot greater than it was today. Years ago, a bookmaker at the track could bet to about one hundred and twenty-five percent and lay most of the horses, which meant he would show a profit almost all the time. Now the percentage was down to between one hundred and one hundred and ten percent, and you could not lay all the horses – apart from some major days with big races, when you could lay between one and four horses per race. Bill said the day of the mug punter and easy cash was over. Everyone was far more switched on now about the prices and horses' realistic chances of success. Bill said there was a lot of professional money about but the absolute guessers with pockets of cash had disappeared over the years. So, Bill thought the real money today was clever money. It didn't mean the horses always won but they were a lot sharper and harder to beat.

Johnny very quickly realised Bill was right; occasionally you had the big days, and you did have lots of families, punters and couples just guessing, gambling for fun, and even just betting horses because of their names, nothing else. On those days the money used to flow in, fill the bag up, lay lots of selections, and it just meant bookmakers did not have to stick their neck out with liabilities. In general, on those days the more money you took, the more you won as a bookmaker. Whereas most days and at the smaller meetings there was only the live money about, and sometimes the more you took the more you lost; it was as simple as that. For some races there would be favourites that you could lay and lay for as much as you wanted to but you couldn't lay any other horses in the same race. So, the only thing that mattered in those situations tended to be, did you want to oppose the favourite and for how much. By laying just the one horse, the bookmaker becomes a gambler. If the favourite wins you can lose a lot, and if the favourite loses you can win a lot. That is not bookmaking. That is gambling. Johnny didn't mind that too much; after all, he was just trying to lay short-priced favourites and hope they would get beat.

Many days would go by with him not making much – sometimes winning, sometimes losing. Bill didn't really have a large enough float or bankroll to trade profitably. He would fiddle about and try and get a day's wages for himself and Eamon, but the daily expenses of trading including Eamon's wages often meant he went home without a profit. Bill had a shop in Brighton, and that was struggling to show much of a profit as well. So, Bill put it to Johnny that he and Eamon would work for him if he wanted. The proposal was that if he paid the expenses, Bill and Eamon's wages were agreed, and then Johnny would just take over full control. Bill would just follow instructions from him about what to do. Johnny would be the bag man and do the prices. Then he would assume responsibility for all the losses or keep the profits. It was illegal, really, but it was going on and no one seemed bothered at all. It would probably be extremely hard to prove. Bill was standing up and doing the trading. It was his pitch. He could have investors. Not sure if he could sell the rights to the pitch on a daily basis, but it didn't matter. So now Johnny had his own pitches, he thought, just not in his name, and he could not stand up and do the trading, but he liked the action and how it made him feel. This arrangement went on for some time but it was not lucrative overall. There were plenty of good and bad days, but every day the expenses had to be paid and over a period of weeks, he slowly realised he was probably not winning or losing overall against the punters; his losses just slowly grew because of the daily expenses.

The best day he had with Bill was Derby Day 1998. He was so excited. Bill had a pitch at Epsom and Johnny was looking forward to it so much.

He and Sophia drove to Epsom in his Bentley. He had no idea about parking but he wanted to get as close to the stands as possible. He drove into the royal enclosure car park by mistake, and for some reason he was waved on and not checked or asked to show a pass. He found a nice spot to park and did so.

He and Sophia then got into the race track and met Bill and Eamon. Everyone was dressed to the nines. A lot of bookmakers had morning suits with top hats. He and Bill had sharp suits on. Even Bill seemed to brush up well that day. Sophia had made a big effort and looked stunning. Johnny had a large packet of cash and was raring to go. The punters got the best of the early results and losses were rising quite sharply, but the weather was beautiful. It was a beautiful summer's day.

Then the Derby betting started. Cape Verdi was favourite, trained by Saeed bin Suroor, with Frankie Dettori booked for the ride. The race looked to centre around four runners and the betting reflected that. The second favourite was Second Empire trained by Aidan O'Brien (IRE), and Michael Kinane was on board, the third favourite was Greek Dance, trained by Michael Stoute and ridden by Walter Swinburn, and the fourth favourite was King of Kings, trained by Aidan O'Brien (IRE) and Pat Eddery was on board. Punters were split in their opinions, and as you can imagine for these four horses, there was as much money available as you wanted. It was one of those days when you could lay lots of horses.

Johnny didn't really have a feeling about the race. Money and bets for the four leading contenders just kept flowing in, and there were bits and pieces for the other runners, but not much. Very quickly, Bill had managed to take a few thousand on the four runners, and they were all losers in the book, so Johnny just kind of went with that and was hoping for a result in the race. There were fifteen runners in total, although some of the runners did look to be just making up the numbers – on paper, at least. It was a great race, very exciting, with lots of twists and turns and different horses taking different positions during the one-and-a-half-mile event. At the business end of the race, there were many horses in with a chance. At the two-furlongs pole, it was hard to see how the race would pan out. Then at the one-furlong pole, a horse called High Rise trained by Luca Cumani and ridden by Olivier Peslier took off and won in great style. All Johnny remembered thinking was that it was not one of the four losers in the book.

When he got back to the pitch after watching the race in the stands with Sophia, Johnny, like all the other bookmakers, was lit up. The winner was a twenty-to-one chance, and only one punter had placed a fiver on the winner with Bill. Johnny remembered thinking, *what a great day to be alive*. Now all the previous losses for the day had been wiped out and Johnny had hit the front by £4k. The sun was shining and everyone was smiling. Sophia had been running about enjoying herself at the track, and she seemed happy. The last few races passed with small wins and small losses. He gave Bill and Eamon a bonus on top of their daily wages.

Johnny and Sophia went to find the car, and it was at this point, when they entered the car park area where the car was, that he realised it was the royal enclosure car park. Beautiful, he thought. Had the best parking all afternoon, and it was free. They jumped in the car. He was on top of the world and decided not to head home but go to his favourite restaurant in London. He had been going to Langan's Brasserie in Stratton Street ever since he met Sophia. He'd taken her there on their first date after the theatre. At the time, Michael Caine had a share in it. Often you might see Michael Caine, Roger Moore, and their wives sitting at the round table near the entrance where you walked in. He knew all the waiters on first-name terms. He used to tip over the odds, and he and Sophia became regulars. In the end, he didn't even have to book. If he forgot, he would pretend he had booked. The staff would never find the reservation, but the waiters would all be over, talking to him and telling the woman on the desk that was fine, they would make up a table for him while he had a drink in the bar.

At the weekends, there was a piano player in the bar, and Johnny particularly liked the selection of nibbles that came with the drinks. There was always a selection of various celebrities dining in there. The staff really did spoil him and Sophia with the service they gave. He first got the idea about pretending he had a reservation when he didn't after ringing one day to book and being told politely by a young lady, 'Sorry, sir, we are fully booked.' He didn't tell Sophia. They just went to the restaurant that evening, and when he was told they couldn't find the reservation, he smiled and looked puzzled, but very quickly Jean Pierre (maître d') came over and started shaking Sophia's hand and talking to her and saying how nice it was to see her and Johnny. At that point he kind of waved at the girl on reception as if to say don't worry about it, it's not a problem. The dinner tasted amazing. Johnny thought he was in heaven, and he was really. A nice drive home later that evening after dinner and a few drinks was the end to the perfect day.

Shortly after that Johnny realised he didn't really use the Bentley very much. It was a beautiful car without a lot of purpose in his day-to-day life. He wanted to get rid of it. He was over at George and Pat's one day in Leybourne and he told George he was thinking of getting rid of it. George had borrowed it before and loved it. George didn't have enough spare cash to buy it but wanted it. Great, Johnny thought, George could have the Bentley and pay him when he could. It suited George and Johnny. He had let it go and George might have a use for it with his business as well as using it himself. George had a large drive with garages so it could just be parked easily enough over at his place. It came with a cover for when it was left outside, or it could be garaged. They agreed a fair price both were happy with. A couple of days later, Johnny drove the car over to George's and George dropped him back home in it.

Later in June 1998 Johnny was offered a bookmaker's shop in Biggin Hill. It was owned and operated by John Summerhayes, who was a bookmaker at Crayford Dog Track, where Johnny first met him. Johnny was often out at the dogs in the evening, with or without Sophia. There were two betting shops in Biggin Hill at the time. The other one was owned by John Humphrys. John Humphrys was a London-based bookmaker with a few shops and was also represented or had pitches at many London dog tracks. John was always sharply dressed and well groomed. Johnny knew John from gambling with him at several greyhound tracks, including Crayford, Romford and Catford. When Johnny bought the shop and John Humphrys knew the shop had changed hands, he came to the betting shop to introduce himself. Johnny hadn't realised that in reality John Humphrys had all the trade and best customers sewn up. The shop he had bought did not have that many customers or a large enough turnover, but he thought it could be improved on and turned around. In reality, that was going to prove very hard indeed.

Sophia had taken a job as the personal assistant to the chairman of the Barrett Group. Geoffrey Barrett was the chairman of a family-run business that was based on car sales, property and hi-fi sales, a successful business with many showrooms and outlets. They were main agents for a number of main car dealers, including Jaguar in Canterbury. His offices were above the Jaguar showroom in Westgate in Canterbury. One morning, Sophia had phoned Johnny to say Geoffrey was threatening to sack her and having a go at her. All Johnny actually heard was he was threatening her. He jumped in his car and drove straight to the Jaguar showroom, went upstairs to his offices, and threatened to throw him out of the window if he hurt Sophia. Sophia lost her job and that was that. It later transpired that she had turned up late for work several times and he was threatening to dismiss her if she continued. Johnny realised he had overreacted in the heat of the moment after listening to a few words on the phone while Sophia was crying. Once he had all the facts, deep down he didn't blame Geoffrey and was grateful that the police had not been called or got involved.

So now, Sophia was working at the shop in Biggin Hill. One Wednesday morning, after she had already left for work, Johnny got up and had a bath. He then went into his bedroom and started to dress. He had put his pants on when he fell over. He thought he'd lost his balance but when he tried to stand up, he couldn't. He then realised he couldn't use the right-hand side of his body. He struggled for ages to pull himself up onto the bed, and managed to after a while. He then phoned Tony McManus using his left hand on the phone next to the bed. When Tony answered, Johnny realised that he could no longer speak properly. It was just like a slur; the clear pronunciation of words had become impossible. Luckily Tony realised it was him, and after a few attempts at a failed conversation, Tony asked if he was alright. Quite quickly, he said to him, 'Shall I get you an ambulance?' Tony realised that was what was needed and put the phone down. Tony knew his address well because he was using it to claim housing benefit from. (Tony lived with Carole in Canterbury, but that was unofficial, and he could not claim from there because they were living together as a couple. Whereas Johnny had four spare bedrooms and Tony just pretended to rent a room there.) The ambulance was quite quick, about 10 minutes, and remarkably, by the time the ambulance had arrived, Johnny had regained the use of his right-hand side of his body and was able to speak again. He had got downstairs and was waiting for the ambulance to arrive. Now he was confused and in a state of shock. What had happened? And what was going on? He explained to the ambulance staff. They seemed to understand and he was taken to the accident and emergency for tests and to be checked.

Johnny explained to the doctors what had happened. They did various tests and could find nothing wrong with him. At this time, he was ok but was shaken by the experience. They sent him home and advised him he would be booked in to see a specialist consultant. In the meantime, if he had any problems he could go straight back. Later that evening, when Sophia got home from work, he told Sophia what had happened. They decided to go and have dinner in the George and Dragon in Fordwich. They were sat in an enclosed area with a table for two and a table for four. They were next to a family of four having their dinner. Shortly after ordering, Johhny collapsed with his head on the table and was slurring his speech again.

As his head was lying on the table, Johhny was looking at the children on the table of four next to them. The father of the children thought he was drunk and was saying to his children, 'Don't look over there. He's obviously drunk,' while rolling his eyes. Johnny was laughing to himself and thinking, *I wish I was drunk.* Perhaps it was an easy mistake to make, considering the circumstances. Anyway, the restaurant staff called the ambulance. When the ambulance guys walked in, they had to put him in a wheelchair to take him out to the ambulance. Sophia was explaining to them what had happened earlier that day. As he was being pushed through the restaurant, which was packed, towards the entrance, Johnny heard the guy pushing him say, 'Don't worry, ladies and gentlemen. It's nothing to do with the food.' It made Johnny smile.

So, back to the accident and emergency department at the Kent and Canterbury Hospital. This time he had not recovered and had several tests again, which again found nothing. He was admitted onto a ward and Sophia went home. The next day they did further tests and again found nothing. Johnny went and used the lock-in toilet on the ward to light up a cigarette. He had his cigarette in the toilet, left it and went back to his bed. By now he had regained use of his body again, as well as his speech. One of the nurses came running towards him and very abruptly told him not to smoke in the toilets. She was furious he had been smoking in the toilets. He denied it. He said, 'I didn't,' and tried to put on his little-boy-lost look. She wasn't having any of that and made it clear. Johnny felt terrible and so embarrassed. Deep down, he knew it was wrong and felt guilty for lying to the nurse, but he couldn't admit it and apologise. The best he could manage was not to do it again. After that he started going to the smoking-room downstairs. It was disgusting. Just filled with people smoking, ashtrays full of cigarette butts, and the walls were yellow, but at least he could smoke in peace in there.

Later that day Sophia brought in some pyjamas and a dressing gown. George and Pat came over to visit. The doctor ordered a brain scan for Johnny, which happened the next day. The results were conclusive. They showed he had a blood clot in the brain. This was the cause of the problem. It was explained to him that as a result of the blood clot, he'd had a transient ischaemic attack (TIA) or mini stroke. The doctor then went on to explain to him that the good news was that the blood clot had cleared itself and everything was back to normal. The doctor then told him that just because this had happened to him, it was no more or less likely that he would have another one than anyone else. He was put on aspirin to thin his blood, and advised to eat healthily and give up smoking. Johhny had been on two or three packets of cigarettes per day since he left school, almost. He went home relieved, didn't give up smoking, and tried to eat a bit more sensibly and healthier for a while.

CHAPTER 11
RACE COURSE PITCH AUCTIONS

JOHNNY WAS BACK at the races in a flash and trying to enjoy life again after his health scare. He was running the cab firm, or at least overseeing the day-to-day running of it, spending time at the Canterbury shop, or at the races if there was any racing on in the south that day. Earlier that year the British Horse Racing Board had changed legislation, and the rules around horse race course bookmaker's pitches had totally changed. Whereas before the pitches could be handed down to a family member, from December 1998 it was going to be possible to buy or sell the pitches at auction. The auctions were going to be managed and run by the British Horse Racing Board. They would be held at racetrack venues in different areas throughout the UK.

Johnny had heard about it all earlier in the year and wanted to get his own race course pitches. This was his golden opportunity to get his own pitches and stop relying on bookmakers like Bill or Chris and being at their mercy, so to speak. Johnny felt like he had served some kind of apprenticeship at the races and now he could take the plunge all on his own. Tower Bookmakers had the permit, which allowed the company to own and operate licenced bookmakers' shops as well as trade as a race course bookmaker. Johnny would simply be representing Tower Bookmakers. He wasn't sure if that stacked up in law, because maybe employees who would represent companies as the bookmaker on course had to have a permit, but everyone thought he was Tower Bookmakers, and it was only Sophia and Johnny that knew Sophia was the director. No one tends to investigate these things or ask questions, and no one ever did. If you pay your bills on time and conform to the rules, why would anyone? Most people are busy enough trying to sort out their own problems and lives, without worrying about other people's lives or business affairs.

The bookmaker who had the number one pitch at Lingfield All-Weather Racing made it known he wanted to sell his pitch. There were lots of bookmakers who had rails pitches and regular pitches that they wanted to sell. All pitches had a number at the race course. It was an old-fashioned system. It meant pitch 1 would pick where he wanted to go first and so on. The bookmaker at Lingfield All-Weather was Peter Johnson and he said he wanted £20k for pitch 1. Johnny was introduced to him and they talked a little. Johnny knew straight away he was a reputable man with integrity. He dressed very smartly but in a casual sense. His family had been at the races for years. He had many pitches at various race tracks and he didn't seem hard up to Johnny. That was just the opinion Johnny got from the guy. Johnny offered him £18k. This was about two months before the auction date. Bookmakers could reach agreement with other bookmakers about selling their pitches prior to the auction date. In those cases, the pitch would be entered into the auction. It would be explained to the auctioneer who had bought the pitch and at what price. That way, all transactions and sales went through the British Horse Racing Board. They would also get their fees for entering and selling of the pitches. Peter turned Johnny down. Johnny knew he wanted pitch 1 at Lingfield All-Weather. There were more race courses meeting at Lingfield All-Weather each year than any other race track. Johnny went back, said he would like pitch 1 and would pay £20k for it. It was a brief conversation. They shook hands and it was agreed on. The transaction could not actually take place until the auction date, but they had a gentleman's agreement at £20k. It was a good start for Johnny. He wanted pitches at the southern tracks.

The auction date and catalogue were published. It would be held on Sunday 13th December at Sandown Race Track. They were also other auctions going on in the Midlands and up north for the various picks. Some reserve prices were for astronomical amounts, over £100k for various different meetings, including Cheltenham. There were also some very low pitch numbers, like 35, that had reserves of about £2k, for the smaller meetings. Everything came down to the pitch number and the venue.

The auction was approaching and Johnny was getting excited about the prospects of having his own race course pitches. He had already ordered the joint with the board and bag. Everything was tastefully printed in the name of Tower Bookmakers.

He had started going to Romford Dog Track recently and enjoyed the racing there. He had been over to Ireland earlier in the year. Tony the dog trainer told him that one of his old employers in Ireland had been cheating with a dog racing at Shelbourne Park. The dog had a lot of time in hand and would win. Did Johnny want to go and back the dog and after the race buy the dog with the winnings? Johnny loved offers like these. The idea of buying a dog with money won from backing the dog was just up his street. He said he would. The plan was, fly to Dublin – no one would know about the dog except him – back the dog, and after it won the race, buy the dog. Sounded like a great adventure to Johnny. It almost went exactly to plan, but not quite.

Johnny asked Tony McManus if he would come and help put money on. It was agreed Tony could back the dog himself as well. Johnny would pay all his travel and room for the night. So, one Wednesday afternoon, Johnny, Tony McManus and Tony the trainer set off from Canterbury to Stanstead to catch the one-hour flight from Stanstead to Dublin. The traffic was heavy on the way to the airport but it was not a problem. They had left in plenty of time. The flight was only one hour long. There were no customs checks or passports required. All that was required was ID to board the flight.

Johnny had never been to Dublin before. They arrived at Dublin after a bumpy flight with plenty of turbulence in good spirits and with high hopes. It was about three o'clock in the afternoon. The dog racing started at seven thirty and the only race they were interested in was race five at eight thirty. Shelbourne Park Dog Track was only about a twenty-minute cab ride from the airport. So, they went into Dublin to find a nice restaurant to eat in before making their way to the track. There was plenty of banter and laughs between them. Johnny was astonished how expensive the drinks were in the restaurant. He thought, *wow, I am glad we didn't come here to get drunk*. They all only had one or two drinks with their food. The cab driver and all the people they met and spoke to seemed really nice, genuine people. Johnny liked the sound of the Irish accent, particularly on women. He found it very attractive listening to Irish women talking.

They got to the track early and just waited for the race. There was a small problem to start with that Johnny had not anticipated: Ireland was playing football at home that evening and a lot of the bookmakers had just taken the night off to go and watch the football. Johnny met the trainer and said hello, then the three of them sat in the bar watching the racing. He always valued Tony McManus's opinion of dogs and asked him what he thought of the race in question. Tony simply said that if the trainer had done his job right and the dog had time in hand, he would win on paper at least.

About ten minutes before the race, they went down to the area where the bookmakers were and tried to find out which layers took the biggest bets in general. It was at this point that some of the locals pointed out that half the bookmakers had taken the night off to go and watch the football. They started betting on the race and they started backing the dog. At a dog track dog prices can collapse in seconds with the weight of money Johnny was trying to get on the dog. He wanted to buy the dog, pay the expenses and take home a tidy profit as well. It was impossible to get all the money on. The dog started trading at seven to two, and before the off there were no offers on any of the bookmakers' boards and some of the bookmakers had hardly laid it. Anyway, there was enough money on the dog to tick Johnny's boxes, even if it did mean not taking home as big a profit as he would have liked. The hare was running, the traps opened and the dog was in trap 6. It came out well enough on the outside, went round the first bend handy, took the race up down the back straight and looked certain to go on and win by a distance. The trainer had the time in hand, the dog hit the front, what could go wrong? Well, the dog never really lived up to expectations. At the third bend it became apparent that the dog was not kicking on and going clear as Johnny had assumed. The other dogs were slowly starting to gain. The distance he was leading by was slowly diminishing and, coming round the last bend, doubt started to kick in. Was he actually going to win? Then, on the final run to the line, a couple of dogs were coming alongside to challenge his position. The dog held on by a rapidly diminishing half a length. A few yards after the winning line the other dogs sailed past him. He had won; there was no doubt about that but it had been a bit heart stopping in the last hundred yards. The dog had not found hardly any time at all, and although he'd won, it was an ordinary middle-grade race and he had struggled to impress.

There was a lot of relief he had won and smiles all round. Tony McManus very quickly made a couple of jokes about everyone having their hearts in their mouths. He then said to Johnny point blank, 'If I were you, I wouldn't buy that dog.' Deep down Johnny knew Tony was right. The problem was Johnny had agreed to buy it if the dog won, and it had. The trainer popped up to the bar about twenty minutes later, which meant he had time to think. Johnny simply said to him, 'Listen, I know the dog won but I don't want to buy it. I am not sure what I would do with it, to be honest. I was not as impressed as I thought I would be.' The trainer kind of knew he had a point. Johnny asked him if he gave the him a good drink and left buying the dog, would he be ok with that? He agreed. Everyone was happy and Johnny gave him £500 for his trouble. Buying the dog and selling it to someone else would have probably cost him a lot more than that, he thought. So, the trainer said good night and off he went.

There was no rush to go. It had been a good and successful night overall, even if it had not gone exactly to plan. It had been a wonderful occasion, and Johnny had really enjoyed the experience, including talking to some really interesting Irish people. The plan was to find somewhere clean and cheap to stay for the night before getting back to the airport in the morning for the early flight from Dublin to Stansted. That shouldn't be too hard in a major city on a Wednesday night, they thought. Maybe they would get a good deal because it was late and the hotels had plenty of rooms to spare. So, there were a few races to go and there was a longer trip race coming up. There was a young puppy in trap two racing over the longer distance for the first time. They watched the race with a passing interest. The two-dog got out slowly, found his stride after a while, went in to the first bend in about third place and followed the leaders around, then, after the second bend, he had got a bit closer to the leaders. As the dogs came out of the second bend, he was getting closer on the outside, then down the back straight, he simply took off passing the dogs in front of him. By the third bend he had hit the front, and he went on to win by a distance. The performance was very impressive. When they announced the winning time, it was just outside the track record at Shelbourne Park for that distance. It had been an absolutely blistering performance for a young puppy racing over that distance for the first time. A lot of people at the track were commenting on the performance. Tony McManus very quickly worked out it was just outside the track record and joked with Johnny, 'I bet you couldn't buy that puppy. It is probably not for sale at any price.' Tony the trainer agreed it had been an amazing performance and the puppy could go on to win anything in Ireland or England. Johnny's brain was doing overtime. Could he buy the puppy? His mum's favourite saying about him was, 'If you want something doing in life, tell Johnny he can't do it.' That had been her experience of him growing up. If she told him not to do it, he just did. It seemed to be part of his makeup.

That was it. He decided to go and find the owners and at least give it his best shot. After all, he'd come to Ireland expecting to buy a dog. What was the harm of trying, he thought. The three of them went round to the kennel area at the dog track to try and find the owner. When they arrived, the trainer was brushing the puppy down and giving him some water to drink. Johnny commented on the puppy's performance through the fence to the trainer. He and one of his kennel hands brought the puppy over to the fence and started chatting. They were two really lovely Irish guys, very pleased with how he had run and in a good mood. Johnny got straight to the point and said he would like to buy the puppy, take him back to England and race him there. They seemed a bit taken aback by his offer. They thought Johnny and his mates were just praising the puppy and wishing them well to start with. The trainer owned the puppy so, quite by chance, Johnny realised he was talking to the owner and trainer at the same time. The man considered his offer. Johnny asked him how much. He asked for £4k. Johnny didn't know how much the puppy was worth but at £4k the deal was on. It was agreed very quickly. He could buy the puppy from the guy at 5 am the following morning at his kennels. They could put the puppy in a wooden dog carry box and take him home on the flight, just pay the charge at the airport. Johnny had never done this before but found out dogs travelled in a certain area near the cargo that was heated and fitted out especially for animals.

So, the evening had ended better than he thought. All they needed to do was find a place to sleep, get to the guys at 5 am, pay and collect the puppy, get to the airport and fly home. So off they went in search of two rooms, a twin and a single, in Dublin. No one seemed to have any rooms available. They enquired and rang a few places. They couldn't understand it. They asked a cab driver and he said, 'Probably won't get a room tonight. Everywhere is fully booked because of the football.' They had forgotten about Ireland playing in all the excitement and didn't realise a lot of supporters would stay over after the match. The cab driver made a couple of suggestions but to no avail. The last chance was Clontarf Castle, which Tony McManus rang. It was now late. The night porter answered and said they did have one room left. It was now approaching midnight and by the time they got a cab there it was quarter past. The night porter confirmed that they still had one room left. They only wanted it until half four, because they needed to get to the kennels, pick the puppy up and get to the airport early.

Johnny was beginning to wonder if it was worth getting a room. Tony McManus did the deal. He explained to the porter, 'We don't want breakfast, we'll be gone by 4.45 am, and we don't want a receipt. Could we get a better price?' The porter seemed to like that idea. The price of the room dropped, it was paid in cash and without a receipt, and no breakfast was required. Maybe no record of the room being rented out got recorded? Who knows! That was not the point. The point was they had somewhere warm and comfortable for a few hours and they could get their heads down. It was a very nice place; a four-star hotel, and they had a great deal. It was a double room with one double bed. Johnny and Tony the dog trainer would share the bed, and Tony McManus would sleep on the floor. No one was getting undressed. It was just a quick sleep, alarm set, up and out in the morning.

It was absolutely terrible, Johnny recalled. Both the Tonys got to sleep quite quickly. Johnny never seemed to sleep quickly. It always took him time to get to sleep. Then it started. The snoring from both of them was something else. He had never heard anything quite like it. Neither of them was drunk. Just a couple of alcoholic drinks had been consumed. After about ten or fifteen minutes, he knew he could not sleep in this room. The noise of these two men snoring was too much for him. It was almost like mental torture, he thought. After about an hour he left the room and just went wandering round the hotel trying to kill time. He went back half an hour later, a lot more tired now.

Maybe he could sleep after all, given time. It was worse. He was now exhausted and still couldn't sleep a wink. He left the room once more and decided to go back half an hour before they were due to leave. He went back, woke the guys up and they booked a cab. He didn't even bother to explain he had not slept, just said, 'I couldn't live with either of you. The snoring was terrible.'

They got to the trainer's kennels just gone 5 am. Johnny paid the trainer the money. They had a brief chat about the puppy. The trainer wanted to pass on two bits of information he thought may be helpful. He said the puppy loved to eat after racing and he loved tracks where there was a long run up to the first bend. He didn't like tracks with a short run up to the first bend. He then gave Johnny £200 back. He said it was luck money. Johnny had never experienced this before. He remembered the gesture. Apparently, it was commonplace in Ireland and other communities. A nice touch, he thought. They put the puppy in the back of the cab on his lead and got to the airport in plenty of time for the flight. He paid the surcharge for the puppy to fly. Within two hours they were walking the puppy around outside a car park at Stansted airport, letting him get some fresh air and exercise after the flight and before the car drive home. They found some water for him and all seemed well. Johnny drove back, dropped Tony and the puppy off at the kennels, then dropped Tony McManus home before going home to bed.

The puppy, who was called Solo Power, settled in well. Tony said he loved his grub. Tony trialled Solo Power in at various tracks and he was doing well. The times were quite impressive and he was definitely an open racer. The first race he was entered into was a maiden open at Rye House. Tony the trainer said he would win. It was straightforward in his opinion. This was music to Johnny's ears. That was the sort of language he liked to hear. When looking in the Sporting Life, the bookmakers saw it as a two-dog race for betting purposes, with Solo Power being the second favourite behind a local dog the papers had made favourite.

Johnny wanted to get £10k on the dog. That would take some doing at Rye House but maybe it could be done. He asked Tony McManus if he wanted to come and asked Peter Flowers if he wanted to come and place money on the dog. Maybe between the three of them it could be done. Peter Flowers had a flower shop in Canterbury with his partner Eileen. He was a regular in Towers in Canterbury and loved the horses and dogs. He loved cards as well. Before racing started, most days, there were card games in Towers in Canterbury. It wasn't allowed or legal, but the game was kaluki. It meant that there was never any money on the table. The scores were kept on a pad and everyone settled up after each game. Peter Flowers, Tony McManus, Tony the manager, Johnny and Mark Cox from the battery shop just across the road from the bookmakers were often to be found sitting at the long table in the shop playing cards in the mornings before racing. Johnny and Mark had become friends as a result of Mark coming in the shop. It was a friendly game and a lot of fun sometimes, Johnny thought. It also added some atmosphere to the shop, he believed.

Johnny, Peter and Tony got to Rye House that Sunday evening with plenty of time to spare. When it came to the maiden open with Solo Power in it, he was priced up at even money favourite to win. They tried to get as much money on as possible but it did not go well. After taking initial bets, the bookmakers were reluctant to take more money on Solo Power. There seemed to be a lack of support for the local dog, and Johnny got refused more bets, as did the other lads. It was that simple; there was no chance of getting all the money on. He was disappointed.

The race went well. The dog came out and ran well. He took

off and won convincingly in a good time. After that, he went to Romford Dogs to be entered into a competition that was for some of the best greyhounds in the country over the longer trip. He did a reasonable first trial. Dogs always tend to improve after having their first run around a new track. The first trial had been a solo trial. The second trial was a three-dog trial, and he was trialling against the favourite for the event and a John McGee runner. All John McGee's runners were always treated with the upmost respect. He had a great reputation for training open-race greyhounds. His most famous winner was arguably Hit the Lid, whom he trained to win the Greyhound Derby in 1988, after being very heavily backed ante-post at large prices and taking the bookmakers for a fortune. He had won all the major greyhound competitions.

The trial went amazingly well. Solo Power beat John McGee's runner and finished two lengths behind the favourite for the competition. The run from such a young puppy on his second run around the track got noted and drew a lot of attention. Then came the first round of the competition. Johnny and Sophia went to Romford that evening. Johnny was convinced he could win the competition, let alone the first-round heat. They were having dinner in the restaurant and enjoying themselves. Solo Power's race came up. The comments about his trial were mightily impressive, he thought. Johnny had found a couple of winners before the race and liked the track. He thought dogs run to form there, or it seemed that way to him. What he really liked about the track was the market. It was easily the strongest betting market he had ever experienced at a dog track. You could shovel money onto dogs in graded or open races. So, he always felt like he could get decent-sized bets on if he was behind. It seemed to him there were a few people being represented there, like Tony Morris and

John Humphrys, as well as others, who were prepared to lay large bets.

Solo Power's race came round quite quickly, it seemed to him. Every time he was enjoying himself, time always flew, as the saying suggests. It was over the longer trip. The hare was running, the traps came up, the dogs ran to the first bend. It was a short run to the first bend and Solo Power had not quite found his stride yet. As they went in the first bend, he was just struggling with the pace a little. The dog on his inside was in front of him. He couldn't get past, he got balked and knocked over, and he ended up on the hare rail at the first bend, not moving.

Tony went to the track after the race, picked him up and carried him off back to the kennels. Johnny shot round to see what was going on. Tony said he thought he had broken his hock. He wanted to get him looked at by the vet and get him home. He had broken his hock, which meant his racing career was over. The next day Tony McManus said, 'I did say to you that the run-up at Romford over the trip was a short run-up. I was surprised Tony ran him there.' He had mentioned it before the race, and Johnny suddenly remembered what the trainer in Ireland had said. He had forgotten all about it. Johnny was furious with Tony the trainer. He was furious that he had run him with a short run-up. After all, he was the trainer.

That was almost the end of their relationship, really. They had some highs and lows together but Johnny always got over the lows. He liked him and relied on him even if he did ask Tony McManus for a second opinion. If the guy in Ireland had never mentioned it, it wouldn't have been a problem, he could have put it down to bad luck or just part of the game, but to just ignore one of only two pieces of advice... Johnny took it particularly badly.

So, after the experience at Romford, Johnny became a regular there for the gambling – not for running greyhounds there. He used to go there on his own or with Sophia for the evening meetings. On Monday, 7th December 1998, he had been to Romford Dogs, was in a good mood, had won a few quid and got home about 11 pm. There was a message on the answerphone from Pat explaining George had felt unwell so he had a lie down but was in pain and so she called an ambulance, to be on the safe side. The ambulance had taken George to the local hospital, which was Maidstone. She was just letting Johnny know. Pat was going to follow in her own car. It all seemed to make sense to Johnny. He told Sophia he was going to Maidstone Hospital to see George, and if they kept him in he would probably stay all night or at least until he knew what was going on. He jumped in his car, put the music on and started driving over to Maidstone Hospital. What he didn't know was that Pat had phoned back after he left and spoke to Sophia. Pat told Sophia that George didn't make it to the hospital alive; he died in the back of the ambulance on the way there. It was a suspected heart attack.

When Johnny turned up at the hospital, he walked in to a rather empty accident and emergency. There was a nurse sitting behind the desk. Johnny had not said a word. She calmly looked at him and said 'Are you Johnny Butler?' He knew in that moment, the exact moment she asked if he was Johnny Butler, he knew in every fibre of his body and heart that George was dead. She looked at him, and he looked in her eyes, which confirmed his very worst thoughts. Then she said, 'I am sorry to tell you…' He never really heard what she said after that; his body just seemed to go into shock.

He was then taken to see Pat, who was emotional, in a side room and they spoke a few words to each other. Pat kind of explained what happened earlier in the evening. Johnny then went outside and was violently sick. After a while he could no longer be sick; he just kept retching on an empty stomach. About twenty minutes later he went back in and asked if he could see George. He was allowed to go into a private room where George was lying on a bed. The body had not yet gone cold, he thought. He knew this was almost the end of his world. What are you meant to do? There is no manual for these feelings and emotions. He simply spent some time with him. He thanked him for being his best friend and the best father he could have dreamed of having. He couldn't hold back the tears. Occasionally he would stop, just keep thanking him for everything, and shared with George his plans for the future. Some people say it is better to remember a loved one as they were when they were alive. Johnny understood this sentiment but he was so glad he went in and spoke to his father and thanked him for everything.

After the chat Pat said he could stay at her place and it seemed to make sense. It was now the early hours of the morning. He was absolutely drained. Pat looked exhausted. Johnny realised he had to let Alex know. When he got to Pat's, he rang his brother at home but he never picked up; it went on to voicemail. They had a phone in the kitchen, not one upstairs, he remembered. Johnny just left a simple message saying that they needed to speak urgently and that he was at Pat's, and to please give him a bell back when he got the message.

Alex rang early the next morning and Johnny shared the news with him. It was probably the most difficult conversation he could have had with him. After conveying the bad news, he didn't know what to say. There were lots of tears and emotion and empty spaces. Maybe sometimes not saying anything is the right answer. The call lasted about 20 minutes. They agreed to keep in touch and sort out the arrangements. There was a post mortem to follow, because George had not been suffering from any long-term diagnosed health conditions. The post mortem confirmed the cause of death was a heart attack. It took nearly a week to get the results and get the body released to the undertakers.

The following Sunday Johnny attended the auction at Sandown Race Course. He had just about composed himself enough and realised if he had not gone, he would probably just sit about at home moping. He and Sophia attended. He knew his budget and wanted to get a pitch at several southern race courses. He was grateful to Peter Johnson for honouring their gentlemen's agreement. A bookmaker said he would go to £25k for the Lingfield all-weather pitch 1. Johnny never even found out until after the auction. Peter Johnson never asked for more money from him. They just shook hands and it was sold to Tower Bookmakers for £20k. After Johnny found out, he thought what a gentleman Peter really was. He would have matched the £25k if he needed to, he thought on reflection, but Peter Johnson never brought it up. It was only after that the other bookmaker told him he'd said to Peter on the day he would go to £25k for it and he turned him down and said, 'I have already sold it.' Not many men have that kind of integrity, he thought. Johnny and Sophia also bought a pitch at Lingfield Turf, Folkestone, Kempton, Sandown and Brighton. So, Tower Bookmakers could now trade at those places in the future. He had spent the money that he had wisely, he thought. Selling prices in general were quite a bit higher than people had expected.

CHAPTER 12
UNSOLVED MURDER

MIKEY HAD BEEN RELEASED from prison in November 1998. Everything had changed between Mikey and Johnny by now. They had started the firm together, had a lot of laughs together. It all seemed to end when Mikey got hooked on cocaine. His personality seemed to change. They earned money together but it was a cooler relationship after that. They had kind of gone in different directions. The financial arrangement they'd agreed on while Mikey was serving his prison sentence stayed in place. Mikey was on parole and had conditions. Very quickly, he wanted to go back to how it was. With a lot of the existing clients and trading partners of the firm, that wasn't going to work. Johnny thought by trying to do the right thing by him when he went away, he had now made a rod for his own back. Mikey kept coming round the office and becoming a liability very quickly, but Johnny knew he did still own half of the business, even after having the money paid to him every week since he went away.

The funeral arrangements for George were made with a very tasteful and professional local Funeral Directors, Clarke and Son, in Snodland. Alex came down to Kent from Manchester to help with the funeral arrangements and be part of the process. George's body was placed in a chapel of rest while waiting for the cremation. Johnny, Pat and Alex all attended Clarke's to make the necessary arrangements. Pat chose the coffin from a selection on offer. Johnny insisted on paying for the affair and asked the undertaker to send him the bill directly. While George was laying in the chapel of rest, Johnny used to visit every day, just to talk to George, who was in a sealed coffin. Although he was emotionally struggling to come to terms with George's death, he used to look forward to visiting every day and talking openly to him. He found a lot of comfort in that.

The crematorium was packed with friends and family who had come to pay their respects. Johnny wrote a speech for the occasion but couldn't compose himself enough to actually read it out on the occasion. He was just in bits for the whole of the service. The reverend read the words out very eloquently on his behalf, he remembered. Alex was in bits too, and the whole affair was very nice but very emotional. Vera managed to attend. Johnny somehow felt for her. She was at the back on her own, and yet had been his wife for 25 years before the marriage ended. Pat was a good woman and had become good friends with him and Sophia, no doubt, but Vera was Johnny's mother after all. Life had definitely changed for Johnny, and the grief that followed was not something he was mature enough to process and deal with.

Tower Bookmakers seemed to be going sideways nowhere, really. Johnny had started gambling for larger amounts again, rather than trying to work at the bookmaking. Most days his gambling results were all that mattered. If he won, everything was fine. Whatever happened in the shops, at the track and at the cab firm seemed to pale into insignificance. He would go to the tracks daily, or the shop in Canterbury, where he was just gambling for large stakes all afternoon. There were some highs at the tracks some days, but not many.

He had amazing credit facilities with Paul Humphry's, the Tote, and Barry Dennis – a bookmaker he often gambled with at the track if he was there. Barry knew Johnny from his time with Chris Lane and Bill Papps. Barry would lay a decent bet and Johnny had become one of his regulars as a punter. Now he was at the track as Towers, everything was down to him in any case. He used to have back bets for the firm and his own personal bets with him. The team at the track was Johnny standing up on the pitch; Tony, Sophia's son, was clerking. He had never done it before but he was a bright lad and he quickly picked it up. Johnny knew he could trust him. Tony McManus asked if his son Dean could be the outside man doing the prices. Johnny agreed. Dean had been off the rails on drugs, caused Tony enough problems as a father, and Tony wanted him doing something honest. It was also an added bonus he was there working with Chris Lane, where he could keep his eyes on him. Dean loved a bet, just like his father. Tony was not really a gambler; he preferred the drugs but was trying to straighten himself out and do something honest, as it were. The team seemed to work well together, and very quickly they looked like they had been there as long as some of the longer-established firms. Johnny did enjoy the bookmaking at the track, especially when it was busy and there was plenty of action and money to be traded. On the days when racing was on where he had a pitch, he used to wake up and actually look forward to the day.

Mikey was going through his divorce with Kelly. It had started while he was in prison but no financial details, child support or financial arrangements had been agreed. He went to see his solicitor, who suggested that because of the children's age, it would be better if he just let Kelly have the house. They had a nice 3-bedroom semidetached in Blean with a very small mortgage. Mikey took the advice and walked away. He had a confiscation order hanging over his head as a result of his convictions. It should have been concluded before he was released but the process somehow got overlooked.

The situation between Johnny and Mikey had become strained. Johnny just wanted to sever his connection with Mikey one way or another. It was now 1999 and Mikey had been talking to a local builder he had met in the pub. Grant was a builder who did jobs in London and lived near Bridge, just outside Canterbury. Mikey had been trying to persuade him that if he bought the cab firm, it could go in his name, and Mikey could run it for him.

Mikey and Johnny met in a pub just outside Bridge, in Pett Bottom. It was the Duck Inn. The Duck Inn at Pett Bottom got a mention in Ian Fleming's novel *You Only Live Twice* as being near James Bond's childhood home. It bears a blue plaque commemorating the fact that Ian Fleming used to sit at a table in there, writing, while enjoying a drink and a smoke. The creator of 007 died in 1964.

Johnny was run down with it all, and with Mikey. Mikey wanted to go back and work with him as it was before but Johnny didn't want the aggravation, as he saw it. That was Johnny's call, in reality. The only thing that was agreed was that the current situation was untenable. Then Johnny said that he would fix a price for half of the business. Once he had chosen the price, Mikey could decide if he was buying or selling. Although all the shares were in Johnny's name, it was an unwritten agreement that they owned half each.

After leaving the Duck Inn, Johnny thought about what he really wanted and, in all honesty, at that time he felt that his love affair with the taxis was over. It had been a cracking business, lots of fun, lots of drama and a great earner. The business was not the same now. The fun had long gone out of it. It was definitely not as lucrative as it had been. Johnny knew if ever anyone found out the truth about how it was run, the consequences could be terrible. It was like a ticking bomb from day one, really. The lying and cheating somehow always got overlooked. So, Johnny pitched the price for the shares at the very low end of what they could be worth. He had decided he wanted to move out.

Mikey went to Grant the builder and put the deal to him that he could buy the business for the agreed figure. It could all go in Grant's name. Mikey would run it and they could be partners. It was also agreed Grant would get Mikey a flat in the Dane John Gardens, a nice area of Canterbury near the cab firm. They all met and it was agreed Grant would buy the business. So, Mikey would get his hands on the business, and Johnny would leave and move on. It seemed to suit everyone at the time. It took a few weeks and it was done. Grant paid Johnny part cash and part banker's draft. Johnny walked away and left the place in good shape, as everything had been agreed earlier.

Johnny got on with his life, was enjoying the racing a bit more and was relieved to walk away from the taxis. The civil claim against the Prudential was taking far longer than he could have imagined and the costs were escalating out of control. He had now given Brabners £60k and there was no sight of a trial date on the horizon. The Prudential solicitors were granted extended time to prepare their case several times and had more investigations to do, they said. A few months later, Johnny received a statement from Brabners that had been served as evidence. Johnny was speechless, didn't know what to think. Mikey had given the Prudential a statement about certain pieces of jewellery, including his Rolex, that he'd lent Johnny to have valued at Anthony Pearce's by Karl Jones many years earlier. It was Mikey who'd recommended Karl Jones, offered the Rolex to him for valuation purposes, and knew about some expensive pieces of Jewellery that had belonged to Sophia.

The statement was damning if true. Johnny couldn't work out why in God's name would Mikey give the Prudential a statement. Apparently, it had turned out that Mikey bumped into Karl in Canterbury one day and Karl had mentioned that the Prudential wanted him to attend court against Johnny. After that conversation, Mikey had gone out of his way to contact the Prudential to assist them with their enquiries. He was then put in contact with the loss adjusters. He met Barry Langford, they talked, and he gave a statement to Barry Langford. Mikey had grassed in court the people he was dealing drugs with to get a lighter sentence. Now he was grassing Johnny over his insurance claim.

Johnny didn't like it. He concluded once a grass, always a grass. After the money they'd earnt, the money Mikey had from the business while he was in prison every week, for him and his wife and girlfriend, all the scams they had got up to – it came to this. Mikey's marriage was over but that wasn't Johnny's fault. Mikey had lost any financial interest in his home, and Nikki had spent all his money while he was in prison. He had been in prison nearly three and a half years and was a broken man, in reality, Johnny reflected a lot later. Johnny had made the firm an attractive deal so Mikey could buy it all with Grant, and this was how Mikey paid him back?

So, after the shock and disappointment, he told his solicitors that Mikey was making that up because they had now parted company. Johnny also thought Mikey and Grant were probably not raking money in at the firm as much as they'd hoped. The business had changed a lot and it was harder now to earn the big bucks than it had been in the old days. The solicitors noted Mikey's convictions and thought they would count against him at the trial, and his character could be called into question. Mikey also contradicted some of Karl Jones's evidence and suggested Karl Jones knew the Rolex was Mikey's and that it was ok for Karl to knowingly value jewellery for Johnny when he knew it was not his property at the time. Karl didn't want to accept this as it would, in effect, implicate him and call his integrity into question.

In about June 1999 Mikey wanted to come and see Johnny and discuss something. He turned up at High Hopes, and Sophia made herself busy in the garden. Johnny told him he knew about the statement and asked him what he was playing at. Mikey was on cocaine again. That much was obvious. He didn't make much sense and was sharing with Johnny how hard he had found it in prison. He ended up at HMP Grendon Underwood. It was a secure prison unit where people who had antisocial personality disorders went. It was in Buckinghamshire. Johnny had visited Mikey there a few times. Apparently, they try to break prisoners and rebuild them again. That was the purpose of the prison at the time. It was for very damaged people. When Johnny visited, they would share snacks and drinks from the cafeteria and talk in the visiting hall. Mikey often referred to other inmates as cop killers (one guy had killed two police officers). He also intimated there were a lot of sex cases there, rapists and so on.

Then, drastically, the conversation took a turn for the worse. Mikey said if he wanted to, he could have Sophia raped and murdered. He could get that done no problem and was going to. The whole thing had got out of hand. Thank God Sophia was outside and didn't hear the conversation. Johnny didn't know what to do. The idea of going to the police didn't sit well with him. That was not his style. It may also not stop bad things happening. Johnny may not have been the best partner to Sophia but he knew one thing: that was not going to happen on his watch.

He never shared the conversation with anyone else. George would have known the answer and could have sorted it out, he thought, but that wasn't an option now. That would never be an option again. Johnny had met a man a few years earlier. He never talked about his work or what he did but you just knew by talking to him what could happen if you needed it. Johnny was lost. He sat with the problem and decided the situation needed to be dealt with. He wasn't going to live in fear or live with the threat hanging over Sophia, which, if carried out, would be on his conscience for the rest of his life. He went and met this guy Joseph. After a brief introduction and sharing a coffee, Johnny asked Joseph, 'If I want someone killed, could and would you do it? And how much would it be?' Joseph was quite clearly taken aback, having had no idea about what the conversation was about. Johnny made it clear, 'If I have got the wrong guy and that is not up your street, I want to apologise for asking.' Joseph took a few moments. They finished their coffees. Joseph said, 'I will get back to you.' Johnny knew it was a possibility. Joseph didn't know Johnny at all but he probably knew an awful lot of people who did. He wanted to know exactly whom he was dealing with before he replied at all.

It was agreed Joseph may be in touch, and if he didn't get back in touch that was the end of the matter. Clearly Joseph went away and did his homework before making any judgment or any further comment. Clearly he got the necessary reference, or references, from whoever's opinion it was Joseph valued. A short while after that, Joseph got in touch with Johnny and said, 'I think we should meet.' The next conversation was short and to the point. Joseph asked Johnny would he get a pull and be questioned after the murder? He replied, 'Yes.' He then told him he would do it. He told him the price. He explained it was payable in cash. The advance payment was non-refundable if he changed his mind. The balance was due on completion of the job.

Johnny then tried to get it done cheaper. He asked if it could be done a bit cheaper. It did seem expensive to him; after all, he thought, this was not *The Day of the Jackal.* Joseph looked at him and said, 'That is the price. Take it or leave it. If you want it done, all I require from you is the money, the name, a description, their address and their place of work.' Johnny agreed. They shook hands. Johnny explained he needed a little time to get the cash together. Once he got the cash he would be in touch. They parted company. He got the cash together, made contact with Joseph and agreed a time and a place to meet. They met, and Johnny gave Joseph the cash and the information. That was it. The hit had been ordered. Johnny felt sad but relieved.

Johnny went home and a day or two later booked a cruise for him and Sophia around the Mediterranean. He was shattered and thought being out of the country would make life less complicated for him and Sophia. He let Joseph know he was going away and when he would be back. It was a marvellous holiday. Johnny tried to relax and just make the most of it. After returning back to England in August, Johnny contacted Joseph. It was just a brief call. Johnny thought that he may have go and pay the balance to Joseph. That was the hope. No, that was not the case. Joseph laughed and said they had met. Joseph was now fully aware of who he was and what he looked like, as well as other certain details he wanted to know. He then said, 'He's not exactly a nice bloke, is he? He will not be any loss, in any case.' That was the end of the call. There was no time frame agreed. It was just in Joseph's hands.

Johnny got on with life as normal. Sophia and Johnny had

been invited to her best friend Mary's wedding on Wednesday 15th September 1999. Mary was marrying a guy called Daniel Gascoine. Johnny had met Mary on several occasions before. She was a larger than life, full-of-herself character who worked in radio sales for Invicta Radio at the time. Daniel worked in the motor trade as a car salesman. Maybe they had met as a result of advertising deals that Mary did for Daniel's employers, Johnny thought, but he never knew how they met; it was just a guess. They had been together some time and already lived together. Mary wanted her wedding to be special, as all girls do, and she had booked the Knowle Country House Wedding Venue in Higham, Rochester. Johnny knew nothing about it but Sophia knew it was a nice place. The wedding was going to be in the afternoon, followed by a sit-down lunch for guests, which would be followed by a reception in the evening for further guests. Sophia had bought a new dress and hat as well as a special gift for Daniel and Mary for the occasion. On the morning of the wedding, Johnny and Sophia got up, lazed about a bit, then got ready to go to the wedding. He put on his best suit and thought he brushed up well for the occasion. Sophia looked stunning, as always. They drove over to the Knowle slightly earlier than the wedding time, the idea being they would get there early and have a coffee or a drink while waiting.

After George's passing Johnny had spoken to Pat and offered to buy one of George's Mercedes cars and the Bentley back, if she wanted, for the fair market price. It did suit her. She wanted to sell the cars. She had a Vauxhall Corsa she used for herself, and she only used that occasionally. Johnny thought it would help her, and George would no doubt approve of the gesture if he was looking down. Johnny used the Mercedes himself. It was a 520 SEL and had been previously owned by Andrew Lloyd Webber before George bought it. Johnny liked the car and liked the idea of driving George's car. George had put an Irish number plate on it to disguise the year of the vehicle. No expense had been spared running and maintaining the car and it was in showroom condition.

Johnny was impressed by the venue and the wedding. It was a blistering-hot day and the ceremony was delightful, followed by a very tasteful lunch, speeches and drinks. It was not a large wedding but a nice group of family and friends from both sides. Johnny didn't get drunk but had a few drinks. He chatted to lots of the guests, met some family members and exchanged pleasantries, as well as getting into some long conversations with some of the guests. In the evening there was music, more food and drinks, as well as dancing. Johnny and Sophia stayed until the end. They left for home just before midnight. The drive back was straightforward, back to Canterbury then along Wincheap past the old cab firm and straight through Thanington to Pilgrims Lane, Chilham. As he turned around the Wincheap roundabout, it seemed very quiet, tranquil almost, to him but it was early hours of Thursday morning and perhaps it was normal. They got home and went to bed. It had been a lovely wedding and an enjoyable experience.

The next day Johnny's phone rang and he was told that Mikey had been shot dead at the cab firm the night before. Apparently, a driver had found him dead in the office. Details were very vague and the exact details were not confirmed. Johnny knew. Fortunately enough, he had the balance in cash ready. He contacted Joseph, arranged to meet, drove over and paid him the balance. The meeting lasted 30 seconds. He managed to borrow a car off Tony, Sophia's son, to use that day. He didn't want to use his own car. Later that day he realised that only Joseph and Johnny knew. That was how it needed to stay. The murder was on the local radio and TV. Johnny never commented to Sophia about it. It was better for her to know nothing at all, otherwise she would be an accomplice, regardless of what she may have thought. Joseph made it clear no one else could know the deal they had. It was a big thing at the time in Canterbury. A full-blown murder investigation was underway.

On Friday, Johnny didn't have much on and he was over at Whitstable, gambling in the Tote shop. It had been a terrible afternoon for him that Friday. It had all gone wrong. He had lost £20k in the Tote shop that afternoon. He was gutted, furious. He drove home, pulled up the drive in his Mercedes and parked up. As he got out of the car, he noticed two men walking up his drive. He knew instantly from the shoes and the clothes that they were police officers. The shoes looked like they were Clark's and the clothes from Burtons.

They introduced themselves as Police Officers DC Smith and DC Falkawoski or (Fuckoffski, as Sophia nicknamed him.) Anyway, they said they wanted to talk to him about the murder of Mikey. He invited them in. They all sat down in the lounge. Sophia made teas and coffees and disappeared. On TV, Sophia had been looking at the news headlines on teletext on the page which referred to the murder. Everyone was keen to know what was going on, including her. Johnny sat on the sofa, with the two officers sitting in armchairs either side. They were to the point, Johnny thought. They said to him, 'You are the number one suspect in the murder of Mikey.' Not quite how he saw the situation, he thought, but he did not comment. *Perhaps they just say that to everyone to see how they react,* Johnny thought. They asked him about his background with Mikey, the business affairs, and he was honest throughout. He had no reason to lie. His relationship with Mikey had always been good. It was based on business and money and they had both done well from their business affairs. Johnny looked the other way when it came to

Mikey's behaviour in many areas. Johnny liked the relationship he had with Mikey. He may not have approved of some of Mikey's behaviour, but it was Mikey's behaviour, not his. Until the conversation with Mikey about Sophia, Johnny always wished Mikey well. In reality, he always wanted everyone to do well. He wanted nice things and a nice life but always wished it for others as well. He was a ducker and a diver for sure, but had a good heart deep down – but everyone has their limits. He was never the kind of guy who would let anyone walk over him.

They explained to Johnny as it was a murder enquiry, they wanted his movements for the whole of Wednesday, not just for the time at which the murder happened. It had occurred on Wednesday evening. Johnny gave them all the answers, explained what he did all day, gave all the names of people he met at the wedding and the time frame around his movements. One officer did all the talking, Johnny noted. The other took notes and kept looking at him. The conversation, which was really an interview, went on for about three and a half hours. They then asked Johnny to attend the police station on Sunday and give a written statement to help in the investigation. He told them he had plans to see Pat on Sunday. It was agreed he would attend the police station Monday afternoon and give the statement, and he did. He arrived and the same two officers said they had spoken to their senior officer about some of the financial activities surrounding the cab firm, which he had been open about, and they could just be overlooked. They were not material to the enquiry, it had been decided. Clearly, they had spoken to Mary and Daniel by now and established that at the time of the murder Johnny was at the Knowle in Higham and there was a large number of independent witnesses to corroborate that fact. So they knew for certain he did not commit the murder.

They changed their attitude a little towards Johnny. They

were particularly interested in Grant Mott, Johnny noted. By now they had become aware of Mikey's background, had spoken to a large number of people who knew him, and knew about his convictions. In fact, the more people they spoke to about him, the more suspects or people with a dislike and possible motive for the murder came to their attention. The whole drug story with informing on a drugs gang gave them a whole host of suspects from the criminal world. Johnny was a possible, Grant Mott was a possible, maybe Kelly sought revenge. There was an endless list of possible criminals or their contacts and accomplices. Mikey had recently upset a guy locally who was trying to have a relationship with his younger daughter – he had a temper and a reputation. It was sad to hear but the police told Johnny they couldn't find anyone with a good word to say about Mikey. Kelly, his ex-wife, told the police Mikey had no friends. The only friend he ever had was Johnny. Johnny reflected in that moment. He was thankful to Kelly for her honesty and realised it was very sad that Mikey had turned on him after all they had achieved together, albeit in a dishonest manner. Johnny felt grateful she had confirmed his beliefs. There had been no need whatsoever for Mikey to turn on him. Still, that was all over now.

Johnny heard Grant Mott had to surrender his passport after telling the police he was going to Paris for the Arc de Triomphe that year. Grant liked a bet and he had become a regular in Towers as well. It made Johnny smile. Grant was probably only a suspect because he was his business partner. He had no real idea how Mikey and he got on. Had they had differences between them over money or work? Only Grant knew that now. At the time, the enquiry reached far and wide, with lots of possible lines clearly being investigated. Large amounts of police officers and resources were being used to try and get a result. All the locals who knew Mikey or worked with him had a theory. It was like one large game of Cluedo, with people all guessing what the motive was and what had happened. There were lots of theories. Some sounded quite plausible, some were absurd, but that's just people, Johnny thought. Some of the police officers involved were going round saying to witnesses and people they interviewed they thought Johnny was a rogue but not a murderer. He had admitted that to them himself, he thought. Mikey's body was not released for a cremation or burial for months. The police forensics and doctors clearly did very thorough examinations and there were long delays. Johnny bumped into Kelly one day quite by chance, and she explained about the delays. She said Mikey was going to be cremated. She told him she would let him know when the cremation was going to be. She was true to her word.

Johnny and Sophia had been invited to Mark Cox's wedding in January. It was going to be held in Sandwich in the afternoon, with a lunch afterwards and a reception in the evening. Mark and Johnny had become close, playing cards in the bookmakers together, gambling together, and he would also spend time with Mark in his battery shop, talking about life, as it were. Mark was going to marry Lorraine. They met when Mark was a battery salesman and used to go to Halfords to take orders, as they were his firms' biggest customer. Lorraine had worked at Halfords and the rest was history, as they say. Mark had a daughter from a previous relationship, which had never worked out. Lorraine had no children. They already had a home together. They both loved skiing. Mark had been a ski instructor in the army when he was younger and was an excellent skier. Mark asked Johnny to be best man at his wedding. Johnny was flattered and agreed.

The wedding was on Friday, 14th January, 2000. Lorraine and Mark had a big thing about getting married in the new millennium. It had been a big dream and wish. They waited for the Year 2000 to tie the knot after having lived together for years.

Mark then added a twist and said Lorraine and Mark would like Johnny and Sophia to go on their honeymoon with them. Sophia thought it was odd to ask people to go on their honeymoon with them but Johnny was keen, as he had never skied before, and neither had Sophia. They agreed. Johnny would be best man for Mark. Johnny and Sophia would go skiing with them on their honeymoon in Austria for two weeks. Then Kelly let Johnny know Mikey's cremation was going to be at Barham Crematorium on Friday 14th January. Barham was halfway between Chilham and Sandwich, so it was on the way. Mikey's funeral was at 12.30 pm. The wedding started at 2 pm. If the service finished about 1 pm, Johnny could be in Sandwich for the wedding at 1.30 pm. He could attend both. He thanked God for that. He wanted to say goodbye to Mikey and he wanted to attend and be best man at Mark's wedding. He told Sophia to travel to the wedding on her own and he would meet her there. Sophia knew Mark and Lorraine well. She also knew a number of the other guests as well, so she would be able to enjoy herself until Johnny could catch up. Tony, the manager from the betting shop, was invited as well, as he and Mark had now become close friends.

On 14th January 2000 Johnny drove to Barham Crematorium, arriving about 12.15 pm. As he entered the car park, he had never seen anything like it. The place was heaving. It was a job to find a place to park. What was astonishing was the number of police officers that were there. Everywhere he looked, there seemed to be men in suits with yellow ties. He thought it strange. He remembered seeing on the films that the murderer always attends the funeral. Was this their logic? Who knew what their plans or motives were? It was a nice service; the vicar used the words, 'We are all God's children,' to describe Mikey during the service. Johnny saw a lot of faces he knew and said hello in passing to them but kept himself to himself. He was mindful he wanted to attend and wanted to say something to Kelly, or at least let her know he was there. Apart from that, he was focused on attending, then getting away sharply to get to the wedding. A lot of family and friends had attended. Mikey's sister spoke about him at the service. Mikey's mother had passed away while he was in prison and he had been allowed to attend the funeral, as Johnny had, but Mikey was handcuffed to a prison guard for her funeral and had to leave straight after.

As the funeral cortege turned up and the coffin was taken in, people went into the crematorium, family first followed by others. Johnny stayed back as he was happy to sit at the rear. By the time he went in all the seats had been taken, so he stood at the rear with some others, surrounded by men in suits with yellow ties. He had already acknowledged Kelly before the cortege turned up so at least she knew he had attended. The service finished, and rather than walk through the chapel and out to see the flowers, he decided he would go out as he came in, get in his car and make his way to the wedding. He had worn a dark suit and black tie for the crematorium. He had the morning suit and cravat they had all hired for the wedding from Moss Bros in the car. Mark wanted green, so they all wore green morning suits and cravats. Lorraine was going to wear a green dress, so Mark, Johnny and Lorraine's brother wore green to match her dress.

After the service, Johnny was approached by a man in a suit, with a yellow tie. He showed his ID and said he was Inspector Fox and was in charge of the murder enquiry. He asked Johnny if he was Johnny Butler. Johnny confirmed he was. He said he wanted to know why he stopped assisting the police with their enquiries. Johnny replied, 'I did assist you. I told you everything I knew and I was honest with you. Then, after that, your officers threatened me with the Inland Revenue and Customs and Excise around the business affairs of the cab firm.' They did that after he said he couldn't help anymore, after assisting at the beginning. He had made his statement and had nothing further to add. He looked at the inspector and said, 'You lost me totally after that.' It was true. He decided he would add nothing to the original statement.

He then jumped in his car and made it in good time. He got changed into his morning suit with some time to spare. It was a civil service, not a church service. After the service, Johnny and Sophia sat at the top table. He sat next to Mark, as is customary. He drank way too much red wine before giving his speech, which drew a mixed reaction from the guests. He spoke about Mark, Lorraine, and as is customary, the stag do. He wished them well. He also took a swipe at the Masons; he knew a few guests were Masons. Mark had been a Mason in Dover for ages. He had put Johnny forward to join previously. As he lived outside the Dover area, it was referred to the Canterbury Lodge, the area where he lived, to see if there were any objections. He had been for the initial meeting at the Dover Lodge and thought it would be a formality. It all seemed to go well, he thought. When the application was advertised at the Canterbury Lodge, it was put to him that the phone rang several times, with several people objecting to his membership. One objection was enough, but there had been several, and they didn't need to say why. He was not told who they were. That was the procedure. He later found out Geoffrey Barrett was the Head of the Lodge at Canterbury, so he kind of understood why he was objected to. He never found out if Geoffrey Barrett did object or not, but it didn't really matter. He didn't really want to join, he thought. It was only because Mark wanted him to join his Lodge for the evenings out and the social events. On reflection, he had gone too far bringing up the Masons, he thought, but some of the guests thought it was funny, as did he at the time.

The honeymoon went well. The skiing in Austria was amazing. It was a new experience and on balance very enjoyable. They stayed in separate log cabin accommodation as part of the hotel. Mark was an excellent instructor and very patient with Johnny. Johnny and Sophia had bought all the ski wear and suits. Sophia went to ski school to learn how to ski, starting with the plough. Johnny slowly picked it up and got more and more confident as the days went on. Then Mark and Johnny slowly went higher up the mountains and on harder runs. At one stage, he was doing well. Then, after about six days, he just overreached himself. They went up on the ski lift. Johnny stopped listening to Mark. He thought he knew how to do it – that was for sure! He started coming down a red run, and as he went round a corner, he totally lost it and ended up with one of his skis in the hard snow area at the edge of the corner. That brought him down and injured one of his legs badly. That was the last time Johnny skied on the holiday. After that, he stayed in the hotel and bar for the duration of the holiday, enjoying the views. Sophia continued at ski school and everyone enjoyed themselves. He was in pain, struggling to walk, but he would survive. It was not broken. He had ripped some muscles, he found out.

Johnny reflected while on his own, he had wanted to ski like James Bond in the movies. He had not quite managed that level but he had tried. He gave it his best shot and had no real regrets. If he tried his best, that was good enough, and he had.

He knew Sophia was safe at ski school and that he would never have to worry about her safety or her life as he had before. He had some peace of mind about her wellbeing. He was grateful for that, and for her never even knowing what had happened. She had not lived one day or moment in fear, and he was grateful she never had to. That was something she definitely did not need to know; he knew that.

So, Johnny was at a wedding on the day Mikey was murdered. He then attended a wedding on the day he was cremated. Two weddings and a funeral in such a short space of time. Johnny never spoke to the police anymore after the funeral. The matter was now closed, as far as he was concerned. A few years later, quite by chance, Johnny heard Joseph had passed away. He had never met or spoken to Joseph after the day he'd paid the balance for the hit. They were not friends. It was purely a business transaction. So the matter was fairly and squarely between Johnny and God now. That was a very comforting thought.

CHAPTER 13
CIGARETTE AND TOBACCO SMUGGLING THROUGH DOVER AND FOLKESTONE

After returning home from Austria with Sophia, Johnny needed to visit a sports injury masseuse in Canterbury to help try to get him up and running again. The murder inquiry was ongoing and just kept rumbling on one day at a time until the police had exhausted all possible leads in their investigation. The civil claim with the Prudential was slowly making its way to the courts.

The bookmaking ventures, namely the shops at Biggin Hill and Canterbury, as well as the race course trading, seemed to be going nowhere fast. The shop at Biggin Hill always showed a small trading profit, but not enough to pay the expenses, so it was a liability every week. The Canterbury shop used to make enough each week to pay the bills with nothing left over. The race course expenses just seemed not to be won each week. The longer the shop at Biggin Hill traded, the more it cost to keep afloat. The race course pitches were the same, really; every week the losses grew. Race course pitch values had gone up since the first auction. So, the irony for Johnny was that he now had his dream lifestyle and career but it didn't pay the bills – *Be careful what you wish for*, he thought. The dog pitch at Central Park had long been given up by now as that had been a loss as well. He decided to close the shop at Biggin Hill, keep the shop at Canterbury – more in hope than anything – and put the race course pitches in the next southern England BHRB auction.

Johnny knew a guy called Eric, a larger-than-life ex-publican from London who lived out in the country with his wife and had a lady friend called Anne whom he used to spend a lot of time with. He had been a bookmaker at Canterbury and Sittingbourne Dogs. He also loved to gamble himself, or play both sides of the fence as Johnny did. To fund his bookmaking and gambling lifestyle, Eric had started tobacco smuggling. Eric later told Johnny that, when he had been a publican many years ago in the East End, London, he had people wanting him to pay protection money for the pub. He told them in no uncertain terms he wasn't paying it. He feared there may be reprisals, so he sat at the top of his stairs the night they had made the threats, with a loaded 12-bore shotgun, all night after pub closing. No one had turned up.

Johnny believed Eric. The more he got to know him the more he realised that Eric was not a pushover for anyone, and that was putting it mildly. Tony McManus was also doing tobacco smuggling, on a smaller scale. Then Johnny and a few guys from the Medway area started doing it as well. On paper it sounded good. There was certainly a market for cheap tobacco and cigarettes. Dover and Folkestone ports were about 20 miles away. A lot of people were buying duty free off the boats bringing them back and saving a lot on the cost of smoking. You also had the others who were bringing them back to sell for a daily wage, so to speak. It probably beat getting a job, and most of them were, or seemed to be, on benefits in any case. The P & O ferries were filled up most days with day trippers or boot leggers, as they were more commonly known. The duty-free prices on the ferries made cigarette and tobacco smuggling a really good living for people, with relatively little risk, and if they were for your own use, it was not illegal. So, by being foot passengers and carrying a respectable amount through customs, they were left alone for a long time.

Then people had started filling the boots of their cars up. They would take the car, arrive at Calais, then drive up to Belgium, which was about a 30-minute drive. They would then buy the tobacco and cigarettes from Belgian tobacco shops and warehouses. The prices in Belgium were lower than duty-free prices, so much less than they were in England. So, they made a greater saving, which could be passed on to their customers back in England. Lots of boot leggers would fill their boot up and drive back to Calais before getting back on the ferry or hovercraft to Dover and then through customs and back home.

There seemed to be an industry of smugglers operating on a daily basis, 7 days per week. There always has been, in reality. The only thing that varied was how much people were smuggling. The bigger players were using lorries to bring the cigarettes and tobacco over. Diesel and alcohol duty in France and Belgium was also a lot lower than in the UK. Lots of lorries were going across the channel to Belgium to fill up because the savings were large compared with UK prices. There was also a large smuggling market in alcohol, but that seemed less lucrative. At the time, a lot of people were going over in vans and filling them up with beer to bring back and sell. Then you had some people who were just employing people, buying vans and doing it on a large-scale basis. Of course, cigarettes, tobacco, alcohol and fuel are all legal products. There was definitely an issue that the customs faced at the time. People just said they were for personal use, and the customs seemed powerless or accepted the fact regardless of what they may have thought, and let people pass for a long time on that basis.

Johnny first went to Belgium with Eric and bought cigarettes, filled the boot of the car up, came back on the ferry via Dover Docks, and drove through customs. He was not stopped and it seemed a simple process, he thought, and a good earner. For the trip, he had made about £500 after expenses for his half-share. They had gone halves for both the cost of the cigarettes and the expenses. Then, later, Eric said he had started going to Luxembourg rather than Belgium because it was a lot cheaper in Luxembourg. It took a few hours to drive there and then back but the further savings were great.

By now the ferries and hovercrafts had started imposing limits on the number of duty-free cigarettes and tobacco that they would sell to an individual. So, a limit of 800 cigarettes (4 cartons) or 20 pouches (1kg) of hand-rolling tobacco would be sold in the duty-free shop to each person, and they would ask for your ticket and stamp it to avoid people using their tickets for multiple purchases. So, duty-free products had firm allowances in place, but because the products from France, Belgium and Luxembourg were not duty free – but duty paid at a lower duty rate – at the time, the personal limit allowance was not specified by quantity. So, in theory, a rich person could go and buy a year's cigarettes for themselves and the family if they intended to give them away as gifts to their family rather than sell them, and simply buy as many as they liked. This was the loophole that everyone was using and exploiting day-in, day-out, to bring back to England as much as they wanted to.

Johnny then started doing trips from Canterbury to Luxembourg and back using the Eurotunnel, as the crossing times were much shorter. Eric seemed to know most of the loopholes and had shared that information about tobacco houses in Luxembourg, and the cheapest and best routes to use to cross the channel.

By now the Biggin Hill shop was closed and the pitches were up for sale at the auction, so Johnny desperately needed an income, as he had to live and fund the civil case with the costs just spiralling out of control – or so it seemed to him. The pitches did all sell at greater prices than Johnny had originally paid. After allowing for commission, there was a profit of about £18k on the original purchase prices. The trading losses at the track in that period were about £20k, so the sale almost wiped out all the trading losses, which was a pleasant surprise for Johnny.

So, in 2000 he had now decided to become a full-time smuggler, or boot legger, as it was known then. There were so many people doing it. A lot of people Johnny knew had changed from importing cannabis, because with tobacco there was no prison sentence involved. A car load of tobacco would not land anyone in jail on its own, whereas with Class C importation – or puff, as it was commonly known – prison would be inevitable. He would keep the betting shop in Canterbury in the hope that it could just earn a bit more again and would show a profit. It also meant he had the business at home, albeit in Sophia's name.

One morning early in 2000 Johnny and Sophia set off for Luxembourg. It was a beautiful sunny day. They crossed the channel using the Eurotunnel without any fuss, then drove straight down to a tobacco warehouse that Eric had shown Johnny previously. It was called Marianne's. It was literally a warehouse filled with cigarettes and tobacco. There was a secure area brick-built in the warehouse, behind reinforced glass, which was where you made your order and paid. All transactions were in cash.

Johnny paid in pounds and was given an exchange rate by the warehouse. This changed on a daily basis in line with the currency markets. He later discovered it would be better to go to a bank in Belgium and exchange the money there. There was always a more attractive rate at the bank, but everything was a learning process for him and at least he was learning quickly about smuggling tobacco. Of course, the only way to learn any trade is to do it, learn from the mistakes and try not to repeat them.

Once you paid, a guy from the warehouse would then bring your order on a pallet. You would reverse your car into the loading area in the warehouse and they would help you transfer the cigarettes and tobacco to the boot of your car. On this occasion, Johnny filled up the back of his Mercedes with Benson & Hedges cigarettes. Johnny had always been a heavy smoker and he knew where he could sell Benson & Hedges. He liked them and they were a very popular brand in England. He managed to get 14 boxes, with 25 sleeves of 200 cigarettes each, packed in the boot by taking them out of the boxes. So, it was 350 sleeves of cigarettes. The markup was about £5 per sleeve, wholesale to buyers who would then sell again wholesale for a small markup, or retail them to customers on an individual basis. So, all things being equal before expenses, the profit was £1,750 per boot load. The cost at the tobacco house was approximately £15, and there were plenty of takers at £20 in England. Then, on an individual basis or price per sleeve, that was generally £25. It took about half an hour to take them out of the boxes then pack them individually in the large boot. They were all laid out like bricks of gold, tightly packed next to each other to make the most of the space available. Johnny had also taken the spare wheel out and left that at home to create the extra space.

Then he and Sophia set off for home. He had always been a fussy eater. Stopping in the services in Luxembourg, Belgium or France had never appealed to him, other than to get fuel or buy snacks and drinks to eat in the car. Some of the food on the ferries was good. They had various restaurants on the ferries. On the Eurotunnel trains, passengers sat in their own vehicles. Apart from toilets, there were no facilities. Johnny would fill up in Luxembourg or Belgium, as the savings on fuel were substantial too.

It was a beautiful sunny day and the way back was mainly all motorways. The customs between Luxembourg and Belgium never seemed to be bothered or looking for cigarettes. There were tolls on the motorways, and sometimes customs would sit at the tolls where people pay just to go through. An English registration would stand out like a sore thumb but Johnny never quite realised that at the beginning. In any case, his car had an Irish number plate on it. The border between Luxembourg and Belgium where Johnny crossed was a main road and it was just a constant stream of cars. The borders in Europe were, of course, down by now, and free trade and travel was opening up in that sense. Europe was slowly becoming one, without all the restrictions and checks that had been in place before. The border between Belgium and France was not manned at all. It was on a main road and the police and customs sometimes sat there in their cars, making spot checks or waiting for certain vehicles or people, Johnny guessed, based on intelligence. The drive back was smooth enough.

Then Johnny entered the Eurotunnel entrance. Johnny had never driven back himself through the Eurotunnel. He didn't know the layout or understand the boarding procedure or layout with the French and English Customs. The approach that would lead you to the Eurotunnel was firstly via a number of booths that were manned by Eurotunnel staff. They were just checking your tickets and asking if you were carrying any petrol or flammable materials, as this was strictly prohibited. If you had arrived earlier than your booked shuttle, they could change the time of the train and journey home if they had space on the next available shuttle. The cheap day return booked at least 24 hours in advance for a car and passengers meant going out early in the morning and being on the last shuttle home before midnight. In any event, if you went over the day, then your return journey had expired. Just turning up at the Eurotunnel and paying to cross would mean paying the advertised crossing rates, which were about six or seven times the price of a cheap one-day return ticket bought in advance. The most expensive way to use the Eurotunnel would be to just turn up and pay for a one-way journey, then do the same when returning. That would cost about ten times the price of the cheap one-day return booked in advance.

Then, the operator in the booth would issue you with your return ticket boarding pass and a coloured paper pass which should be hung on the rear-view mirror, indicating the shuttle you were booked on. So, Johnny and Sophia turned up at the booth, had their return time booking changed to the next available shuttle, and were issued with a new ticket and boarding pass. There was a shopping and toilet area where you could stop, grab a coffee, use the toilet or buy some cheap perfume or alcohol at French prices before boarding the train home. This complex was still in France. Then you drove through the French Customs area. Then, after the French Customs area, there was a short drive and you would go through English Customs, which was situated in France. The two governments had an agreement that just before the English Customs area, this part of land was under British control and seen as entering England.

So, as Johnny approached the French Customs area, there was no one in the passport control booth. Johnny should have just driven on but at that moment a French Customs officer walked across Johnny's path, so he slowed down. He looked at Johnny so Johnny stopped and offered him both Johnny and Sophia's passports, mistaking the procedure and thinking he may be passport control. He then asked where they had been and the purpose of their journey. Johnny lied and said shopping in France. He then looked at Johnny, holding both passports, and said, 'Fine. Please open the boot.' Johnny got out of the car and opened the boot for the Customs officer. He asked Johnny where he bought the cigarettes. Johnny then told him in Luxembourg. He asked for the receipts. Johnny had been given the receipts at the tobacco warehouse in Luxembourg but the last thing he thought about was keeping them. He had thrown them straight into the bin in the garage on the way home. In his mind, they could be used against him and be incriminating, or at least definite evidence. Johnny told him he didn't have receipts. At that point the French Customs officer accused Johnny of buying them off a boot legger in Calais. Johnny tried to explain that was not the case, but without receipts and Johnny not understanding the law on tobacco duty, smuggling, or what the French Customs guy meant, he was asked to drive into a French Customs garage area.

At that point Johnny explained they were for personal use. Whether the French Customs believed him or not was not the issue. Without receipts, it was pure and simple tax evasion, as far as the French Customs were concerned. It was explained to him that the cigarettes were going to be confiscated. A receipt would be issued. He then had the right to return within seven days and pay the French Customs Duty indicated on the paperwork and receipt that they issued. If he chose not to return, pay the duty and collect them, then that was the end of the matter. The duty was just under £2k. So, after the cigarettes had been confiscated, counted and the note of seizure issued, Johnny and Sophia were free to go and their passports were returned. An electric roller shutter was raised, Johnny and Sophia exited the garage area, and from there you could see the English Customs area. It was just a short drive before going through passport control and approaching the English Customs area, which they proceeded through without being asked to stop. Then a short drive towards the shuttle boarding area. Then back on the shuttle for the 25 to 30-minute return journey to Folkestone. Once arriving, they would disembark and there were no checks at all in Folkestone. Johnny just exited the shuttle onto the link roads which would take you to the local roads and motorways.

So, the day and trip had gone nothing like planned. It was an experience. The £2k fine, as English boot leggers and Smugglers saw it, or French tobacco duty as the French Customs saw it, seemed a lot. Of course, it ruined any potential profit on the journey, but it was a great opportunity to pay the duty, get the cigarettes returned and limit the losses. So, after reading the paperwork and speaking to Eric about it, Johnny returned a few days later, paid the duty and collected the cigarettes. It turned out Eric had been through the same experience; it was just part of the rough and tumble of the game, as he saw it. As he drove off from French Customs, Johnny suddenly wondered if the English Customs could now present a problem. They never stopped him or searched the car. After passing through passport control, he boarded the Euro Shuttle for the journey home. He sold the cigarettes having just learnt some of the pitfalls of the job.

One day after chatting with Tony McManus about the experience, Tony explained to him he was buying Luxembourg cigarettes off a northern lad, George, in Calais. They were using the ferries daily, boarding as day passengers, meeting George in the car park just as you left the French terminal, buying the cigarettes in the car park, then returning back to the P&O

terminal entrance to board the next ferry home. It was a thriving business, Johnny found out. Tony had been told about George by someone else buying from him. He used to turn up in a Belgian registration car, park up towards the rear of the car park, outside the ferry terminal, and wait for a variety of customers off different ferries to serve up in the car park. Johnny saw it one day after going on a ferry as a foot passenger and thought it was unbelievable. George was like a magnet for the boot leggers. They would run toward his Belgian estate car, and he had all their separate orders waiting for them in carrier bags. You could order any brand of cigarettes you liked from him and he made the orders up in carrier bags of 8 sleeves each. The carrier bags were all from a local French supermarket, he noted. Most customers were buying 16 sleeves of cigarettes from him in 2 carrier bags. They seemed to think that walking through English Customs with 16 sleeves of cigarettes meant they could claim they were for personal use and therefore be allowed to keep them rather than having them confiscated. At the time, the personal-use argument seemed to favour the boot leggers because it was so unclear and had no real definition attached to it.

Of course, in reality, a lot of these guys and girls were claiming benefits and it was a great way of earning cash to improve their lifestyle without actually getting a job or starting a business. It was almost a readymade business or job for many people, and was paying cash in hand; the sort of crime or loophole that was not reportable. It was a victimless crime. Of course, the Treasury would disagree. They would argue the loss is to the Treasury, therefore everyone in the country suffers as a direct result of this type of crime. Nevertheless, Johnny definitely felt more comfortable fiddling the Customs and Excise than causing havoc in people's lives.

He got George's mobile phone number and started buying

from him. George was dearer than going to Luxembourg. Of course, George was going to Luxembourg himself and bringing them back to Calais and selling them in Calais to English bootleggers. That was his business model. The benefit of dealing with George was that he was in Calais and selling them cheaper than French or Belgian prices. You could drive over to Calais, load up and do a trip per day, whereas the Luxembourg trip from Canterbury could be about 12 to 16 hours, depending on roads and crossing details on any given day. Johnny did this a couple of times and all went well. He would take Sophia with him. The logic was that a couple looked more like day trippers than a single male, he thought. Everyone wanted to look like day trippers rather than boot leggers, obviously.

Johnny actually started talking to George about life, as you tend to, and found out he was a really wealthy guy who had been importing cigarettes and tobacco into England for ages. He started by driving to Belgium, filling his car up and driving back to Newcastle and selling them for great profit. Then he just started selling them for less money to people in the Dover and Folkestone area but was doing it daily. He'd had an incredible run of good fortune which ended in really bad luck. He preferred the Eurostar to ferries because it was so much quicker. He'd crossed on the Eurostar in different cars over a two-year period 272 times. Then, one day, he was stopped by the English Customs at the Channel Tunnel. He had a boot load of Golden Virginia in nets of 100 pouches, which is how they are sold at tobacco warehouses. He said it was for personal use. He had about 50 nets so; that was 5000 pouches of tobacco. They disagreed. They seized his car and the tobacco, which was not such a great loss in reality. He was in a new hire-car, which would have to be returned to the hire company, and George would probably be billed more for their troubles, either in hire days or time spent recovering the car from the Customs. Of course, he lost the money he spent on 50 nets of tobacco, but that was all very small beer compared with the run he'd had prior to being stopped.

What the English Customs did was go to Eurostar and check how many times George had crossed previously. They got lucky – George had not anticipated or considered this. George had simply been booking all his trips with Eurostar on his credit card. Very quickly, they could prove he had crossed the channel 272 times over a period of about 17 months. They assumed that, without a reasonable explanation for this behaviour from George, he had been successful 271 times before being stopped. Of course, that assumption was very close to what he had been doing, with a few exceptions. They then investigated his personal situation in the UK. He was a married guy from Newcastle without any income on his tax records, who was not working and who owned two beautiful properties in England without any mortgages. He and his wife had a nice home just outside Newcastle, paid for, and a beautiful home in St Margaret's at Cliffe, an exclusive residential area a few miles down the road from Dover, that was worth a small fortune. His wife drove a Mercedes Sports but had no job or income. Then, as they investigated further, they found large amounts of cash in bank accounts. He was charged with tax evasion and had all his assets frozen pending the outcome of the trial. George knew he was not going to be able to explain it to a jury, and so may face prison. He was going to argue about the assets, as everyone seems to in a confiscation hearing, at least to start with, until they realise that the confiscation hearings are designed to strip criminals of all their assets and ill-gotten gains. Fighting the Crown after a conviction seems very futile.

So, on the back of all this, George decided to keep fighting and delaying his trial as much as he could. It wasn't really with the expectation of winning, although there was always that chance. He wanted time to then go over to Calais and trade as he was building up new money, which he and his wife would now hide and keep. That was his plan. He achieved it as well. He delayed his trial by about a year and a half. In that time, he traded nonstop in Calais and stashed the cash separately out of sight from the Customs and his asset-seizure order.

Then, one day, Johnny asked Sophia to go on her own as he had plans of his own for the day or was off gambling somewhere. Sophia met George, the boot was filled up with Benson & Hedges, George helped Sophia pack, George was paid, everyone was happy. Sophia then went back on the Eurotunnel. She went through French Customs all ok but was stopped by English Customs for a routine chat and then a routine search. They found the cigarettes. She claimed she had never seen them before and someone must have put them in the boot while she was shopping at the French Hypermarket. After all, she now remembered she forgot to lock the car. They were not amused, not buying that old chestnut, and seized the cigarettes and car. They were allowed to seize the vehicles on the basis that they were being used to commit the crime. Sophia then rang Johnny in front of the Customs and explained her shock at someone putting all the cigarettes in the boot while she was shopping and the fact that the Customs did not believe her. Of course, in reality, any story or excuse is irrelevant. What a boot load of cigarettes looks like to English Customs is exactly what it is, cigarettes to be sold for a profit, not for personal consumption. So now the loss was the cost of the cigarettes from George, which was 14 cartons of Benson & Hedges, which was about £6k, and Johnny's car, which had been his dad's car (he had sentimental attachment to it), as well as the £10k he'd given Pat for it after his dad's passing.

All he heard on the phone call in reality was, 'You've just lost £16k and I need picking up from Folkestone,' as Sophia was now crossing without the car. He went down to Folkestone, picked Sophia up and thought, maybe this smuggling business wasn't as lucrative as he'd first thought. If you get stopped at Customs, it seemed like a bad day at the races or in the bookmakers all over again. The idea was great. In theory, you just keep importing and making a profit. In reality, it was nothing like that – if it went wrong, the losses were severe.

He thought it was just a different form of gambling. That was how he saw it, but if you lost gambling, you didn't face arrest, prison or a confiscation order; you lost your money and had to go away and take it on the chin. So maybe Tony McManus had the right idea, crossing each day as a foot passenger, getting 16 cartons and signing on. Not exactly living the dream, Johnny thought, or the life he wanted. It seemed a very small way to play, and somehow very unsatisfying. It certainly wouldn't fund the life Johnny wanted. Tony and Johnny certainly had different aspirations, which was evident in all areas of both their lives, from the homes they had, their gambling stakes, the restaurants they ate in, the cars they drove, the holidays they had, and their partners.

CHAPTER 14
ENGLISH TOBACCO DEALER IN CALAIS

TONY DID, however, make one interesting suggestion to Johnny. He asked him, 'Have you ever thought about setting up in Calais and selling over there?' Interesting idea, Johnny thought. Tony said if he did, he would use him to buy from and encourage everyone he knew on the ferries to do the same. Tony did seem to know an awful lot of the people on the boats doing the same thing. Johnny did take on board what had been said. In reality, Tony was looking for a discount, but Johnny didn't know that at the time.

He didn't really have many options that he liked. He never wanted a job – or a real job, as he would have called it. The idea of waking up, having breakfast, driving to work and being stuck in traffic, working for someone's dream, doing something boring, driving back home in traffic and waiting for the weekend, then repeating it for 50 years was Johnny's worst nightmare. After a few days he decided he had two choices: start a business in England or give it a go. He decided he was going to give it a go. He could hire a Belgian car, set up in Calais, find somewhere to stay on the cheap, and trade in France. He wanted a Belgian car because in Luxembourg, Belgium and France, an English registration plate almost seemed like taking an advert out that he was a boot legger, he thought. All the big hire firms were situated at Brussels Airport. George had told Johnny he flew to Brussels airport. After landing, he hired his car and did it like that. Johnny decided it would be easier to drive to Brussels airport with Sophia. She could then bring the car back to England without a boot full of cigarettes and he could hire a car and that would be that. He knew he wanted an estate car. EuroCar seemed the best firm to use. They offered vehicles at a flat fee with unlimited mileage, they had diesel estate cars and seemed more competitive than the rest. Johnny agreed to give Tony McManus 50 pence a carton or sleeve discount if he got him the customers off the boats as he said he would. Sophia could also travel across as a foot passenger on the ferries daily and carry 16 cartons back, which would help as well. She would also be bringing back money to England on a daily basis.

So, one day Johnny and Sophia went to Brussels airport and it started from there. Sophia came back to England. He picked up the estate car he had ordered at Brussels airport and went to Marianne's Tobacco House in Luxembourg to fill up. After filling his car up with tobacco and cigarettes – he had some advance orders from Tony – he would drive to Calais and find a nice, discreet, cheap hotel where he could base himself. That was the plan.

He chose the Formula 1 hotel just outside Calais in Coquelles. It was cheap and cheerful, he thought. It was located almost between the ferry port at Calais and the Eurotunnel. So, it ticked all his boxes, and if he was discreet, he could just blend in with the local holiday makers and guests at the hotel. He got to the Formula 1 hotel at Coquelles about 8 pm that evening. He went in, got a downstairs room, and parked his car outside the room. That seemed like a good idea. The room had a conveniently positioned window, and maybe he could put things in and out of the room via the window without anyone noticing. The Formula 1 was a large hotel on three levels. It offered very limited services but it was cheap. There was no restaurant or facilities to speak of. A double room was a bunk bed. Rooms were small, with no ensuite. Toilets and showers were shared by several guests on the landing. The hotel was built like a T-junction, then reversed, so the check-in desk, drinks machine and food machine with a few chairs with tables was at the front centre, then it had two landings either side, with rooms on both sides and one behind it.

So far, so good. Johnny had no idea what he was walking into. He had exchanged his money in the bank and got the best exchange rate, got the Belgian car, was getting the best deal possible in Luxembourg, and now had a base just outside Calais and a few orders and customers for the next day. He had two mobiles on contracts with 02; one for him and one for Sophia. He had just a few clothes in a bag, mainly socks and pants, which he took into the room. He then went into the reception area for a coffee from the machine. He felt good. He had his first carload in Calais and was just winging everything, really. After about an hour, he opened the window in his room. He then went out to his car, opened the boot – which was literally just a few feet away from the window – threw a few cigarettes and nets of tobacco through the window, then closed the boot and locked the car using the keyless remote. He thought he had been discreet and not been seen. He was cute – so he thought. Then he went into the room and stacked the cigarettes and tobacco.

He did it again, being careful not to be seen or attract any unwanted attention; after all, he was just a tourist who happened to be staying at the Formula 1. This was the image he wanted to portray. After a couple of trips in and out of the hotel and slowly transferring the cigarettes and tobacco to the room, a guy with a Middlesborough accent walked up to him laughing and said, 'I am Dave. Would you like a hand to unload your car? We have been watching you and laughing at what you are doing.' Dave said, 'We are here doing the same thing.' Anyway, to cut a long story short, Dave and two other lads with northern accents went out to the car, opened up the boot, told Johnny to get in his room, and just threw the whole boot load through the window in about two or three minutes. Johnny was in the room, just trying to throw it to the back of the room to make space for the cargo coming through the window. Once they finished, they shouted, 'Shut the window,' locked the car and the job was done. Then Johnny neatly arranged his stock in the room.

After that, he left the room, went to reception and thanked the lads, and started chatting to them over coffee. Very quickly, he learnt the hotel, or the ground floor of the hotel, was full of English tobacco dealers, literally. He had been fortunate to get a downstairs room. Dominique the manager knew what everyone was doing but didn't care. They were all booked in constantly and just kept paying in advance. The hotel was almost always fully booked. The chambermaids liked it because none of the English people expected their rooms or beds to be made because of the tobacco. Then, occasionally, the English lads would borrow hoovers from the chambermaids and hoovered their own rooms.

Everyone was at it; Johnny was just a late arrival to the scene. Jock and Andy had helped Dave empty Johnny's car through the window. Andy, it turned out, was a driver for a small firm already in the hotel. He was from Middlesborough as well. Jock was a giant of a man. He was about 6 foot 5 inches and solid all over. Johnny had listened to him speak in reception before trying to unload. Jock spoke with such a heavy Scottish accent, Johnny could not understand a word he said. He had assumed he was French or possibly Belgian. Jock was in business with Keith, a massively overweight guy from up north who wore glasses and was always walking about in his underwear in the hotel. Astonishing, Johnny thought. Keith was a man of very few words, never had much to say, just laid on the bottom bunk all day in his underwear or occasionally walked around the hotel. He reminded Johnny very much of Jim Royle played by Ricky Tomlinson in the TV show *The Royle Family*. Keith's son Freddy was something else; maybe a learning-difficulties person or brain damaged. Bless him, he thought. He never made any sense. It turned out he was always off his head on heroin, so he was living in another world.

Johnny remembered when they first spoke. It was like talking to someone who couldn't really talk. He just kept waving and gesturing with his hands and grunting, almost communicating in some sort of physical language using his hands while not being deaf or blind. It was a little bit frightening, because he did have a naturally dark side to his character, Johnny felt. The vibes were not good to say the least, or at least that was what he picked up on. Then, within a few minutes of meeting Freddy, he invited Johnny to his room to show him something and help him. When they got to the room, which was full of tobacco, Freddy pulled out a loaded hand gun from under his pillows and said, 'Get one; you need one here.' Johnny said thanks and walked off. Was Freddy threatening him or trying to help him, he wondered. Carrying a loaded firearm in a foreign country was not on Johnny's radar or in his plan. He wanted to sell some tobacco, make some money, go home to England and live to tell the tale.

Then, other Belgian-plate vehicles started turning up at the hotel, quite a few of them in quick succession. The lads in reception were watching out for them. When they arrived, it became like a military operation. They all knew each other's rooms and were working together, albeit for themselves or different firms. They would have one person in the room open the window, three lads at the back of the car, and the car would be emptied in about three minutes. Everyone was mucking in and Johnny was happy to help everyone else. He admired and liked the spirit in the hotel, and wanted to be part of, not separate from all the other tobacco dealers. They had helped him, and now he could help them.

He took to the hotel with the other lads like a duck to water, he thought. He seemed to settle in well. He respected the rules and ethos. He wanted to learn the tricks of the trade very quickly. He knew the whole thing, like everyone's individual operations, was probably operating on thin ice, so try not to jump up and down was his logic. Then Keith and Dave explained about the BAC. He had never heard of the BAC; what were they talking about? They were a group of people, mainly two or three men, who would arrive in a car. They carried guns and they would tax English tobacco dealers by taking their tobacco or cash from their room and no one argued. They would even pull up while people were unloading, wave their guns about, and after everyone scarpered, finish unloading the cars – but not into the room; into the boot of their car – before driving off. My God, it sounded like the Wild, Wild West. It was just how it was. The dealers saw it as a form of taxation and accepted it; after all, who were they going to complain to? They were all breaking the law in a foreign country, and didn't speak the language either. Johnny thought it sounded a bit like drug dealers robbing drug dealers in England. They couldn't exactly report it to the police, could they?

It also very quickly became apparent that if dealers ran out of stock, they were all borrowing and buying from each other. It seemed more important to everyone to keep their customers happy. After all, if their customers went elsewhere, then they might not come back. This was going to help Johnny a lot but he didn't realise how much at the time. Very quickly, people were asking to borrow and Johnny lent. He felt it was the right thing to do and he could do the same in the future. It was an unwritten rule in the hotel. Johnny's biggest problem was volume. Yes, he had a few foot passengers who were day trippers on the ferries, but he had to build them up very quickly. The name of the game was customers, volume, getting to the bank and doing a trip a day to Luxembourg, and selling it daily, not every other or every 3 days. So, very quickly, he said he would sell his stock to other traders, because he had it sold already. It wasn't true but they didn't know that. They were happy to just buy it and sell it at cost to keep their customers happy; after all, their initial stock had gone for the day. So, Johnny started off with a few customers but very quickly could sell everything he had towards the end of some days. There were also a few lads from England he had met playing cards previously. They heard he was dealing out there and asked to deal with him. Some of them were sending drivers, not going themselves, and Johnny always used to turn up on time and help them load it up really quick to try and keep them happy, like George had with him in his early days. They were bigger players and were buying car loads at a time, which was just what he needed.

It was not too long after arriving at the Formula 1 hotel. Johnny was sitting in reception one evening when one of the lads shouted BAC. Everyone jumped up from their seats and disappeared at what seemed 100 mph. Johnny knew he wasn't known yet, or so he thought. He didn't want to go to his room, because he thought they might spot him or work out what his room was. He sat in reception and watched a French car turn up in the car park. Then these two really tall men jumped out. They were carrying guns in holsters around their waists. The car was marked BAC. This was not what Johnny was expecting. They walked into the front entrance of the hotel by reception. Johnny sat there drinking coffee on his own and not saying a word. How could they know he was English, he guessed? He didn't make eye contact but listened to them talking in French before walking down the right-hand side section of the hotel.

Johnny disappeared back to his own room. He left it ages before coming out. Everyone was in reception again. It turned out the BAC was the Bureau Agency de Crime – the French equivalent of the CID. Johnny didn't see that coming. It turned out they had gone to see Keith in his room and threatened him with a gun for money, if Keith was to be believed. He said he gave them £2k to get rid of them. It was a bloody madhouse. A few of the local officers clearly realised how much money was being made by some of the players in the hotel and wanted a cut. They were nothing short of bent coppers on the take and knew no one would complain. They carried fire arms; they were officers of the law and the English tobacco dealers were breaking the law. They could have come round and confiscated everything if they wanted to make it official and do their job properly, but it was more of a Customs matter, really, since the tobacco was not illegal. The tax evasion and the buying to sell were. So they were just bloody liberty takers. The BAC had been taxing English lads at the hotel ever since they had started. Now Johnny finally understood what and who they were. Avoiding them and the Customs would become his two main priorities. He later found out Keith and Jock had found lorry drivers to take tobacco back to Scotland for them and they were paying the drivers for letting them put tobacco in the trailers. They were literally putting 2 pallets of tobacco on the back of a lorry and sending it to Scotland if it wasn't stopped at Customs. They had their fair share of losses and successes over time but had made hundreds of thousands of pounds over a period.

So, very quickly, Johnny took on a full-time driver rather than drive to Luxembourg himself. He offered the job to Tony, Sophia's son. He could be trusted, he was a good driver, he would pick the job up quickly, and if he came over daily rather than living in Calais like the northern lads who were drivers, he could take back cigarettes as well, which would improve his daily earnings. The rate for a driver at the time was £100 per day or trip. It was just an added expense. Johnny had very quickly found customers from everywhere, really, and then if there was a shortage at the hotel, as there was from time to time, literally everyone in the hotel would start running around getting stock from everyone else and everyone would sell out. It was so quick, he realised. Once the biggest players sold out, if they had customers waiting or on their way, he could just sell anything and everything to anyone in the hotel. Since he got on well with most of them, he was one of the first they might ask. The tobacco would sell quicker than toilet rolls in a supermarket during early Covid. It was just simple supply and demand; once there was a shortage, panic set in instantly.

Johnny decided he was going to trade 5 days per week, from Monday to Friday. He would leave Dover as a foot passenger on a ferry Sunday evening and return as a foot passenger Friday afternoon, or on the odd occasion Saturday morning. Soon he decided to get another Belgian hire car and another driver. He took on one of Dave's friends, Geoff.

Geoff was down from up north, living and working in Dover. He was carrying cigarettes back on the ferry or hovercraft daily.

Dave told him he could get him a job driving in Calais and he took it. He used to travel backwards and forwards from Dover daily, do the Luxembourg run, then go back home to Dover on the ferry. Geoff seemed a really nice, straight-up guy and he never once let Johnny down. Johnny had found his feet, and with another car would double his earning potential if he could sell it. He was regularly earning £10k per week all-in, after expenses. The room at the Formula 1 was paid for 7 days per week, was secure, and the cars seemed safe, locked up at the hotel or in the free car park at the ferry terminal over the weekend.

Carrying cash through customs was also a problem. If you had over £10k in cash, that could be confiscated, in theory, without a proper explanation. Johnny could ask people to carry cash back for him, and he also dealt with a guy called Acker. He liked Acker and trusted him. He knew him from years ago. So, he used to let Acker pay at the weekends rather than when he sent drivers over for tobacco. That way he was getting paid in England, and the cash was already at home. So, it suddenly crept up on him but he now had the best paying job he had ever had. It came at the right time precisely. He had to give Brabners Solicitors about another £80k for barristers and further expenses for the civil proceedings. He used to do this in payments of about £4k at a time in cash. He would get a handwritten receipt from the receptionist in the office in Dover. He also wanted to pay off the mortgage on High Hopes, which he did. He then sold the property to an offshore company called Oak Trading. Oak Trading was based in the Turks and Caicos. Johnny was the sole shareholder, but that information was hidden from the English tax authorities. Johnny had spoken to his accountant at Singh and Co. He said the ownership could not be traced. The company had a Barclays business account in the Isle of Man. His accountant said that if Inland Revenue wrote to the Turks and Caicos and enquired about any company details, they threw the letters in the bin and never replied. Legally they never had to, and so they never did, and Inland Revenue never asked anymore after that. Johnny liked the sound of the Turks and Caicos. He felt his home was now fully protected in any event from the British authorities.

Johnny was gambling at the weekends in Coral's in Canterbury and hit a purple patch several weekends on the trot. He was winning large amounts and walking out. A few weeks later, he walked in one Sunday afternoon, picked up a betting slip and started looking at the horse racing, when the manager walked over, gently tapped him on the shoulder and quietly said they don't want any more, thanks. He did a double take. He wasn't barred from the shop but the powers that be told the manager to tell him that they didn't want his bets anymore. That was that.

In a flash, he couldn't even have a bet in there. At the weekends, he was regularly taking Sophia to the theatre and Langan's brasserie for dinner. It was a great way to live if you could afford it. They even used to stay at the Savoy as well. He would drive up to London in his Bentley with Sophia and live in pure ecstasy for a day or two, then go back to the Formula 1 cheap and cheerful for the week.

Another way of hiding money or keeping it safe was at the tobacco house. By now he had an excellent relationship with Marianne, the owner of Marianne's tobacco warehouse in Luxembourg. Johnny could just send all his money there with a driver. She would keep the balance after charging for the car load of cigarettes or tobacco and make a note of his credit balance on the receipts so he could keep track. It worked both ways, as well. After a while, he could send drivers with no money and pay later, so he now had a credit facility in Luxembourg with the tobacco warehouse, as well as a deposit facility. He was just treating the place like a bank as well as a place to buy stock.

Life and good fortune were very good to him at this time. The job was a bit of a laugh and a giggle, he thought. All the earlier fears he'd had at the start had proven to be unfounded. He spent most of his week sitting in a hotel reception, smoking and drinking coffee, chatting to people taking orders on the phones, then driving and delivering orders to customers as well as picking up and dropping the drivers back to the ferry terminal. One morning, Dave caught him a treat with the chambermaids. He asked Johnny if he would get him some clean towels off the chambermaids. Dave said, 'Just go up and say je t'aime.' Johnny had not put two and two together. So, he walked up to a young, attractive chambermaid and said 'Je t'aime.' She burst out laughing and ran off, so he chased her round the hotel and kept saying it to her. Then he saw Dave and some of the lads in bits, laughing their heads off, and he realised something was up. It then got pointed out to him that he was telling the girl 'I love you.' After a few moments, he saw the funny side to it all.

He had seen the BAC a few times and saw what they did and how they treated people, but thankfully he had managed to avoid their attention and he never got challenged by them. One evening, everyone in the hotel was waiting for their drivers to return from Luxembourg and no one turned up. After a while everyone knew something was not right. It had never happened before. Drivers' phones were turned off and everyone was a few hours past the time they would usually return by. Then, suddenly, Geoff came round the corner and parked up, but not by the window of the room; just in the car park. He then explained what had happened and what was going on. It turned out that there had been an armed robbery at Marianne's. A lot of people were going there daily. There were two main warehouses you could use in Luxembourg – Marianne's and Paul's. Paul was actually an English guy who used to smuggle tobacco to England and had set up in competition with Marianne because he could see the potential, knew all the English smugglers who were doing it at the same time he was, and knew it was a legal way of trading rather than an illegal way. He moved to Luxembourg and just opened a warehouse. Johnny'd heard he had a lot of lorries being sent there by English people who were doing it in lorries rather than as foot passengers or in cars. Johnny did notice himself on a few occasions how much cash was behind the counter, which was fully enclosed and protected by bullet proof glass, he thought, or at least reinforced glass. It seemed they just had large piles of cash laying everywhere. He didn't think any more of it. Everyone was paying in cash and it was a very busy place but it certainly was not put out of sight. They seemed very relaxed around cash, maybe because they were turning so much over. They counted people's money using counting machines, which Johnny thought was a novel idea.

Geoff reversed into the warehouse to pay and load up. As he got out of the car, armed police handcuffed him to a rail. Geoff never knew it until a little later but he was the first person to turn up after the armed robbery. A member of staff had been shot and taken to hospital and another one threatened with a gun and was in shock. It turned out that the armed robbers went into the warehouse and, to get the cash given to them or gain access to the secure payment area, they threatened to shoot the lad in the warehouse. They put a loaded gun to his head and said they would shoot him if they weren't let in to get the cash. They did gain access but were challenged by a member of staff, and they either shot him intentionally or the gun went off in a struggle and he had been taken to hospital. He later died. So, the armed robbery became murder very quickly, but when Geoff arrived, he knew it as armed robbery. Geoff was questioned as to what he was doing there, why he went there, and so on. Then Marianne herself started vouching for the drivers who turned up, explaining they were customers. What no one knew, as it was not advertised or obvious, was that the whole area was recorded by 24-hour secret surveillance cameras, so the police were able to watch exactly what did happen. They also had the evidence and testimony of the staff at the warehouse, so after a few hours, checking people's passports and running checks on them, as well as starting their investigation, they started releasing drivers and telling them to just go. No one argued, naturally, so they all came back without any tobacco. The local police in Luxembourg were astonished at the trade that was going on and the obvious implications of it but didn't get overly interested in that side of things. They were there to catch armed robbers, and when the guy died, catch a killer or killers.

There was a large scouse element involved in the tobacco trade. A lot of lads from Liverpool were staying at the Formula 1. They seemed a good laugh during the day but Johnny realised a lot of them were out of control in the evenings. Johnny would mind his own business and sit in the hotel, mainly. Some of the scouse lads who seemed to follow a lad called Ben about a lot and listen to him were down the local bars and night clubs in Calais, getting drunk, taking drugs, causing fights and chasing the local French girls. They were young, had money to burn in their pockets, and were causing mayhem. Often the police were getting called, and they seemed to think it was a big joke. The local police probably knew they were selling tobacco and were just a bloody nuisance, really.

At the time there were local elections in Calais, and one of the candidates for Mayor of Calais fought his campaign on cleaning up the town and chasing the English criminals, tobacco dealers and thugs out of Calais. Everyone was oblivious to the campaign but Johnny did use to think, 'I wish they wouldn't draw unwanted attention to us.' Anyway, so the candidate who fought his campaign on cleaning Calais up and running the English out of town won. No one knew of this but with hindsight it was hardly surprising. It turned out that Keith and Freddy had Interpol warrants out for their arrest since the murder at Marianne's. Keith and Freddy had gone in there with guns to rob the place. It turned out Jock and Keith had been dealing with the Belgian mafia and had lost a lot of money. They were being financed by the Belgian mafia and it had all gone wrong. So they were skint and in debt to the wrong people.

Johnny realised you never knew the truth or got all the facts in any case, but he had seen them at the hotel, turning up in two cars at a time. All Johnny knew about these guys was they had "don't mess with me" written all over them. Everything about them, from the cars they drove to the clothes they wore and the way they walked and conducted themselves just said "mafia – keep away." If ever Johnny had seen the mafia in real life, or at best, organised crime figures, this was them. Johnny had never spoken to them or even really looked at them. They were definitely not for Johnny's attention. Freddy actually got stopped by English Customs after returning to Dover as a foot passenger, and so the story goes he was off his head on drugs and was carrying £72k in sterling and Belgian francs. Keith was later picked up in France and both were extradited to Luxembourg to be remanded in a Luxembourg prison while awaiting trial for murder and armed robbery. That was the last Johnny ever heard of Keith or Freddy, but the police had the tape of the whole thing as evidence and eye witness testimony from staff at Marianne's. Apparently, because they thought there were no cameras, they didn't even try to hide their identity by wearing masks or crash helmets. They were desperate for the money, wanted to get the cash and get back home to England. Jock just seemed to disappear at the same time.

Marianne's did open again as usual, after the murder, but somehow the whole business seemed a lot colder now. Tobacco dealers in Calais were being robbed and targeted by gangs. English criminals were now running round Calais with guns and robbing the tobacco dealers. There was so much cash involved, and the tobacco was as good as cash. Not at the Formula 1, but some players who were renting large detached houses in the area, had staff in them and were trading from them, were literally being robbed by their customers. Some scouse lads ordered a few car loads of tobacco from one of the larger dealers in Calais, then turned up to get it at their rented house. There were two guys there, minding the shop, so to speak. They tied them up, and took all the stock and cash. In reality, no one really knew who they were dealing with. It was all Christian names, cash, and no one knew where anyone lived or their surnames. It had become like the Wild, Wild West, exactly as Johnny thought. Johnny had lost his passion for the business and enthusiasm. He'd had an amazing run while doing it and had used at least some of the earnings wisely, as well as gambling a lot and living in the fast lane, as one of Johnny's later therapists liked to refer to it.

About a week later everyone was sitting in the reception area at the Formula 1, one morning at about 10 am, when a procession of police vehicles and customs vehicles just filed into the car park and sat there. No one, including Johnny, had ever seen anything like it. Johnny was on his own. Sophia and the drivers weren't there yet. In a split second, he nipped into his room, and grabbed his passport and cash. That was enough for Johnny. The stock could stay there. He knew when the game was up and just wanted to get out. The police and customs vehicles filled with officers just sat in the car park. After about 10 minutes, two officers got out of one of the vehicles and walked into the reception area. Before they got to the entrance, everyone had done a bunk. Johnny didn't want to go anywhere near his room, that was for sure. The room and stock were a bloody liability and just proof he was a tobacco dealer. Johnny, fully clothed, locked himself in a shower. Middlesborough Dave saw him and said, 'Can I come in with you?' He let him in and they stood there without speaking for ages. Just trying to stand in silence.

After about thirty minutes they hatched a plan. If they were challenged by anyone in authority while leaving the shower or hotel, they were going to say that they were lovers and were sick to death of being picked on, so they came to France to get away from prejudice that existed in England and they shouldn't be discriminated against in France just because they were gay. They had a right to be left alone. It was the best they could manage in the short time they were locked in the shower together.

When they opened the door of the shower the place was deserted. All the vehicles had left the car park. They then found out that the two officers had walked into the reception area and asked to speak to Dominique. One of the guys was supposedly head of Customs in Calais. He told Dominique the local mayor was sick to death of English tobacco dealers in Calais breaking the law, abusing the locals and generally being a nuisance. He then told the local customs and police it all stopped immediately. It was as simple as that. That was the order. So, it turned out, he told Dominique that he knew that all the English residents in the hotel were selling tobacco and he was leaving but was coming back four hours later. When he returned later in the afternoon, he wanted the name of every English guest in the hotel, a copy of their passport and their room number. After he left, Dominique told everyone in no uncertain terms that they had two hours to leave, they could not return, and if anyone didn't leave, he was giving their details to the head of the Calais Customs when he returned.

That was it. It was just a mass exodus. No one knew where they were going, and no one cared. Everyone had a lifeline and they were going to take it. So, the reverse was now happening. Everyone had their cars parked up outside their windows and was transferring their stock from their rooms to their cars and leaving. Johnny managed to load up a car quite quickly. He didn't have a great deal of stock, and what he did have, he sold later that day. He parked the other car up in the car park with nothing in it and locked it up. He sold the stock that day and decided that was enough for him. He was going to quit while he was ahead.

He left the hotel, sold his stock, then took a car back to Brussels airport. He got Sophia to follow him to Brussels airport in the other car. He returned one hire car after cleaning it inside and out. They then went to Marianne's to collect the money he had there on deposit. After getting the money, he took Sophia back to Calais and said to her to book a car return the next day, come over in a car, they could then go down to Brussels airport together, drop off the second hire car and return to Calais. At the time, he had bought a Peugeot 405 diesel to run about in, so Sophia drove that over. Johnny knew the cash he had, a total of about £42k, would be a problem if the Customs stopped him but there was nothing he could do about that. Johnny and Sophia returned on a P&O ferry and had dinner in Langan's as they often did. They drove through the port of Dover without being stopped or checked, so there was a huge relief when he started driving up the Jubilee Way after exiting Dover Docks.

A few weeks later he was curious to know what was going on in Calais. No one seemed to know very much. Johnny had let all his customers know he was finishing. He decided to go over to

Calais and just take a look and see what was going on and how the land lay, so to speak. He and Sophia went over on a ferry and bumped into a couple of guys they had met while over in Calais. It was Bill and Ruben. They were travellers from the Crawley area. Ruben had a stunning-looking girlfriend called Jayne. Jayne was involved in running brothels near Crawley and Ruben had tried every trick in the book to make money. Bill was a tall, slim family guy who clearly loved his wife and family dearly. He always had his son close by and was teaching him the ropes, as he saw it. Neither of them was educated at all but they were both very street wise and knew how to earn. Ruben had a certain charm, charisma and way about him. Every time Johnny saw him, he was always wearing the same sheepskin coat. Johnny thought it was sewn onto him but he generally wore it well and looked good. One of Bill's favourite sayings was, 'If you've got a donkey, go to work with the donkey until you can afford a horse.' Johnny always translated it as make the most of what you have got until you got better. It turned out Ruben, who got on well enough with Johnny, had rented a farmhouse further away from Calais and was dealing from there. It was out in the country. After chatting for a while, Ruben said Johnny could deal from there, pay half the expenses, and they could try and help each other out where they could. Johnny was in. He didn't have to think twice; he missed the money and the action. So, it was back down to Brussels a few days later, picking up a Belgian registration diesel estate from EuroCar, then off to Marianne's to load up and drive back to France again. The farmhouse Ruben had rented was out in the country, just off the main road, about halfway between Calais and the Belgian border. The drive was long enough out of Calais, Johnny thought. It was all motorway, apart from the last mile after exiting the motorway. The location was great. Ruben had certainly done well to get this place.

The first Sunday evening Johnny returned after the first week, he was at the farmhouse on his own when he thought he heard voices outside in the barn near the farmhouse. He rang Ruben to see where he was; after all, he may just be down the road on his way back. Ruben answered and told him he had been delayed and was still in England. He then said to him if they come in after the money and or tobacco and are armed, it's better if they are wearing balaclavas or face masks. That means they don't intend to shoot you; they just intend to rob you. If they are not covering their faces, you might have a serious problem. That wasn't exactly how Johnny thought the phone call would go. He sat there on his own and realised what Ruben had just said kind of made sense. At this point, he kept looking through the window but could see no one. Later he got a bit bolder and went outside. There was no one there, thankfully, but in the barn next to the farmhouse the wind was blowing signs that were creaking. Maybe that was what he'd heard earlier on.

Anyway, off to work again. Johnny knew he didn't have the customers he had before. Everything changes very quickly. He had a few but there was no trading in the hotel or comradery as there was in the hotel. He also realised for the first time how secure the hotel had been compared to an isolated farmhouse. At the hotel everyone wanted to avoid the BAC. When you are on your own, you just want to avoid everything and everyone. Johnny decided not to meet customers at the farmhouse, not to invite people there. That way no one knew from his end where he was based. He never really knew how Ruben and Bill covered their backs or tracks but Ruben's son, young Ruben, who was like a mini-me of his father, was out of control and like a homing beacon. He carried on like some of the young scouse lads. Wherever or whenever he drove, he was screeching around like he was on a race track, and he had no tact or people skills whatsoever.

Customers were harder to find now, and Johnny thought Bill and Ruben were ok to share with but they never had a great deal of customers, so there wasn't much trading he could do with them. Johnny met Al at the port one day and managed to secure their custom. Al was as hard as nails, from Glasgow, and trying to earn the best he could. When Johnny had first met him in the Formula 1, Al explained he and a couple of mates would come to Calais, go to Luxembourg and get a car load, plot themselves up at the Formula 1, and they were all taking it back to Dover as foot passengers in small amounts, leaving it at a place in Dover. Once they had taken the car load over, they used to take it back to Scotland. That was how they operated. In Scotland they were selling in small amounts and getting top dollar return on their trip. They stopped going to Luxembourg and just started buying from Johnny in Calais, taking over to Dover and then back to Scotland. Johnny got quite close with them in the short time he was back out in Calais. Sophia would come over on the same ferries as them sometimes and travel back together.

Card games became the big thing at the farmhouse. Ruben, Billy and Johnny loved 3 card brag. They used to play for hours. There was nothing else to do. Everyone had cash on their hip. Johnny had not played 3 card brag for years. He loved the game. Over the years, the whole world seemingly started playing poker. It was a nice change from 5 card stud or 7 card draw poker. Johnny found it hard to beat them both. He could hold his own at the cards, and although they liked cards, they definitely did not have the gambling bug like he did. Still, it passed the time away. After a few weeks, it wasn't really working out that great for him. He could earn, but nothing like what he had done in the past. Bill and Ruben were somehow a little boring after a while.

Johnny had enjoyed their stories and banter when he first met them but that novelty soon wore off. He'd quit while ahead the last time, and so decided to call it a day again. He had earnt some money, with no dramas or huge losses. He had now had a date confirmed in 2001 for the civil trial with the Prudential at Canterbury Crown Court. He asked Tony, Sophia's son, if he wanted to trade from the farmhouse. Tony decided to give it a go for a while. He and his girlfriend Rachael plotted themselves up at the farmhouse. Johnny never really knew how it went for him but he seemed to make a go of it for a while before deciding enough was enough.

After Tony returned to England, he was explaining to Johnny one day about how he could buy drugs in Holland, bring them back home and make a tidy profit. It was a really expensive type of cannabis called pollen, not widely available in England. It was about four times the price of soap – or basic cannabis, as it is known – and it came in very slim bars that could be hidden easily. Johnny liked the idea. It was a simple plan. Tony knew a guy in Folkestone, Gary, who would drive a car from England to Amsterdam. Tony and Johnny could follow in a separate car. In Amsterdam Tony would buy the drugs, hide them in the car, or at least attempt to hide them, mainly under the bonnet and in various spaces. Then Gary would drive the car back through Dover Docks. Gary was being paid £2k for driving the car. The figures sounded good and Johnny agreed to get involved.

A Montego was bought for the job. It was a tidy-looking vehicle with high mileage, a cheap purchase. They decided to cross on P&O Ferries on an early ferry from Dover to Calais, then drive to Amsterdam. So far, so good. Johnny and Tony followed Gary to Amsterdam. After arriving, they all parked up. Then it became apparent Tony didn't know where he was going to get the drugs from. No deal was in place in Amsterdam. Tony just kept going in coffee shops trying to buy large quantities without much success. After a few hours a deal was struck; he found someone willing to do a deal. They bought just under forty thousand pounds' worth of drugs, which couldn't really be hidden well in the car – more just placed in the car as best they could. Gary drove the car back to France, and they agreed, no stopping on the way back. Tony and Johnny followed in Johnny's car.

They boarded a ferry at Calais and set sail for Dover. The drugs could not be concealed that well. If Gary got stopped and the boot or the bonnet got opened, it would be game over. Gary, by now, was a bag of nerves and falling to pieces. It turned out he had never done it before and was just a drug addict who was desperate for cash. Johnny wasn't happy at all with how things were going on the ferry. At one stage, Gary wanted to back out. Tony managed to calm him down and Johnny thought Tony and Gary had a joint to calm the nerves. Johnny was frazzled with the day's events. The ferry docked at Dover and Gary had agreed he was going to drive the car through Customs. That was something Johnny thought, although by now he realised Gary looked like a drug addict on a suicide mission going through Customs, which didn't inspire confidence one bit.

Everyone went down to the car decks to await disembarkation from the ferry. Johnny was parked just a few cars behind Gary, on the same level. Since loading up at Amsterdam, he didn't want Gary out of his sight with the car full of drugs. Gary got in his car. After a few minutes and the docking procedure being completed, drivers were being waved off the ferry. Only one problem. Gary's car wouldn't start. He came and told Tony and Johnny. Everyone was driving round them and leaving the ferry. It just wouldn't start. They managed to push the car off the ferry and down the ramp into Dover Docks with the assistance of some P&O staff. The car was sitting at the bottom of the ramp with Gary in it and still wouldn't start. Then Tony said the tyres had marks on them, which may have been placed on them by Customs, who had gone round the vehicles with a drug dog and marked the car for a search. It was just a belief, not a fact.

After about 15 minutes, they managed to get the car going. Now Gary was on. He needed to drive through the Customs hall with Johnny and Tony following. It was now late at night and dark. As they approached passport control, the only thing that was obvious was there were no other cars at all. It was Gary being followed by Johnny. Everyone else was gone. There was no one there at all checking cars. Gary drove through and as Johnny followed. As he drove, he looked in the Customs area and saw several cars being searched by Customs officers. Johnny was not going to let the Montego out of his sight now, that was for sure. Gary then drove the car back to Folkestone, followed closely by Johnny. At Folkestone, Gary got out where he lived, Johnny paid him, Tony jumped in the car and drove it back to Canterbury. It had worked. It had been a success after all. Never again, Johnny thought. It was definitely more luck than judgement.

CHAPTER 15
CIVIL TRIAL WITH THE PRUDENTIAL

IT HAD LITERALLY BEEN years getting to court. The original claim on the Prudential insurance policy had been made in 1993. At the time Johnny had envisaged it would take a month or two for the claim to be paid. He remembered thinking £49k would be a very handy deposit for a house at the time. It was now 2001. There had been the investigation and arrests followed by the criminal trial, which took two to three years to unfold. Michael Mann QC had offered to help Johnny get paid when he was walking free from Crown Court. Johnny never forgot that or the connection he had made with the judge in the criminal trial. In fact, he smiled after the first day of the criminal trial when Michael Mann had said to him, 'I am the only loser here today.' He had been paid his retainer for taking the case, and his daily rate was £2k per day. He was referring to his loss of earnings for the next week or two. Of course, when the case collapsed on Tuesday morning, as Michael Mann knew it was going to, he had no work lined up for a couple of weeks.

When it came to finding a barrister to fight the case for him,

Johnny had presumed he would instruct Michael Mann again. That made sense to him, but a few years later it was suggested that Michael Mann was a little older now and had peaked in his practice a few years earlier. He had been an excellent advocate in criminal matters, but for civil proceedings a different approach would be required. Of course, Johnny had listened to the solicitors all the way through. He did not know or understand the legal process or which barristers were better. Brabners had recommended Michael Mann in the criminal matter, and he had turned up and got the job done. Now Peter Watson at Brabners was suggesting Richard Broadhouse. Johnny wanted a QC or leader as well. He thought that a QC had more chance of winning, and better to turn up in court with a strong legal team. The name Stephen Hillman QC had been suggested.

Richard Broadhouse was a large Scottish gentleman with a beard and a wicked sense of humour. Stephen Hillman was a very small man who wore glasses and, as you would expect, he was a very experienced, educated man with great passion for the law. Stephen Hillman drove a Jaguar sport car XJS, which made Johnny smile. Mr Hillman behind the wheel of a large 2-door sports flying down the road conjured up memories of Atom Ant to Johnny. So, Johnny instructed Richard Broadhouse and Stephen Hillman. Brabners had been doing all the work necessary to get a case to court for a civil trial. There had been countless hearings at court about disclosure of documents, best estimate of time frame for trial, more and new evidence being added by the Prudential, availability of witnesses and barristers, etc. It did seem that finding a date to suit every witness on both sides as well as the barristers, the serving police officer, the judge, and then fitting that date in with a date available in the court was a very long and drawn-out process. The original proceedings had been issued in the High Court but transferred to the County Court on the basis that the original claim had been for under £50,000.00. The court estimate was one week and it would be heard at Canterbury County Court, which was in the same building the criminal trial had been heard in. The combined court centre at Canterbury is in Chaucer Road. It was a lady judge presiding over the case.

The case would start on a Monday and finish on a Friday. As the case began, the first thing Johnny realised was that it was never going to finish in a week. The last thing you could accuse anyone of in court, he thought, was rushing. All barristers speak and allow the judge time to make notes they feel appropriate, and then speak again, so the questioning of witnesses is always a slow, methodical, thorough process.

Johnny had asked Al from Scotland to come down for the week to tag along and keep him and Sophia company. Al had seen the very hard side of life on the streets in Glasgow, and had now given up on the smuggling. The customs at Dover and Folkestone had started targeting boot leggers and were confiscating cigarettes and tobacco nonstop. They had finally got wise to the smugglers and were just confiscating off anyone who was a regular traveller. They just went to war with them and very quickly wiped most of them out.

Johnny didn't know how things would play out with members of Sophia's ex family. He knew Arthur had a reputation for being a handful and violent if he wanted to be. He also knew that apart from the claimant (Johnny), no one else who would give evidence in the case would be allowed to sit in the court until they had given their evidence. So, Sophia would have to wait outside the court on her own. Would Arthur play up or not? Who could know or tell? Al was the insurance policy he had in place for any such unwanted or unwelcome behaviour, whether that be verbal or physical. Al sat with Sophia all the time until she had given her evidence. Then Al would sit in the court with Johnny and Sophia, listening to the case. They all travelled in the same car to and from court, and Al stayed at their place for the week. There was no trouble with Sophia's relatives. Whether that was Al's doing or not, Johnny would never know. Maybe having Al there had been an overreaction, but it did the job.

There did not seem to be any more shocks or additional information for Johnny or Sophia to look at or explain. It was just a simple process of going through the whole case step by step from the beginning. Statements from all witnesses had been disclosed. The barristers were now presenting their witnesses to the court and taking them through their evidence step by step to be heard by the judge before they could make their final arguments.

In the criminal matter the Crown Prosecution Service had to prove to a jury of 12 randomly selected strangers that Johnny and Sophia had attempted to defraud the Prudential, beyond all reasonable doubt. That is the level of proof, and that burden falls on the Crown. The defendants do not have to prove anything. In a civil case, the matters are decided on the preponderance of evidence. If no settlement is agreed in advance and a claim goes to trial, then that is the basis on which a judge will make their judgement. At trial, the person suing (the plaintiff) usually must prove that the other party (the defendant) is more likely than not liable for some harm the plaintiff has suffered. The legal term for this "more likely than not" standard is "preponderance of the evidence."

So, after day three (Wednesday) in court, the only thing that was clear to everyone in the court was that the case would not be finished by Friday. Johnny had realised quicker than everyone that a week was too short for the case. It clearly needed a lot longer. When the time frame had been set and agreed for the trial, obviously everyone had totally misjudged the matter. Johnny thought the trial would just continue day-in, day-out until it concluded, so he presumed everyone was coming back on Monday the following week, to just keep going until the case was concluded, as it would in any criminal matter. No, it would not be anything like that. The judge and the barristers had other cases on the following Monday. The case was clearly going to have to be heard up until Friday afternoon, then it would be listed as part heard. Everyone would then have to agree when they were available again for the trial to continue. Everyone agreed the case needed to be listed for another week. No date was agreed or set because none of the judge, barristers or witnesses knew when they would be available.

Johnny had never heard anything like it. The solicitors explained that as soon as everyone checked their availability and confirmed it with the court, a new listing date would be confirmed to all parties. It felt very unsatisfactory to him, but what could he do, apart from accept it? By this time, he had already paid over £100,000.00 to Brabners, and now they diplomatically explained that they would need more funds for them and the barristers for the second week of the trial. Johnny was still flush from his time in Calais, so paid the additional funds to Brabners. In total he had paid £140k, but it was only an investment, as after the matter was concluded, he would be entitled to his £49k as well as £140k costs. So, it was more of an investment rather than a risk, he thought.

Tony, Sophia's son, was back dealing drugs again in England. Johnny had always steered clear of that. He knew people who had made a lot of money in that business, he knew people who had lost a lot of money in that business, and he knew way too many people who had been to prison or had lost their lives in that business, whether they were dealing or using. Also, lots of people just ruined their own lives, as well as the lives of their families and the people who cared about them.

Johnny was looking for something to do. He was speaking to Tony about prices one day, and he also started speaking to Al in Scotland. Al could get puff, or cannabis, at £800 per kg for a bulk order of 50 kg. At the time there was a shortage around Kent and the prices were a lot more. Johnny realised that by getting it down from Scotland, he and Tony could make a quick killing. He ran through all the details, and then told Al he wanted 50kg at £800. Al said to leave it to him. He would get back to him and let him know. Within a few days it was agreed. 50kg for £40k cash. They agreed to meet halfway, at Woodall Services near Sheffield. Al and Johnny both agreed they would set off at the same time, Al from Glasgow and Johnny from Canterbury. Woodall Services was halfway up the M1, near Sheffield, and Johnny knew it was a three or four-hour drive. He only had one problem: he didn't have £40k in cash. He got together every last penny he had and it was just over £32k in cash. Then he realised he had some money in the Standard Chartered offshore bank account he had set up previously. He wrote a cheque for £8k and left it blank. This was his first drug deal and he never quite realised no one takes cheques. He thought 32 and 8, that would be acceptable.

It was a Monday evening and Johnny set off about 5 pm. The plan was to meet up about 9 pm in the services, not hang about too long, a nice steady drive back, and he should get home for about 1 am. He enjoyed driving and the drive up there was straightforward enough. He had the music on and was singing along. About an hour before the meeting place, he and Al spoke on the mobiles just to confirm progress. It seemed to be going according to schedule. Johnny was northbound on the M1 and Al southbound.

When Johnny arrived, Al was there with a couple of mates. They had coffee in the services. Then it was agreed Johnny would drive up the motorway, turn around and come back down the M1 to meet Al on the southbound side. They would wait in the car. They would give him the puff and he would give them the cash. It seemed to all go well without any hitches. He pulled alongside them, got out of the car, and paid with the cash and cheque in a carrier bag. They then took the drugs out of their boot in a large holdall and he put the drugs in his boot. He closed the boot and jumped back in again. He was driving Sophia's Toyota Yaris. It was a very inconspicuous car and he like the idea of just blending in when picking up drugs. He certainly knew he did not want to stand out. So, as Johnny pulled out of the services, he now knew what he had in the boot and every fibre of his body tightened up. He now felt really uncomfortable and paranoid. Of course, his nightmare would have been getting stopped on a routine traffic stop by the police and him not coming across too well, and for some reason they look in the boot. He knew prison would be inevitable.

The drive home was nothing like the drive up there. On the way up there, he didn't have a care in the world. Carrying money hidden under the seat wasn't stressful, as he could explain that on some level, not that any police officer had ever stopped him before and searched under seats for money. In fact, he did nothing but worry on the drive home. He decided not to speed but just stick to the maximum speed allowed, not too fast but not too slow either. He would put the tunes back on and just chain-smoke the whole way back. After a while he started counting the miles back, and after an hour or two he just kept singing and talking to himself. So, when he got down the M1 turned on to the M25 heading for the Dartford Tunnel, he felt relieved and less stressed. After that, it was back down the M2 towards

Canterbury and Chilham. He turned into the drive at High Hopes in Pilgrim's Lane and parked up. It was about 1.30 am. There was no one about, no cars, and it was pitch black. Emotionally exhausted, he got out of the car and went in. He left the large holdall in the boot.

Sophia was in bed. Johnny made a coffee and got a cold drink and just sat in the lounge, relieved but totally stressed out. It took a while for him to calm down. Then, after about another half an hour, he went out to the car, grabbed the holdall and took it into the dining room. He opened up the large holdall and grabbed a 9-bar of puff. That's when he realised that there were a few 9-bars of puff on the top and everything else was like bricks of plasticine or brown modelling clay shaped into bars the same size. He knew instantly he had been turned over. There were 10 bars, which was 2.5kg of puff, and 47.5kg of modelling clay. They had even put the right amount in for authenticity with weight and size. Was it Al's doing or his friends'? He rang Al straight away and told him. Al said he didn't know anything about it. He had just put the deal together with the guys. As far as he was concerned, they were on the level. He would speak to them and find out what was going on. He didn't understand it but would get to the bottom of it. Johnny knew Al had either put it together himself, which was highly likely, or at least was in on it. Al never got back to him. It was the last time they ever spoke. He was pleased he'd put the cheque in and he had 2.5kg. He had just done £30k in an evening driving up the M1 and back. The next day he cancelled the cheque he had written and left blank. *Thank God for small mercies*, he thought.

Then he sat and thought about the events that had just occurred. When Johnny met Al in Calais, both were wearing jeans and jumpers and getting on with life. Al lived in a really rough part of Glasgow and had a son who had, as he had himself, been addicted to heroin. They met, they chatted, they got on. Then Johnny had asked him to come down and stay for the week and he would pay him for the week. Johnny had a large house set in the country up a private lane, a Bentley on the drive, and kept going on about the costs in the insurance claim and how much it was worth. Al was living in a rough council estate in Glasgow. Johnny realised he had virtually taken an advert out to Al and brought it on himself. So, the first drug deal had been a complete disaster from start to finish. Johnny ended up knowing his name was Al, he lived in Glasgow and had a non-contract mobile phone number for contact purposes. That was it. The matter was closed, he and Al both knew that.

Johnny had now been informed of the new date for the civil case. It would be in another two months, about three months in total since the first week at Canterbury County Court. The venue would now be Maidstone County Court. Johnny was amazed that the venue was not Canterbury. Apparently, the judge was going to be sitting there and that was that. It was all a learning curve for him—part heard, and now a different venue. Still, at least he had that to look forward to. He decided to sell the Bentley again. He'd only bought it back for sentimental reasons, really. The Mercedes had been confiscated by the Customs. He now needed cash, so he let the Bentley go. He had no real reason to keep it or use it. It had been nice to own and drive but it wasn't really his thing. It would just be a pleasant and expensive memory to have. It certainly wasn't an everyday car, that was for sure.

So soon the trial date came around for a second time. At Maidstone County Court, Johnny met Richard Broadhouse and Stephen Hillman QC again. They had not met or spoke since leaving Canterbury County Court a few months earlier. Mr. Hillman said to him he was pleased with how the first week had gone. Everyone, including Johnny, thought the case was going well. He certainly thought the defence team had spent most of the week on the back foot. He said that he wanted to get back in that space again where they had been before. Everyone was getting on well. All the mini conferences in private rooms at the beginning of the day, after lunch and at the end of the day had gone well. Johnny would go through witness statements and the points that needed to be challenged or covered. The barristers were listening and ticking the boxes.

The second week went well, Johnny thought. The only main concern he had was time again. Time seemed to be running out again, and it did. The witnesses did all manage to finish giving evidence by Friday afternoon. However, it was obvious and agreed by all parties, including the judge, that there would not be time to prepare and give closing arguments. The evidence all got heard but then the judge decided both parties would have to do written closing arguments and submit them to her within six weeks.

Johnny couldn't believe it. Both parties were given six weeks to write and submit their closing arguments? There was never going to be a judgement on Friday, then. The judge was always going to need time to go through the evidence and weigh up her views and the law before reaching her judgement. Mr. Hillman said he was pleased with how it had gone, and so was Johnny. One of the very last remarks from the barrister representing the Prudential to the judge was, 'If you find for the claimant, please note quantum has been agreed.' Up until then, nothing had been agreed. Johnny virtually saw that as a concession of defeat. He thought the defence barrister simply got let down by his witnesses, who did not come across well or as being honest; that was his view.

After leaving court, the barristers and solicitors wanted more funds for the written final arguments. Johnny thought the barristers were bigger crooks than he was. They certainly knew how to ask for money. It was several thousand pounds. He just ignored the letter when it arrived, thinking it could all get sorted out when the matter concluded and the costs issue was dealt with. He was sent a copy of the closing argument which was submitted by the barristers. It just seemed a straightforward explanation of why the plaintiff should succeed and the defence fail in this case. The judge did not set an exact timetable for her written judgement but indicated it would be in the region of about two months after receiving the written arguments. It was more of a guideline than an exact date. Johnny found out the judgement would be sent to the solicitors, not him. Then, about six or seven weeks later, he received a phone call from Peter Watson at Brabners. The judge's clerk had informed both parties in the case that due to the passing away of her husband she was taking time off to deal with the matter. Johnny asked Mr. Watson how long that would be. There was no answer to the question. She was not taking a set period of time off. It didn't have an end date. She was not under any pressure to return until she felt comfortable and able to do so. It did even get mentioned she may never return; at that moment no one could tell. Johnny actually asked, 'If she does not return to work for any reason, what would that mean? Would another judge go through her notes and write a judgement?' 'No,' was the answer. The case would have to be heard all over again by a new judge. That would be the outcome in that event. It was left that as soon as the solicitors knew anything, they would let him know.

You couldn't make this up, Johnny thought. It was now 2002 and the judge who heard the case was off work because of her husband's passing and no judgement had been written or given, and now there was no date for one.

A couple of months went by and Johnny got a phone call

from Brabners Solicitors. The judge's clerk had let both parties know that she had now returned back to work and would let her judgement be known when she finished it. Johnny was out shopping for Christmas presents for his nephew and nieces on a Thursday afternoon in early December when he got a call on his mobile from Peter Watson at Brabners. He was in a good enough mood, looking forward to Christmas. As soon as Peter Watson spoke, he knew it was not good news. Some people speak in monotone so you cannot tell if they are happy or disappointed in a conversation. Peter Watson was not one of those people. He was an up and a down guy, like Johnny, really. His tone told Johnny it was not what he had expected or wanted to hear long before he said, 'Not good news. The judge found for the Prudential.' He told Johnny it was a 25-page written judgement which concluded the plaintiff's case had failed, in her opinion, because of the way it was presented to the insurance company. It covered lots of areas of evidence, law, and her opinion. The Prudential was awarded costs on the basis of her judgement. Peter Watson said he would stick a copy in the post for him to read but wanted to let him know straight away. Johnny was grateful for that – and shell-shocked. He sat and had a coffee and cigarette, tried to digest what he had been told, and just kept shopping with a numb feeling.

The written judgement arrived in the post within a day or two. The judge just simply found against Johnny – that was that. He had discussed the possibility of the appeal process when speaking to Peter Watson. There was no right to appeal. The only right to appeal was if the judge had lost the plot or her mind and misinterpreted the law. The bereavement process may have affected her emotionally but she had not misinterpreted the law. She just chose on the preponderance of the evidence to find for the Prudential and not Johnny. Simply disagreeing with her opinion was not a basis for appeal. With the written judgement came a reminder about the outstanding costs for the written arguments. How much would the Prudential's legal bill be? Johnny had no idea but he knew it would be substantial to say the least.

CHAPTER 16
JOHNNY FACING BANKRUPTCY

JOHNNY WAS skint and was facing the bill for the Prudential costs and the outstanding costs from his solicitors. He did have a few credit cards, including his American Express platinum. He realised he was facing financial ruin so thought, *might as well enjoy the credit cards*. The first thing he did was find a small one-bedroom place to rent. He was looking for a cheap flat but ended up renting a small log cabin in Westwell, near Ashford. He needed an address to live at where he could pay council tax and get a receipt for rent payments and tenancy agreements, but not actually live there. He told the owners who lived next door he worked abroad and was hardly ever at home. He threw a few clothes in there and started going over occasionally and collecting any mail that started turning up for him. He then booked a 3-week P&O Ferries cruise for Sophia and himself from Southampton across to America, around the Caribbean, before returning back to Southampton. It departed on Sunday 5th January 2003 and would return on Saturday 25th January.

The cruise was amazing. It left Southampton, cruised to the

Azores, where it stopped, before finally arriving in America. Johnny always remembered the lady at the Azores telling the passengers that the Azores was where the weather was cooked up. He smiled and remembered thinking, *what a lovely choice of words for how the weather is created.* Johnny had been a little seasick for the first two days. The ship was really comfortable, and the cabin was very elegant and tasteful. The food in the various onboard restaurants was very tasty and unlimited. There were bars everywhere, a wonderful boutique, and really a quite good selection of entertainment. There were lots of onboard daily activities, as well as a casino. Johnny remembered one afternoon seeing a sign by a lounge, which stated "Friends of Bill W Meeting at 2 pm." He had absolutely no idea what that really was or meant. He just thought Bill W, who must be a passenger, had just hired the lounge to entertain a few friends and guests. Perhaps it was his birthday or an anniversary and it was a private party. He didn't know Bill W stood for Bill Wilson, one of the co-founders of Alcoholics Anonymous in America in 1935. Later, he would find out exactly who Bill W was and come to understand that the gathering on the cruise was an Alcoholics Anonymous meeting.

Johnny and Sophia had spent their first holiday together many years earlier on a Caribbean cruise. He had booked a Cunard cruise around the Caribbean. They flew direct to Miami on that occasion, stayed in a hotel overnight, and picked up the cruise ship from Miami port. They had been on several cruises over the years on different cruise lines, either around the Caribbean or the Mediterranean. Every cruise he went on, he always blew his brains away in the casino. He had loved casinos. Roulette, blackjack and dice had been very expensive habits over the years. He'd had some great wins over the years in casinos in Kent and London, but he was a loser overall, as are most people.

He never gambled for pleasure – he gambled to win. He needed that feeling of winning and getting out in front with the cash. He'd had the gambling bug in him since he was a child, whether in casinos, bookmakers or in business. His father knew at a young age he had a problem gambling. Johnny had later met a woman called Tina. She'd told him, 'Gambling is just in your DNA, Johnny,' and she didn't know him that well or for that long before reaching that conclusion. Maybe she had meant in his behaviour in general. She suggested to him he liked cruises because of the casino onboard, not for the other stuff. He had never considered that idea until then. He certainly hadn't known there was a casino on board the first time he booked, so maybe that was not exactly true. The travel, the entertainment, the food, the bars and the casino seemed more fun than sitting on a beach trying to get a tan.

The cash setup on all the cruises was exactly the same. You could not spend cash anywhere on a ship. When you boarded the ship, you would hand over your credit card, and after they had recorded your details, they would issue you with a charge card for the cruise. When the cruise finished, they would present you with your bill, which you paid before disembarkation. That way it avoided any cash transactions or payments on board and virtually did away with all fiddles, Johnny thought, as well as giving passengers the simplicity of one payment method for everything on board. All the cruise liners he travelled on charged for everything in US $. There was only one limitation on the charge card. Each passenger had a daily limit that he or she could charge in the casino for chips. This always made him smile. He could only imagine what some gamblers had charged to their charge cards before daily limits applied to their accounts in the casino on cruise liners. There were probably some really funny and horror stories with no daily limit being applied.

Johnny told Sophia, as usual, that she could spend what she liked on her card but he wanted her daily allowance in the casino. The limit was $250 per passenger. So at least Johnny now had a $500 limit per day. He was determined to enjoy the cruise, but at the same time he could win a few dollars in the casino and get $500 per day, so by his calculation he could get 18 days @$500 that would give him $9000, and if he won say $3000 over the trip, that would mean he would have $12,000 at the end of the cruise. He could get cash for that and charge his card. In reality, every day he and Sophia got their $250 allowance on the cruise charge cards, then he lost it very quickly in the casino. Whatever he tried did not work. There was only roulette or blackjack, and he was just running cold. He never even got any type of winning run together at all. So, he just lost the $9000 in the casino.

Apart from his disastrous run in the casino, it was a nice holiday. When they got to the Caribbean, there had been several chances to disembark for a day or the afternoon and go on organised trips on the various islands. There had been a shopping trip in the Dominican Republic, a show at a hotel in Puerto Rico, drinking local rum on an old sailing boat around Barbados, and he had rented a jet ski off a local guy in the Bahamas. When they were arriving at an island, there were several jet skis going up and down. Once Johnny and Sophia reached the beach area, they found a few guys offering to rent out jet skis. Johnny had never been on a jet ski but it looked appealing.

He rented one jet ski for $30. That seemed reasonable enough, he thought. All you needed to do was put a life jacket on and off you go. Sophia didn't really want a jet ski so he said she could go on the back of his. He and Sophia set off, went out a bit, and then Sophia said she would be ok back at the beach, so he dropped her back at the beach and then shot off on his own. He just thought, *well, I will have a look round the island and see what is going on*. He was totally oblivious to the fact that the hire was for 30 minutes and there were two markers or buoys just off the island to show the area for jet ski use. You could drive around the markers and go backwards and forwards and enjoy your time.

Johnny set off to his right and started going around the island just off the coast line, just exploring, really. He didn't think too much of it. He knew Sophia was on the beach and just went on his way. It took him about an hour and fifteen minutes to go round the island and get back to the beach area where he had set out. The local guy he'd rented it off was waving ferociously at him. Johnny went back to the beach and met the guy. He then started waving at his watch, asking him where he had been and pointing out the markers representing the area for use. He then said the $30 was for half an hour. He wanted more money. Johnny just said it as he saw it; he said he had no idea about the time limit and the area for use and asked the guy why he had not said something at the beginning about time and use. He had never said a word. How was he seriously supposed to understand anything if he had not been told? The guy spoke broken English and just said $30. That was it. He had said yes and off he went. There did appear to be a certain relief that he had returned with the jet ski and no real harm was done. He just kept going on about more money. Johnny thought *bloody cheek*, and told him that he had no more cash on him. It was clearly a terrible breakdown in communication but he had taken umbrage with his shouting and screaming and decided not to pay any more.

By now Johnny knew he was going to struggle with his plan in the casino. That was not working out at all. In Barbados, he noticed a duty-free shop which included jewellery. He started having a look. He had some nice watches which he hardly ever wore. While he was looking, he saw some really expensive Rolex watches, tax free and priced in dollars. He saw a his and hers matching Rolex watches with diamonds. The salesman was keen to help him and, after a while, Johnny had let the salesman convince him that they would be great for him and Sophia, and because they were tax free, the savings meant it would be the cheapest price anywhere in the world. He had his American Express platinum in his back pocket with no pre-set spending limit, so he could charge the $59,000.00 to his card and he would have a receipt as well. With the receipt, in England, he could cash them in anywhere for a decent sum, he thought. After a short sales pitch, Johnny agreed to purchase them. He gave the salesman his card. He put the card through and it came up to call for authorisation. For a large sum like that, it made sense; probably checking it was him using the card. It had certainly been the largest purchase he had made on the card in one transaction. They then asked if they could speak to Johnny, and he was invited behind the counter to a small room with a phone hanging on the wall. He was handed the receiver and left on his own for privacy for the conversation. It all started simply enough. American Express asked if it was him. They asked security questions including name, date of birth, address and other security questions to confirm he was who he said he was. Then they asked about the purchase amount and the purpose of the transaction. After a brief conversation, they advised him that his separate credit card with them had nearly reached his limit and had not been paid recently. He apologised and explained the only reason for the delay in the payment was the fact that he was on holiday in the Caribbean for a month and would correct that when he got home. The American Express representative said in the circumstances, they could not authorise the transaction. They explained to him that once he got home and paid his credit card, they may review their decision, which he took as a nice way of being told, 'You are taking the biscuit, mate.' It was suggested he should not use the card again until he got home to England and settled his other account.

He returned to the main shop and said that unfortunately they would not authorise due to complications in England that he had overlooked. The salesman smiled and said, 'No problem, we can use another card to complete the purchase.' Johnny thought, *as if*, and he politely explained he did not have another card on him he could use. The salesman said, 'No problem, if you give me your details, you can ring and pay when you get home, and we will send them to you.' At this point Johnny and Sophia left the shop. Deep down Johnny admired the man's persistence. He must have been on commission, he thought. Johnny had offered his American Express platinum as the preferred payment method for Johnny and Sophia's charge cards on the cruise. Straight away, he realised that was going to be declined as well now.

So, after the Caribbean Islands stops, it was back up to America and back home across the Atlantic, stopping of at the Azores on the way. The trip back and the entertainment were good. The food was always good, and they had a few days left to enjoy the end of the cruise. He told Sophia just go and get whatever you want in the ladies' boutique and shops. Unless he hit the jackpot on the last two days in the casino, he knew he couldn't settle the bill. About three days from home, he had a polite message left in his cabin that he needed to go to reception and ask for a certain lady. He didn't think anything of it. When he got there, she politely explained to him that the American Express card he'd lodged at the beginning of the cruise had now come up as unable to be used. He politely thanked her, and explained that while he was in Barbados there had been an issue with the card which he could not resolve until he got back home to England. He then gave her a credit card that at least was still in use. She thanked him and that was that. Clearly, they were not keeping tabs on his spending, he thought, while he was on the cruise, and for that he was grateful. Of course, in reality, why would they? People were there to enjoy themselves and spend money.

The cost of the cruise had been an arm and a leg to start with, so there were probably an awful lot of affluent people on the cruise. He had met one such lady on the cruise in the casino. She walked about like she owned the ship. She was tipping all the croupiers more than he had been gambling. She was an unremarkable-looking woman about 50 years of age, not particularly well dressed, but whenever she entered the casino all the staff, including waiters and waitresses, as well as croupiers, could not do enough for her. She and Johnny never really had a conversation but when she was not there, he asked one of the croupiers who she was. He told Johnny she was an heiress to an American oil company. She was the only daughter of the founder and stood to inherit everything one day. She had travelled on the maiden voyage and liked the ship that much that after that she did a deal with P&O Cruises. The deal was she would pay a fixed fee for one of the penthouse cabins with butler service on the ship, 52 weeks per year. It was her place for the year. Then she just got on and off as she pleased. She had a list of all the destinations the ship would be at on what dates and just got on and off at her convenience. She literally spent a few months a year flying round the world meeting the ship wherever it was and coming aboard. She paid for the whole year and did what she wanted. She always ate in her cabin and rarely visited the restaurants, apparently.

The table Johnny and Sophia were allocated in the main dining hall for breakfast and dinner had accommodated an unusual but colourful group of people, all from different backgrounds. Johnny and Sophia were one of four couples.

Generally, Johnny thought they had been fortunate with the table they were on for breakfast and dinner. They consisted of an Irish colonel and his wife, who seemed to be in their late seventies or early eighties but were good company. That was Liam and Mary. Mary was very elegant, softly spoken, and didn't say too much. She always dressed very well. Liam had served in the Irish army all his life and reached the rank of colonel before retiring. He told Johnny that everything the Americans ever did was always over the top in matters of war. He said that if an operation needed 20 men, the Irish or English armies would send 20 men in two or three vehicles or choppers. If the Americans did the same operation, they would send 250 men and a fleet of vehicles. He just always believed they were over the top.

Richard and Sue were from Hackney. Richard was the finance director of Fiat UK and was clearly very successful. Johnny and Richard got on quite well, passing time away with light conversations and stories. Johnny never really hit it off with Sue, his wife, but Sophia liked her and they got on well enough. Then there was Ray and his Elaine. Ray was a lawyer and had worked all over the world, in Hong Kong, Russia, and was a tax exile in England. It meant he could only live in England so may days a year because he worked abroad and paid no taxes on his income in England. It was Ray who told Johnny about his friend who was also a lawyer falling in love with a Russian prostitute, then agreeing to buy her out of her employment with the Russian mob so they could be together and marry. After he paid the agreed price, they killed both of them as an example to others. Sophia actually swapped numbers with Sue and Richard and agreed to have dinner when they were back in England. Canterbury and Hackney were not that far apart, and they did meet up and have dinner on one occasion at the Bridgewood Manor hotel in Medway. The food was nice but it was a kind of one-off thing that never went anywhere after that.

Johnny never hit the jackpot in the casino, and by the time they got back to Southampton, they had packed all their clothes. All they needed to do now was settle their bill and find their car after disembarking the ship after breakfast. Johnny went over to ask for his bill. It was extremely busy, with everyone just paying their accounts before leaving the ship. He had to queue and wait his turn to get the opportunity to pay. When a cashier became free, he gave the cashier the charge cards back. She found the right cabin and started printing off the bill. The printer kept printing. After a while she looked at him, smiled and said, 'Perhaps it's a mistake.' The bill was several pages long. Then she looked at the total, which was $14,000.00, and politely said, 'Would you like me to get that checked for you?' He looked at it and replied, 'No, thanks, it seems about right.' She then raised her eyebrows. Johnny then pulled out his credit card and presented it for payment. The payment was declined. The cashier seemed more embarrassed than he was. He explained he had intended to use his American Express but due to a technicality in the Bahamas, which he could not foresee, that was now not possible. His credit card probably didn't have sufficient funds available on it to cover the bill in pounds. How was this going to pan out, he thought. She simply smiled at him and said 'I understand. Would you like us to send you the bill?' 'Yes,' he replied. 'That would be great.' He gave her his Westwell address and thanked her for her time. Johnny and Sophia then got off the ship for the drive back from Southampton Docks to Chilham.

The drive home was about 140 miles, depending on traffic, about two or three hours. After about an hour driving, Johnny was hungry again, which made him laugh. All that food that was available on the ship 24 hours per day, virtually, including room service. Within two hours of leaving the ship, he'd stopped in the KFC in the services, hungry. When Johnny and Sophia got home, there was mail everywhere. After unpacking, Johnny started opening the mail. There was the outstanding account at the Brabners Solicitors. Then there were a few credit card statements that he had not transferred to Westwell yet. Then he opened a letter from a firm of solicitors in Ashford representing the Prudential. They were attaching a copy of the costs incurred in legal fees as a result of the civil case. Johnny couldn't believe it. The total bill was £270,000.00. That seemed a bit steep, he thought, not that he was in the mood to argue about the total. They asked for payment or proposals of how the bill would be settled within a certain time frame.

On Monday Johnny was feeling in a sarcastic mood. He picked the phone up to the solicitors, thanked them for the bill, and told them he would need time to pay. Could they give him a few weeks to sort things out; he had not realised how much the bill would be. The guy on the other end of the phone was so polite and took him so seriously. He said, 'Of course we can give you a few weeks to sort your finances out.' Johnny had just been bored and was playing with the guy, in reality. He never did settle his American Express credit card, and very quickly they started threatening legal action by post and phone. He just kept living on his credit cards. There had been some credit left on some of them and that was just paying the bills, so to speak. A few weeks later he phoned the solicitor back and let him know he could not settle the bill. That was it. He told him, 'I will leave the matter in your hands.' Then he received a threat of bankruptcy from American Express. They were clearly not impressed by his behaviour and wanted paying. American Express were good to their word; soon after that, they launched legal proceedings in the

County Court at Canterbury, petitioning for him to be made bankrupt.

Johnny never argued about the facts and was declared bankrupt in 2003. He had to show all his assets, explain the circumstances, and the rest was up to the Official Receivers. He made the mistake of wearing a nice watch to the meeting with the Official Receiver, and the man asked for it and took it. Johnny had not allowed for or thought about that, but after that meeting he very quickly realised they wanted anything and everything of any value, including jewellery. He explained to the Official Receiver he was unemployed; he had signed on after coming back from the cruise, otherwise he would have to explain how he lived. He explained he'd lost the civil case in 2002. He had solicitors' bills, credit card debt, and he left it all with them. He would be bankrupt for a period of three years, and any substantial income or money that he got during that period would need to be declared to the Official Receivers and paid to them for his creditors.

Johnny had no money at all. Thank God the house was owned by Oak Trading, otherwise that would have been gone. He was fresh out of ideas and had lost the plot, really. It had all come tumbling down quite quickly, with the gambling, the loss of the court case, and now being declared bankrupt. He agreed a fair price and valuation for his watch and was able to buy it back for that valuation. He liked the watch and still has it today.

He didn't really have any zest or desire to start a business, so he thought he would sell the house and use the money to make a fortune, either by trading in stocks and shares or gambling. That seemed like a logical plan to him. He put the house on the market for £325,000.00 with Ward and Partners in Canterbury. He agreed a fee of 2% for a sole agent basis. A few prospective buyers turned up, but none of them seemed too keen to put forward an offer. Then, one day, a guy made an appointment to view the house. Sophia was out so Johnny was going to show him round. The doorbell went. He answered, and standing there was a young man about 30 years of age, well built, very polite. Mr Salmon. Johnny introduced himself. Mr Salmon soon identified himself as Steve. Steve stood on the doorstep and they chatted for about 10 to 15 minutes about the area, the local services, the garden, the home and life. Steve had a partner and they were considering buying the house together. Steve was clearly a go-getter, Johnny thought. He had a very positive attitude towards life. Once the conversation had finished, Johnny invited him in and showed him around the house, then finished up by showing him the three quarters of an acre gardens and the shed where he kept his Honda tractor for cutting the large lawn area at the top of the banks. Steve asked if the Honda would be for sale as well. The small Honda tractor was perfect for cutting the grass, and the shed had been converted at the front so the tractor could be driven in and out and parked up when not being used. 'Yes,' he replied, the tractor was for sale. Steve seemed keen on the tractor at the time, and Johnny realised that was a bonus, because he probably wouldn't have a use for it in the future. Steve said he was interested and left to discuss it with his partner.

Johnny said, 'If you want to come back again, here is my mobile. Give me a ring and we can agree a time and day. He told him no point ringing the agents. Steve rang back a day later and wanted to come and view it again with his partner. They agreed a time and day. They turned up in a new Volvo estate and jumped out of the car, a young couple full of life. They looked like they were young and in love, Johnny thought. After viewing the house and the tractor, they ended up in the garden again. She clearly liked it and almost gave Steve the 'I want it' look. Steve and

Johnny spoke on their own, and Steve made an offer. It really was not a long conversation. After a few minutes they agreed on £320k and no agents fees. The end of the two months was nearly up, and Johnny asked the agents next day to come and collect their board and take it off the market. Steve and Johnny also agreed £750 for the Honda. The deal proceeded with not too many hitches. They had nowhere to sell. It was a straightforward valuation and mortgage application, which once approved meant the sale could proceed. It took about ten weeks from agreement to completion.

To live and have some cash during that period, Johnny had borrowed £10k in cash from a local money lender he knew. The weekly interest seemed reasonable and Johnny told him he was selling a property and he would pay him back on completion. So, once the sale went through, he paid the loan back. Johnny and Sophia then rented a 3-bedroom semidetached house in Chestfield, which they moved straight into on the same day the sale of High Hopes completed.

CHAPTER 17
BUYING AN INDUSTRIAL UNIT IN WHITSTABLE

ONCE HE HAD PAID six months in advance on the property in Primrose Way, Chestfield, and the loan back, Johnny had £300k in the bank. That was his stake to gamble and invest with, which meant he could get in front again and buy another house. One night he went to a dog track in Milton Keynes. He didn't have much cash on him. A friend had a dog racing there, and he went for the evening out with no great expectations of anything, really. After all, with no cash in his pocket, what could happen? He had never been to Milton Keynes Dog Track before. There were a few open races on the card that evening. When he arrived, Johnny thought what an unremarkable place it was. It was a small principal dog track. The facilities were mediocre at best.

Before the first race, Johnny went out of nosiness and looked at the betting market. There was a line of about eight bookmakers, and one of them was T&F Racing. He knew these lads from the horse-racing days. There were two partners who were like chalk and cheese. Mark seemed really intelligent, educated and cultured. Robin just seemed so rough and ready and down to earth. They came from such different backgrounds, but both had a great love and fascination with bookmaking. The only thing Johnny knew about them for certain was that they were loaded and players. If you wanted a chunk of money on a horse at the race track, these guys simply had a reputation for accommodating you. Lots of bookmakers will lay bets only up to a certain size. They seemed to want to have the reputation of laying any size bet. They had always laid him at the race course. He had done a lot of business with Mark and Robin at Lingfield all-weather race meetings previously. T&F must have been their surnames. They had started at the horses at the same time he had, but they had invested a lot heavier in pitches at places like Ascot, Newmarket and Cheltenham. They gave over £100k for their Cheltenham pitch alone.

They offered to lay him prices off the tissue for the dogs, which meant he could see the prices in advance and get accommodated. Johnny smiled and said, 'I haven't got any cash on me this evening, so I will not be playing.' They simply said, 'That is not a problem at all. You can have what you want with us and just call the bets and we can settle up later.' Johnny thanked them and walked off. Suddenly, he was off and running. No money in his pocket but unlimited credit with the biggest layers he knew for the race meeting. He smiled and thought, 'Great, a good opportunity to win a thousand or two.' He was now happy he had gone. He left the first race and had a coffee at the tea bar. He started slowly after the second race, and by the end of the evening he had not found one winner. He walked out owing T&F Racing £20k. Mark said, 'You can bet on the phone with us at the horses.' He thanked them. Within one week, Johnny had not backed one winner at the horses. He only needed one winner, because he always rolled up the size of his bets. He now owed them £100k. Johnny couldn't walk straight or get out of bed. He had never lost £100k in a week before. Shortly after that he paid them, in a total meltdown and panic by now. He felt depressed, suicidal, and that life was not worth living anymore.

Soon after this Johnny got in a conversation with a guy he knew called Lee. He didn't know him that well but he knew he was in the transport business. Lee explained he had managed to get a container load out of Tilbury Docks. He had a contact there and it would become a regular thing. The containers were from China. The first one was a container of hedge trimmers. They were a Chinese make and all new. Johnny didn't think this through properly. All he heard was that regular containers were going to be coming out of Tilbury Docks and he could get in on it.

Johnny just bought the whole container load for what seemed a good price at the time. In reality, they were a low end, bottom of the range, cheap product to start with. He had nowhere to put them or no one to sell them to. Very quickly, he realised they were just a headache. No one he knew even wanted them, really. They were a brand that no one had ever heard of. They did work ok – he tried them out – but he kept meeting people who would say they would have one or two, but that was not what he was trying to do. In the end, he was giving people he knew loads of them on the basis they could pay after they sold them. He ended up taking a loss on the stock he had. To store some of them, he had filled up the home at Primrose Way with them. It was just chock-a-block; there was not even any space to live in left.

He'd been playing cards in Medway one evening and was driving home when he got pulled over by the police on a routine traffic stop. It was late at night. Johnny didn't think too much of it. He got out gave his name and address. He knew the car was taxed and insured. He was driving Sophia's car. He had not been drinking, so nothing to worry about. It turned out there was a warrant out for his arrest for failing to attend court for traffic offences. There had been confusion around his old address and the new address. Then there was confusion around permission to use Sophia's car. Had he stolen it, they asked. The situation very quickly seemed to get out of hand at the roadside. Next thing, a van full of police turned up and he was arrested and taken to the local police station. He had been handcuffed and taken into the custody area. Johnny couldn't believe the way he was being treated. He had been arrested for traffic offences or not turning up at court for traffic offences. He had been man handled in and out of the van in a very aggressive manner, he thought. He was marched into the police station like some sort of armed thug, he thought. With his hands still in handcuffs, he just said to the custody sergeant, 'I want to make a complaint. I know why I have been arrested but I am being treated like a terrorist.' At that point the police officers changed their attitude. They stopped holding him and took him out of the handcuffs, and slowly left the area.

He started to try to explain to the custody sergeant that it was Sophia's car, they had lived together at the previous address, they lived together now, and he had her permission to drive the car. The custody sergeant then asked Johnny if he sent some police officers round the house to verify everything, would that be ok with him? It was at this point Johnny realised and remembered the house was full of the stolen hedge trimmers. He couldn't say no, otherwise it would make matters worse, but the last thing he wanted was the police round at Primrose Way knocking Sophia up out of bed to clarify and verify the situation. He then said,

'You can ring her if you don't believe me.' He had her number with her name on in his mobile. The police rang and she said who she was and confirmed that he had permission to drive her car that evening. That had saved the day. At least now he didn't have to worry about making up a story about the origins of hedge trimmers, and neither did Sophia.

He was kept overnight in the police station and taken to court the next morning to answer to the charges. It turned out that the matter had just totally got out of hand because of his failing to attend court. The motoring offence allegations against him were not true. He could prove it and did. He did have a licence and had not been banned, and the vehicle he was previously driving was insured. He was free to go after explaining about moving homes. His version of events was checked with DVLA while he was in the local magistrates by the clerk.

Johnny met a guy in Medway called Steve. Steve had made a lot of money out of prostitution – or massage parlours, as they are often referred to. After speaking to him and hearing how he ran his business, he decided he was going to give it another go. The only experience he had in this area was the one previous experience with Mikey and Doug in Gravesend, but after speaking to Steve, he saw that type of business in a new light. Johnny didn't know much about him but he had a Mercedes AMG and owned an awful lot of properties in the Medway and Maidstone area. Johnny decided to open a massage parlour and give it a go.

Sophia found an industrial unit for sale on the Joseph Wilson Business Park just behind Tesco's in Whitstable. The idea of owning the industrial unit appealed to him; that way there were no landlords to please or leases and agreements to sign. In an ideal world, the industrial unit would have been bigger. It was a little on the small side, but after gaining access and taking the exact measurements, Johnny did a quick sketch plan of how the layout could be inside and it was just about big enough, he decided. The unit was in total disrepair and needed totally rebuilding inside, as well as some work outside. It did have a number of factors in its favour. It was freehold, it was cheap, it was on an industrial estate opposite a factory, and while it didn't come with much parking, there was unlimited parking very close by on the industrial estate. It was only connected to one other building, and that was an optician's.

Johnny made an offer for the freehold and it was accepted. He used the offshore company, Oak Trading, to buy the unit. So there was a landlord on paper, but it was just an offshore company that he owned; perfect, he thought. After having the offer agreed, both parties instructed solicitors. The unit had previously been used for storage and had been left empty for years. It would need a change of use for the building. It was going to be a health club. The application was submitted to Canterbury City Council. Having a small health club on an industrial estate should not raise any concerns at the council, and it didn't. The purchase and change of use application were ongoing. In the meantime, Johnny was granted access to the unit with various builders and tradesmen, to get quotes for the work that was needed. He had never project-manged any building work before.

Sophia knew a carpenter called Tony Green. He had done some work for her previously on one of the flats she owned at Hersden. Tony came out and gave a quote to do most of the work apart from some electrical work, re-tile the whole place and rebuild one side of the unit which needed to be rebuilt and have some new windows installed. Johnny also got a quote from a local builder called Colin to do the building job at one side of the unit. He also got an electrician to quote for the electrical work.

He got a price from a local flooring firm and found a new spa he could get, as well as a new sauna. They both ticked the boxes in terms of size to fit in. The rest of the accessories and furnishings could all be bought locally. Johnny accepted all the quotes from the tradesmen and asked them to just tell him how much the bill would be for the work done. He really didn't mind what the figures were but was on a budget and had no real idea or interest in the difference between quotes and estimates. Johnny thought he was simple to have a deal with, and in reality he was; many people had told him that. In all his business affairs, he always paid the price agreed for anything but would take it really personally or badly if people tried to change the agreed prices.

By the time the purchase was completed by the solicitors and the change of use had been granted by Canterbury City Council, Johnny had a detailed plan for the layout, down to the last inch, had ordered the spa and sauna, and had given the tradesmen the deposits they required to start the work. It didn't go as exactly according to plan as he had hoped. Johnny and the builders were probably not a match made in heaven.

Tony had a partner whom Johnny knew nothing about called Herbert. Tony and Herbert had a gang of lads they employed between them. After a while, Tony said he needed more money to do the job. The whole floor was uneven and needed levelling up. Johnny couldn't believe it. More money? The guy sounded like Oliver Twist, Johnny thought. He was about to learn about the difference between a quote and an estimate. Johnny was not amused. He said, 'I am not interested in that stuff. I told you exactly what I wanted. I told you I wanted a price for the whole job. So that's your problem.' There was a big disagreement about this term, "extras", and Johnny being told that it was another few thousand just to have a level floor. Very quickly he agreed he had to have a level floor, and so agreed to more money, but made it clear that there were no more extras at all. The building had not changed in any way. Tony pointed out he could not see certain things when he gave the price. No real harm done, but it was totally agreed that the job would be completed as agreed and for no more money from that point on.

Colin came along and started the other building job, which was rebuilding a wall of the unit and installing windows. Very quickly it became apparent that Colin was not up to the job. He had a relative with him who was doing the brickwork. It was embarrassing. Even Johnny thought he could do a quicker job than that guy was. He was laying one brick, having a cigarette and looking at the job. He was so slow. Everyone was laughing, including Johnny, but it was not funny. Colin had not been recommended by anyone. Johnny had just picked him out of the local paper in Whitstable and assumed he was up to the job.

Then Tony and Herbert let him know that the work was not up to scratch and the bricks and the windows were not even going to be level. The wall had not been built straight. Johnny knew they were right but had never factored this into the equation. A builder who couldn't build. Perhaps he was just like Johnny when Johnny got in the roofing business as a teenager. Johnny did know Colin was a family man with a home and family in Whitstable, so he questioned how a grown man supporting a family could pretend to be a builder or take on jobs he could not do. Anyway, perhaps that was a bit deep; the reality was he couldn't do what he had agreed to. Johnny had paid him a deposit. That was that, to be blunt. He could see the job was no good with his naked eye, but Tony and Herbert went over the work and wrote down in builders' terms exactly what was wrong with the work to date.

The next day Johnny approached Colin, who had seemed a very reasonable nice man to Johnny when they first met. Colin did not take the criticism well and very quickly they fell out. Colin took it all very personally. Johnny just kept saying, 'The job has got to be right, and it isn't.' Then Colin asked for more money. Johnny was speechless. It wasn't going well.

The next day a friend of Johnny's, David, came to visit and catch up. They met for breakfast and Johnny started showing him the unit and what he was doing and telling him about the builders. David did not know any details at all about Mikey's murder but there were rumours and people had their own opinions, of course. He looked at Johnny, laughed and said, 'The way it is going, you may end up with a few dead bodies in the cellar.' Without more money to start again Colin was not going to continue, he was so two-bob, Johnny had realised. They fell out and parted company. He was glad to get rid of him and accept the loss, as he saw it. He needed someone else to put the job straight and finish it. Tony and Herbert said they would do it all when they finished what they were already working on. Great, Johnny thought, and agreed it. They would complete that work after they finished their own. Then Colin turned funny with Johnny about money. He said Johnny owed him more money for what he had done. He said the original deposit had been spent on materials and he was owed for the labour costs of the work that had been done. Johnny hadn't seen this coming. Labour costs for people who did work that was sub-standard at best and appalling at worst. It certainly wasn't what was agreed at the beginning.

He agreed to meet Colin on site on Saturday morning, when no one else would be there, and discuss it. He still had the list of what was wrong with the work that had been done to date. So, Saturday morning came around and Colin turned up with two massive guys. Johnny had never seen these guys before. Who were they, he wondered. Perhaps they were builders or colleagues, or perhaps not, he very quickly thought. He thought maybe they were there to intimidate him. It looked like that and felt like that. They didn't speak but were standing next to Colin and listening. Colin did the talking first. He was saying that he was owed money for the labour and wanted paying. Everyone was listening. By now Johnny was furious, absolutely seething. He was listening to a builder wanting money for a proper lash-up job, and to make the whole matter worse, it felt like Colin had brought a couple of heavies along to intimidate him. After Colin finished, he brought out his list and ran through it, with Colin in front of these guys and them listening to the disagreements. At the end of explaining to Colin again what was wrong with it all, Johnny looked at the two heavies and said, 'I have no idea who you two are or why you are here but if you are here to intimidate me or apply pressure for money, please remember this. I can't fight. I am not paying him or you any money. Just remember, whatever you do to me, I promise you, I know someone who is going to do three times worse to you, and you know he will find out where you live and who you are, because Colin will tell him. He will go to Colin first and Colin will tell him.' He meant it as well. That was the end of the matter. They all got back in the car and left. Johnny never heard from Colin after that.

He was starting to play cards again a lot in Medway. He went to a game one day and there were a few new faces there. Most people at these games were either car dealers or involved in criminal activities one way or another. There were large sums of cash involved. Importation of drugs seemed to be a common occupation. Part time or full time, half of them were at it and would quite openly discuss it. Johnny realised half of them were doing business together. When George was alive, he had told him a lot of car dealers he had known were into drugs as well. It just seemed to be how it was. When everyone used to and you could trade openly in cash in really large amounts, it was a very easy way to clean money up, whatever the amount. Some of these guys had massive second-hand car sales and could fill them with hundreds of thousands of pounds of stock quite easily. It was a great way to clean their drug money up, as well as building properties and paying everyone in cash.

Johnny was introduced to a guy called Lee Glazer. He had never met him before. He knew nothing about him. Lee was a car dealer who was in business with his uncle Paul in the Medway area. He wasn't into the drugs in any way – taking them, importing them or buying and selling them. Johnny and Lee got on instantly and agreed to swap numbers for future card games. He and Lee would become close friends over the next few years. They were both hooked on gambling. That was the instant connection and common language. It turned out Lee lived in Rushenden on the Isle of Sheppey. Johnny knew the Isle of Sheppey well from when he used to go to work with his dad, George, when he was younger. He had spent a lot of time in Sheerness Docks and Sheerness Steel Mill as a child when George had been in the haulage business. He and Lee even knew a lot of the same people.

Johnny and Sophia split up and stopped living together. It was an acrimonious split. Sophia pointed out she had not changed or done anything wrong. She was right. It wasn't about her. It was about him. He just wanted to move on and start afresh. He went and stayed with his mum before getting a flat in Canterbury. Sophia decided to go and live with her relatives in Guernsey and work there.

The work at the unit did get completed. The flooring contractors turned up, did a great job, and Johnny paid them. If only everyone had been so easy to deal with as they were. It should always be like that, but life just doesn't seem to go that way a lot of the time. Perhaps it would take the fun and the drama out of life if it did. One of Johnny's friends said to him one day, 'You do like a drama,' and he knew a few stories about him. Perhaps Johnny was addicted to drama as well. How much was enough? How much was enough of anything? Interesting questions. Johnny had never really thought about the answers that much! The electrician turned up and did the work. There was a problem about paying him and that got out of hand for a bit but got resolved without any real drama.

So Tony, Herbert and their team finished the wall, installed new windows, as also did the additional building work they had taken over from Colin. They did a good job. Then Tony told him how much extra he owed him for the extra work. Johnny was shocked. He had not asked for a price. That had been a mistake. So, a disagreement followed about the bill. Their bill was substantially more than Colin's original quote had been, and they had taken the job over with all the materials for the job and part of the work done. Johnny couldn't work out how, for the time spent on the job, the bill could be so much. Very quickly Johnny and Tony disagreed about the figure. Johnny tried to haggle and put his case. He thought he was being reasonable, offering to pay a certain amount for the job. Tony was adamant that was not enough and Johnny owed what he wanted. Johnny felt like they had done the job, so he did owe them, but by now everyone knew it was not going to be a health club and he felt like *he* was being priced up, not the job. He had always paid them in large amounts of cash and on time for what they did. It really felt to him that they were trying to get a large bonus on completion. They never did agree a figure in the middle or strike a deal. They just quickly fell out and it got all personal.

There were no more phone calls about it. Then, one day Johnny was driving through Canterbury with his tunes blaring out on the radio and he noticed behind him Tony and Herbert in an estate car. Johnny was heading to his flat over at Wincheap but was totally on the other side of the city. Was it just a coincidence? Tony lived locally. Johnny didn't know where Herbert lived, they both worked locally. So he did a few left and right turns and was just driving to see if they were following him. Every time he turned off, they followed. Whichever route he took, they were always behind him. At this point he knew they were following him. Perhaps they saw him driving, decided to follow him and surprise him and talk about the outstanding matter. Now Johnny knew that they were following him, he turned into Nunnery Fields, and drove up there a little until the road got a lot wider and cars could pass easily on both sides. Then he pulled over on the left-hand side of the road, parked up and got out. They pulled up behind him and Herbert got out of the car. Johnny had no idea until many years later, when he would meet Tony again in very different circumstances, that Herbert told Tony he was going to kill Johnny. Did he literally mean it or was it just a figure of speech? He was extremely angry and an intimidating figure. They argued in the street about the amount and didn't reach agreement over a figure. Whether he was right or wrong, Johnny was offering to pay something. He just felt that they were trying to take advantage. After a while he told Herbert where to go. If Herbert had haggled and negotiated, it could have been agreed and paid. Herbert tried to intimidate him. Now it just meant they were both extremely angry and shouting at each other. Johnny got back in his car and left. He got out of his car where he lived and walked in. They had followed him again but when he went in, they drove off. He never heard from them or saw them after that.

The unit did open shortly after that. The opticians next door, owned by Joe and his wife, were clearly aware of what the place was going to be. Over the time Johnny had started talking to Joe on and off. Joe had a lot of experience dealing with builders. Johnny had shown Joe the work and inside as time had gone on. Joe pointed out a few things to him about certain parts of the work that Johnny then pointed out to the builders. Joe also said to Johnny that he was getting a good job done, which was reassuring to hear from an impartial third party. It turned out Joe had a lot of building work done on properties over the years and was a very successful business man who had a beautiful large country home a few miles away in Herne. One day he and Joe were standing on one side of the unit, looking at the building work and talking in general. Joe said to him, 'Have you thought of putting a red light on top? You might earn a few quid.' Johnny didn't comment and Joe said, 'Good night,' before getting in his car and driving off.

The layout had been based on Steve's place at Medway and was going to be run on the same basis. Since Johnny had started buying the unit and converting it, Steve and his partner Hannah had been arrested and were facing various charges ranging from brothel management to money laundering, as well as other financial crimes. Johnny basically copied his business model and admitted to borrowing a few ideas from him. Steve told him that one of his biggest headaches and problems was that he had taken credit cards and it was all traceable and could be proven, whereas all the cash would be gone and there was no record of it. For that reason alone, Johnny decided not to take credit card payments. He advertised for a receptionist. Sophie, a young woman from Canterbury, was the best of the candidates, he thought. She had no idea or experience of running a brothel but was keen and willing to learn.

Trade was slow to begin with. All the ads were put in the local free papers, on websites and in the Daily Sport, which used to show adverts from a lot of people in the business. Johnny took out ads for staff as well. Slowly but surely, the phone did ring and staff applied and turned up as well. It seemed a slow process. He knew the first month was the hardest and slowest month, because there was no repeat custom, obviously. Steve had pointed this out to him.

CHAPTER 18
PROSTITUTION AND DRUGS

THE GENERAL CONSENSUS in the brothel and escort business is that a good woman is what is required on the phone as the receptionist or the maid. That made sense to Johnny. A man expects to talk to a woman before deciding if he wants to be a customer or not. Sophie was not a natural on the phone to start with, but she was a woman and she picked everything up quite quickly. She had cards and telephone scripts to follow. She had all the required information for people to visit or escorts to visit. Johnny would sit with her in the office and kitchen area at the unit and encourage her as much as possible to smile when talking on the phone and try to inject some passion and enthusiasm into her voice, including when giving out girls' descriptions. He knew it would all come across a lot better for potential customers.

He had never quite understood how much drink and drugs played a major part in the industry. In the years that followed, he realised that about 90% of the people involved in the business had drug habits, alcohol issues, or possibly both. In all honesty, most women only do the job to finance drug and alcohol addiction. There were a few who did it purely for the money for a specific purpose – maybe single mothers supporting their children, saving to start a business or possibly a deposit on a house – and then would stop, but they were a minority. So 11 am was the daily opening time and by 11.15 am he and the staff were either drinking or up at Tesco's getting the drink. After a couple of glasses, everyone loosened up and it just became normal. Johnny didn't want anyone drunk, but being tipsy seemed quite normal after a while. Sophie couldn't drink too much, and she didn't drink much in any case. He had security cameras installed for security purposes and to record how many clients came in each day.

After a while Sophie started running the place and trade started to pick up. New staff turned up and it slowly started to become a business. He would keep out of the place and just go back at the end of the day to lock up. Sophie had his phone number if she needed to speak to him. Johnny started going out with one of the girls at the unit after closing. It was just to drink and get high together after work. Her name was Rebecca. They only went out a few times. That soon fizzled out. Then, one day, Johnny wanted some skunk. He had never tried skunk before. In fact, he had never taken drugs before. Johnny had always been a heavy smoker. He asked Tony, who was back in the drugs business, if he could get him some skunk – and he did. It was just enough for one joint. Johnny tried it for the first time one Sunday, when he was in the unit covering the phone if Louise – whose working name was Sian – was busy. He loved it instantly. He got the giggles and just could not stop laughing. He then went into a state of meltdown and was totally paranoid. He rang Tony and explained. Tony said to him he was high as a kite. He advised him to eat chocolate. Just keep eating chocolate – and he did. Very quickly Johnny had the munchies and could not stop eating chocolate he had got from Tesco's. Later that day he felt relatively normal again. He rang Tony again and bought some more for his personal use. He was just about to become a daily user and a drug addict.

The magic of the drugs for Johnny was in that all his real problems went away the moment he inhaled. Wow – the power of drug addiction and running away from his own reality. The skunk was a bit too much for him, because once he smoked a joint his day was over. He never really lit a spliff and just had a couple of draws or tugs on it and let it go out. If he lit a spliff he would smoke it, so he tried not to smoke spliffs until later in the day. So now Johnny was a daily drinker, heavy smoker, and would smoke drugs in the evening. Often, he would sit at home and drink and drug himself to oblivion to end the day. Johnny lived on his own in his flat in Canterbury. He had a spare bedroom and a sofa, so if any northern girls came down to work for a few days, as they did, he would put them up at his place overnight.

One morning Sophie said to him there was a new girl coming in for an interview, so he hung about. In walks this woman in her 30s and says she is Carly but uses Kate as a work name. She brought her passport for ID purposes, which no one ever had before. *It's not that sort of job*, he thought. So, they were standing in the kitchen at about 11.30 am and he just opened a beer and started drinking from the can. He offered her a beer and she had one. She had previously worked for an escort firm in London and was working as a dancer in a club in London but moved down from London and was looking for a job. She had the long blond hair extensions, implants, and looked good, he thought. She certainly knew how to make the most of her appearance. So, they agreed a start date and Johnny finished his beer and left. After the unit had been open for a while, there were a lot of staff who turned up and gave it a go for a while. A lot of the staff tended to stay at places for a few months and move on. There were lots of different girls turning up from all over, with different backgrounds and experiences in life.

One girl, Kadine, left school one day and started the next. She was bang on the cocaine, it would turn out, but you don't exactly talk about that at the informal interviews, and it almost becomes a blur in the end – who is on what, who is admitting to it, who is doing it and not admitting to it. Everything is just a web of lies in reality. Johnny remembered one day a really stunning girl turned up from Tunbridge Wells. She said her name was Sammi. She looked like a model, he thought. Anyway, she started with two other girls that day. It was a really busy day and she had seen most of the clients. At about 7 pm she said she was just going to Tesco's and threw her coat on. When Sophie went to meet a new customer at the door, Sammi took the whole takings for the day from a box in the drawer in the office and skipped off, never to be seen again or answer her mobile. When Sophie returned, she realised the money had gone and so had Sammi. Johnny was far from amused but it was all a learning curve and it only happened once. Johnny paid the other girls for what they had done. It was not their fault, he realised that.

After about two or three months, there seemed to be a very good mix of staff who were reliable, or as reliable as can be expected in that business, some good regular customers, as well as daily passing trade. The business actually started to earn money. It wasn't what he had hoped for but it was beginning to work out, and he realised you needed several places to make some serious cash. Sophie was pregnant with her first child and decided to leave. Johnny advertised for a receptionist. Camilla turned up. She was young and lived in her parents' pub in Whitstable with her boyfriend, who worked for P&O Ferries. She picked the job up quite quickly and got on well with most of the girls. She liked drink and drugs as well, but kind of had it a bit more under control than most, Johnny thought.

One afternoon Rachael, Tony's girlfriend, phoned Johnny and told him that Tony had been arrested for a drug offence and was unlikely to get bail because of his antecedence. He had many previous convictions and had spent time in prison for drug offences. At that time there was a copper in Canterbury who seemed to have Tony on his radar 24/7. He clearly knew what Tony was doing, and Tony had upset him a few times by evading capture in his car and on foot. Tony had given him the slip once too often and the pair seemed to be in constant battle with each other. Johnny didn't think anything of it. Then she said he had taken 40k of skunk from a guy called Connor and it was on bail, which simply put meant he hadn't paid for it yet; he would pay as he could when he sold it. It turned out, he in turn had sold it to a number of people all over the place who would pay him on the same basis. It was normal practice for puff or skunk, Johnny learned. Most people didn't have large amounts of cash lying about, so credit was an absolutely essential part of the business, whereas with other drugs, like cocaine, credit is very limited or not available because people can get in too much trouble too quickly using it themselves and then can't pay, which Johnny would later find out happened all the time. Tony once said to Johnny, 'In the drugs business everyone has got bad debts. It just goes with the territory,' and to minimise those was everyone's best hopes. It turned out Tony had sold about 6k of skunk and had 34k left hidden at home in Herne Bay. Rachael explained he owed Connor for it and who Connor worked for.

Johnny had never had any previous dealings with the family from London that she talked about but everyone knew their name and their reputation. Everyone just referred to them as the A

Team. Allegedly, they were responsible for major drug importation, dealing and various murders, as well as a whole range of other unsolved crimes. She asked him if he could help sort it out with this guy called Connor. She gave Johnny the 34k of skunk and Connor's mobile telephone number. She also had Tony's strap list, which was simply a list of names on a piece of paper. Beside their names was an amount of money, depending on what they owed. Johnny rang Connor, explained he was a friend of Tony's – who had been arrested – he had something that belonged to him and was just wanting to return it. This Connor was worried about who he was and why he was phoning but he agreed to come and meet him and collect what he had. Johnny never mentioned drugs or money on the phone. He talked in general terms about things but Connor clearly understood what he was saying. They agreed to meet at the unit one evening.

Johnny had everything for him in a holdall. It was 9.30 pm. Up turned this hyperactive nut case who was in his late twenties or early thirties. He was wearing trainers and bounced everywhere rather than walking, Johnny noticed. Johnny later discovered he was a raging cocaine addict as well, and with hindsight, he was probably totally off his head when they first met. Johnny invited him in, showed him the 34k's worth of skunk, and explained about Tony. Then he explained about the other 6k and the strap list, which he said he would try to collect when they had it and pass it on.

Then Connor started asking what the place was. Johnny explained and showed him round. It turned out Connor used escorts and prostitutes all the time. After looking round and chatting for a while, Connor asked Johnny if he wanted the 34k's worth of skunk himself. Johnny said, 'No, thanks, it's not my thing. I don't know anyone to sell it to.' Connor explained he could have it for £3,200 per kilo, which was a good price, and he could earn out of it. Johnny did know the price was good, because Tony had previously mentioned how much stuff was. What Johnny never realised was that there are not that many people that will take 40k's worth and have got the customers to sell it to. Connor had lost his best customer, it turned out, when Tony was arrested, but Connor was not declaring that he would have to take it back and explain what had happened and return it himself. He told Johnny if he had it, he could pay when he could, no time limit. Johnny agreed to give it a go. He would try to sell to the people on the list.

Johnny spoke to the people on the list and explained he would collect the money and he had some more if they wanted it. Johnny had now officially become a drug dealer. Collecting the money seemed a very slow process, but slowly they were paying and taking more and he was passing it on to Connor. The drugs were being paid for and the situation had been resolved, at least in principle. Connor seemed happy enough, he thought. Connor started using the unit and booking escorts, which was handy, because Johnny just knocked it off the bill.

One night Connor and a few of his friends were going out for the evening and wanted about 6 girls to go to his place afterwards. A price was agreed and Connor said to get the girls a limo to come over in. Anyway, it was arranged 6 girls and a price agreed. Camilla said she wanted to come along. She had met Connor a few times at the unit and knew he always had a lot of white powder on him. She wanted the cocaine; it was pure and simple. She quite liked Connor but what she really liked was the fact that whenever she had met him, he would always offer her, as well as the other girls, cocaine. To her, he was like Tony in Scarface. That was his main business, selling cocaine. Puff was a secondary line – so it appeared at the time.

So, the limo turns up. Connor lived over the other side of

Maidstone, near Aylesford. All his friends were like business associates really, and all in the same business. The limo was early so the plan was to stop in Maidstone and have one or two drinks before going to Connor's place. After getting to Maidstone, they all started on the drink and drugs, apart from Louise. She was not on the booze or the drugs. She was doing the job as the result of a bad relationship breakup and trying to get straight and support her daughter. They went in a pub and got a drink. All the girls, including Camilla, had really dressed up for the occasion. Connor then phoned and said he had to cancel. He had problems to deal with and would pay for the limo and give the girls a drink for messing them about. Johnny told everyone and they all decided to go clubbing in Chicago Rocks. Johnny was already off his head and the plan was for everyone to act sensible and sober while waiting to get in, otherwise they would be turned away.

So up turns this limo at Chicago Rocks in Maidstone. They all jump out. Johnny had the driver's number for when they wanted him again. They all managed to get in no problem, so once inside, everyone was drinking and dancing. Some of the girls had guys after them within minutes, offering to buy them drinks, get their numbers and take them out. Johnny had been creeping outside in an alley and smoking a joint on his own. He was high as a kite. When he got back, Kadine was with a guy. Johnny walked over to her and whispered in her ear, 'Don't forget to give me half.' She was laughing and so was Johnny. The guy had no idea who he was but he knew Kadine was with him. Then Johnny went up to the bar on his own and there were two either Australians or New Zealanders standing at the bar just staring at him. They walked over to him and said, 'Do you mind if we ask who you are? We noticed you earlier coming in with the girls.' Then he realised how it may have looked to an onlooker. He walked in with seven girls all done up to the nines, various ages from about 21 to 35, in dresses, skirts or trousers, all trying to look their best. So he started speaking to them and said, 'I am Johnny. Those girls will not leave me alone. I can't get rid of them; you know what it's like.' These two guys were standing at the bar on their own and clearly had no idea what it was like or at least the idea of how they thought it was. He told them he was in business and they just all tagged along with him for a good time. Their jaws dropped and they were speechless, he remembered. Later that night, before closing, they got the limo back to Whitstable where he dropped everyone off. Some went home and some went in the unit for more drinks until the early hours.

Carly and Johnny had been getting on well. They both liked drink and drugs and would often chat at work. Johnny had dropped Carly back at her parents, where she was staying, on several occasions. It turned out she had a 14-year-old daughter from a guy she met in Turkey many years earlier. Then she had met a guy called Noah, who was doorman at the pole dancing club where she'd worked in London. The club was owned by the same crime family that Connor worked for. What a small world, Johnny thought. Carly and Noah had a long-term relationship and he had taken her daughter on as his own. He couldn't have children himself – a 'Jaffa', as Carly would say – but he had done his best by Mia. They had hit the rocks, so she moved back home to her parents' place after leaving the club. A few days later, on a Sunday, she was leaving work and getting all dressed up. She was going to see Noah and it seemed like she wanted to sort out the current situation with him. She wasn't due back at work for a few days.

Tuesday morning, she rang Johnny and said she wanted to talk to him about Noah. She said things had not worked out with

Noah as well as she'd hoped and wanted some advice. She had taken a room in the County Hotel in Canterbury High Street rather than go back to her parents. He agreed to go and chat with her. He said he could make it a couple of hours later. So, he went to the hotel and her room a couple of hours later. After chatting very briefly, Johnny and Carly ended up getting passionate for the afternoon. When he left, she asked if he wanted to come back later and have dinner. He did, and that started a few days of staying in different hotels together. After that, she stayed at his flat for a while. Next thing, they agreed to get a place together, which they did.

Talk about a small world. They found a 3-bedroomed terraced town house to rent in Chestfield. Johnny spoke to a woman called Julie and they agreed to view. He didn't know it at the time but Julie was running a brothel in a flat she owned in Margate, and had been for years. She had bought properties to rent out and invest in or buy-to-let mortgages. She lived in Faversham herself. This would all come out later after they moved in. They agreed a six-month tenancy and it was available straight away.

Once Mia came along and moved in and the initial passion had faded, it was clear this was not an ideal situation for anyone. Mia would constantly moan about her mother's drinking and the fact that she believed she was an alcoholic. Johnny preferred the term "she likes a drink occasionally." Mia was, of course, more on point, but the whole situation daily was fuelled by drink and drugs. Noah, Carly's ex-partner, rang Johnny and told him that if he did anything to Mia he would go berserk. Johnny respected his attitude towards Mia and thought rightly so. Then Johnny said to Noah, 'Since you are so concerned about her, will you be supporting her financially? And coming to take her out?' At that point Noah changed his attitude a lot. Johnny pointed out talking on a phone is one thing. 'Let's hope your actions are actually as keen as your words.' Johnny was never going to do any harm to Mia but made it clear to Noah that if you want to play a role, you should take real responsibility. Of course, in reality Noah never contributed a penny. He was not her father and, like a lot of men, used Mia to find out about Carly and Johnny. He seemed more interested in Johnny and Carly than her. Johnny thought it was the old thing – he didn't want to be with Carly but didn't want her to be with anyone else or happy either. He was mindful Noah was a doorman for the wrong people in London and probably could have a real tear-up, if necessary, otherwise he wouldn't be working for them.

One night Johnny and Carly were driving home after being out when the police officer who had arrested Tony for drugs charges spotted Johnny driving. He pulled him up and started searching the car. In the boot of his car, Johnny had a hose pipe he used to drain the spa at the unit in Whitstable. The officer thought the hose pipe was some sort of a piece of equipment being used to grow cannabis, which made Johnny smile. He just said, 'No,' and pulled a face of shock and 'I have no idea what you are going on about, mate.' He could hardly explain what it was really for!

Tony used to drive the police mad in Canterbury with his interviews under caution for drug offences. Tony had created a character in his mind called "Ginger John" and he would often say he was only doing it under threat and duress from Ginger John. Tony knew he could walk if he was being threatened and in fear for his life. It meant he had a defence. The idea came from the film *The Usual Suspects*, where the Kevin Spacey character called Virgil talks about Keyser Soze and creates an elaborate fabrication of events in which he creates and describes himself as another person and acts like he is a poorly educated cripple in fear for his life.

Next thing, Johnny gets a call from Hayley, Connor's wife. Connor had been arrested and remanded in prison. She didn't say what for and he didn't ask. He had met Hayley at Connor's place once or twice, so at least he knew who she was. She simply asked if he could let her have the money when it was available. That made sense to Johnny and he said, 'As soon as I can I will ring you and pop over.' Connor and Hayley were having a lot of building work done at their place and she said she would need to be able to pay the builders to keep them going. Johnny popped just over £9k over to her in cash in the next couple of weeks. He just made notes of dates and amounts on the list of the debt for the drugs. Then one day Johnny gets a call on his mobile from a guy who says that Connor had been arrested and the stuff Connor gave Johnny is his and it's his money. He was one of the brothers of the family, Johnny later found out. So, they chatted and Johnny told him he knew about Connor. Hayley had let him know and he had been paying her since. At that point the guy says, 'Stop paying her anything. It's not hers. I will come and see you.' So, they agreed a meeting.

This guy turns up in a new Mercedes Sports with a driver that looks like he is not employed for his driving skills. If ever Johnny saw a picture of what he thought the family members looked like, this was it. It wasn't the car, the driver, the brother, or the clothes and jewellery. It was just absolutely everything about how they drove, walked, talked, and looked. They didn't need to introduce themselves; it was written all over them.

It was all very civil and quick, really. Johnny had all the details, some more cash for him, and a balance outstanding. They then discussed the situation and it turned out Connor had been released from prison on a licence for the second half of his sentence, and part of the licence conditions were that he visits his probation officer and reports to them. He had just stopped going and it triggered a recall to prison. So, the guy checked the figures, looked at Johnny and said, 'Let's just be clear about all of this – everything you are telling me and have told me about these payments and figures is true.' Just after he finished saying it, Johnny felt really grateful that what he had written down was the truth. He then said he was going to check with Hayley and Connor. At this point the man said, 'Ok, no worries. Please give us a bell when you've got the balance and we can meet up.' Then he jumped back in the car and they left. He rang Johnny later and told him that he went and saw Hayley and she said he had not given her that much money, but when he showed her a record of the payments, she'd said 'Yes, he did give me that.' Apparently, her maths just wasn't that great. Johnny was just grateful that she had been honest about it.

A week or two later he had the balance. They spoke. He said he was going to come down to the Crab and Winkle with a friend for dinner in Whitstable the next evening. It was a Wednesday. They agreed a time to meet. Johnny turned up and saw his car in the car park. He went in the restaurant and they made eye contact. They both left the restaurant, went downstairs, Johnny gave him the balance in an envelope and that was the end of it. Johnny left and he went back up to the restaurant.

One Sunday afternoon Johnny was with Carly at the unit. Sophia called and Carly answered. She shouted out to Johnny, 'It's for you, honey.' When he got to the phone, Sophia started down the phone with both barrels. 'Honey – who is she?' It turned out Sophia was coming back to England from Guernsey and wanted him to hire a car for her for her stay.

He agreed to pick her up at the airport, and took her to a car hire company in Medway. He knew the guys from his smuggling days and could rent a car with her as a named driver. So, it came out he was living with Carly. Johnny and Sophia spoke about it one evening. She asked Johnny not to go back to Carly's that night. Johnny agreed. He said he would go to his mum's. Sophia knew Johnny better than Johnny knew himself. He did intend to go to his mum's but thought, *what's the difference and what's the point,* so after leaving Sophia he drove back to Chestfield.

Carly was already in bed. Johnny got into bed and got off to sleep. About 5.30 am there was this massive banging noise. It was a quiet residential neighbourhood and all he could hear was the loud thudding noise.

He looked out the back window and saw Sophia in the hire car ramming his car. Then reversing up and doing it again. She had already done it several times. He went down. Then a screaming match started and Johnny wished he was somewhere else, preferably about 100 miles away. Then Carly came down and started. Then a neighbour came out and said, 'I have called the police.' Very quickly, the situation had escalated and now the police were on their way and Carly and Sophia were talking. The police turned up and asked him if he wanted to press charges. 'No,' he said, 'it's not a problem. Let's just forget it.' The police said the disturbance had to stop. Carly and Sophia said they should all go inside and discuss it. Johnny was not having anything to do with that. He wasn't going to complain about Sophia, but sit in the living room with both of them, and discuss it? He wasn't that stupid or keen on the idea. He simply said, 'I am off.' He walked round the corner and got a cab to the local Little Chef, where he had coffee and breakfast and sat on his own for hours. Carly and Sophia did go in and chat about him and his behaviour, generally criticising him to each other and sharing a few stories. Some were, no doubt, true and some were embroiled with their perspectives.

A few hours later Johnny went back and tried to carry on as normal, then Carly started and they talked. He just wanted to brush it under the carpet, as usual. Carly told him about some of the things that got talked about. He thought, can we move on, but Carly seemed hell-bent on having her say. Johnny denied some of it and shrugged some of it off. Neither of them had been angels was his recollection. We are all good at judging other people's behaviour. Johnny was too. He could tell you all about other people's behaviour, without looking at himself honestly. A lot of people who sin just do it in different ways; that was certainly true in his experience.

Still, a few days later he had invented a hit-and-drive off story in a car park for the hire car and paid the excess. He thought that was the end of that story, but it was only the beginning. Sophia went back to Guernsey. Carly now didn't trust Johnny, and that was the end of that. Johnny left and went back to good old mum again. Johnny let Julie know he had left and that after the six months he was no longer going to be responsible or staying there. The original agreement was in joint names and for six months.

Julie came out with a cracking remark, which made him smile. 'I thought you were an odd couple when I first met you.' The hire company and the insurers were not convinced about Johnny's version of events with regards to the damage on the hire car he'd returned. He stuck to his guns about the imaginary story. The insurers could tell that the car had not been hit once and that the hire car was the car that had caused the damage and it appeared to be more than one incident. A big disagreement ensued. He just denied it and said they were wrong.

By now Tony was back out of prison again, Connor had also left prison and was trying to get Johnny and Tony to deal with him together. Sophia had decided she wanted to leave Guernsey and run the unit herself. Johnny and Sophia had agreed a deal for that to happen. Sophia did come back from Guernsey and started running the unit. Then one day Johnny went to see Carly about something to do with them. Noah was staying there, it turned out, at least for a few nights. A large argument started on the doorstep and it was agreed to calm down and leave it for now.

Johnny overreacted. He went and saw Tony and said he needed a gun. Tony knew where he could get one and got a price. Apparently, there was a guy in Herne Bay – and that was what he did. He literally lived just down the road from Tony. Johnny agreed to the price and said to Tony, 'That gun needs to work. If it doesn't, I will shoot the bloke you get it from.' What a stupid thing to say, he thought afterwards. What was he going to do that with? Although the point had been made.

The next day he met Tony and picked up the hand gun with five bullets. Tony went out into the woods with the seller the previous evening and shot a tree to check it worked. That was reassuring to hear, he thought. Tony said that was standard practice, to check if it worked or not. So now Johnny had his hand gun and knew it worked. It wasn't exactly a Magnum 45, more of a cheap Eastern European import – or so it appeared. Tony explained that guns were like cars; if they had ever been used in a crime, the bullet or bullets for that crime could be traced to the gun by the police, so when you bought the gun, if you got caught with it, the police would then assume you were involved in any previous crimes.

Of course, there was no way of knowing if it had been used in a crime or crimes previously or what the crimes were. Sounded a bit like Russian Roulette to Johnny; better not get caught with it, then. He hid it in the loft in the unit, in the little leather wallet it came in.

He and Noah had spoken on the phone and agreed to meet

and talk about the situation with Carly, and Noah staying there. Johnny knew if it turned violent, he had no chance with Noah. Now he had resolved that issue, or at least was not concerned about meeting him anymore. Johnny spoke to Connor about Noah and said they had a problem.

Connor said he'd heard; Noah had spoken to his boss at work, who told him, 'We do business with Johnny, so whatever happens, it doesn't want to get out of hand.' Then Connor said, 'Don't worry – he might give you a slap but he's not going to shoot you,' and laughed. Maybe he had not totally overreacted, Johnny thought, but he'd never considered that he was more important to them than a doorman at one of their clubs. He took that on board.

A few days later he and Noah met and sat in Noah's second-hand Mercedes. Johnny had loaded the gun and took the safety catch off. He wore a black leather jacket and had it in one of the inside pockets. Then he started thinking, *if it goes off accidentally, it will shoot me in the leg.* They both jumped in the car and started talking. There were no real issues to be resolved, in reality.

Noah was going back to his place in London on his own. Carly was going to stay until the end of the six months, then move out. She'd decided she didn't want to stay, and Noah didn't want to move in either. It was a very brief conversation, and the only thing Noah wanted was Johnny to promise that he would not go round there and cause any trouble until she moved out. Johnny agreed and that was it. He never pulled the gun out.

Noah never knew what he had in his inside pocket. He had not got the gun to threaten him. Johnny had the gun as an insurance policy. If Noah had turned violent, he was going to pull it out and point it at him. If that didn't do the trick, he was intending to shoot him in the leg, then point it at his head and tell him the next one was going in his brain.

Johnny had no real experience of firearms, but he knew two people who did: Connor and another guy called Stephen. Connor asked him, when they met up one day, to collect some of the debt on Tony's strap list. There was a local traveller, Tommy, and another guy who Johnny thought may present a problem.

Johnny had contacted them to collect the debt. Connor came down to assist in collecting from the two guys and Johnny sat in his van for a brief period, talking to Connor, after he turned up at the Victoria Hotel in Canterbury. Connor then pulled out a handgun from the glovebox. 'If there's a problem, I will put the first one in the leg and then point it at his head. That will get their attention and they will know we are serious.'

The other guy, Stephen, had said many years earlier that the only thing he knew about a gun was, if you bought a gun, you needed to make sure you were prepared to use it. Don't buy one to wave about at people.

When Johnny sat in the hotel with Connor, he never realised he was going to be carrying a gun just in case. The place was full of cameras and he felt really uncomfortable. Thank God that Tommy walked in with an envelope and just paid the outstanding balance. After 5 minutes everyone left. After that, they went up to the Mill House pub in Canterbury and Connor sat in the van.

Johnny walked in. The guy was with a few friends at the bar. Johnny walked up and said, 'I need that money.' The guy said, 'Let's not worry about that. Let's have a drink.' Johnny walked slowly up to him and spoke quietly in his ear. He said, 'The guy whose drugs and money we are talking about is in the car park and if there is a problem, he is going to come in here and shoot you.' The guy sobered up immediately and said, 'There is no problem. I will pay you in a few days,' and he did. Connor didn't have to come into the pub – job done. A few weeks later, a day or two before the 6-month tenancy agreement expired, Carly booked a man and van from London who turned up and loaded up. Johnny and Julie went round just to finish everything off. Carly and Mia moved back to London. That was the last time he saw Carly or Mia.

CHAPTER 19
THE MEN BEHIND BRITAIN'S BIGGEST EVER ROBBERY

BY 2005 SOPHIA was running the unit under her own steam. She ran the business how she saw fit and the agreement was a 50/50 split of all profits on the basis that Johnny owned it, and she ran it. She picked up the ropes quickly and turned it into a successful business. Johnny kept away from the day-to-day running of the business.

Johnny started putting money into a car sales business as a way of earning more cash. There were two brothers in Gillingham who had a large car site and were short on stock. Johnny knew Russell from previous gambling experiences at card games, dogs and horses. He couldn't tell the truth if his life depended upon it. Robert was more honest and less full of himself. The brothers were from a large family of immigrants.

They were characters Johnny could relate to and they knew a lot of people locally with dark backgrounds. It wasn't a get-rich-quick scheme but he felt his money would be relatively safe there and generate a cash income. The deal was Johnny would buy the cars, leave them on the site, and the brothers would sell the cars after doing any work required, putting an MOT on them and marking them up. They offered warranties and finance. The business had lots of potential but just not enough stock, so Johnny kept putting cars on there. Some sold quickly, some sold slowly, but they always sold in the end and he got a cash profit on each car.

It worked quite well for some time and it suited him because he never had to be there or do anything. In those days there were plenty of car traders bringing vehicles in all the time and wanting to trade them to car sales. So, it wasn't particularly lucrative but it was safe and steady and the cash was always in the vehicles. It was all done on a cash basis and records just kept in a book.

Part of the site, the brothers rented to two guys who had just started a van hire business. Gordon Rose and Melvin Cullen started Medway Van Hire in Gillingham. Johnny knew Gordon Rose from the tobacco smuggling days, and everyone seemed to know Melvin Cullen, although he knew nothing about him and had never met him. Gordon was a loveable rogue. He had a nice side and manner about him. He always had a cigarette on the go and he was another one who just couldn't tell the truth about anything. His business partner in the tobacco smuggling had been Lyndon. Lyndon had described Gordon to Johnny one day. He said, 'If he told you what the weather was like outside, you would have to check.'

Johnny was at Russell's house one evening, and Mel was there. They sat and chatted for hours about everything, including the world and his wife. Mel was a musician who, in his early days, had played with some big-name artists, including Edison Lighthouse. He had loved music, as well as drink and drugs, for an awful long time, Johnny would later find out. He had written a new album, which he then went into the studio and recorded on a CD as a demo, for promotion.

It turned out he had spent a lot of time in Thailand, running a radio station. He then got involved in a drugs racket and was convicted of drugs charges in Thailand and sentenced to 20 years in prison. He shared some of his stories about prison life in Thailand. It was amazing for Johnny to listen to the experience that Mel shared, especially that without money in a Thai prison you simply don't eat, and the general conditions in which prisoners are kept, including overcrowding, poor sanitation, and lack of medicine and medical care. It was an interesting first meeting. Johnny didn't swap numbers with Mel but would later bump into him again at the car site in Nelson Road, Gillingham.

After meeting Mel in the new van hire office, and going out for dinner and having a few drinks together on a couple of occasions, it turned out that both of them were living in temporary accommodation. Johnny was again living at his mum's in Canterbury, while Mel was staying with a friend of his, Jo, whom he had known for many years, at her place near the maritime dockyard in Chatham. Jo was also an interesting character to bump into. She had divorced after her 20-year marriage ended and she had been doing reception and telephone work at flats used for prostitution in London. She had the sexiest voice Johnny had ever heard – her voice was her biggest asset. Johnny thought she sounded similar to Joanna Lumley. So, Johnny and Mel agreed to rent a place together and share the rent and bills for a period of 6 months. They grabbed the local paper and found a few interesting places locally. They found a place in Station Road at Halling, a 4-bedroom semidetached place with plenty of parking and a nice garden. It was out of the way, with a nice feel to it, and was available straight away. After viewing, they both decided it ticked all their boxes, so to speak. Rather than going through the referencing process, they just agreed to pay the rent for the full term in advance, which just left a few ID checks. The letting agent took about a week or ten days to process the application, and ten days later they both moved in.

They both had their own separate businesses and it should have worked quite well in theory, but it was a difficult experience for both of them for different reasons. The fun and novelty lasted about six weeks before it became evident they lived in totally different ways and their behaviour and habits were going to start annoying each other. People who love each other can live together and struggle to cope with each other's behaviour. In this position, it was two guys that hardly knew anything about each other. It was meant to be a convenience, and cracks started appearing quite quickly. But they got on quite well, regardless. If they were both in together in the evening, very quickly, they would end up drunk and high, talking for hours about things that they could not even remember in the morning.

Johnny had been offered a Renault Espace seven-seat people carrier and thought it was a good deal. He thought he could put it on a car site and it would be a good earner, but it was high mileage and it turned out not a good deal at all. He decided to clock it, just trade it to someone and get what he could for it. He rang Lee Glazer to see if he would buy it, and he agreed to come and have a look at it. After looking at it and making a reasonable offer, Lee bought the vehicle. Johnny was taking a loss but at least it would get it out of the way. The next day Lee rang Johnny and told him the vehicle has been clocked. Johnny stated he knew nothing about that, and the conversation went not too badly considering the circumstances. At the end of the conversation, they agreed to meet up and go out for a drink sometime. Within a week or so, Johnny went out with Lee and his crowd from the Isle of Sheppey. They were all heavy drinkers, some on drink and drugs; he fitted in a treat. Whenever they went out, after the first hour, no one could ever remember what happened. Everyone was drink-driving and playing up in bars and clubs. It was like a bunch of children being let loose for the evening. One guy called Tony Macaroni lived in Rushenden and worked for his brother at his London cab office. He and Johnny got on particularly well. Tony drank large whiskeys all evening and Johnny was drinking large vodkas.

Johnny started going out to the pubs and clubs seven days per week. He met a girl called Claire at the Grasshopper, near Westerham. They used to have an over 30s night every Friday evening. She worked in the beauty industry and Johnny managed to get her phone number at the bar one evening. He had never met her before that evening. He phoned her the following Sunday and they agreed to go out for dinner.

Mel was driving about in a new BMW M3, and Johnny borrowed it from him to take her out. When he picked her up, it turned out she herself had a BMW and loved them. By the time Johnny met her in a pub at Coulsdon, where she lived, he had already been smoking some skunk. He drove into London. They had dinner. She loved drink and smoked puff as well. After dinner they were both the worse for wear. He took her to Stringfellow's dance club. Lee Glazer knew the doorman there and the guy remembered Johnny. He was so drunk he got the dancers dancing for Claire, which they both enjoyed. When they left, Claire said to Johnny, 'You can take me anywhere you want; I don't mind.' He didn't even realise what he had done. It was their first time out together.

Johnny had driven back to the pub at Coulsdon and Claire invited Johnny back to her place to have a joint together. Johnny followed her back to her place, went in, had the joint, then drove back to Halling, getting there about 6 am. He couldn't remember a thing, apart from the fact that he'd had a good night and was probably lucky to have driven through London and back home without getting stopped by the police. After that evening, Claire and Johnny started seeing each other. She had her own place in Coulsdon and two grown up children who had – kind of – moved out.

Johnny had been drinking and driving since he was a teenager. When he was young, it seemed to him that drink-driving was against the law but everyone did it; they just took the chance. The real crime was getting caught. On 19th August 2005, Johnny left a club at Rochester, absolutely legless, jumped in his car and started driving home. He got stopped about 2.30 am in a police check and was over the legal limit. He blew over in the breathalyser. In desperation, he gave a blood sample, hoping it might go missing or prove he was under. The blood sample was over as well. Johnny knew his fate. He knew within a week or two he would be banned from driving, once the paperwork had been processed. He needed his licence. So, he asked Sophia to buy a new Toyota Avensis in her name, insure the car, and add him as a named driver. She bought it and he paid for it, so it never was in his name. It was taxed and insured. It was a neutral-colour Toyota that should not attract any attention.

When he got to court, he explained to the magistrates that it had been a one-off misjudgement, which he regretted. He pleaded guilty after the blood sample came back positive. The magistrates banned him from driving for 16 months, fined him and offered him the drink-driving rehabilitation course which would reduce his ban from 16 months to 12 months if completed. He drove the Toyota as usual and just forgot about the ban, tried to put it out of his mind. He used to drive to the drink-driving rehabilitation course in Maidstone on a Monday evening and hide his car round the corner. He completed the drink-drive rehabilitation course and drove successfully for the first 11 months of the ban. Then, one evening, with one month of his driving ban left to serve, he was driving home up the Tonbridge Road in Maidstone. It was late and he was on his own. He glanced in the rear-view mirror and saw a police car, two officers in it, just behind him. There were no other vehicles about and he was convinced they were going to pull him over. He kept driving within the limit and, just before the entrance to his place, he indicated right to turn in. As he turned right and drove into the Coachyard, they kept driving on the Tonbridge Road. When he parked up outside his place, Johnny was so relieved that he decided not to drive for the last month of the ban. He never did. He parked the car up and left it there for a month, until his ban expired.

While living at Halling, Johnny found a mortgage broker in Larkfield so he went in to find out what was required to buy a home in Maidstone. The owner of the mortgage brokers was Mark Chipton. He was keen to do business with Johnny and was very helpful at explaining everything. Johnny had the deposit but needed to know about the requirements from the lenders. Voter's roll and wage slips, as well as regular employment. He asked Mel if he would pretend to employ Johnny for 3 months. Mel agreed, and June in the office knew Johnny was officially on the team if anyone rang and asked for him. June had his mobile and she would always say he was with clients and he could return their calls. June thought the whole thing was funny and got on well with Johnny. He would often sit in the office talking to her about life in general

Things at the van hire business were not going as well as they could have. Very quickly, Mel and Gordon parted company. Gordon decided to go off and do something else on his own. Johnny sometimes helped out in the office. After about 5 months of shared living at Halling, Johnny bought himself a beautiful penthouse apartment at the Coachyard in Maidstone, Kent. After buying a home in Maidstone, Johnny decided he wanted some properties and arranged a mortgage using Mark Chipton on a flat in Hillbrowe Avenue, Sturry, which still had a tenant, Stuart Fallon, living in it. Johnny and Stuart did a further deal after the terms and conditions of the original purchase and agreement. By mortgaging that property, Johnny released a lot of the equity available in the property, which he could use as deposits on other properties. Johnny used Medway Van Hire to confirm all his details again, and the mortgage got approved after a few small delays.

One night Johnny was drunk at the bar in the Inn on The Lake, just off the M2, near Gravesend. It was a Wednesday evening. Every Wednesday was over 30s night, and he was in there most Wednesdays. He met a woman called Tina. She looked like an American Indian woman. She was very intelligent, very smart, and a divorcee who ran her own business. She had been educated at Benenden School. She was plausible, and he thought on balance she was telling the truth. She took an instant like to him and was laughing a lot with him. Anyway, he got her number and started taking her out as well after that evening.

Johnny then agreed to buy a property from Lee Glazer in Rushenden and keep the tenants he had, so that was the first place he intended to buy once he had the deposit. It was a three-bedroomed terraced property, and they agreed the deal at a card game one evening.

He then bumped into Louise from Sittingbourne, who had worked at the unit in Whitstable. Johnny had always had a soft spot for her, and they started to date as well. So, he had lost the plot, really, by now. He even started to have the cash from the unit paid in his bank rather than going and collecting it, as he had always done previously. He was drinking and drugging constantly, totally out of control.

Johnny gave a copy of any keys he had to his mum, so if he ever lost them, he would be able to go and pick a set up. He used to just leave them at her place in a drawer. He gave his mum a set of keys to his home in Maidstone too, and said to her, 'You can pop in whenever you want. If I am not there, please let yourself in if you want.' She never came over unannounced and, in reality, Johnny would visit her, not the other way round. One night, Louise stayed at Johnny's place. They shared a bed but Louise wasn't having anything going on at that time. She made that clear and he never pushed the point, although he did try, obviously. The next morning Louise was walking about in the front room with just her blouse on, after getting out of bed. Johnny was mumbling about in a t-shirt and a pair of pants. The front door opens and his mum says, 'Hi, Johnny. Just thought I would pop in and see you. I am meeting friends in Maidstone for coffee later.' Then Louise pops her head round the corner and very sheepishly says 'Hi.' Johnny weighed the situation up instantly and said, 'I am just going to have a bath.' He couldn't believe the day his mum had picked to just drop in. Louise and Vera spoke briefly in Johnny's absence before Louise had to go to work. She was a nurse by now.

After Louise left, Johnny and his mum had coffee. Vera said, 'Nice girl, very down to earth.' Johnny ignored the comment and moved on with the conversation.

In 2005 Johnny also decided he wanted to mortgage the unit at Whitstable and use that money to buy property as well. He went to see Mark Chipton again to organise the mortgage. Mark told him he didn't do commercial mortgages but his friend, Nigel Steel, did. Johnny got in touch with Nigel Steel and organised a fake lease to support his application with regards to income generated through the Abbey National. When the application was submitted to the Abbey National commercial department, they instructed a valuer to value the property. Johnny agreed to meet the valuer at 10.00 am one morning. He had spent a few hours that morning converting the unit so it looked more like a health club. The guy turned up and they argued about the valuation Johnny had put on it as a result of the lease. The valuer seemed to accept it was a health club, but not the rental figure. Due to the size of the property, the valuer valued the property at £120k, whereas Johnny had valued it at £250k, arguing that £250K was a fair value based on the rental income that it generated. Once the valuer left, he quickly changed everything back to how it should be in time for the 11 am opening of the brothel. He had no choice but to accept the valuation. He could borrow 75% of the valuation, so he could raise £90k before expenses on the deal. That mortgage application was a lot slower to proceed to completion than residential mortgages were. Johnny had an arrangement with Sophia that if anyone ever enquired or there was a problem in the future, the unit was being rented by Mel Cullen. The fake lease agreement details had been drawn up quickly, and Johnny inserted Mr Melvyn Cullen as the tenant and signed and witnessed the agreement.

By December 2005, Johnny was still dating Claire, Tina and Louise. He used to regularly think to himself, *I wish I could meet a girl with Claire's looks, Tina's brain and Louise's body.* That would be the ideal partner for Johnny, or perhaps, if Carlsberg made women, the Carlsberg woman. Sophia was certainly going to be hard to replace. In reality, Johnny was just addicted to the chase, as Tina often pointed out to him. Johnny's mind looked for the negatives rather than the positives in the women he met, he realised. The biggest irony of all, Johnny thought, was that he was sleeping with Claire and Tina but Louise would not sleep with him because she knew him better than the others. She said to him a few times, 'You are only after the chase.' It was true.

At the beginning of December, he got drunk one night, and by the morning he had finished with all of them. Tina laughed and said, 'What, again?' Louise and Claire moved on. Of course, about a day later he realised what he had done and wanted them back, but drink and drugs had ruined it all, in about one hour of madness.

Things had gone very well for Johnny in 2005, on a financial level at least. With the money from the mortgages Johnny could buy more cars to put on car sites, buy some properties, and he even started investing in lorry loads of drug importations through Dover Docks.

On the 21st and 22nd February 2006, the Securitas depot robbery in Tonbridge, Kent, was committed. It began with a kidnapping on the evening of 21 February 2006 and ended in the early hours of 22 February, when the criminals left the depot with almost £53 million. It was the UK's largest cash robbery, and the gang left behind another £154 million only because they did not have the means to transport it. After planning the heist for some time, doing surveillance and putting an inside man to work at the depot, the gang abducted the manager and his family. That night, they tricked their way inside the depot and tied up fourteen workers, threatening them with weapons. The gang stole £52,996,760 in used and unused Bank of England sterling banknotes. Most of the getaway vehicles were found in the following week, one containing £1.3 million in stolen notes. When details of the robbery were released, it became the talk of the town for weeks. It was in the newspapers and on the radio and TV daily.

One morning in May 2006, the robbery squad, who were put in charge of investigating the Securitas robbery, turned up out of the blue at the unit at Whitstable. Sophia was totally thrown. They wanted to know everything about the unit and what it was used for, who owned it, who rented it, what went on there, and so on. Sophia stuck to the massage story and they quickly realised what type of business it was. It turned out that a number of phones they had traced calls on had been ringing the unit landline for months before the robbery was committed. Their original thinking had been that the unit was used as part of the planning for the robbery. It turned out that, literally, a number of the suspects for the robbery had just been very good customers for some time. After a while they accepted that Sophia was not involved and it was likely, on balance, that they were just customers, whether they had discussed any plans there or not.

They wanted to speak to Johnny urgently and find out all about him and what was going on. There was a security tape from the video camera which recorded every day, but unless needed for any reason, it was just recorded over again the next day, so the security tape only showed the previous day's visitors to the unit, which was no help at all to the squad. To clarify everything that they were being told, they left two officers in the unit, who watched the people who came in for about a week. Some of the officers were even trying to get the girls' phone numbers and take them out after work.

A detective sergeant rang Johnny and explained the situation. Johnny was grateful the first point of contact had been on the phone; it gave him a good chance to get his act together and figure out exactly what he wanted to say when they met. They arranged to meet the following afternoon at the Malta Inn just outside Maidstone. By the time Johnny had arrived the following afternoon, he had spoken to Sophia and basically had some understanding of what was going on, what was being asked and the nature of the enquiries.

They had a list of several suspects they wanted to speak to. They knew their names, had recent photos of them and were after certain people. They were not just being nosey about who went in there and what went on. Johnny, as always, told half a truth. He said he used to run the place but decided it was not for him and rented it out. He told the detective sergeant he hadn't been involved in the running of the business since the new tenant took over. Whether the detective sergeant believed him or not seemed to be immaterial. He read a list of names to Johnny and asked him if he knew them or had any dealings with them whatsoever. The irony of that business is that, like the girls, most customers only gave a Christian name – and generally that is a made-up name, not their real name. So, after being asked about the names, Johnny could honestly answer that he had never met any of them and knew nothing about them. That was the truth.

Then he was shown pictures of men and asked if he had ever met any of these people. The first couple did not look familiar at all. Then he was shown a picture of Tony, a local builder in Whitstable. Tony had been coming to the unit since it opened. He was a very regular customer for massage. All the girls liked him. Johnny had several conversations with him over the previous couple of years and thought he was a regular guy. Johnny said he had met Tony before in the unit and knew he had come in from time to time. It was at this point the detective sergeant pointed out that Tony was Sean Lupton. He was a builder and lived locally in Herne Bay, and was suspected of being involved in the planning and the robbery itself. Tony, aka Sean, was a fit-looking guy, middle aged, with short hair. He often used to help teach lads to box. It turned out a few of the suspects lived in the Herne Bay and Tankerton area, just a few miles down the road from Whitstable.

The robbery squad did catch up with Sean Lupton a while later. He was questioned over the £53m Securitas cash depot heist in Kent and later was released without any charges and bailed to return. In December he went missing, and as a result never answered his bail. After he went missing his home was searched. He has never been seen since. Stories of his whereabouts vary wildly from him living in Cyprus with large amounts of cash from the robbery to him having been murdered to guarantee his silence.

One Wednesday, shortly after this, Sophia had somewhere important to be and could not open the unit on that day. She asked Johnny to run it for the day. She had three girls lined up to work and didn't want to shut for the day. She asked Johnny and he said no, just close it. Then, after a while, he agreed to do it on the basis that it was a one-off.

He remembered the day quite well, considering. He turned up early, got organised, and all the girls turned up. Johnny was smoking a joint and drinking by about 11.30 am, half hour after opening. The girls all looked stunningly beautiful to Johnny once he'd had a few drinks. It was like being drunk in a night club. He was on the phone, telling everyone who rang that the three girls today were all like Miss World contestants. Suddenly the door started opening, and in came this continuous flow of men. Then, as he got more and more drunk, he was asked about services provided by the girls and he said, 'You can get whatever you want in here today.' The girls all told him not to say that. They took the phone off him and did the phone between them until he sobered up a bit. Two of the girls were drinking as well. Johnny went back to saying 'Three Miss World contestants,' and they all agreed to stay late because it was so busy. They ended up closing at 11 pm, not 9 pm, and it was the best day's takings ever. Johnny did the wages and when they all left together, he was saying to the girls, 'We have all earnt more money than the prime minister today.' The girls liked that line and what they had earnt.

CHAPTER 20
CODE NAME OPERATION OPERA, SERIOUS ECONOMIC CRIME UNIT

In 2006 Johnny bought Lee's place at Rushenden on a buy-to-let mortgage and kept the tenants on. By using a 15% deposit, he didn't have to have his income verified, as the rental income from the property would cover repaying the loan.

In early 2007, he decided he wanted more flats to open as brothels rather than buying property for tenants. Renting was always going to be a big problem with most landlords. So, Johnny bought a flat in Ashford and one in Faversham. He put 15 % deposits down and did them on buy-to-let mortgages through Mark Chipton in Larkfield. He then got them up and going. He put maids in them and did 50/50 splits with Jo and Anne, who ran them for him. They were both ex-working girls, it turned out, and knew the ropes.

On 31st March 2007, he was in a night club in Rochester and had drunk so much he could hardly stand up. He vaguely remembered leaving the club and that he could not see his car properly. He managed to get in the car and started driving home.

He knew he was struggling; he was almost driving while unconscious. He ended up taking a wrong turn and driving towards the paper mill in Snodland. He drove straight through the security barrier at the entrance to the paper mill, then drove for a bit in the mill, before parking up and just collapsing behind the wheel. He just stopped the car and passed out. The security man phoned the police. They came and got him out of the car, arrested him and took him to Tonbridge Police Station.

Johnny genuinely couldn't remember the next few hours. He was taken to the police station, failed the breathalyser and so was put in a cell. About 7.00 am he woke up in the cell and heard the door being unlocked. Once he saw the officer and realised where he was, he really began to panic. He wondered what he was doing there, and more to the point, what had he been arrested for? Then the police sergeant told him he was being charged with drink-driving, which he couldn't remember – but he was relieved it was only drink-driving. Then he remembered that after his first drink-driving offence, they told him for a second drink-driving offence the ban would be a minimum of 3 years. Johnny didn't want that. What could he do? Then he remembered the car was still in Sophia's name. He came up with this chestnut. He asked Sophia if she would say she had been driving and he was just a passenger. They had a disagreement because he was drunk. She drove in the paper mill because of the argument, got out of the car and walked off and made her way home. If the security guard couldn't be certain who was driving the car when it entered the paper mill, he was home and dry. The paper mill was private property, not a public road.

She agreed to help. So, he pleaded not guilty at his first appearance and a trial date was set. The trial was at Tonbridge Magistrates Court. Johnny decided to represent himself. He had one witness – Sophia – and himself to give evidence. When the Crown presented their case, the only part Johnny wanted to cause confusion and uncertainty around was who was driving, nothing else. He tried to suggest to the security guard that he couldn't be certain who was driving in the early hours and the dark. The security guard said he was certain it was just one person in the car. The magistrates convicted him after hearing from everyone. They banned him from driving for 3 years and fined him £1,400 plus costs. Johnny quite liked his story and appealed the conviction. The appeal process took ages and he continued to drive, in any event.

In June 2007, he decided it would be a good idea to go into therapy. Deep down, he knew his drink and drug issues were out of control. He'd seen and heard a lot of talk about therapists to talk things through. Johnny didn't really understand therapy. He had watched all the complete box sets of *The Sopranos* and saw Tony was in therapy, and rather thought he liked the idea of getting a therapist similar to the one Tony had in the TV series. He had a soft spot for Tony's therapist, or at least the character on TV.

Anyway, he found a therapist in Maidstone, a nice guy, but he wasn't an alcoholic or an addict himself. If Johnny had understood therapy at all, he would have found an addict or alcoholic in recovery who had chosen the path of counselling as a profession. It would have been helpful if the therapist had some experience of drink and drugs and been a bit more direct with him. Still, he never understood. He thought that by talking to the guy, something would happen. He still had not faced the truth about his own behaviour and why he was doing it.

He explained that he had broken some laws and the therapist explained about his legal responsibilities with regards to counselling. So, they worked on that basis. In other words, Johnny had to lie about a lot, or rather than lie, just not talk about it. He went every Tuesday evening, and after leaving therapy he always went straight to his favourite wine bar in Maidstone before ending up in a club later. He was now out every night in Maidstone or somewhere else getting legless. He had been drinking and driving since he was a young lad, really, and always took the chance, or, if he was out in Maidstone, he would get a taxi into and out of town. He was known in all the places he went in and would often get asked to leave after a few hours. He regularly got barred for the evening from lots of bars and clubs in Maidstone.

Johnny was quite good with girls in bars, getting their phone numbers and getting them out or back to his place. He had the chat, a pocket full of cash, and after a few drinks was a good laugh and fun to be around. Tony Macaroni would often come over for the evening, or if not him, a crowd from Sittingbourne and Sheerness whom Lee mainly knew. There was a lot of fun being had, and at the same time, drugs and booze being taken. Even Johnny's therapist said to him one day, 'You are living in the fast lane, Johnny,' which made him smile. Sophia told him he only went to therapy to show off. Interesting perspective. He wasn't really convinced about that one. If no one else was going out that night, he just went out on his own. He preferred that sometimes. It was a lot easier to dress up smart and chat to women and girls who were out. If he was out in the crowd, generally a few of the lads were behaving terribly, which ruined all chances with the girls.

One night a new bloke turned up with Lee. Everyone knew him as Adam, a traveller from Sittingbourne. He was a tall, young lad full of life, bang on the drink and drugs. He and

Johnny starting having a laugh. Lee said he was a right handful. If there was any trouble or it kicked off, he was up for all of that. After a couple of hours, the group went from Chicago Rocks to the Source Bar just up the road and down a small turning. Adam knew an investor in the bar very well and all the bouncers knew him, so they were all drinking and dancing and generally being a nuisance, dancing with drinks on their heads, which was Tony and Johnny's party piece when drunk. So, Johnny was on the dance floor, dancing with a large vodka and red bull on his head, which was what he was drinking most nights, but he lost his balance and the drink went all over the place on the dance floor. He didn't know it but there were two guys at the bar that he had upset. Apparently, they said they were going to get him barred and drag him outside. Adam was standing at the bar and listening to them. As they approached Johnny, he just grabbed them and hit the pair of them. He only hit them once each and put them on the floor. Then a bouncer walked up to Adam and said that they were both off-duty coppers. Adam told Johnny. Next thing, the police were called. Johnny and Adam slipped out and ran down this turning to get back to the High Street. While running, all they could hear were sirens. As they got to the High Street, they stopped running, Adam turned right and started walking down the High Street. Johnny turned left and started walking up the High Street. As they did, up screeched several police cars, with officers jumping out and running down the turning to the Source Bar. It had been a close-run thing, that was for sure, but they were both clean away and met up later on in Chicago Rocks again.

Johnny was earning well and spending it every week, but he always made sure his mortgages were paid. After that, he didn't worry too much about anything. He was investing in cars, drug importation and prostitution. Life was good and in full swing.

It was one Wednesday morning in June 2007. He had been out on the Tuesday evening as normal, got back to his penthouse late and crept into bed on his own. He had never been an early riser but about 8 am the next morning he woke up with a terrible pain across his chest. He manged to get down the stairs. He sat on his leather sofa, drinking water and hoping the pain would go away. It wouldn't, so he thought if he had a spliff, that would do the job; that would calm him down and take away the pain. He rolled the spliff and lit it. That didn't take the pain away either. He realised very quickly now this was serious. He phoned 999 and asked for an ambulance on his mobile. The telephone operator said she would send an ambulance straight away. She asked him if he could make it downstairs. She told him not to use the lift, to stay on the line and she would talk to him while he walked downstairs. Johnny got downstairs and the ambulance turned up within a minute or two. The paramedics quickly got him into the back of the ambulance, did some checks and tests, told him they thought he was having a heart attack, then laid him down in the back of the ambulance and connected him to monitors and wired him up. The Coachyard in Maidstone was not that far from Maidstone General Hospital – about 2-3 miles – so in less than ten minutes he was arriving at the accident and emergency department at Maidstone General. He was taken in and the pain was getting worse.

He was in an enclosed area in the accident and emergency, and some nurses were inserting central catheters in his arms. The pain was so bad, at some point he thought it was all over. He thought he would be dead in seconds, or minutes. He very quickly thought, *I wish I could say goodbye to my mother and brother* and started thinking about some of the women he had known, which made him smile. A doctor walked straight up to him and said, 'We think you are having a heart attack.' He quickly explained that he could be treated with drugs instantly but Johnny had to consent, because there were possible side effects, which were explained to him. It was a no-brainer, he thought – die of heart failure or possibly live but maybe have side effects. He consented and signed the forms.

The doctor and a nurse started injecting him with drugs. Within moments the pain subsided a little. At that moment he genuinely felt like just maybe he had a chance. He had experienced the most peaceful moment of his life when he had accepted his life was over. Total peace and serenity came with total acceptance that his number was up. Then, slowly, the pain eased again and disappeared. Within a few minutes he was totally drained but the pain in his chest had gone. He was taken to the Intensive Care Unit. He was given a bed, and as he was being transferred into his new bed from the trolley, he started to panic. He had this amazing panic attack. He started fighting the staff and trying to wriggle. The staff held him down but not in a forceful manner, more in a controlled way that allowed him to move just a little. The doctor told Johnny to calm down. He said he was having a panic attack, which was a relief, because he thought he was having another heart attack. Johnny shouted at him, 'I can't calm down,' but after a few minutes of being restrained, he stopped panicking.

He stayed at Maidstone General until Thursday, when it was confirmed that he did have a heart attack, and on Friday morning he was transferred to St Thomas Hospital in London. The ambulance went from Maidstone Hospital to Tonbridge Hospital, where it picked up another gent who needed to get to St Thomas Hospital. On arrival at St Thomas Hospital, they were taken up to a ward. Johnny got to see a doctor, who told him there were several possibilities. He needed to be taken into the theatres and have a camera inserted through his groin. The camera would be able to show exactly what had happened and they could see the damage and what needed to be done. The doctor explained that they were really busy. They didn't do procedures at the weekend. They were doing the operations from Monday to Friday. They were full up and he would be seen when they had a cancellation or could squeeze him in.

So, Johnny knew he didn't have a time or an appointment but would just get slotted in when they could. He thought maybe in a week or two. The place was full up, after all. Literally all the beds were taken. On the Sunday, Alex and his family came down to visit for the afternoon, and it was nice to see them all. Monday morning, Johnny was woken up by a nurse who asked for his name and date of birth. It was about 6.30 am. After confirming his details, she told him he had been placed in the first two operations of the day. He couldn't believe his luck.

He was rolled into a lift with another patient and sent down to the theatres. He was put on the operating table and it was explained what they were going to do. The procedure started. Johnny was just lying on the table and looking at a monitor. He was half awake, under a local anaesthetic. After about an hour or so in the theatres, he was taken back to the ward. The surgeon explained that they had found the damage and inserted stents into two of his arteries. He was told that out of his three arteries, one of his arteries had totally collapsed, one had partially collapsed, and he was surviving on one and a bit and was 'lucky to be alive.' About two hours later, Ravi Singh, Johnny's accountant, popped in with some fruit. He was shocked to see him. He explained that he heard what had happened and where he was and decided to jump on a train, pop up and say hello. Johnny was very touched and pleased to see him. Nice touch, he thought. At that moment he realised, whatever he was up to now or in the future, Ravi would always be his accountant.

He was prescribed various drugs, everything that had happened was explained to him, and he was told that this was in fact his second heart attack. He said, 'No, it is my first,' but was told they found the damage from the first one. The first one had been a mild heart attack and he probably thought he was just having a rough day with indigestion and not feeling too good. The consultant explained it was alcohol related, and Johnny immediately thought it was the drugs, not the booze. The prescription medication had "not to be taken with alcohol" written on it.

It was all over, he thought. The 3 packets of Benson & Hedges per day, the vodka red bulls to black out daily, and the skunk. He would give it all up.

On Wednesday he was allowed to go home. He got a minicab from St Thomas Hospital back home and started talking to the woman driver about his life and what had happened. She said to him, 'At least you have lived. I bet you wouldn't change it,' and he had to agree. Although he'd nearly died, he had another chance and decided to make the most of it.

He got home and had to rest a lot. After about two weeks, he was bored out of his mind at home. He decided to go out clubbing but not drink. That meant he could get out and socialise without all the rest of it. He dressed up and went to the Grasshopper. He was drinking diet coke as his healthy choice. After about an hour or so, he saw a rather attractive woman smoking and smiling. The ban on smoking inside pubs and clubs was due to start on 1st July 2007, but that was still a week or so away. All Johnny thought was that it would be nice to have a cigarette. She had looked so happy. He went to the vending machine and bought one packet of Benson & Hedges. Within an hour he was chain-smoking again. Then the diet cokes turned into large vodka diet cokes rather than large vodka and red bull.

He imagined that would be healthier and better for him. He was now drinking again. Within a week he was back on drugs, smoking, and drinking every day. It was almost like the heart attack had never happened. He now just took the medication and thought he would be fine. It was total madness, really. He just couldn't see it.

Johnny was back out in Maidstone every night drinking again. After the clubs used to kick out, sometimes, he would end up in a kebab house or chicken shop getting something to eat before going home. Then, one morning, he ended up in a Subway sandwich bar. It was a new one in Gabriel's Hill, Maidstone, and it tasted really good and different to the dodgy kebabs and chicken shops that were open around that time. More to the point, it was absolutely mobbed and you had to queue for ages to get served, but people didn't seem to mind that. Then he realised that this place was opening up early in the morning and stayed open until late at night, until about 4 am Thursday, Friday and Saturday, the busy nights for the clubs, and taking a fortune. He was very impressed with what he had seen, and he got to thinking it would be a great business to get into. At that time Maidstone was thriving during the day and there were so many bars and clubs doing a great trade in the evenings.

So now he had this idea – open up a takeaway, turn that into a chain and get out of the crime business. That way he could walk away, move into something that was at least legal, and just cheat the VAT and tax, as in those days most people were still paying in cash rather than card. He spoke to Sophia and asked if she wanted a slice of the business. They agreed a deal and how it would become reality. The finances were agreed. Premises were required – a complete shop probably – and that would be the first of a chain.

As a result of a possession with intent to supply charge that

Tony, Sophia's son, was convicted of and served a prison sentence for, he had faced a confiscation order under the Proceeds of Crime Act 2002. It was a new act in the UK. The British Government had copied America, who had introduced it to pursue the massive amounts of money made from drugs and financial crimes. It is a very deep and complicated law; the whole act is often referred to as a legal minefield. Before the 2002 act was introduced, criminals used to face trial for the crimes they had committed, serve their sentences, then come out of prison with just a criminal conviction. Under the 2002 Proceeds of Crime Act, if a person or persons were convicted of crimes, then the Crown had the right to confiscate the proceeds from that crime or other crimes. The idea was, and still is today, that if you earn money illegally and do not pay tax on it, then the Crown has the right to take everything, whether it is cash, property, assets or just possessions.

Tony and his mum had bought a few properties and were letting them out to tenants. One of them was a home for Tony and his girlfriend Rachael. Tony and Sophia were fighting the confiscation of his assets on the basis that the deposits had been put down by Sophia and the money was not the proceeds of crime. So, as a result of the confiscation order, the Serious Economic Crime Unit started Operation Opera. Operation Opera was a financial investigation which started as an investigation into the financial dealings of Tony. As they started investigating his assets, they added to the investigation the financial dealings of Rachael, then Sophia and then Johnny had been added to the investigation as a result of his financial links with Sophia. No one really knew the extent they were going to in uncovering all the financial records and tax records of the people under investigation.

In September 2007 Johnny met a girl at work again. This

time it was Magdalena, a beautiful Polish girl. They started dating. He had chatted to her a few times and they got on. She had fallen out with her guy because he had been violent towards her. It all started off very well.

Johnny had been looking for premises for the takeaway and found a great place, which ironically was only two doors down from Subway in Gabriel's Hill. It was exactly opposite Madison's, a very busy bar and club on Gabriel's Hill, and between the kebab house and Subway. It had been a jeweller previously. It had a large 3-bedroomed flat above it, which was not ideal. He would have preferred a shop only, but the flat entrance could be made separate to the shop and the flat rented out.

He made enquiries, explained what he wanted to do, and did a deal through the agents with the owner. The owner came down, met him and agreed it would all be good. Johnny would take a twenty-five-year lease, and the terms and conditions were agreed in principle, subject to planning permission being granted by Maidstone Borough Council for a change of use from retail to a takeaway. Solicitors were instructed and a planning application was submitted to the council. The deposits required were large but they were only deposits, and the premises were ideal. Johnny was allowed access with builders to get quotes for the work required for the conversion and to plan the design of the takeaway. He and Sophia agreed on the name Express Kitchen.

Within a month or so Johnny had got prices for all the building work required. Sophia had a niece, Kylie, who was married to a guy called Steve Burke. He was a builder who could do the job. He had a good reputation. Anything he could not do, he could bring in people and get all the building work done. Johnny very quickly realised the costs were already spiralling out of control, with the equipment and shop fitting which would follow the lease costs and the building work. At the time he was still drinking with a lot of guys Lee knew. One of them was Mick Kendell. He had just been done for drink-driving and had his own transport business over on the Isle of Sheppey. Johnny and Mick were regularly out, drinking together. One afternoon, Johnny persuaded Mick to lend him £40k to finish the project off. They agreed a deal and it was formalised by solicitors. So now he had the funds to take the project to completion and get it open and off the ground.

Life seemed to be going well for Johnny in late 2007, and he saw it as a big chance to get his life straight. He was still in therapy, drinking and taking drugs daily, but had a plan to get out of the crime business, settle down with Magda and make a life for himself. Magda wanted to go back home to her parents in Poland for Christmas. Johnny was invited. He considered it but she wanted to return in January, so he declined. He wanted to stay in England and concentrate on getting the lease sorted and Steve Burke on with the building work.

He had only made two mistakes with Steve Burke. The first was not getting a time frame for the work. Prices had all been agreed, so that was not a problem. The second was getting a quote from him at all. He really didn't come up to scratch in so many departments. His attitude was not great from the off. Johnny went off him for his attitude from the beginning. He had given him the date that the solicitors would complete on the new lease. Therefore, he would have access and Steve could start, but Steve said he couldn't for a while, which Johnny couldn't believe. He was giving him notice. The rent and rates were £1,700 per week and he just wanted the job getting on with.

So, there was now a delay before Steve could get in. They agreed a start date. After Steve started, it was clear that Steve knew his trade but some of the sub-contractors he was using were not up to the job. Johnny tried not to lose his temper with Steve a few times. He wanted the job done and he knew Steve was married to Sophia's relation. He certainly was not worried by Steve but he realised Steve thought he was a bit of a boy and a lad, so to speak. Johnny was busy ordering the shop fittings according to his design and had everything ordered ready for delivery as soon as Steve finished. The counter area needed to be built around the units, and a carpenter would need a while to finish off once everything else was in place, but everything else was stainless steel and fitted units and work surfaces.

Johnny was in Madison's with Mick Kendell and both were the worse for wear. They were both standing on the steps outside the bar, looking at the new sign, Express Kitchen, which had been put up on the facia, had lighting above it and looked amazing. This guy walks out the pub and says to Johnny and Mick, 'All these takeaways and kebab houses are owned by criminals into drugs and prostitution. They are all fronts, really.' Johnny certainly had heard of rumours that half of all kebab houses were set up and run by people involved in the importation and supply of heroin. Mick was on the floor, laughing his head off. Johnny tried to keep a neutral look on his face, preferring to pretend he hadn't heard what he said before he shuffled off up the road.

When Magda came back from Poland in January 2008, Johnny called it off with her. He had been drinking nonstop since she went away. Very quickly he ruined that relationship which had so much potential, and they did talk after that but they never got back to where they were in 2007. It had all been his doing. It all started the day he picked her up from the airport when she got back.

Steve didn't quite finish the job off properly but wanted paying in advance. By now Steve had worked out that being a bit of a boy was not going to get him very far with Johnny. Their relationship had deteriorated but Johnny tried to keep his cool. Some of the people Johnny was knocking about with and drinking in the bar opposite with probably told Steve more of a story than he realised. Steve knew Johnny was very disappointed with how he'd handled the shop fitting. Tempers flared a little, and Johnny told Steve where to go in no uncertain terms. Then, to keep the peace and get everything done, he agreed to give Sophia the balance, which was about £4k. It was agreed that as soon as Steve completed the work, Sophia would pay him.

That was a good solution. So, Steve goes in to complete the work and finishes it off, then causes some damage which looked to Johnny like it had been caused intentionally. Johnny went to check the work and was absolutely astonished. He rang Sophia and told her not to pay Steve as he had caused damage to the property. She told Steve what Johnny had said. She had not seen it but was going to take a look herself to see if he was overreacting.

It was on a Monday, and Steve phoned Johnny. Johnny was driving through Maidstone when he answered the call. Very quickly it turned into a slanging match. Then Steve said he was going to go over the shop and chuck a brick through the window and cause some more damage. The red mist came down for Johnny. He could not believe what this guy had just said. He was so angry. He rang Adam and asked to meet him and John, his cousin. John was totally unbalanced and Johnny and John had got on when they had met before. Johnny knew John was a handful. They met in a pub in Iwade and he explained to them he wanted to go to the builder's and pour petrol over him and burn him. He knew where he lived in Gravesend. They all jumped in Johnny's car and drove up the M2 to Gravesend. On the way they stopped in the services and Johnny bought a plastic petrol can, filled it up with petrol and put it in the boot. When they got to Steve's place in Gravesend, Johnny parked up just round the corner and rang Steve. Steve didn't answer. He left him a message saying he was just round the corner and was going to burn Steve alive. He made it clear to Steve he would not be going to Maidstone to cause any damage at all under any circumstances. Then Johnny rang him back and said if you come out, we can discuss it. Steve never answered or phoned back. They all left and drove back. Later that night, Adam told Lee, 'I have never seen him like that before.'

The next day Johnny was in therapy, telling his therapist about the goings-on. As no one had been hurt, the therapist was not under any obligation to report it to anyone. The therapist said to him, 'You had control when he put the phone down on you.' Johnny didn't really understand the remark at the time but it did sink in what he had said, and later he would understand the significance of the remark.

In March 2007 he was confident of winning his appeal for drink-driving and went out and bought an Audi A5 sports car from Audi in Maidstone. He insured it and simply overlooked the fact that he was on a ban. It was in March that he was watching the local news on the TV one evening when there was a report on a police operation all over Kent. The two previous days, the police had targeted brothels in the Kent area. Johnny thought how fortunate he had been not to have any problems as a result of the raids. He never realised no one at work wanted to tell him about it. Sophia just didn't tell him. Jo had opened late, and when they arrived no one was there at all, so they left. Anne was working on her own because staff had let her down, and a woman working on her own cannot be classed as a brothel. A brothel must be used by more than one woman to sell sexual services from.

Finally, in April 2008, the shop was coming together and could open. It was going to open on Wednesday 16th April, after a few deliveries had all been arranged for Tuesday and all the stock was in place. The shop looked amazing and was good to go. Johnny was so pleased and relieved. It could finally start to trade and earn. On Tuesday he was celebrating the shop opening with Mick Kendell. Johnny and Mick were going to open it together on Wednesday morning and run it together until all the staff had been taken on and it was up and running.

Tuesday night Johnny had been drinking heavily but he set his alarm for 06.30 am and managed to get some sleep. The next morning there was a really loud, continuous banging and knocking at his door. He ran downstairs in his pants, looked through the peephole on his door and saw this man's face. He didn't recognise him at all. He was half asleep and only saw his face. He undid the door and opened it. As he opened the door, he saw the man was wearing a police uniform and was a police officer. Then it became apparent there was a line of police officers out of sight. Some were in uniform and some were in plain clothes. Then a warrant appeared and they all walked in. Johnny had never seen so many police officers. There must have been about 9 or 10 in total. They came in explained they were from the Serious Economic Crime Unit and had a search warrant issued under the Proceeds of Crime Act to search and remove any property they saw fit to assist their investigation into Johnny Butler.

The sergeant in charge was on the phone to other police officers who were raiding other properties and suspects homes. The officers trying to search Sophia's address couldn't find her or get her up. He asked Johnny where she was. Johnny laughed. He thought, *the last thing I am going to tell you is anything.* Then, when he was on the phone, they had got her up. She had been in bed. Johnny was slightly embarrassed to say the least, because he had all the properties he owned in separate folders on his dining table, which he thought probably didn't help. Next thing a thorough search was going on, and his computer, documents and all sorts were being seized. He was allowed to go and get dressed with an officer in his presence. As he was getting dressed, the alarm went off and the copper joked, 'It was nearly time for you to get up in any case.' Johnny had two mobiles. One of them he definitely didn't want them getting their hands on. He managed to get it in his jean pocket without being seen. The other one was seized. He was then arrested and taken to Maidstone Police Station while the search continued. Three officers took him out to a Volvo. As they left the building, Johnny launched his phone into a bush. It hit the wall and made a bang. There was not a person about and no other noise at all. He thought they must have heard it but they were all involved in a conversation. Everyone just kept walking towards the unmarked Volvo. He was relieved about getting rid of that phone.

When they arrived at Maidstone Police Station, he was booked in the custody area and put in a cell. He was offered one call and he asked the sergeant if he could call Mick Kendell on the number stored in his mobile and just say 'Johnny has been arrested and will not be at work today.' Johnny felt awkward and a little embarrassed. The shop was going to open and he had been arrested. He didn't know it but Sophia was going to be brought to the same police station and questioned later on at the same time. In fact, it was clearly done on purpose, but before he was interviewed, he was taken into a custody area and was left in a room on his own with the door open when Sophia was brought in and booked in. He realised what the point of this was, and just totally ignored her. He just acted like he had never seen her before in his life. Johnny and Sophia were questioned all day about various offences. He just gave a “no comment” interview from start to finish. He had a local solicitor and it was agreed let them prove their case while he said nothing. Later that day they were both bailed to return to the police station in six weeks and released at exactly the same time. They walked off at the same time together towards Gabriel’s Hill. As they crossed the road, Johnny glanced behind and saw two of the officers just watching them walk off together. What a day it had been.

He had not realised it but when they’d searched his home, they found the keys to his new Audi, which was parked in one of the two parking bays allocated to the apartment, and had searched that as well. Later that day they realised he was banned from driving. Very quickly they worked out he was driving on his ban. On 25th April, Johnny walked out of his home, jumped in his car and drove out towards the gate. He didn’t know it but the police were waiting in an unmarked car for him. As soon as he turned right on to the main road, they had indicated to other officers that he had left, was on the public highway, and had turned right heading towards Tonbridge. As he turned right, the lights were red and he stopped. Traffic was particularly heavy that morning. When the lights changed to green, Johnny drove off but was just sat in traffic. He heard a siren but didn’t think anything of it. It seemed like a long way behind him. Then, on his outside, a police car appeared after overtaking several vehicles. The passenger window was wound down and he recognised the officer from the search at his house. He said to him, ‘Pull over. You don’t have a licence.’ Johnny replied, ‘Yes, I do.’ Then the officer said, ‘You are banned from driving.’ Johnny pulled over. He was arrested and one of the officers drove his car back to his place for him and parked it up outside his place. He was taken to Maidstone Police Station where he explained he had appealed his driving ban and was driving until the appeal had been heard. He had launched the appeal – that bit was true. They explained to him that he was not allowed to drive before the appeal was heard. He was charged on 25th April with driving while disqualified and driving with no insurance. The sergeant on the desk looked at Johnny and said to him, 'I bet no one has ever called you boring.' Johnny smiled and said nothing.

CHAPTER 21
ORGANISED CRIME CHARGES AND TRIAL

When Johnny got home, he decided to stop driving for a while, as he now knew they were onto him and perhaps it was best to leave it until the appeal against his drink-driving conviction was heard. He attended Maidstone Magistrates Court to face the charges and explained that he was waiting for the appeal to be heard and it was simply a misunderstanding. The magistrates thought it would be better to deal with the matter after the appeal had been heard. The Crown knew the appeal was in the system and waiting to be heard, so this matter was adjourned until a date had been set for the appeal of the drink-driving conviction.

After returning a month later, the Crown knew that the appeal against drink-driving was to be heard at Maidstone Crown Court on 8th August. There had been a delay because of witness availability, they explained. So, it was agreed that the matter of driving while disqualified and driving with no insurance would be dealt with on 10th August.

Bail for the organised crime allegations was continuously being extended and the police were speaking to the solicitors and agreeing new dates while they continued their investigations. Express Kitchen was now open and trading, and life seemed to be just rolling on. Johnny met a girl called Debbie in Chicago Rocks one night and they agreed to go out for dinner.

She seemed really nice. She looked good, liked a drink and lived the other side of Maidstone. He got her to come round his place in her car and they would go from there. She turned up and parked her Mini next to his sports car. Johnny wanted to impress her so took her out in his Audi. The whole evening went well. Dinner in West Malling went well. Then they went back to Maidstone and hit the pubs and clubs. He was a bit uncomfortable driving. He was totally paranoid, just in case he got pulled up.

He was also drunk again. So, later that night, they ended up back at his place. After a couple of hours, they decided to go back to Debbie's place. She drove through Maidstone over the limit and he followed in his car, also over the limit and on drugs. He really felt uncomfortable. It was about 4 am and there was no traffic whatsoever.

He knew his car would flag up as not insured and with a driver on a ban, or thought it would, but they got to her place without being stopped. He stayed at Debbie's for a few hours and then went home. He managed to get home ok but didn't feel comfortable with the experience, even if he was out of it on drink and drugs. He decided to stop driving and started using cabs and buses again. He only took the car to impress Debbie, and it had worked.

Late one night Johnny had run out of vodka and fancied some nice food for the fridge. He jumped in his car just to nip up to Tesco's and get a few bits. It was about 2 am on 6th August. He was driving up the A20 towards Tesco's at Lunsford Park. He drove past the Kent Police Tactical Operations entrance on the London Road near Allington.

The road was very quiet, not a lot of traffic at all. Johnny was driving steadily, sticking to the speed limits. Then from nowhere he saw flashing blue lights in his mirrors. He pulled over in the lay-by. No need to panic, he thought. One of the police officers got out of the car and approached him. He seemed quite genuine and just said it was a routine stop because there was a large number of high-performance sports cars, including Audi A5's, being stolen to order, so they were just checking it was his car. He said yes, gave his name and explained it was his car and in his name. The police officer went back and checked. He came back and asked him to get out of the car. He said, 'You are banned from driving.' Johnny tried to explain that he was not banned. He had appealed the conviction and a date had been set to hear the appeal. He was then breathalysed, which he passed but only just. The police then said that they were getting the car towed to the police pound and arrested him. The breakdown truck came shortly after and Johnny was taken to Maidstone Police Station, interviewed and charged again with driving while disqualified and driving with no insurance. He now had to attend Maidstone Magistrates the next day and face the charges. The magistrates looked at him with disbelief and shook their heads. They told him this was a very serious matter. He kept his composure and said politely, 'I am confused. Am I allowed to drive or not?' At this point the male magistrate in the centre of three told Johnny, 'If you drive again, you will be going to prison.' Johnny thanked him for explaining and now said he understood he should not drive and would not until the appeal was heard. This new case was adjourned until 10th August, 2 days after Johnny's appeal and the date set for the other matter to be dealt with.

So come 8th August, he was ready for the appeal. All he had to do was create doubt in the mind of the appeal judge as to who was driving the car when it crashed through the security barrier. Sophia had agreed to give her evidence again, that she was driving her car and he was only a passenger, they argued and she just walked off. The Crown relied on the testimony of the security man again. Johnny knew the Crown had to prove their case beyond reasonable doubt, and he believed he had a defence which created reasonable doubt. The case did not take too long to hear, just over an hour or so. Then the judge said the appeal had failed. He called Sophia and Johnny bare-faced liars. Sophia was not in court now. She preferred to wait downstairs. When the judge said it, Johnny thought, 'Whatever you do, don't mince your words.' Then, remarkably, the judge reduced the fine from £1400 to £900 as he thought the original fine was excessive. Johnny wasn't too worried about the fine reduction. That was not the point of the appeal. He was fighting for his driving licence and had lost that fight.

On 10th August he attended the Magistrates Court in Maidstone to have the outstanding driving matters dealt with. When he attended, the duty solicitor from Burroughs Solicitors, who had represented him in his no-comment interview earlier in the year, was there. He looked at him and said, 'Strange. You have no criminal convictions whatsoever up until drink-driving, then all this,' obviously referring to the driving matters and the organised crime allegations. Johnny shrugged his shoulders and said, 'Mm.' He had a long list of arrests, charges and "not guilty" convictions, as well as cases collapsing and not being pursued. He would later meet a woman called Elizabeth, who worked for the Government, who had seen Johnny's full list of arrests and convictions. She described Johnny to one of her colleagues, Andrew, as 'Al Capone with the gift of the gab.' Johnny only had his original defence – that he thought he could drive until the appeal was heard. The solicitor spoke for him and he pleaded guilty to the four driving offences, with his mitigation being that he thought he could drive until the appeal was heard. He was sentenced for the four charges together. He was given a community service order for 18 months, a supervision requirement, unpaid work for 200 hours, disqualified from driving – obligatory 3 years and driving licence endorsed. The real positive was that after taking the biscuit, so to speak, he had avoided prison.

He would simply have to stop driving. Express Kitchen was struggling to make its mark as he had hoped it would, but he could now concentrate on that. One Friday evening, Johnny and Mick were in the shop and meant to be serving but it was quiet so they nipped over the road for a few drinks. Mick had gone too far on the Jack Daniels and cocaine. Johnny was still holding it together slightly better when they returned to open the shop again about 11 pm. It was now a lot busier. In walks this young lad up to the crisps stand, grabs a few packets of crisps, looks at Johnny and Mick, who were behind the counter, then just walks out with them. Johnny and Mick were speechless. They looked at each other and burst out laughing. Then Mick fell over in the shop and couldn't get up. The police were passing and popped in to see what was going on. Johnny explained there was no problem. Mick was working in the shop with him. They were both in charge. This copper looked at Mick and told him he was drunk. Then he asked him if he had been drinking. He said no, then the copper said to Johnny, 'He is not working in here tonight. I am not having drunk people serving drunk people.' Mick started laughing. So it was agreed Johnny would serve on his own. After the police left, they locked up the shop again and went back over the road.

The police kept extending bail and then in October 2008 dates were agreed with the police and the solicitors for Johnny, Sophia, Tony and Rachael to answer their bail and attend the police station. It happened over a two-day period and everyone got charged with various offences ranging from management of brothels to drug offences, handling the proceeds of crime, money laundering, various frauds, deception and concealing criminal property. They all got charged individually but all the charges, a total of 34, were put on one indictment so they would all face trial together and at the same time. When Johnny returned to the police station, the sergeant from the Serious Economic Crime Unit asked him how he got on with his driving ban and offences. Johnny looked at him and said, 'No good. I got convicted.' Then, after Johnny was charged with nine offences, the sergeant said to him, 'We call you Lucky.' Even Johnny smiled. The original hearing for the case was at Maidstone Magistrates Court. Then after that, the case got transferred to Canterbury Magistrates Court. Johnny parted company with his solicitors after the first hearing at Maidstone Magistrates Court. Whatever was going to unfold, he didn't want them representing him. The police officer explained that most of his cases were dealt with at Maidstone Crown Court but they did some at Canterbury Crown Court purely based on court availability and so on.

Johnny had a regular probation officer for his driving offences supervision order. He walked into the probation office for the next appointment and was waiting in reception to see her when she walked past and said, 'You have been a busy boy.' Johnny had not realised she would be aware of his charges. He hadn't thought that through. When he went into her office a short while afterwards, he calmy looked at her and said, 'They are only allegations – not convictions.' She raised her eyebrows. He certainly wasn't going to discuss it with her.

The second appearance for the case was at Canterbury Magistrates Court purely for the matter to be sent to Canterbury Crown Court to be dealt with. Johnny turned up, one of four defendants. He was not being represented on this occasion. Everyone had dressed up very smart for the court appearance. It was while waiting outside court that he bumped into Kerry Irwin Mitchell. Kerry Irwin Mitchell knew from the charges on the list on the wall what was going on. He asked Johnny how he was. They spoke. He said to Johnny, 'You should have rung me when you got arrested.' Johnny hadn't thought of it, really. He knew he would offer "no comment", so the other guy had ticked the box, so to speak. Anyway, he agreed to have Irwin Mitchell & Co act for him, so he was now represented. Kerry Irwin Mitchell knew all the magistrates and did have an excellent reputation for criminal work. He already knew him from many years ago, from when he had first represented Mikey and him in various matters.

When all the defendants walked into court, the first thing that happened was the Crown handed each one of them a large A4 envelope. The day before, a judge at Maidstone Crown Court had signed various orders and all the defendants' assets had been frozen. None of them were aware of this until that moment. Johnny read the order and realised his properties and his bank accounts were no longer within his control. Everything he owned had been frozen. His order was clear – the only people he could write a cheque to for payment was HM Government, Inland Revenue or Customs and Excise. How thoughtful. He smiled; he couldn't do anything apart from pay the government money he owed if any.

The court was full of various journalists. Clearly the case was going to attract a lot of media attention. He and his co-defendants sat behind a glass screen and the thirty-four charges got read out. At one point, after about twenty-five of the charges had been read out, one of the magistrates glanced over at the defendants with a look of 'My God,' on his face, 'how many more charges?!' All the defendants were granted bail to appear at Canterbury Crown Court in 2009 for the next hearing. Their assets had all been frozen and now they had to work out what they were going to do. After the hearing a journalist said to Johnny, 'You don't look the type.' Johnny said to him, 'It was all just a misunderstanding,' and walked off. After saying his goodbyes, he nipped up the bank a bit smartish to get some money out but it was too late. None of his cards worked. They just came up with "refer to branch for details." Johnny went into the branch and was told there was an order on his accounts, freezing them. That hadn't taken long to take effect, that was for sure.

So, December 2008 he sat at home, potless, with a Fray Bentos steak and kidney pie for Christmas lunch. By January he could get some rents paid to him in cash and work out where he was going now.

By January the Crown had handed over all the disclosure to the solicitors. There were boxes filled with reams and reams of papers. The investigation had certainly been thorough. Johnny and all his co-defendants all had different solicitors representing them, and when he attended Irwin Mitchell & Co, they recommended Lewis Trent as a barrister. He took their recommendation and another meeting was set up with Mr Trent at the offices of Irwin Mitchell & Co. They started sifting through the evidence and Lewis Trent recommended pleading guilty. Johnny was shocked and disappointed. He had been trying to explain to Mr Trent he was innocent. Clearly Mr Trent wasn't listening to him. Then, after considering more evidence, Mr Trent said to him, 'You protest too much, Mr Butler.' Johnny wasn't amused. He wanted a barrister who would fight for him.

Pleading guilty and losing everything he had didn't seem like a plan at all to him. He wanted to fight and win. He thought pleading guilty seemed like a total surrender. It just wasn't in his nature. He knew criminal cases can and do collapse all the time for various legal reasons. He knew a couple of the witnesses were lying to protect themselves and just totally disregarded the other witnesses and evidence. He didn't want to hear the truth. What he did know was that if he had always pleaded guilty, he would have been sent to prison in his twenties for fraud and other various crimes, so surrendering or pleading guilty, as Mr Trent put it, was a nonstarter. A defence statement had to be submitted to the Crown prior to a trial date so they could see what his defence was.

One night Tony was driving home down the Thanet Way on his own and ended up hitting the central reservation, losing control of his motorbike and crashing. Tragically, he died instantly, which broke Sophia and Rachael's hearts. At the next hearing the indictment was reduced to three defendants as a result of the tragedy. Following the accident, the coroner concluded it was death by accident.

Johnny had not quite worked this out yet but he needed a magician, not a barrister. Simple, he thought. He would defend himself. That would solve any problems. He could write his own defence statement and defend himself in court. At least he understood the case against him and what his defence would be. He certainly believed in himself and his defence more than Mr Trent did. So, he told Irwin Mitchell & Co and Mr Trent he no longer required their services. The solicitors had a legal responsibility to inform the courts, and so they did. A hearing just to deal with this matter was set up at Canterbury Crown Court in April 2009. By now Johnny had written and served his defence statement to the Crown. When he got to court, the matter was listed to be dealt with in front of Judge Adelle Fulton. He remembered her from when she was a barrister and had represented Sophia in the attempted deception on the Prudential trial many moons ago, in which they had both been acquitted. At the time, Sophia had told him she had the reputation of being a rottweiler. After Irwin Mitchell & Co explained that he had terminated their instructions and intended to represent himself, she looked at him and went mad. She certainly had a loud voice and almost starting screaming at him, 'This is a large trial that will last some time and there are other barristers involved. All you will be doing is delaying the proceedings and it will not serve in your best interests to act for yourself even if you are capable.' She said that the solicitors and barristers had years of experience, which could and would be used in his best interests. She urged him to go away and reconsider. That was how it was left. After leaving the court, Johnny said to his legal team, 'If you want to fight the case and defend me, then you can. If you just want to keep knocking me, and asking me to plead guilty, then don't bother, that simply will not be happening.' It was agreed they would act for him again and they would let Mr Trent know he was back on the firm. The pleas would be "not guilty" and the matter would proceed to trial, and it was suggested to Mr Trent he needed to start fighting for him a bit more. Johnny wasn't disappointed by the outcome at all. He had made his point and at least now everyone knew where they were.

The next hearing for the case was at Canterbury Crown Court in June 2009. It was in front of the judge that had been given the case. As all defendants had bail dates, it was less of an issue because if defendants are remanded in custody, their cases have to come to court within a certain time limit. The judge happened to be a regular customer at the industrial unit at Whitstable. Sophia remembered him. He would always turn up with his driver and see the same girl. This might be a stroke of luck, Johnny thought. Then, after reading the papers and hearing the charges, the judge explained he had holiday commitments which may well affect his ability to hear the case, so he would have to let the case be reallocated to another judge. Neat idea, Johnny thought. He didn't blame him in the circumstances.

The case got reallocated to Judge James O'Grady and was listed to start on Tuesday 5th January 2010. Monday 4th January was a bank holiday. The Tuesday was the first day in the new year that the court would be open again after the Christmas break.

The rest of 2009, Johnny spent working on his defence as well as staying with his friend Tony, on occasions, and Sophia. He was still smoking like a trooper, drinking and smoking the joints. On one occasion he went out with a few lads he knew and they ended up on the cocaine that night. About midnight he collapsed and just passed out. The stress and drink and drugs had just knocked him spark-out. He remembered coming to the next morning and hearing a hoover. There was a woman hoovering the bar and all around him. She said his friends said he would be fine to be left there until morning. Adam knew the owner and explained it would be all right, and the owner had been fine with that, it turned out.

Tuesday 5th January 2010 soon came around. It was agreed everyone would arrive early to have a conference with their legal teams before the case started in court. Johnny and his two co-defendants entered pleas of "not guilty" to all the charges. Rachael was only facing one charge, and that was almost out of spite to get guilty pleas and do a deal. She had not really been involved in the financial crime that she was accused of. A jury was selected. There were only a couple of people that could not serve on the jury. One knew Sophia from many years ago – that was him excused – and the judge excused another woman based on the possible length of the trial. There were two barristers prosecuting the case: Mr Kindell and Mr Hind. The opening statement from the Crown sounded bleak, apart from the fact that Mr Kindell chose to make it a matter of two different stories representing the facts of the case and said, 'It will be a matter of whom you believe.' Mr Trent and Johnny quite liked that part, because he could prove a couple of their witnesses were lying or at least being economical with the truth. Early on in the trial, Sophia had been looking at the jury, and one of the female members of the jury said she felt threatened d by the look as it was intimidating. A note had been passed to the judge and he reprimanded Sophia for her alleged behaviour.

As the prosecution witnesses took the stand, Mr Trent said there were certain witnesses whose evidence could just be accepted. 'No need to challenge everyone,' he said. 'We can simply let the Crown know which ones, and their statements can just be read out.' That was like a red rag to a bull. Johnny was off again. They did finally agree on a few witnesses that didn't need to attend and could just have their statements read out. They tended to just be from people who collected information and data, or at least what they had to say had no real bearing or weight on guilt or innocence. After about eight or nine witnesses had given evidence, Rachael's barrister argued to the judge that in the circumstances about what evidence had been given it would not be reasonable to allow a jury to consider her innocence or guilt, as there was already a lot of doubt as to what she actually knew. The Crown didn't really even argue that much and Judge O'Grady agreed with her barrister. The Crown dropped the charge against her. She was free to go.

After a few more witnesses, one of the mortgage brokers said in the witness box that for the buy-to-let mortgages, employment status was irrelevant. If anyone had the 15% deposit, they would get the loan. It was just about the deposit and the rental value of the properties. The judge looked surprised at what he had heard. The witness was just being very honest. A lot of this was going on just prior to the financial crash in which banks would have been wiped out without government support. As result of this, Sophia and Johnny had some mortgage fraud charges dropped. Then, at the same time, the judge said he thought two of the charges that Johnny was facing were in fact a duplication of charges for the same crime. That meant a further charge got removed from the indictment. At this point Johnny quite liked the fact that the case he was facing seemed to be less severe. Mr Trent disagreed and said, 'I am not sure about that,' even if now there were less charges.

Then a week or two later it was blatantly obvious to everyone that Mr Cullen was lying in his evidence. He denied it but the damage was done. The prosecutors could not repair that damage. It was at this point Mr Kindell lost confidence in the strength of the prosecution case and Mr Trent realised it. After a casual chat, Mr Kindell let Mr Trent know that if his client pleaded guilty to two charges, the rest could be dropped. It was explained to him that Mr Kindell would recommend that to the people in the office as a result of how the case was going, and since they were not there hearing the evidence in court, they would take his recommendation.

One officer in the case followed Johnny in the toilets one lunchtime and just said, 'How is it going in there?' Johnny looked over, smiled and said, 'It depends which side you are on.' Johnny realised they were rattled a little, especially when Johnny declined any deal. Whatever they thought, they knew that it was going to be a real fight rather than a walkover.

Mr Trent said to Johnny that he was a natural-born trader.

This was the moment to do a deal. He said, 'Mr Kindell thinks he's struggling. I am not totally convinced but he thinks he is. This is bargain, basement time to buy the stocks.' Johnny liked that saying. Things had certainly started to take a turn and Johnny's confidence was now through the roof. If he pleaded guilty to two charges, Mr Trent thought he would get about two years in prison and a confiscation order. He couldn't agree to that – a prison sentence and a confiscation order with him admitting two charges. He declined the offer and decided to continue fighting. He knew he could talk once in the witness box and put his side across. Maybe he could create reasonable doubt; that was the standard.

By now the case was front page of the local papers every week. One lunch break, Johnny and Sophia left the court together and there were photographers with long-range lenses about 100m away from the court entrance. He saw them but didn't realise they were there to photograph them. He certainly didn't put that together until seeing the photo covering the whole of the front page. There were always various headlines about the allegations in the case.

One witness Johnny particularly remembered from the trial was a woman from Faversham who was giving a small piece of evidence about one of Sophia's charges. She referred to everyone on trial as "bloody criminals". Johnny thought, *I hope she's not talking about me – I have not been convicted of anything.* Maybe a little bit presumptuous of him.

Every day after the proceedings finished, Johnny and Sophia would go out to eat and drink or just for a drink. One evening they ended up drinking in the Red Lion in Bridge. In walked Grant Mott, the builder who'd bought the cab firm with Mikey many years earlier. Johnny and Sophia were not drunk but had had a few by the time he appeared and he was putting tracks on the jukebox. He had found a few Perry Como tracks, which Johnny had not heard for years; in fact, it was probably since his childhood. George, his father, had 8 tracks of Perry Como and would often play them. Grant smiled at him and said, 'They don't play tracks like this in Parkhurst.' Johnny never replied; he was more intent on enjoying the music, although deep down he thought it was funny.

By the time the Crown chose to close their case, Johnny had his version of the truth absolutely engrained in his mind. It was one simple acting job. If he was plausible, they had a chance. Sophia decided not to take the stand on advice from her barrister. Johnny took the stand. It was now February. Mr Trent asked Mr Kindell how long he thought the cross-examination would last. Mr Kindell said something like, 'until I have covered everything.' The direct examination from Mr Trent didn't last too long. Just a couple of hours. He led Johnny through his statement and then rested. So, after lunch, it was now Mr Kindell's turn. Mr Trent's advice had been, 'Dodge the bullets,' before the cross-examination started.

Johnny's cross-examination took three days. He knew the case inside out. He knew the Crown's weaknesses and would continuously refer to them at every opportunity. Mr Kindell accused him of making up evidence in the lunch break at one point. On a few points, Johnny was scoring well, he thought. Then Mr Kindell asked him how he saw his relationship with Ravinder Singh. When Ravi had turned up to give evidence for the Crown, Johnny and Ravi had lunch together upstairs in the court canteen, in full sight of everyone. He didn't realise they shouldn't be talking. Ravi pointed out at the beginning of the conversation that he couldn't discuss his evidence. They didn't discuss his evidence. They simply had lunch and caught up.

Ravi had had another child and he spent most of the time

talking about that. Ravi had always been more than fair to Johnny. Eighteen months earlier, a detective from the Serious Economic Crime Unit had rung Ravi and explained he had a warrant to seize any records he had about the business or tax affairs of Johnny Butler. He made an appointment for the following afternoon to go and collect the records. Ravi phoned Johnny straight away and suggested he go over. Ravi explained certain records obviously had to be handed over and why. He then left some folders about some of Johnny's business affairs on the desk and explained he could not destroy any documents or contents of those files, obviously. He then had a call of nature and had to leave him in the conference room with the folders on the table, while he went to the loo. Johnny simply picked the folders up and walked out of the office, saying to the receptionist, whom he knew very well, 'Nice to see you. Please let Ravi know I had to shoot off and I will hopefully see him soon.' What a touch, he thought as he drove home. Maybe he was The Carlsberg Accountant. He certainly couldn't have been any fairer or loyal.

Johnny explained to Mr Kindell that, originally, Ravi had been his accountant, and as a result of that over the years they had become friends. Since Ravi had not changed his evidence, he decided to move on after Johnny admitted he saw him as a friend today. Johnny noted that Kerry Irwin Mitchell came into the courtroom and listened for a few hours during his cross-examination.

At one point, Mr Kindell was accusing Johnny of knowing and being involved in the management of brothels. Johnny denied all knowledge of this and said, 'It was nothing like that at all.' When he was challenged further, he tried to put his little boy look on his face and said, 'If that is what has been going on, I feel I have been let down.'

Then, when presented with his bank statements and all the cash payments that had gone into his accounts every day at certain bank branches, which were also timed at generally 10.30 am, just before opening time, he couldn't really explain them properly. He knew he was weak in that area. He used to collect cash, then, through laziness, stopped doing that, preferring to have the monies paid directly into his accounts. Then Mr Kindell, who had all his bank statements in front of him, said to him, 'You like eating in nice restaurants, don't you, Mr Butler?' Johnny agreed that he did and knew he'd mainly paid by card. He took it as a compliment but Mr Kindell was confirming to the jury that Johnny had expensive habits, including eating out all the time in nice and, more particularly, expensive restaurants.

Some of the texts read terrible at face value but he felt he had managed to offer credible explanations and alternative interpretations to their real meanings.

Mr Kindell hit a few genuine brick walls with him. Johnny tried to rewrite the testimony of some of the witnesses and the judge actually went back over his notes to quote what they had actually said for the avoidance of doubt. At one point, Mr Kindell was struggling a little and Johnny knew the correct answers. He stated that he thought Johnny was very intelligent. Johnny didn't mind that. After three days of cross-examination, Mr Kindell accused him of lying about his evidence. Johnny denied that. On redirect, Mr Trent just introduced the fact that for part of the time Johnny was unrepresented legally and had submitted his own defence statement, which he felt might assist the jury in their deliberations. That was the end of the evidence. It was now just left for the judge to sum up the case before sending the jury out to deliberate. At one point during his cross examination, there had been legal arguments and Mr Trent said to him, 'I think the judge isn't really worrying too much about whether you are guilty or not. He is more concerned if there is anything you haven't done.' All through the trial, Johnny had been going out the front of the court to smoke during any breaks. He had quickly realised that some of the jurors were there as well. He had always tried to open and hold the doors for them, and on occasion had been able to light their cigarettes for them. He thought he might score a few brownie points with that.

The next day the prosecution and defence barristers put their final arguments to the jury. Sophia's barrister suggested to Sophia he would not rely too heavily on Johnny, just in case he was not believed. That was followed the next day by the judge summing up the case for the jury and giving them legal instructions. Johnny believed it had gone well. Rachael had walked, various charges had been dropped, as well as the charge the judge believed was a duplication. Mr Trent did prove two witnesses were lying, and he had given a full alternative version for the jury to hang their hat on if they wanted to in acquitting. At least he had given it his best shot. He had brought his mother to court to hear the summing up by the judge, he was that pleased with how it had gone. His mum was in the public gallery and listening. At lunchtime Vera said to Johnny the judge suggested his behaviour had been organised crime with a parachute plan. She said it sounded more like disorganised crime to her, and laughed. Then she said she wasn't best pleased by some of what she had heard. Johnny overlooked that remark and took her out for lunch before dropping her home later that day. The judge sent the jury out to deliberate on Thursday 11th February.

At this point it just became a waiting game. Mr Trent looked at Johnny and said, 'Well, you did what you could.' He then smiled at him and said the jury could come back at any time from now on. He wished Johnny good luck and then said that a barrister he trained with when he was a pupil always said to his clients, 'Whatever you do in the morning before you leave home to come to court, don't forget to turn the gas off – just in case.' Interesting remark, Johnny thought. After a few hours the jury had made certain requests about certain parts of the evidence. They were asking questions about tenancy agreements, which he had presented as his defence for purely being a landlord.

Then they came back on Monday 15th February and were asking questions about advertising and how that could be interpreted as proof.

On Tuesday 16th February the jury let the judge know they had reached their verdicts, apart from on one charge against Johnny, which they did not fully understand. The judge said he would hear their verdicts before commenting on the single charge that they did not understand. So, everyone was called together and gathered in the court again. The judge asked his clerk to get the jury back in. They came in and all sat down. It was about 3 in the afternoon. Johnny was first on the indictment. As all the charges were read out against Johnny and Sophia, all Johnny kept hearing was "guilty." The jury had found them both guilty of all the charges except one. At that point the judge suggested to the prosecutor that he would leave the charge on the file. The charge was against Johnny and it was Conceal/ Disguise/ Convert/ Transfer/ Remove Criminal Property. Then the judge thanked the jury for their time and verdicts. He stated he understood the verdicts after the overwhelming amount of evidence presented against the defendants in the case. The judge said sentencing would be the following day and if any of them wanted to return to hear the sentencing, they were more than welcome to, but they didn't have to and they were now excused from their service. The judge then looked at Johnny and Sophia and withdrew their bail. He said the temptation to abscond after being convicted may prove too tempting. Johnny was thinking to himself, *I wonder where he thinks I would run off to with no money*, but in any case, Johnny and Sophia were remanded until the following day for sentencing. The judge just said, 'Take them down.' Johnny and Sophia were led down the stairs to the cells before being taken away in prison transport. Mr Trent and Miss Taylor from Irwin Mitchell & Co came down to speak to him. Johnny commented that he thought, based on the fact that two of the prosecution witnesses had lied, that he had a chance. Mr Trent said, 'The jury probably thought you were as bad as each other and relied on the other evidence to convict.' Then, after a while, they said they would see him tomorrow and left. Johnny was taken to HMP Elmley on the Isle of Sheppey with an order that he be produced at court in the morning.

He didn't sleep that well and was up early the next morning and taken back to Canterbury Crown Court. He appeared in the dock at 10.30 am and was shocked the public gallery was full of people. Mr Trent had told him the judge was going to read him the riot act now that he had been convicted. It turned out Sophia's prison transport had broken down and alternative arrangements were being made to get her to court but she would not be there until lunchtime. The judge said he felt sentencing should take place at the same time and delayed sentencing until 2 pm. Johnny was surprised all the jury had returned to hear the sentencing. He thought, *why on earth would they want to come back again?*

At 2 pm on Wednesday 17th February, Johnny and Sophia stood in the dock to hear their sentences. Johnny was now aware that the people in the public gallery were police officers involved in the case and members of the Crown Prosecution Service. Judge James O'Grady said they would both go to prison for four and a half years, then the judge went through the various convictions, sentencing for various criminal offences ranging from 12 months to two years and making some sentences concurrent and some consecutive but making the final sentence four and a half years for both of them. Their crimes and convictions were different but the judge said he thought on balance he would treat them the same. Then after the sentences for each crime had been passed down and recorded, he said they could now sit down. Then he flew off the handle, in Johnny's opinion, about the case, going into a speech about both of them and their behaviour, which lasted half an hour. Mr Trent said the purpose was to keep the Crown Prosecution Service happy and act as deterrent to others considering similar behaviour.

Johnny could only really remember two remarks from the speech. He said Johnny didn't recognise the truth when it was staring him in the face. Johnny thought to himself, *is he calling me a liar?* Then he said Johnny had become a very wealthy young man as a result of his criminal activity. Johnny didn't mind that. All he heard was "wealthy young man." He was highly critical of Sophia as well. Then he praised the police involved and the Crown Prosecution Service for all their hard work in the case. Now Johnny understood it was just like a theatre production, with the judge thanking all the people in the public gallery at the side of the court. After that, he agreed to sign and start the confiscation proceedings as a result of the convictions for both defendants. He then rose and left the court before Johnny and Sophia were taken down. Mr Trent said he wouldn't come down to the cells. Johnny understood entirely. There was no point. He knew he would serve half in prison and half on prison licence.

Johnny was taken back to HMP Elmley in the prison transport with a few other people. He remembered getting a plastic container of drinking water, a cheese sandwich and a packet of ready salted crisps for the journey. When he got to the entrance of the prison, there was a slight delay in the gates being open and the lorry was just sitting outside, waiting. Johnny had the following thought, *if you could go back and change your life and live differently and avoid prison and a confiscation order, would you?* He sat and thought honestly and instantly decided, 'No.' On that basis, he had no complaints or reasons to moan. The gates were opened a few minutes later and the lorry drove in.

CHAPTER 22
PRISON LIFE

JOHNNY WENT into the reception area when he was allowed to leave the prison transport. A prison officer looked at his convictions and asked him if he had ever been to prison before. He said, 'No.' Then he asked him if he had any issues. Johnny didn't really understand what that question meant. He said, 'No.' Then he read the convictions and saw one was in contravention of a certain sex act, i.e. management of brothels, and he said, 'Do you want to go on the numbers or a separate wing of the prison for your own protection?' Johnny was stumped, looked at him and said, 'What for?' The officer asked about the one conviction and Johnny explained about brothel management. He said, 'Ok, that's fine, you won't have any problems for that.' Then, as a result of the medication he was on for his heart, first time in prison, the confiscation order and him saying he had no issues, Johnny was put in the hospital unit at the prison. He found out later from a person he knew that he was on suicide watch. He never knew that at the time. He was just thinking a spliff and a few vodka and diet cokes would be nice. So, after a medical and a quick lecture about prison life, he was placed in a large cell with several beds, on his own in the hospital ward. He had been given a free letter and some tobacco. The first night he wrote a letter to Tony, his friend, letting him know the outcome. Tony would tell everyone else. They all saw it in the papers in any event. The only line from the letter to Tony he remembered writing was, 'The judge said I cannot come out to play for four and a half years.'

The cell he was in was a complete tip, he thought. It had graffiti everywhere, was not particularly clean, and the toilet area was not the best he had seen. Maybe he had better start adapting to life and conditions as they were rather than how he thought they should be. The doctor came round with a large trolley full of prescription medication. He was flanked by 4 prison officers. The contents of the trolley were very valuable in prison, he kind of guessed. It was an African doctor. Johnny had his own medication with him when he went to prison. His only real priority was to make sure he had a good supply of his medication, as the doctors at St Thomas's Hospital had told him in no uncertain terms, 'If you don't take your medication you will die.' One of the officers was commenting on the size of his bag of medication. The doctor said to him, he is lucky he is not in some countries in Africa. They don't have that medication there and he would die.' Food for thought, he thought, but he realised the doctor was telling the truth.

The next day Johnny got out of bed about 10.30 am. He had a strip wash at the sink. He had cereals and milk left out for him for breakfast. He noticed they were not Kellogg's, just plain clear packets without any writing on. He then saw his door had been left open a little and he ventured out. He saw nearly opposite a room and some lads playing pool in there. He walked in. There were three younger lads around the pool table. Johnny looked at them. He could play pool, he thought and kind of wanted to settle in. So, he said to them, 'Is it winner stays on? Stick my name down on the list for a game, can you?' They all looked at him and started mumbling. Oh my God, he thought, they can't even talk properly. They were looking at Johnny and blurting out things like babies might try to talk. Not ideal, he realised. They just kept looking at him. Johnny started thinking two of them had cues and all the balls on the pool table. He had a vision of it kicking off very quickly. The atmosphere was not good. He didn't know what to do, so he sat on the floor and looked at them. It seemed to make it worse. He couldn't understand what they were saying and thought, well, if they want to act stupid, I will do the same. At this point a woman's voice shouted, 'Lunch! Get back to your rooms.' That was music to his ears. He was up on his feet and straight back to his cell. It was the dinner lady who was bringing lunch around on the trolley.

After lunch he was told he was being sent to the main prison wings. He got taken to the induction wing. He was given an English test and a maths test. He scored 60 out of 60 on the maths and 59 out of 60 on the English. He was disappointed with getting one wrong in the English test. He had not thought the tests were too hard. He got a strange look and realised that a lot of people in prison could not add up or read and write. He shared a cell with a Belgian lorry driver on the induction wing. He had been stopped at the customs at Dover and after a search, a large quantity of drugs had been discovered amongst the contents of his cargo. He said to Johnny he knew nothing about them. He was awaiting trial for importation. Johnny apologised to the Belgian guy about the state of the cell; it was worse than the hospital unit.

Very quickly, he realised the food certainly wasn't up to what he was used to, which made him smile. Then Johnny laughed to himself and thought, *I am apologising about the state of a prison in England to a guy smuggling drugs into England, or at least allegedly*. Anyone remanded awaiting trial would always say they were innocent. He got that. He would have as well. There is a language in prison, he very quickly realised. He would soon pick that up. *When in Rome*, he thought.

After being processed as a convicted prisoner he was sent to House Block 2, waiting to go to House Block 5, which was full up. There were certainly some characters in there. Everyone wore the same green trousers and jackets and plain blue t-shirts. You would never tell from looking at the people in there what they were in there for. He very quickly started meeting people he knew and had met before, even customers of his. He even met people who knew people who knew him. A young lad, Paul, he shared a cell with knew Adam and said to Johnny, 'You have gone from up there (pointing to the top of the world) to down here (pointing to the floor).' He had a point. Another guy Johnny didn't know asked him if he was a millionaire, which made him smile. The first time Johnny went up to get lunch on the wing, it all looked terrible to him. He asked what it was. After being told, he said, 'I can't eat that' and didn't get any. Then, at the end of the servery, standing on his own, was a guy who used to work for him on the cabs, Grahame. He laughed at Johnny when he said he couldn't eat that. He said to him, 'I can give you a load of doughnuts if you like.' That was his job, giving out doughnuts for dessert. He said he would look after Johnny. Johnny looked at the doughnuts and laughed. They looked terrible. They were the palest doughnuts he had ever seen and couldn't believe they had any real jam in. Still, it was nice of Grahame to offer. After a day or so he just ate the food and picked what he preferred and fell in line with everyone else. After a couple of weeks, when he was ordering a week in advance, he very quickly realised he had his favourites to look forward to some days. He was certainly learning to adapt very quickly.

The second guy Johnny shared a cell with was Gavin from Gravesend. Johnny knew nothing about him. He asked Johnny for a burn. Johnny said yes but he had no rizlas so he couldn't. Gavin said, 'No problem. We can use the Bible.' He ripped pages out of a small Bible in the cell. They were very thin and made excellent papers for rolling cigarettes with. Johnny liked that; they could smoke tobacco rolled in Bible pages. So that was handy. They now had a book full of papers. Gavin showed him a few prison tricks on that first night, including how to get electrical power from the light above to use. Johnny was learning fast. Gavin had been in prison several times previously and knew all the ropes. Gavin was in prison for driving without a licence and insurance again. He had never passed his test. He asked Johnny what he was in for and Johnny told him. After that he said to Johnny, 'I am the link man for the IRA and the Mob. If they need to talk, they get me to make the arrangements.' Johnny thought, *you are a bloody liar,* but didn't challenge him on it. It was one of those stories that can never be proved or disproved, a bit like how many women some men think they have slept with – pitiful, really. The only thing he knew for certain was that if such a person existed, they would have the job because they never told anyone anything, not spouted their mouth off about it.

Johnny bumped into a guy called Mario. An Italian guy who could talk for England. He had only known him 10 minutes and he said to Johnny, 'You are obviously a slippery so and so.' He was serving 14 years for robberies in London. He was clearly as hard as nails. He grew up the hard way in Italy. He was one of nine children from a poor family. He used to see people driving about in Ferraris when he was a child and he knew he wanted that life but didn't really have a plan on how to get and live that life, so he just went out and took the money from banks. He was old school, in a bank with a shooter and just trying to grab as much as he could as quick as he could. At least he was entertaining to talk to and listen to, Johnny realised. He spoke broken English but Johnny could understand him. Johnny had some money when he went into prison – not a lot but it was enough in prison terms. His canteen sheet got messed up and he couldn't buy any tobacco. For a heavy smoker, that was a problem. He very quickly found tobacco lenders on the wing that would lend for a week and want one and a half back or one and a quarter. He just kept borrowing from them for the first two weeks. The first week he paid back but ran out again so did it again. After two weeks he had that sorted. He didn't know anyone himself that were tobacco lenders but they were everywhere if they thought you were good for it.

Johnny knew deep down he didn't have any real grounds for appeal against his convictions. The judge had said after the verdicts while looking at him, 'I have been more than fair to this defendant,' and he had, really. He probably gave him a lot more leeway than Johnny realised at the time he was giving evidence. He'd only really corrected him personally once during three days. Mr Kindell had got confused over some business matters, including ownership of companies. Johnny had corrected him and told Mr Kindell he was wrong. The judge stepped in and said, 'We don't understand business, Mr Butler – we understand law.' The judge clearly understood he was right and protected Mr Kindell, but apart from that gave Johnny a free rein with his defence whatever he had thought.

He could appeal the sentence, though. He had a chance, he thought. Once he was in prison, he realised that if his sentence was reduced to 3 years 11 months total on appeal, he could get a tag before the end of the first half of his sentence. Any defendant that gets a sentence over 4 years cannot be eligible for a tag. Johnny did launch an appeal against his sentence on the grounds that it was manifestly excessive in the circumstances. The solicitors did the paperwork and the appeal against sentence was lodged.

Johnny got moved into a three-man cell after about another week and was sharing with two young black guys. One of the guys asked if he could borrow some tobacco from him until canteen day. He said yes and lent it to him. When canteen day came, he never offered to pay Johnny back. Johnny left it for a couple of hours and then said to him about it. He said he didn't have enough to pay him back but would the next week. Johnny knew straight away he fancied he wasn't paying him back. Anyway, what was he going to do? It wasn't about the tobacco. It was about the principle. Then Johnny found out he would be going to House Block 5. So, he went to see Mario and told him he didn't want the tobacco but he couldn't let it go. Could Mario promise to collect it, and if he did he could have it? At least Mario wasn't trying to rip him off. Mario walked straight up the stairs on to the first landing and said to the guy, 'You owe that tobacco to me, and next canteen day you will be paying me. Do you understand?' The guy totally changed his attitude and said yes, of course. Mario had said it to him in front of a crowd of prisoners to make the point.

Johnny got sent to House Block 5, which was for convicted offenders who would serve their sentence in HMP Elmley or be transferred to other prisons, depending on their sentences and crimes. He was put in a two-man cell with a young body-builder type who was full of himself and in the gym every day – Peter, from Folkestone. It didn't work out at all from the very off. Johnny got put in the cell while Peter was not there. He settled in. The cell was extremely tidy and clean. He had OCD. This person definitely had that and some more; everything was immaculate. It takes one to know one, that is for sure.

Johnny was on the top bunk and stood on the bottom bed to get on the top one. He lay there reading a book. Then this Peter walks in and says, 'Why have you been standing on my bed?' in a really aggressive tone. Johnny didn't look up and said, 'I didn't.' That was it – a blazing row with Peter accusing him of doing it and Johnny denying it. Then Johnny saw him and thought, *this is a problem, definitely*. Within a few hours the mufti squad – or riot squad – were at the door asking what the hell was going on. Johnny said, 'I am not staying in here with him.' Then they opened the door and said to Peter, 'It is always you, every time this happens.' Johnny was relieved. It made a change from him getting the blame. They knew the situation was at boiling point and put him in a cell opposite on his own. It was a two-man cell but was empty.

Johnny was watching his telly late that evening, the roulette, thinking and feeling not too good. He had come off the drink and drugs and was missing them, really. He did have tobacco and was settling down to prison life slowly. The very next day he got up and remembered Peter in the opposite cell. There had been no real harm done but Johnny fancied it wasn't over. He sounded like a raving lunatic the way the officers had spoken to him. Johnny walked out of his cell and virtually bumped straight into John, Adam's cousin, with whom he had always got on well. It was a bit of a shock to bump into him and they got chatting and laughing straight away, and laughing and joking. Then Peter came out of his cell and started looking over at Johnny and John. John was asking Johnny how he was doing. Johnny said, 'All right, apart from the incident with the guy across the landing,' and they both looked at him. John said to Johnny in a loud voice so Peter could hear, 'Do you want me to go over there and chuck him off the landing for you?' Johnny looked at Peter and said, 'Not at the minute; it might not be a problem.' Peter walked off and never spoke to or looked at Johnny again.

Within a day or so, Johnny met a few guys on the landing he knew and just started knocking about and around with them. They were the wrong crowd and Johnny got on well with them. He never had any trouble at Elmley after that. John would often go round for a burn and a coffee with him in his cell. John said, 'If you've got any problems, let me know I will sort them out.' Johnny thanked him and told John that if he needed anything, to let him know and he would get if for him.

Johnny stayed in the same cell and never had anyone put in with him, which was lucky, while he was at Elmley. He started his first job at Elmley, which was headphones in a work unit. It was all for Virgin airlines. He would go and stand at a bench and take the old earpad foam sponge covers off the headphones, replace them with new ones and put them in new, clear, Virgin airways bags, ready to be put out again on the aeroplanes and used again. He thought that Richard Branson didn't miss a trick, he even got his headphones recycled for pennies by prisoners. About right. He may argue it provides prisoners with employment – there are always two sides to any story.

The chaps who had been there a while were like machines. They didn't even look at what they were doing. They had it off to a fine art and could do hundreds every day. Johnny couldn't even begin to keep up. It was a rate per hundred. He wasn't going to earn a lot but at least it got him out of his cell and he could chat to all the others as well. After about two or three weeks, he could nearly keep up with them. It really was just a matter of practice.

Johnny used to have to go to the pharmacy in the morning and evening while at Elmley. There he met an old guy called Roger, who was on a different wing to him. Roger was a pensioner and had just been sentenced to life for a third arson offence. He talked about it like it had no meaning at all; it was just how it was for him. Roger and Johnny used to sing songs together on the way back, which was a long walk, including "I want to Break Free" by Queen, "I am an Innocent Man" by Billy Joel and "Jail House Rock" by Elvis Presley. Roger had all the moves. It was just a way of amusing yourself and made for a good laugh, Johnny used to think.

One day he was returning from the pharmacy on his own and the alarm went off on his house block. About a dozen officers were running towards him as he got to the House Block entrance. They shouted at him to move out of the way, opened the door and ran onto the House Block. Johnny followed in afterwards. There was a guy lying on the floor in a pool of blood and a guy with his legs cuffed together and his arms behind his back, handcuffed and being carried off by about six officers. The guy being carried away had cut the other guy's ear off. The next day Johnny found out the victim had stolen his attacker's mobile, so that was how he dealt with it. That was an eye opener.

Johnny had his confiscation hearing coming up at Canterbury Crown Court. Half the prisoners in the prison had confiscation proceedings as a result of their convictions. It was now just an everyday part of the legal system. One day before he was due at Canterbury Crown Court in July 2010, he got told he was being sent to HMP Highpoint near Newmarket, in Suffolk. Before he was getting on the bus to go, he tried to explain that he was due at Canterbury Crown Court for a confiscation hearing tomorrow. The officer was not in the least interested. Officers were not there to change plans; they were there to follow orders. They didn't even have the discretion, he realised.

He went to HMP Highpoint, and when he arrived, he was told they had a production order for him to go to Canterbury the next day. Johnny explained he'd tried to tell them. They said he should never have been sent. He was sent to the induction wing and had no idea the prison had a nickname of Knife Point because of the amount of people who had been stabbed there recently. There had been a lot of drug problems and other issues, and prisoners were getting stabbed left, right and centre.

Johnny was sitting in a cell on his own when a black guy walked in and said to him, 'Give us a burn.' Johnny took an instant dislike to him. He was not in the best mood and he was rude. His ask was more like a demand so put his back straight up. Johnny told him he didn't smoke. Then, within a few minutes, another one of these three guys hanging about outside comes in asking for a burn. Johnny looked at him and said, 'I don't smoke.' He just didn't like how it was going and was furious. He then rolled up a cigarette and lit it up and started smoking it within view of the three guys. Then the third one walks in and says, 'Give us some burn.' Johnny took a drag on his rollup, blew it out and screamed at the bloke, 'I told you I don't fucking smoke.' They all walked off. That was the end of that.

The next morning, he had to be up at 04 00 am. He got to reception. They had sent a small van for him. It was a few hours' drive to get to Canterbury and they had to be there by about 09.30 am. The driver flew down to Canterbury from Suffolk. It was only Johnny in the back. On arriving at court, he realised it was not for the confiscation hearing to take place. It was just an appearance for issues to be discussed. He met Mr Trent again and they went through some documents. Mr Trent told him he looked 10 years younger. No doubt, giving up the alcohol and drugs had started to show. Johnny actually felt better by now and had kind of got used to prison life. Mr Trent did emphasise the need for him not to lie in his replies to written questions he would need to answer from the Crown Prosecution Service. He said if he lied or did not disclose everything that was asked of him, it would very quickly get out of hand, because if the Crown Prosecution Service could prove one lie or failure to disclose, they could then say anything they wanted about his finances and the judge would have no option but to believe whatever they said based on his behaviour. Johnny understood that and was fortunate they had not missed one thing when checking his assets and bank accounts. They had even found an Abbey National Child Saver account, which he'd opened when he was about 15. He'd lost the passbook and forgotten all about it. He had initially deposited £1 in the account and it now had a balance of £4.25.

So, the idea on non-disclosure of assets or lying had totally been taken out of his hands. All his properties and bank accounts were already frozen and they knew about them all. The Crown just wanted to be sure they were aware of everything before presenting the facts about his wealth to the judge. Sophia was also in court and both confiscations were being dealt with at the same time. So, Sophia and Johnny grabbed a few words before and after the hearing, which lasted about an hour and was in front of the original trial judge. After the hearing and later on that day, at the end of court, he was taken back to HMP Elmley again and back on House Block 5.

The biggest advantage to being in the local prison to his area was prison visits. Whenever he was at Elmley he had a few visits from friends and family. Lee, his mate, very kindly sent him a large cheque, which got credited to his account and made prison life a lot easier. Each week money could be transferred to his spends account from his savings account and spent, as well as any wages. When there was no work, a prisoner's total daily income was 50p or £2.50 per week. Jobs were paying from £10 to £25 per week.

One day when Johnny was in the showers, he was listening to

a conversation between two white guys. One said to the other, 'Well, it all kicked off in this brothel one night. I just got out. You know what the people are like who own them places – they will end up murdering you.' Johnny looked the other way and started laughing.

He had no idea where he would be moved to next, or maybe he would stay at Elmley until the confiscation hearing had been concluded. After about a month he was sent back to HMP Highpoint (Knife Point) again. At least he had an idea about Highpoint now and knew what to expect. The only difference this time was that he was taken to HMP Chelmsford, dropped off there for an overnight stay, and the next day he and three others travelled to HMP Highpoint together. The only thing he found out about HMP Chelmsford while he was there was that it was at that prison that *Porridge* was filmed.

On arriving at HMP Highpoint, Johnny spent a short period on the induction wing. Here he came up with a cunning plan. No, not to escape, but to get his time back that he was going to spend in prison, so he decided to quit smoking. While he was on the induction wing, he had his hair cut by a young guy who just started chatting while he was doing it. By now he was just simply having a number-one haircut with clippers. The rate for a haircut in most prisons was half ounce of tobacco. Lots of people in prison become barbers. It is a very simple way of earning tobacco, and most people in there need regular haircuts.

Johnny was walking round the wing and asking about haircuts, and came across this young guy. He asked him how much for a haircut. The guy said, 'Give us what you can.' Johnny said, 'Ok, but how much is the minimum?' He said, 'There isn't a minimum.' Johnny said fine and asked him to do it. It was a straightforward haircut. He took his time. It may have taken fifteen minutes in total. During the haircut, Johnny and him started talking. Johnny just asked him about life. He was sitting in a chair facing the landing and the guy was behind him with the clippers. The story about his childhood and life was so heartbreaking, Johnny was crying inside for the guy. After he finished the haircut and was sweeping up, Johnny said, 'I will go and get you some tobacco.' He went back to his cell and realised he could give him enough for a few rollups. He knew that was not the point of the exercise here. He gave him all his tobacco apart from the pouch he had open. He gave him six ounces for the haircut. The guy was blown away. He just wished him well and walked off. Johnny never saw him after that. After finishing the pouch he had, he decided to give up smoking, and he did. Two days later he was informed by the solicitors that the appeal against sentence had been turned down but they had not increased his sentence, which they could have in the circumstances. Johnny borrowed some tobacco and started smoking again. Two days later he laughed at himself and decided to quit again, and this time he gave up smoking for good.

He left the induction wing and was put on a regular house block. There was a shortage of jobs available so he never got offered a job, which he preferred. It meant that all day he could just stand and chat on the wing to a few inmates. He preferred that. It was while Johnny was at Highpoint in October 2010 that George Michael, the singer and entertainer, got sent there to serve some of his sentence. His partner used to visit him, and it was something to talk about for a few days. It even lifted the morale of the prisoners for a while when he arrived.

Johnny would spend a lot of his time talking to a guy called Smithy. His name was Alan Smith. He had been caught smuggling large quantities of drugs through Dover. He had a trial at Canterbury Crown Court as well. He used to drive to his trial every day in a new Aston Martin. He got nine years after getting convicted, as well as a confiscation order. He and Johnny got on well and shared many stories and hours chatting on the landing. The first thing Smithy used to do every day was ring his wife and get her to put his bets on for the day, which made Johnny smile. Smithy had been at it all his life and knew the drug importation business inside out. Just couldn't stop; there was so much money involved.

It was at the end of October that Johnny had his next appearance at Canterbury Crown Court for his confiscation. He was taken back to the court for the day, and the process to take a further step towards completion, and then sent back to HMP Elmley again. He was back on House Block 2 and recognised some old faces. There were a few new ones too. People go to and leave prison every day. It is just a conveyer belt – one in, one out… almost.

Johnny was waiting to get on House Block 5. He thought he might end up going to HMP Highpoint again. He was sharing a cell with a young guy called Dennis. This guy had a drug deal going down, which was nothing to do with Johnny. In prison terms, it was a large deal. Dennis had agreed to buy a 9 bar of puff from a northern guy who looked and spoke like a mad monk. Dennis had been put up to it by some guys on the wing. He was going to rob the mad monk. The deal went down. The mad monk guy, who was from Newcastle, could not get on the wing, so they were going to trade through the bars in pillow cases. They did. The guards were not that interested. They tried to make out they were swapping laundry. Dennis got the drugs; the mad monk got a load of dirty laundry. Ooops, not a good move by Dennis. Within about ten minutes, the mad monk was at the bars on the wing and in front of the guards, screaming at Dennis, 'When I get on there, I am going to kill you.' He was shaking the bars and screaming. Everyone went out to listen.

Dennis told Johnny what had happened. Johnny said, 'You need to give the drugs back and start talking very quickly.' Then Dennis said he gave the drugs to some lads on the wing and got a cut. That was it. Unbelievable, turning a complete psychopath over drugs and getting a small cut. Anyway, within a few minutes the mad monk was on the wing. Johnny had no idea until he heard him screaming, 'I will find you.' He didn't know which cell Dennis was in. He started searching. Very quickly, he was at the cell door. Johnny suggested to Dennis that he hide in the toilet and stay still and silent. When he got there, he asked Johnny if it was Dennis' cell. Johnny said, 'Yes.' The guy went straight in and saw it was empty. He was totally in a rage. If he had found Dennis he would have pulverised him, if not more. He then looked at Johnny and said, 'Do you know where he is?' He replied, 'I think he went for a shower; I am not sure.' The monk was off to the showers. A few minutes later it was end of recreation and everyone would be locked in again. Johnny opened the toilet door and said, 'He is gone.' Dennis had turned white, which did not surprise Johnny. The mad monk left the wing and everyone was back to their cells and locked in for the night. That night they discussed his predicament. Johnny suggested to him that he go and tell the guys he gave the drugs to that he wanted them back and was going to give them back, and go and apologise with the drugs and explain. Dennis did. The next day he got the drugs back and went and found the mad monk early and quickly and apologised, gave them back. It was all over, no drama.

Shortly after that Johnny got sent back to House Block 5. Within about 10 days, one morning, Darren, a guy he had met once before prison, came running into his cell and said, 'We have both had a right touch. We are going to the Verne.' Darren had been a career criminal all his life. He had been sentenced this time for robbing cash machines from various banks, including the HSBC. He and a gang of three others simply used to drive JCB diggers into the walls of banks in the early hours of the morning, scoop up the cash machines into the back of small trucks and drive off with the machines. They did it so many times they had it down to a fine art. They would then drive the machines off to a private warehouse and lock themselves in before taking all the notes out and scrapping the machines. He said sometimes they could get three or four hundred grand in one go if the machines were near full, sometimes a lot less. Darren said he used to do the JCB driving as he loved the rush he got from it. After about 24 successful heists, HSBC were losing so much money they decided to install trackers on all their cash machines. One morning they did an HSBC in the Medway towns. It all went well. They were in the warehouse counting the money at about 5 am and they heard on speakers, 'You are surrounded by armed police. Come out now.' They were literally surrounded by armed police and had been caught red handed. The police were alerted when the tracker went off and just simply followed it. The game was up. They had to plead guilty, but only to the one they were caught on. The police could not prove the others. They only had a vague idea and no real evidence. They were all facing confiscation proceedings as well. Darren had been in prison several times and was up early that morning, went down to the notice board and saw his and Johnny's names down for transfer to HMP The Verne. He told Johnny to get packing, which didn't take him too long.

Next thing, an officer came and found Darren and Johnny and told them to be ready to go in an hour. They made their way down to reception with their prison clear bags with a few possessions in. They were told the journey was too far for one trip so they would stop at HMP Highdown, which was about half way, stay there overnight and be taken to HMP The Verne on the Isle of Portland in Dorset the following day. Darren said it was a really good prison, whatever that meant. It was a C category prison, but was open and more like a C/D category prison because it was half used for English prisoners and half used for prisoners waiting to be deported back to their own countries after their sentences had finished. So it was a very diverse-population prison to say the least.

The prison was situated at the top of a hill. Once on the Isle of Portland, Johnny realised they were nearly there, because the prison transport just started going uphill and just kept going and going. Once inside the prison, Johnny could see a lot of African guys walking about in prison green, which made sense because of the deportation aspect of the prison. Once the van parked up, Johnny and Darren were allowed out and told to go into reception. A large sign saying racism would not be tolerated was located behind the counter, clearly visible. The officer told them to wait in the waiting area until shouted for. Johnny didn't reply. Darren said 'You like a nigga in here – don't you?' Johnny couldn't believe he'd said it. The atmosphere was terrible. There was just a deathly silence. About ten minutes later a couple of officers came and got Darren and told him he was being shipped out. That was it. He was out. He wasn't going in. Johnny later found out he was taken to HMP Parkhurst on the Isle of Wight as a result of his comment.

It turned out Darren had been right about The Verne. There were no 3-man cells. All cells were singles, except for just a few doubles. Prisoners were given their own door keys. The toilets were at the end of each landing, not in cells. Cells were not called cells; they were called rooms. The food was like staying in the Ritz compared to the other places. It really was a very high standard. There was a lot more freedom. Half the prison was open. Most of the officers were older and waiting to retire. It had a good feel to it, as prisons went. It was a working prison and everyone worked. At the first work board, Johnny didn't understand or care about asking for a certain job. He said anything would be fine. He didn't understand you needed to ask for the better jobs – or that you could. The woman talking to him said, 'Fine, I will find something for you and let you know.' He said 'Fine,' then left. He got given the wood factory, which had the reputation of being the worst job. The real problem with the job was there was hardly any real work, but to provide employment for all, they gave anyone a job. So, when you got there, you ended up standing around or sitting down – in Johnny's case waiting for the break, then lunch, then the break, then finish. Occasionally there was a little bit of work, but it was very boring. Lots of people took books to read. He very quickly realised he needed to transfer but you had to do a job for several months before you could change or ask for a transfer. He found out the only exception to that rule was education.

He managed to get a transfer to education after a while. He was learning to use photoshop on an education course which was taken by a tall Scouse teacher called Ray. Johnny was sitting next to a guy called Yuri. Yuri was Ukrainian. He had come over from Ukraine years ago, trained in accountancy. He had met his wife in England and they had their own accountancy firm, which had a great reputation with all the foreign guys. He was simply fiddling all their records and tax returns and charged them accordingly. He knew a few loopholes in the tax law and was exploiting them all to the maximum. He and his wife lived in King's Hill near Maidstone and had built up a portfolio of properties. It was all going wonderfully well until the Inland Revenue cottoned onto what he was doing for his clients. It had just been a large fraud, really. He and his wife both got 10-year sentences and were fighting confiscation proceedings of everything they owned between them. Yuri didn't need to be on the course. He could have taught the course. Johnny was trying to learn, listening to Ray and watching Yuri while talking to him. For a couple of days, he just couldn't get it. Then Yuri helped him a bit. By the following afternoon Johnny could do it. It was this afternoon that Johnny had now found his feet and his face lit up. He was so happy after days of struggling. Ray walked over to him and said to him, 'That is why I teach. What's just happened to you is the reason I decided to become a teacher.' Johnny understood what he meant. He felt great in that moment, when he had thoroughly understood what the guy was teaching them all.

After photoshop he was on computer courses with a new teacher called Silvia. She was such a laugh. She was not particularly happily married and used to enjoy her work and a good laugh. When Johnny told her what he was in there for, she used to say, 'You don't seem the type.' Then she would often joke with him and say, 'When you get out, I will come and work for you.' One day Silvia was talking to an African guy called Samuel, who was rude to her. She told him not to be so rude. Samuel said, 'In my country I am a prince and I have three wives. You are just a woman; you should do what I say.' Johnny and Silvia burst into laughter and couldn't stop. They were in hysterics for ages, and for a while after that neither of them could keep a straight face.

After a while in The Verne, Johnny realised trouble was rarely seen or heard about. If anyone started any trouble, they were out; it was as simple as that. Everyone was told at the beginning, 'You are being trusted. If you mess up, you are out.' While he was working in education with Silvia, Johnny was given his prison plan. He didn't know he had one or would get one. On his plan, he was told he needed to complete an offending behavioural course, which would allow him to be considered for a D category prison. Up until this point he'd never considered his behaviour a problem. The courses were always busy and you had to wait to get on them. He said to his offending behaviour manager, 'Perhaps there is someone else who might need the course more than I do?' She looked at him and said, 'You are on the course and it starts Monday.' That was that.

Johnny found out that the Prisoners' Education Trust would pay the entire cost of education courses for prisoners if they thought they were appropriate. There was a long list to get considered, and the list was forwarded by a prisoner. Johnny spoke to him, a slippery character to say the least. He told him he wanted to be at the top of the list, not the bottom. He didn't want to wait. They agreed he could be top for four ounces of Golden Virginia. That seemed reasonable to Johnny. He got accepted straight away after writing a letter which was dictated to him and then backdated. It was a business course. He quite liked that one and got it. After receiving the course, he was told it was a mistake. He would not be allowed to have internet access, which was required to study for the course. He said he would do it without internet access and that was agreed.

By chance, before starting on the course for addressing his behaviour, Johnny and Dermot, an Irish lad, Johnny chatted to occasionally and realised they were both on the same course starting on Monday. Johnny knew very little indeed about Dermot, apart from that he was a good laugh and generally seemed quite happy. Dermot told him the course was for five guys. It was taken by very clever people. The class was fully recorded by cameras and they were looking to catch them out lying. Dermot made it sound like the Gestapo without the possibility of torture. Dermot and Johnny decided to stick close together and to go to the course together – like two school kids, really. By this stage, Johnny had not realised Dermot could not read or write. When they arrived for the course, which would last several weeks, at the designated classroom, they saw it was being taken by two ladies, Susan and Mary. They did see multiple cameras too. Johnny realised Dermot had half a clue about it. Five lads were taking the course, and Johnny only knew Dermot, and not well. There was a lot of talking about rules and conditions and the purpose of the course, work sheets and booklets for everyone.

The first morning was taken up with introductions, really. Then, in the afternoon, they started the work for the course. They wanted people to talk openly about their crimes and sentences and behaviour and see what had been learnt, initially. A tall lad called Trevor started talking. He was the first of the five to openly talk to the group and the tutors. He said he believed he'd clearly made a mistake and regretted what he had done. He was praised for that remark and asked to explain further. He said he had poured petrol over a man and tried to burn him alive but regretted his actions because he got the wrong man'. At this point Johnny thought it would be wise to not say a word or even look at him. He couldn't believe what Trevor had said. Then Trevor goes on to say that he was trying to kill a paedophile but he got the wrong flat number so ended up trying to burn the wrong man. Johnny was speechless. Trevor went to the wrong flat. He was only sorry because of that, not because of his actions. Johnny decided it might be a good idea not to talk too much.

The next day he was going back to his wing after lunch and he saw Trevor fighting with some officers. That was the end of Trevor. He was shipped out and then there were four. Most evenings there was a little work to be done on your own for the next day. At this point Dermot suggested to Johnny it would be a good idea to do it together after dinner. Johnny agreed. Then Dermot hinted he wasn't good at reading and writing, not particularly educated like. Johnny understood. Dermot was in for drugs and burglary. Johnny said, 'We can do it together.' Johnny and Dermot used to talk his stuff through. Johnny would write out what he needed to say and Dermot copied his writing, so at least it was in his own handwriting. There was another guy on the course called Allan. He didn't like talking much. He seemed a very private guy. He always said, 'Let Johnny talk. He likes talking.'

Johnny got talking to the two tutors after a while. The atmosphere on the course was quite good after Trevor left. Mary had problems with her husband and Susan with her boyfriend. Johnny gave them some good advice and tips about how to change their situations, as he saw it. They were ever so grateful. Oh, the irony, he thought. Anyway, he did his work and realised he should obey the law in future. Or at the very least present that picture at that time, regardless of what happened in the future. He knew it was about changing his behaviour and so ticked the boxes. Dermot passed his course with flying colours and was very grateful to Johnny. Johnny passed and got a glowing reference, and as a result of that would now be allowed to go to a category D prison, or what was more commonly known as an open prison.

Due to the location of the prison he was in and the distance from Canterbury Crown Court, his solicitors agreed with the Crown Prosecution Service and the judge that he could be excused from attending further hearings with regards to the confiscation proceedings, until the final hearing when he must attend. All other enquiries until then could be dealt with by letters and post, which they were.

After the course finished, Johnny changed his job, so now he was placed in charge of the prison newspaper, which was published once per month. He was offered a move to HMP Ford Open Prison but decided the location had no benefits to him. It was so far away from his mother and friends he couldn't see the point. He turned it down and said he wanted to go to HMP Standford Hill on the Isle of Sheppey. It was the closest open prison to home. He was told he may not be able to get in HMP Standford Hill, because it was full up and there was a long waiting list. He said, 'Fine. If I can go, great. If not, I understand. I will stay here.' He was put on the list for HMP Standford Hill on that basis.

The job running the newspaper simply meant asking students – who were mainly African drug dealers – to write an article about something in their life, an event which would then be corrected if required, maybe have pictures added and then be printed. There was some information for prisoners about situations and events in the prison. The woman in charge of the newspaper trusted him to help the lads if they needed any help and used to slip off to the staff room for the lessons and come back before the end. He was left in charge and he told all the lads, 'Whatever you are doing, don't get caught.' He was busy typing up his course work for his business course, which he wasn't allowed to do but he had it on a PC and made sure he just didn't get caught doing it. Maybe Claire knew. Maybe she didn't or maybe she didn't care. It was very obvious she didn't like being there at all. She was a slightly older woman and very full of herself. She always said she had work to do in the staff room.

By March 2011, Johnny received a letter from his solicitors which did have positive news in it. There had been a hearing about Johnny's assets. The Crown were putting the details together. The judge remembered he had money paid in cash in his accounts and said as a result of that, the Crown could not argue hidden assets in his case, as the proceeds of the crimes had been paid into accounts and not hidden in cash. Johnny understood the significance of that remark. It meant he would lose everything but not have to serve further time in prison if the Crown had alleged hidden assets.

Off Claire's classroom, where the paper was published, there was a separate room for all the stock for the prisoners for the education department for the year. It was locked and was full to the brim with paper, envelopes, pencils, pens, rulers, scissors, as well as an awful lot of general stationery required for the classes. The whole situation with Johnny and Claire got so lax she stopped locking it and told him to give the students whatever they needed and always keep the door shut. He was so into his business course he hardly paid any attention to what was going on in the classes. Then, after finishing module 1 of his course, he realised that that had to be sent off for marking and then he would receive the next module to do, so there was going to be a delay. At this point he started trying to get the articles together for publishing. The lads kept asking for stuff and he kept handing it out. He knew these African guys were very good at speaking English when they wanted something and not understanding and speaking their own language when it suited them not to understand. So he came up with this master plan as he was now bored. He was going to sell the entire contents of the stockroom to the students. That was a challenge. He negotiated with them and they paid in tobacco. That was handy. He was no longer smoking, but in prison everyone pays in cash outside for drugs or with tobacco or tuna inside. They simply took almost everything from the stockroom. They got a good deal but Johnny was happy. He was selling prison property and it was all a bonus to him. The next day Claire went berserk, asking him what had happened. He pulled his little boy lost look face and said, 'I have no idea. I am not sure who took it. It was nothing to do with me.' She hit the roof. She knew he was lying. So was everyone else. He was smiling, thinking, *how are you going to explain why you didn't lock the room or you didn't see what happened?* She said to him, 'I could lose my job over this.' He realised his time working in the education department needed to come to an end sooner than later.

Johnny only ever cried openly in prison once, even though he'd tried not to. One Sunday his brother Alex had driven from Manchester to Canterbury, picked their mum up and brought her down to visit for the afternoon. Johnny asked them not to come because of the distance. They had insisted. The visit went well. All prisoners had to wear prison shirts and prison jeans so they looked smart and all the same. At the end of the visit, Alex got all emotional and burst into tears. It set Johnny off. They left and he manged to compose himself but, on the walk back to his room, he got all emotional and tearful again. When he got back to his room, he had a good cry and got it all out. His brother apologised but said it was how he felt. Nothing you can say to that. After that Johnny told them there was no need to visit again as he now was a D category prisoner waiting to be transferred to an open prison.

So now he knew his goose was cooked in education. Steve the laundry man had been given a D category and was going to HMP Standford Hill in two days. Laundry was the best-paying job, because you got a wage and everyone paid to have their laundry done. Johnny knew Steve. Steve was so bent and dishonest he could never look at anyone when he was talking to them. Steve was serving an 8-year prison sentence for timeshare fraud. He simply sold timeshare agreements on properties that were never built and did not exist, except in his brochures. The irony of him meeting Steve was that years previously Sophia was interested in the idea of buying a timeshare. There was an event advertised at Broome Park Golf and Country Club, and it was for timeshares. It was one of Steve's events. He simply never told anyone the truth. None of his staff or sales team knew about the scam. They thought it was all above board. When Johnny and Sophia went, it was well put together and presented and they were nearly tempted to buy, but the idea of going to the same place every time wasn't that appealing, really, which was handy. Steve was nearing the end of his sentence but his confiscation order was for millions of pounds and the Crown were alleging hidden assets as well, so he could be facing a further sentence, but that somehow got overlooked and he was allowed to go to the D category prison. Johnny told Steve he wanted his job and would be grateful if he got it. Steve told the officers he was off and recommended him for the laundry. They gave it to him. Johnny gave Steve two ounces as a thank you. He was now neatly out of education and in the laundry.

One lunchtime Johnny was going to leave the wing and didn't realise the door had been locked. So, as he approached the door at speed, almost jogging, he pushed the door and kept going but the door did not move. He put his face straight into the glass plate, which was wired glass, and smashed his face on it. The pain was horrendous. Johnny felt like he had just been hit in the face with a hammer. Instantly he fell to the ground and held his face. The area was busy and all the prisoners were laughing. He could hear them. He was on the floor, holding his face, but managed to get up and brush it off… almost. Not the time or place to show emotion, obviously.

Johnny enjoyed working in the laundry. He got obsessed with it and very quickly his cupboards and room were full of tuna and mackerel, the main currency for laundry payments. One day a Nigerian chap walked in, Mr Ndou, and said to him, 'If you give me your name and address, I will send you the money for my laundry when I get out, to save me paying as I go. What do you think?' Johnny looked at him and said, 'I was telling better lies than that when I was 10.'

A lot of the African lads asked him if he would read at their church service on Saturday afternoons. They knew he could read and invited him along. He went for a couple of weeks and was amazed. During the service they all danced various dances while he was reading the Bible. He had never seen anything like it. On the third week the service was raided by officers because of alleged drug dealing. They all denied it but it was so funny for Johnny to witness from the front. All the African guys were dancing, he was reading from the Bible, and the officers were chasing prisoners around the church and searching them at the same time. The reverend was trying to keep the peace and be diplomatic with the prisoners. He knew, even in the church of God, that security overrode everything so the officers were fully in their rights to raid at any time they wanted to.

Next to the church was a large field, which was often used for exercise and relaxation if the weather was ok. The field had a tower and security post that could be manned by officers. There were outside cameras as well. Johnny, on several occasions, witnessed parcels wrapped up in brown paper or plastic bags suddenly arriving on the field after clearly being thrown across the large brick wall surrounding the perimeter. That seemed to be the most direct route for drugs getting into The Verne, and there was a bad drug problem in there as there is in most prisons. If no officers saw the parcels arrive, sometimes a prisoner could just pick one up and slip off. Johnny guessed it was about the time; a time would be agreed and that was that. On several occasions he saw prisoners pick up a parcel and be chased by officers. One such time, a guy picked the parcel up and had four officers chase him but managed to get away and get the parcel into the wings. They knew who he was but he denied it was drugs. They did need to catch the culprits red handed. Sometimes parcels would come over and the officers would get to them first. It really was a game of cat and mouse.

Johnny would regularly go for walks around the field, and started to improve his fitness and health after giving up alcohol, drugs and cigarettes. On one occasion he bumped into a pensioner called Ron. When he first met Ron, he seemed such a nice harmless guy Johnny assumed he might be in there for non-payment of council tax or maybe a fraud of some kind. After they started chatting, Ron said he was a single guy, bored and hard up. So he used to be a driver delivering cocaine for drug gangs. That all went well, and once he had some of his own cash, he started buying and selling cocaine himself. He built up a round of good customers and was earning a small fortune. Then he couldn't stop, and after a while too many people knew what he was doing and he was put under surveillance before being caught. He admitted his crimes and was now facing a confiscation order as well. His favourite saying was, 'If you can meet with Triumph and Disaster and treat those two impostors just the same, you found the secret to life.' Ron said he had heard the founder of Ferrari say it one day.

Johnny had a deal with Ron. He had some hair clippers from Argos in a box and told Ron he could have them if he brought him the equivalent monetary value to the cost of the clippers on his canteen. He did. Ron was taking the bag to Johnny when he got stopped and asked where he was going with his clear bag of canteen. He told the officer what Johnny and he had agreed. The first rule of prison is no trading. Next thing, the officer tells Ron to go and find Johnny and come to the office. Ron finds him on the field and explains what has happened. Johnny can't believe what Ron told the officer and what had happened. He went in and was accused by the officer of trading with Ron. Johnny never knew this officer so he started speaking in a manner which suggested he had learning difficulties and was a bit thick. After a couple of sentences the officer said to him, 'Are you a bit simple?' Johnny shook his head in agreement and with a confused look on his face. The officer said, 'I can see that. You don't understand, do you?' Then he said to him, 'Ok, on this occasion I am not going to do anything. Don't do it again. You can go.' He told Johnny's personal officer, who smiled at Johnny and said, 'He said you are a bit thick.' Johnny shrugged his shoulders and walked off.

One Tuesday in July 2011 he was working in the laundry. His personal officer came in and said, 'You are off to HMP Standford Hill tomorrow. I am pleased for you. Good luck.' Up until then, he didn't know if he would get a place before the end of his sentence or would see it out at the Verne. The next day he had said all his goodbyes and walked up to reception with his clear bags. The route back to Kent was the same as it had been on the way there from HMP Elmley, which is in a cluster of three prisons on the Isle of Sheppey. It was an overnight stay at HMP Highdown. Johnny was on his own, and the next day it was off to HMP Standford Hill.

Johnny arrived on Thursday at HMP Standford Hill. He had never been to an open prison before. He just thought, *you come and go as you please*. It was a lovely sunny day. After lunch, he just walked off the wing he had been put on and found a field to walk round. He never knew that the door had been left unlocked by mistake. After walking round the field, he thought it seemed really peaceful and quiet. He lay down in the middle of the field and started sunbathing. He was lying on the grass with his eyes shut. After about 10 or 15 minutes, a guy in a shirt and an officer walk up to him and say, 'What are you doing?' Johnny looks up and smiles and says, 'Sunbathing' and shuts his eyes again. Then they say 'Why?' He says, 'Because I want to relax and enjoy the sun.' At this point they ask him how he got off the wing. They explain that one of them is a governor and he should be on the wing, and that he was not allowed out in the field after lunch. Then they tell him he is to get back on the wing.

After that experience, he settled in and found his feet in a day or two. He didn't really want a full-time job. He was put on B wing, or Stirling House, as it is called. He took a cleaning job so he could start going to the gym regularly and use the Olympic-size swimming pool that was open every day. That seemed like a far better idea than working. He was not into weights but got into cardio and swimming and lost weight. The cleaning job he had could be done in about 15 minutes in the morning and 10 minutes in the afternoon, which gave him the spare time. It was while he was at HMP Stanford Hill that he completed and passed his business course. He got a distinction and was pleased with that.

The final date for his confiscation proceedings had been set. It was going to be in August 2011. Johnny was taken to Canterbury Crown Court on Thursday 25th August 2011. He was unaware that Sophia was having her order dealt with at the same time. On arriving at the court, he was locked in the cells downstairs. Then, after a while, he was taken to a room where he met Mr Trent and a lady from Irwin Mitchell & Co. They said their hellos and then Mr Trent started telling him how it would be. He didn't want to hear that and started disagreeing. Then Mr Trent went a bit far in Johnny's view he said, 'Your parents really should take some responsibility for not teaching you to be responsible.' Johnny didn't mind whatever he called him but no need to bring his parents into it. He was way too emotional for that stuff and would have chinned him if he wasn't a barrister and in a court room, even if he was right. So now his back was straight up and they just started arguing about the details of the order. Johnny accepted and knew he would lose everything but wanted to at least try and make some sort of stand on one or two points, rather than show a total surrender. Then Mr Trent said 'You really are your own worst enemy.' So, Johnny simply replied, 'I do not need you representing me anymore, and don't want you to.' The conversation ended abruptly and the lady said, 'Us as well?' Johnny said, 'Yes.' He was put in the cells again, waiting for the start of court. The matter was still being dealt with by the Right Honourable Judge James O'Grady. So, at 10.30 am everyone is back in court with no one in the public gallery this time. Mr Kindell started talking. Then Sophia's barrister spoke. Then Mr Trent said, 'My instructions have been terminated.' The judge said, 'I remember Mr Butler from the trial. The matter is a legal minefield,' while looking at Johnny. The prosecutor said 'Let's hope Mr Trent enjoys his day off.' The judge said he would hear the matter at 2 pm. Johnny knew the judge and Mr Trent knew each other well and probably wanted to understand what had actually happened. He was taken back down to the cells until 2 pm when he would represent himself. Sophia had her order dealt with after that.

At 2 pm Johnny is taken back to court to represent himself. The security guy standing next to Johnny in the dock says to him, 'So what is it like in HMP Standford Hill?' He replies 'A poor man's Travelodge.' The guy laughed at that, Johnny remembered. The prosecutor then spoke about the benefit figure from his crimes and his available assets. The benefit figure was 4.1 million pounds from his criminal behaviour. The Crown Prosecution Service had seized all his assets and that total was £768,000.00. After that, he was allowed to speak for himself in the matter. Johnny knew, whatever happened, he could not affect the outcome, but he just made a couple of minor points about the order. The judge listened and took on board – or appeared to take on board – what he had said and then went through the final details of the order before finalising it and signing it. When the prosecutor explained the time frame of the order, the judge looked at him and said, 'Well, Mr Butler has very graciously accepted the majority of the findings,' and he made two minor variations on the order, which slightly favoured Johnny. He had been more than fair yet again, in reality. Clearly, no one understood that if Mr Trent had not challenged Johnny and his parents and had made the slightest effort, his instructions would never have been terminated. Johnny always knew he would leave skint, but there are ways of walking away and accepting situations, he had thought, and he was never going to forgive personal attacks on his parents. The matter concluded with Johnny losing £768,000.00 in available assets.

After the judge and the prosecutor had finally talked through the final details of the order, the judge finalised it and signed it off. Then he looked at Johnny and said, 'When do you get out of prison, Mr Butler?' Johnny looked at him and wanted to say, 'You sent me there; can't you remember?' but instead replied with the exact date in 2012 for his release after serving half the sentence. Then the judge looked directly at him and said, 'When you get out of prison, I wish you well.' Johnny could not believe what he had heard. He was absolutely astonished. The security guard on his left said to him, 'I have never heard him say that to anyone before.' He then got up and left the court.

After returning to HMP Standford Hill, Johnny felt quite good about the day's proceedings even if he was potless. At least he had stood his ground and not accepted what was being suggested to him without challenge. About a week later, he received a copy of the confiscation order.

Johnny was soon going to be able to have home leave, two days away from the prison, as well as being allowed to work outside the prison. He was walking round the field exercising one day when he heard a very distinctive voice that he thought he recognised. He was walking behind two guys. It was not a friend, more like someone he had heard on TV. Then Johnny walked past the guy and recognised him instantly but couldn't put a name to his face. Johnny smiled at him and he smiled back. Later that day he found out that Lord Taylor had just arrived in the prison. He was the only Lord in the House of Lords who was convicted of fiddling his expenses. A number of MPs were in HMP Standford Hill for fiddling their expenses. Johnny used to sit in the library some days if he was bored and just passing time. They would often come in for a book or to read the paper. He knew them by face but not name. He would often jokingly talk to the librarian in a raised voice and say things like, 'What a joke this country is. All those MPs meant to be running the country and they are all busy fiddling their expenses.' They used to look at him but never bit. One day he got to speak to Lord Taylor. He told him he couldn't wait to get out and get back to the House of Lords. Johnny said, 'Is that to put right what you did wrong and do some good work?' He looked at Johnny and said, 'No, it is for the money.' Johnny thought, *how refreshingly honest is that?*

Johnny started working outside on the vans, as it was called. There were two vans that went out every day and did clearance jobs for Swale Borough Council. It got him out of the prison and was like going to the gym, because it was physical work and he would often finish the day shattered. Just before Christmas 2011, Johnny received a letter from his eldest niece, Helen. She was complaining that every day her dad was drunk on the patio.

Johnny was astonished to read the letter. He decided to speak to his brother about it and brought the conversation up on the phone at Christmas 2011. Alex wanted to know which one of the children wrote to him. He neatly evaded that question and they got talking about daily drinking. Johnny said he used to drink vodka every day. Alex said he used to drink whisky. Johnny had never seen Alex drunk. Alex said he went to AA and stopped drinking. He then stopped going to AA and started drinking again. It just registered with Johnny for the first time ever that he'd had a terrible drink problem. He knew that when he left prison, he needed to stop drinking so he could earn some money again and get back on track again. He couldn't earn if he was drinking, he thought. As they say in AA, the seed had definitely been planted. He put AA on his to-do list for when he got out. He never realised there were AA meetings in HMP Standford Hill for prisoners every week in the church opposite Stirling Wing. Slowly but surely, his release date came round in 2012. Good old mum had told him he could stay with her in Canterbury. He was also allowed to open a Co-op cash minder account, which in his circumstances was the best he could get. All his other accounts were empty and closed. He walked free from prison in May 2012. He left the reception area in the morning and saw his brother and mother waiting in the car park opposite in his brother's new Jaguar.

CHAPTER 23
RELEASE FROM PRISON – CHANGE

Johnny left HMP Standford Hill and the first thing that went through his mind was that prison had saved his life and gave him a new one, if only he could get honest and see the wood for the trees. He was released with about £68, and that was all the money he had. He had asked Mum to stay with her again, and that was fine. The real problem was that Vera had the early signs of dementia now; not a diagnosis, but all the signs were there. He didn't have a mobile, and a guy said to him he probably would struggle to get a contract phone. How times changed, he thought. Still, Vera said if he got turned down, she would get him one in her name or go guarantor if required. Johnny went into a phone provider and got a new Apple iPhone on a two-year contract without too many issues. He just used his mother's address. He didn't have a driving licence. He applied for a new one after his second drink-drive conviction had expired and was told he had to go for a medical with a DVLA doctor to see if he was physically well enough, as well as see where he was in relation to alcohol misuse as a result of the second drink-driving conviction.

He had to meet his probation officer, who was based in Wincheap, in Canterbury and would have to serve the second half of his prison sentence on a prison licence, which meant if he broke the law or the terms of his licence, he could be recalled to prison.

Johnny had no real idea what he wanted to do but he knew he wanted to go to Alcoholics Anonymous and check it out. He rang the AA help line number and spoke to a woman called Lil. She told him he needed to go to a meeting. There wasn't one that night. The next one was on a Thursday evening in the Age Concern building in Canterbury. He turned up and had absolutely no idea what to expect. He walked into his first AA meeting and was greeted very well by a whole group of people. It was a busy meeting with about thirty people in it. He sat down and was advised to listen for the similarities, not the differences. He sat there and listened as best as he could. When he got there, he was told he was the most important person in the room. He didn't realise he was important because he was a newcomer. He thought he was the most important person in the room because it was him. He slightly misunderstood that point. He could relate to an awful lot of things that people were sharing and talking about. At the end of the meeting, a guy called Mark told him there was another meeting tomorrow night at the Quakers' House in Canterbury, just near the Marlowe Theatre. Johnny had enjoyed his first meeting. He had been made very welcome. He didn't understand too much about it, apart from 'keep coming back'. So, he did. On Friday night he went to the meeting at the Quakers' House. This meeting had a slightly different format to it and different people in it. The secretary of the meeting was very attractive, he thought, and she kept smiling at him, so now he really was beginning to like the AA. He had been in prison for over 2 years and now he fancied his chances with the secretary of the meeting, an attractive woman called Lucy.

After the meeting a guy tapped him on the shoulder. It was Shaun, who'd worked at the cab firm years ago. Wow – Johnny had not noticed him in the meeting. He had been sitting behind him. He and Johnny said their hellos, then Shaun took him over to the literature table. He introduced him to Craig, the literature secretary, and Craig gave Johnny his first little Big Book, which was a gift from the group. Shaun then said to him, 'You are the problem. The steps are the solution.' He then gave him a list of 5 daily suggestions, which he recommended he do every day. Johnny looked at the list. Prayer to God or a higher power of my own understanding, ring two people from AA, read the Just for Today card, read two pages from the Big Book, and make a list of 10 things that you are grateful to have in your life. He asked Shaun, 'Does everyone come back next week?' 'Yes,' Shaun said. Johnny took one more look at Lucy and said, 'I will be here.' Then he found out there was another meeting on Saturday night at the Age Concern building again. He went again the next evening. He didn't quite know it yet but he was hooked on recovery already. He heard words whose meaning or relevance he didn't really understand but everyone was laughing and telling stories about how they had ruined their lives on alcohol, and a lot were addicted to other substances as well. They had come to AA and rebuilt their lives and were happy leading a spiritual life and not drinking. Everyone said they all only just did it for today. It was like living in the present moment, not in regret or resentment about the past, and not living in fear of the future. People were just trying to live in the day and enjoy serenity and emotional sobriety. After the Saturday meeting, Mark told Johnny he was going to a meeting in Deal on Sunday night and would pick him up if he wanted a lift. Johnny said yes. He had no licence or car yet and there were no meetings in Canterbury on a Sunday.

Mark picked him up on Sunday in a Toyota sports car he had recently got and was showing off in it really, Johnny thought, but it was a kind offer and gesture. The meeting at Deal was different again – more new faces, a different format – and after the meeting Johnny, Mark and a guy called Chris ended up having coffee in the Royal Hotel on Deal seafront. During the conversation, Chris said 'I like the peace of mind.' Johnny couldn't believe what he had just heard. Peace of mind. He had never experienced or had peace of mind. He never knew it existed. He was hungry to learn more about this AA and these alcoholics. This definitely needed further examination. He just started going to as many meetings as he could. He was lucky he was living in Canterbury. In those days there were five per week. He took some part-time work in a local cab firm, Cab Co, which gave him some pocket money every week, and his mum never robbed him for staying there.

After a few weeks of going to AA and going out for fellowship and coffee after the meetings, including with Shaun and a guy from Liverpool called Paul who was working down this way, Johnny realised he was an alcoholic. In lots of meetings, people were talking about getting sponsors, someone who had been through the steps and got a sponsor, and going through the steps. Johnny asked Shaun if he would sponsor him, and Shaun agreed. He told Johnny he needed to get some service. That very same night, the tea service came up for grabs at Canterbury Friday night meeting. Johnny stuck his hand up but Lucy didn't see him. A lady called Jacqueline did and gestured towards him. Johnny got the nod. He was now doing the teas on a Friday with a woman called Alex. He started the steps with Shaun. He was chatting with Shaun one day about his mother and how her memory was going. He said she probably needed care full time. Johnny had arranged a doctor's appointment for Vera to get a confirmed diagnosis for dementia, because at this stage there had been no medical intervention. Shaun said to Johnny, 'You will never get your time back with your mother.' That was Johnny's Higher Power working in his life. For some reason, that really sank in and he knew he was right. Johnny'd had excessive amounts of money in the past, gambled for England, and had done drink, drugs and sex to death. There had been amazing highs and lows but he'd never understood about being grateful for what he had, peace of mind and contentment in his soul. Shaun got Johnny to step 4 and then unfortunately lost his dad – and the plot a bit, understandably so – so Shaun had been very helpful with what he had done in his life but maybe it was time for a change of sponsor. Shaun had enough on his plate.

Johnny passed the DVLA medical in Margate and got his licence back later in 2012, so he could now drive again, which was handy, because his mum had a little Vauxhall Corsa but didn't want to drive anymore. She wasn't capable, in reality, and knew it, but she put him on her insurance so he could now be the chauffeur.

Johnny was doing his step 4 mainly when he went to work at the cab office. He worked nights, and after about 2am he was virtually left on his own with not much to do until 6am, when he would finish, rush home, grab some sleep, and get up to care for Vera. Johnny was on the verge of completing his step 4, which was in his own handwriting and it had shown him the truth about himself. He couldn't deny it as much as he would have liked to, at least some of it. He asked a guy called Arthur if he would sponsor him and Arthur agreed. They didn't go back to step one. They started on step 5. He had been very thorough on his step 4. The only thing he left off was the contract killing of Mikey. He wasn't going to burden another man with that, but after doing steps 5 to 9 with Arthur, Johnny found a monk at a monastery a long way from home and shared that one thing with him before leaving very quickly. After he finished reading his step 4, with Arthur on step 5, Arthur said, 'Your reality was better than any fantasy.'

Johnny and Arthur started doing prison service together in AA. Arthur had a chequered background and had been in a few scrapes. Every Wednesday evening for a year, they would go to HMP Standford Hill and take the AA meeting for prisoners. They would take the meeting in the church opposite Stirling Wing. Father Frank was the priest and would let them in and lock up afterwards. Johnny used to look up at the room he was in when he had been in there and smile to himself. How times change!

Johnny had always believed in a power greater than himself. He had never really been connected to it before. This was certainly an interesting journey to be on for him – where he came from and where he might be going. A woman he knew on social media called Barbara, whom he used to chat to about AA, said to Johnny once that, 'God has put you right in your mother's life exactly at the right time for both of you.' What an amazing observation, he realised. His whole program and recovery were based on being of service to others. He had decided he would take good care of his mum and do his best for Pat if he could. The rights and wrongs of parenting aside, since no one has a manual for that, he knew deep down that his mother and father had definitely done their best for him with the tools that they had. He just knew it was the right time to be there for her and, because he was single, he could.

One afternoon Johnny and Vera spoke about care homes and so on. Vera said, 'I don't want to go into care.' He said, 'You don't have to; I will look after you.' He signed on benefits as his mum's carer. It wasn't enough to live on but that somehow didn't seem to matter. Every day he would take his mum to Waitrose for coffee and cake during the daytime, then out for dinner in the evening.

The appointment with the doctor prompted a brain scan appointment at the hospital, and the scan confirmed an early diagnosis of dementia. Vera was now under a psychiatrist at St Martin's Hospital and put on medication. They would go to all the courses about living with dementia and caring for people with dementia. It was confirmed the medication may slow down the rate at which the dementia would spread but there was no cure. Of course, half the time Vera never knew what was going on but Johnny used to call it forgetfulness rather than dementia. She could cope with the idea of a bit of forgetfulness, but not dementia and a care home. There is no manual for caring for your mother with dementia, really, but Johnny just wanted to see her laugh and smile so they would often sit chatting and making up stories and jokes. By now, some days she did not know who he was but she knew he was a friendly face. Alex and his family popped down occasionally to visit and go out for lunch and did the best they could in the circumstances. One day Johnny was sitting at a coffee table in Waitrose with Vera, laughing and joking, when a very elegant lady about 60 years of age walked up to him and said, 'Excuse me, are you her son?' Johnny looked at her and replied, 'Yes.' She looked him straight in the eye and said, 'I watch you and your mother all the time in here. I wish I had a son like you.' He absolutely melted inside. What a compliment from a complete stranger. Vera jokingly said, 'Are you my son?' then said to the lady with a laugh, 'I will sell him to you if you want.' It had certainly been a beautiful moment. The lady smiled and walked off.

One night about 1am Johnny was in bed when he heard a

moaning sound. Now fully awake, he ran into his mum's bedroom but she was not there. He noticed the light on downstairs. He went down the stairs and saw his mum laying on the floor in the living room. He asked if she was ok and she said yes, so he suggested she sit on the sofa but she could not lift herself up. He lifted her up on the sofa. Then he realised she couldn't walk or go to bed. He called an ambulance and it turned up quite quickly; it was the early hours of the morning. Two paramedics, a lady and a man, came in and spoke to her and asked her what had happened. Then Johnny explained she had dementia and couldn't lift herself up or walk and was in pain. Vera denied it all and said there was nothing wrong with her. The lady then said to her, 'That's fine. I just want to see you walk and then we will be off.' Vera couldn't so she became all stubborn and obstinate. Shortly afterwards, when it was obvious she couldn't and she was telling porkies, the paramedics brought a wheelchair in and took her to the Queen Elizabeth The Queen Mother Hospital in Thanet. Johnny could have gone with her but it was agreed he would follow in the car so he could get home afterwards. By now he and Alex had full power of attorney over all her affairs. She made it so either of them could make the decisions if needed, so he knew he had full power of attorney over her health and wellbeing. Once she got to the accident and emergency, after a short while and x-rays, it was confirmed that she had broken her hip. She had got up, gone downstairs, fell over and then shouted for help, it turned out. She was admitted to the hospital and put in a ward awaiting a hip operation to repair her hip. It had been a clean break, which was some good news in a bad situation. Johnny went home and, in the morning, went back with some personal items for Vera and he also let Alex know.

Vera had to wait about 10 days for her hip operation. Johnny visited every day and Alex came down at the weekend with his family. The hip operation went well and she needed to rest before she could try walking again. She was transferred shortly afterwards to the Whitstable and Tankerton Hospital, which was for a period of rest and for rehabilitation. After a couple of weeks there, she had a problem when trying to learn to walk again. It became apparent that she could not remember her physio or rehabilitation exercises, so Johnny was told she should now go home. He asked how she would get up the stairs at home to use the toilet or go to bed. He was advised she could sleep on a camper bed downstairs and use a potty. He thought and took it as a total insult. She was being sent home very prematurely in his opinion. He objected and raised his concerns with the staff. She was in her late 70s and had dementia. So now he found himself at odds with the ward manager and the hospital manager. He was going to do anything and everything to keep his mum in the hospital until she could walk and live upstairs and downstairs. It was not as if she could not walk in the future; it was a question of time. Johnny avoided the hospital staff for a few days when visiting, then they set up a meeting so her future could be discussed – or effectively, she could be sent home. He was considering taking legal advice or considering just not picking her up. No one else was going to, and she didn't have her own keys on her. He knew deep down in his heart that she needed about another six weeks in the hospital. At that point returning home would be a much more satisfactory experience for her, and more appropriate in his view. He had a massive stroke of luck and found out he could appeal any decision in the NHS. The stroke of luck was that he found out that the appeal process at that time took 13 weeks and while the appeal process was ongoing no decisions or action would be taken until the conclusion. What a great piece of good fortune, just to find that out. So, because he had power of attorney, he was invited to attend the meeting with his mother.

He turned up and thought the best way to play it would be cool and very respectful. He thought by staying calm he could present the facts as to why Vera should stay in there far more convincingly. Johnny and Vera sat in the room and Johnny was surprised how many members of staff were in the meeting. The manager took control of the meeting and invited everyone to speak. Vera said, ‘Whatever Johnny wants is fine by me.’ That was perfect. It was all he wanted to hear, even though he had the legal authority and responsibility to speak for her.

It was a total ambush and kangaroo court style meeting in his view. They just simply wanted to send her home for the bed. Johnny had her best interests at heart. They had the NHS waiting lists and interests at heart. He knew it wasn’t personal. It was just their job. At the end of hearing all the reasons why she should go home, he was invited to speak. He spoke about Vera’s best interests in the situation, the manager didn’t listen or certainly didn’t appear to listen or show any interest in what he said. After he spoke, the manager instantly said she will need to be discharged and go home the next day. Johnny looked at him, absolutely furious, but was never going to show his frustration, anger or disappointment. That was not going to help anyone. He simply looked at Vera, smiled and said, ‘Don’t worry, Mum, we are appealing. Leave it to me.’ He said it quietly and smiled but just loud enough for the manager to hear. The manager looked at him and realised that, just maybe, he was not going to get too far with Johnny. Johnny just smiled at him. Then the manager said, ‘Perhaps we can agree a date in the future for Vera to go home. Johnny said, ‘Yes, perhaps we can.’ The manager then said he would leave it to Johnny and the ward manager to agree a date. Johnny thanked him and went backed to the ward with Vera.

A date was later provisionally agreed for six weeks after the meeting. Johnny felt that would give his mum the best chance. In the six weeks in between, a handrail was fitted on the stairs, with two pull-up bars at the top. Six weeks later to the day, he took her home. She could now walk with walking sticks better than she could before. More importantly, she could now get up the stairs with Johnny standing behind her just for insurance purposes, and could sleep upstairs and use her own toilet, which also had a frame installed around it to assist. It was only a few weeks later and she was almost steady with just a walking stick and his arm, then just with a stick after a while. Carers started attending at home to administer Vera her medication, as she used to laugh at Johnny when he asked her to take the pills. If he gave them to her, she would say, 'I don't want them,' and he couldn't really argue with her but knew the medication would help her. When he used to give her the pills, she would drop them on the floor or fling them away in front of him, laugh and say, 'I have taken them.' With her carers, she would take them because she was afraid of them and didn't want to argue with them. The carers were great, Johnny thought, and it worked well.

Johnny and Vera were now back out daily, having coffee again and going out for a nice meal in the evening. He knew his mum was losing her mind and maybe her freedom, as well as her life ultimately. He wanted to make sure she enjoyed her time. Every day, it just became his mission to try to put a smile on her face and take care of her the best he could. Johnny and Vera couldn't afford to live how they were but that was irrelevant to him; he was just racking up credit card after credit card. He would worry about that later. Vera had her home, and that could be sorted out later. The quality of her life was far more important than worrying about her assets. After all, she was only going to pay it in care fees or leave it to Johnny and Alex. Johnny would rather they lived while she was alive than having any regrets if she passed away.

One day they were walking down into Canterbury and she didn't know who Johnny was. He was walking alongside her and she knew he was caring for her but she couldn't remember it was Johnny. They were laughing and joking, as usual. Then she started telling him about her son called Johnny. It was one of the most magical experiences he would ever have. She literally just started talking about how naughty he had been as a child, laughing about the times she had spent with him and how much she loved him. He listened patiently and absolutely. He would have done absolutely anything to have walked down the street and listen to his mum that day. It was simply priceless to him.

Johnny was in AA as much as he could be. He was grateful Shaun had taken him through steps 1 to 4. He was grateful Arthur took him through steps 5 to 9, at which point there had not been any guidance around steps 10 to 12. Johnny enjoyed the experience with the steps but it somehow felt incomplete. Arthur actually said to him one day, 'You know, we should have started at the beginning and gone from step 1 together.' That made sense to Johnny. He was surprised that they had not, really. So, he meet this guy called Richie who was in AA and CA. He had something Johnny wanted. He seemed very at peace with himself and Johnny always got good vibes and energy from him. Johnny got his phone number and rang him up one Sunday. The purpose of the call was to ask him if he would take him through the steps from start to finish. He left him a message as he didn't pick up. The next day Richie rang Johnny back. The Sunday had been his wedding anniversary and he was out with his wife. They agreed to meet and discuss it. After meeting for a coffee and having a brief chat, Richie said if Johnny was prepared to do the work which Richie had outlined in full to him to avoid any misunderstandings, then he would take him through the twelve steps as outlined in the Big Book and they would use the 12 steps and 12 traditions book as well (the 12 & 12) for the process. Richie had been a lot more thorough than Johnny expected. He appreciated that. Richie said, 'Sit with it for two days and let me know your decision.' Johnny rang him up two days later, thanked him and said he would be prepared to and would like to do the work. So, it was agreed that they would start.

Johnny and Vera had been part of the furniture at the restaurant for a long time by now. They were in there more than most of the staff and they were treated like royalty in there. Lots of staff would say, 'Nice to see you, we were talking about you earlier and wondering what time you would come in.' Not all but a lot of the waitresses would make a real fuss of Vera, make her feel special and have a good laugh with her, which was nice to witness. Johnny got to know a lot of the staff in there very well, all talking about their lives, families and so on.

He started going through the steps with Richie and had such an amazing experience. Doing step work with Richie was a real treat and a pleasure. Richie was working night shifts in a treatment centre and had access to a computer and email. They would often exchange 20 emails in the early hours of the morning while he would sit up doing his step work after Vera had gone to bed. He did the steps again, thoroughly and to the best of his ability. It changed his life entirely. He had new glasses on after that. His perception and understanding of life, as well as his own unrealistic expectations, had caused him lots of emotional pain in the past, which he didn't want to talk about and had avoided with active addiction. Richie was such a great sponsor and he was up for the work. They had met at the right time. Richie had been his teacher.

The irony of meeting Richie and putting him in his life was

never lost on Johnny. It felt like God had put Richie right in his life just at the right moment. After doing step work with Richie, Richie said to him, 'You have had four lives already.' In many ways it was true, Johnny thought, and smiled before hugging him and thanking him on that occasion. After going through the rest of steps' general talking, experiences and completing his list of amends, which had taken Johnny about four or five years, Richie said to him, 'You have had a full healing experience.' It felt like that way to Johnny. He felt amazing about himself, his life, and had been free from active addiction for years. He was literally existing on food and oxygen and felt good and, more importantly, alive again. There were more similarities than being alcoholic and addicts between Richie and Johnny than Johnny had first realised. Richie and Johnny were both of a similar age, had both gone bald, were both born within a couple of miles of Arsenal Football Club, were both lifelong Arsenal fans, had both had new Mercedes cars in their 20s. Johnny had bought his and Richie stole his. That was the only difference, which made Johnny smile and laugh.

Johnny was walking down through Canterbury with Vera one day. He saw the Jaguar showroom and smiled. He was in debt up to his eyeballs and couldn't afford a car service, let alone a Jaguar. One of Johnny's biggest fantasies as a child had been to drive an Aston Martin and seduce a beautiful Russian spy. He saw a few James Bond movies as a child and thought he wouldn't mind living like that. It seemed rather appealing to him at the time, and Johnny later realised half of the lads his age also probably wanted to live like James Bond. Lots of glamour, excitement, great gadgets and toys, beautiful women, exotic locations and excitement and escapism from a regular lifestyle. He said to his mum, 'I am not sure whether I should get a Jaguar or an Aston Martin – what do you reckon?' She looked at him and said, 'Don't mess about, get the Aston Martin.' Nice advice, he thought.

Alex had season tickets for Arsenal, and one week when they were playing in the Champions' League midweek and Alex couldn't make it, he asked Johnny if he wanted the tickets. Johnny thanked him and accepted. He wanted to take his mum to the football and go back to where the old greengrocer's shop was, just off the Holloway Road. They wrapped up warm and off they set. He knew everything may take time and be difficult, so they set off with hours to spare. He wanted to try and take her back to times she remembered well. It would almost certainly be the last possibility of watching the Arsenal live with his mum. Everyone in the family had been Arsenal fans. Johnny told Vera, 'If at any moment you do not feel comfortable, we can leave.'

The walked up to the stadium and up the stairs. It took a couple of hours but there were lots of breaks and time to sit and talk while resting between walking. He was pleased that they had managed to get in the stadium and upstairs with plenty of time to spare. When they managed to get in the seats, which were high up in the stands, the view down could be daunting. Once they got seated, Johnny hoped she could settle, but it was too much for her. So, after about five minutes, he smiled and thought, *well, at least we tried. That is the main thing.* So, they got up out of their seats. They got back to the main aisle and started walking down the steps to the area where they could begin to exit the stadium. They slowly got down the steps and turned to go down the last few steps before they would reach the food section again. A steward said, 'Are you all right?' He replied, 'Yes, thank you.' He then said, 'We are leaving. I brought my mum to watch the game but it's a bit too steep so we are going to leave it and shoot off.' The steward looked at Vera and said, 'Don't go. There will be some spare seats down there at kick-off and I will find you two. Wait down at the food area and come back at kick-off.'

Wow! Another real gift from a Higher Power. Johnny smiled as he looked up in the sky. Johnny and Vera went downstairs, took some photos, and went back up at kick-off. The steward found them two lovely seats right down the front, a lot lower down. The view was a lot better without the drop. They both enjoyed the full game and Arsenal won; a beautiful experience and memory to treasure. After the game, Johnny drove his mum round to where the shop used to be. It was now a block of modern flats, but they did visit the place and spoke about the shop and many good memories before setting off for home. It had been another memorable evening with his mum. One Johnny could stick in his heart and hold on to forever.

Looking after his mum had taken its toll on Johnny by now. He wanted to keep his mum out of a nursing home but he wasn't fighting her. He was fighting the disease of dementia, and it was relentless. It was very hard for him to witness his mum losing her mind. Mentally and physically, he found it overwhelming by now. He didn't realise he would be tortured as a result of looking after her. He explained to Alex that he couldn't cope anymore. Alex said he was considering buying a lot larger home and she could go and live with him. Wow, what a relief that was to hear for Johnny. The only problem was Alex had to sell his home first and then buy another one. That may take some time, but at least there was light at the end of the tunnel for him. Johnny and Vera just stuck to their daily routine and he found some clubs at Age Concern and other local support groups where Vera could go and spend some time, which meant he could get a couple of hours' break here and there. They continued to go for coffee every day in Waitrose and out for dinner in the evening. Vera clearly had no real idea what was going on but she really enjoyed going out and having fun with Johnny. They made the most of a terrible situation.

Alex's house sale and purchase had actually started. A buyer had been found and an offer accepted, and they in turn had found a place and after a while agreed and had an offer accepted. It seemed to go quite smoothly. Not particularly quickly, but it was continuously ongoing and, after a few false starts, contracts were exchanged on both properties and completion dates agreed. Once the move had taken place, Johnny left it for a few weeks and then spoke to Alex. They agreed a date for Vera to go and stay with Alex for one week, just as a trial, and it was agreed after that, a date for a permanent move would be agreed. They met at the services on the M1. Vera jumped in with Alex and Johnny had a full week off to himself. He had made plans to go to Bournemouth for a break, just to unwind and relax. Tuesday morning, Alex rang him and said he couldn't cope with Mum and asked Johnny if he could go and get her. Johnny was absolutely speechless and gutted. He said he couldn't, he had made plans for the week, which he had. Clearly, she was not going to be allowed to live there in the future. At the end of the week, Johnny went and collected Vera. Alex had ideas about getting full-time staff in to care for Vera. There had been the biggest breakdown in communication and interpretation between Johnny and Alex. The agreed-upon idea about keeping Mum out of care clearly meant very different things to both of them.

A couple of weeks later Alex came down to Canterbury one Sunday. He shared his ideas – if she lived with him, he'd have full-time carers in to look after her, and clearly that meant staying at home with them all day, or she could go in a local care home near him. Johnny wasn't amused to say the least. Johnny and Alex offered Vera the choice of going to live with Alex or staying with Johnny. Johnny accepted that Vera having full-time carers at his place was better than a care home. He just wanted her to be happy. She said she would decide. A couple of days later he asked her what she really wanted to do. She said, 'I want to stay with you.' Johnny was made up on one hand, the way it had been put to him, but knew he would struggle. He decided to knuckle down and do the best he could. Vera stayed with Johnny and they carried on. By Christmas 2016 Johnny was shattered, broken, and couldn't cope. One night he slipped off over to the Friars at Maidstone. Johnny had taken his mum there before and they'd prayed together. When they prayed, Vera said to Johnny, 'This is the sort of place that when you pray, you feel like it has gone up and been received,' pointing up to the heavens. He simply asked for help. He had no idea what he could do. He just said, 'Please give me a sign and help for what to do.' He got home and Vera was still asleep, so he went to bed.

Hours later he heard a banging on the front door and thought it was the morning carer who'd come to give Vera her medication being too lazy to open the wall safe and get the key out. The banging on the front door continued. Johnny was so tired he rolled over and went back to sleep. The banging on the front door stopped. Shortly after that, the light was on in his room and there was a massive police officer standing at the end of his bed. Johnny wondered where he was and what was going on. Was he hallucinating or dreaming? Was it all a dream? The policeman asked if his name was Johnny. He said yes. He then said, 'We found Vera in the High Street. We brought her home.' Johnny was absolutely shocked. He ran downstairs behind the police officer. It was freezing outside and his mum was standing just outside the house in her nightdress, carrying her hand bag and talking to a lady police officer. Quickly she came inside, in the warm. Johnny thanked both the police officers so much for what they had done. Thank God they had spotted her and no harm had come to her.

It turned out she was walking down the High Street with her handbag at 5am and when they stopped in their patrol car and asked her what she was doing, she said, 'None of your business.' Then they said they were the police and she said, 'How do I know that?' By now they'd worked out something was not quite right and asked her to get in the car. She refused, saying she didn't know who they were. After a while, she agreed. They then managed to work out where she lived and who with. When they got into Ivy Lane, they couldn't work out which house it was. They knocked on a few doors and after a while knocked on Claire's, next door. She said, 'She lives next door with her son Johnny.' The policeman broke in when Johnny didn't answer the door, knowing it was her home. The main thing was she was safe and sound. She had come to no harm whatsoever.

After getting back into bed – after Vera had gone to bed again – he realised she had never done that before. He had gone and prayed and asked for a sign and help. Next thing, she was out in her nightdress in the middle of the night and anything could have happened to her. Johnny took that as a sign that the whole thing was out of control now and he couldn't stop her walking out in the middle of the night again. Yes, he could lock the front door a bit more securely but that may not prevent it, and the worry was simply too much for him after that. After some serious thought, he decided he had kept her out of care for nearly four years and enough was enough. In the New Year he contacted social services and explained. A care home was agreed and a place found for Vera in 2017.

He had done his best. In the years that he had been caring for her, he had always been honest with her and she trusted him implicitly. In 2017, he told Vera she was going on holiday for one week only. He felt bad about the lie. She asked him if she was coming back after a week and he said yes. She agreed to go on that basis; otherwise she wasn't prepared to go, she had told him. She was now in care and Johnny and Alex got to visit all the time. They had fallen out by now over various issues around Vera's care and the finances. It was a sad experience, Johnny thought, but he had put his mum's best interests first and decided he would be comfortable living with that. His brother Alex could do whatever he wanted.

Once Vera went into care, Johnny slept constantly for almost two weeks. Apart from visiting his mum, he just got up to eat and slept most of the rest of the time. Of course, she never knew where she was, almost from the moment she'd arrived at the care home. It had been the most traumatic and difficult experience in his life, with the exception of losing his dad, George, years earlier. The grief from that nearly killed him. This had been terrible, but it had also been the most rewarding experience of his entire life. Some of the best memories were simple moments in coffee shops laughing and singing songs from Oliver Twist. Their favourite one to sing together was "Got to pick a pocket or two". Special memories he could reflect on and carry in his heart forever.

When visiting Vera, the brothers took their mum out for lunch and tried to make a day of it. After a while, Vera couldn't really manage going out for lunch. It was too much for her, walking and leaving the home. So instead, on visits, Johnny would sit in the lounge and talk as well as listen to the music or watch TV together. There were still some laughs and good memories to be made. Even though Vera didn't know her own sons by now, she always knew Johnny was a friendly face and was somehow related or connected to her. She often thought he was her father and the war was still on. On one occasion she sat in the lounge and said in front of Johnny, 'You are the biggest fiddler I have ever met in my life.' He was quite pleased with that remark. She was laughing when she said it. Then, on another occasion, she said rather loudly, he thought, 'All the police know my Johnny,' and was laughing at the time. Probably the greatest memory Johnny would have to treasure from when his mum went into care was one day when she was in bed in her room. Out of totally nowhere, she looked at Johnny and said, 'Thanks for what you did for me.' That one moment made the whole thing so worthwhile, just to hear those words from his mum and see the expression on her face when she said it. She passed away in the care home in 2018.

Since then, the 12-step program that Johnny was in, which he had used to give his life purpose, love and kindness shortly after leaving prison, has been copied by so many different fellowships. Spirituality is the only worthwhile way of life. Of course, it's all about balance, but he knows that he has a soul sickness that can only be filled with the spiritual way of life. Today his life is nothing whatsoever like his past. He attends regular meetings, does service and just tries to help other addicts and alcoholics recover from the selfish disease of addiction. The highs and lows are not there for now for him, but he has a more balanced way of life, and he practices gratitude, prayer and meditation on a daily basis to try to stay connected to his Higher Power which he believes is love, self-love and love and tolerance of others. It has been an amazing journey and now his experience can help others. They can relate to him because he can relate to their madness and behaviour. He can't save them from themselves but he can show them how they can help themselves, and for that he is grateful. He is not certain that he has the gift of contentment today but he is the closest to it he has ever been.

At the beginning of 2020, Covid 19 hit England and the

lockdown came along. In 2021 Johnny had another heart attack and had to have two heart operations, one in October 2021 and the other in January 2022, which meant he could not work. One day, as lockdown restrictions were lifting again and Covid 19 was beginning to become just an acceptable part of life, so to speak, he was walking into Canterbury. He met a guy he knew from AA called Ryan. Ryan had stopped going to the rooms now but they started chatting about life. Ryan explained to him that he had an experience in his life which inspired him to write a book during lockdown and he had just got it published. After speaking to Ryan, Johnny went home and just sat at the computer and started typing. What would he call it? Then it came to him. The title would be, *The Butler Did It.* He liked that one. He could write a crime novel based on some of his own life, experiences and events as well. He could be honest about certain facts and events and would change others for entertainment purposes. After all, even liars tell the truth sometimes. He could also change the names of certain people he met in his own life and create characters based on those people, as well as creating one or two new ones as well. Then he could get it published as a novel.

A lot of people in life don't see the need to change. Neither did Johnny before going to AA. Now his outlook and attitude towards life and people have changed. He realised he had a soul sickness which he needed to fix on a daily basis with spirituality, not multiple addictions. Johnny Butler's real vocation in life was to be of service to others. That was the best feeling in life he had ever experienced and he continues with that way of life today. How ironic, he thought, the Butler being of service.

THE END

ABOUT THE AUTHOR

'The Butler Did it' is the author's first novel. Born and brought up in London. Travelled the world. Now lives a quiet life in Kent.

Printed in Great Britain
by Amazon